"Toni Blake's romances are so delicious, so intoxicating and addictive, a good night's sleep isn't even an option.... No one does it like Toni Blake."

—*NEW YORK TIMES* BESTSELLING AUTHOR ROBYN CARR

USA TODAY BESTSELLING

# TONI BLAKE

*the*
# love
# we
# keep

*A Summer Island* NOVEL

ISBN-13: 978-1-335-00881-7

EAN

# Praise for Toni Blake

"Toni Blake's romances are so delicious, so intoxicating and addictive, a good night's sleep isn't even an option.... No one does it like Toni Blake."
—*New York Times* bestselling author Robyn Carr

"The perfect small-town romance."
—Eloisa James, *New York Times* bestselling author of *Born to Be Wilde*, on *One Reckless Summer*

"With sizzling sensuality and amazing depth, a book by Toni Blake is truly special."
—Lori Foster, *New York Times* bestselling author of *Driven to Distraction*

"Toni Blake's *One Reckless Summer* is one wild ride! This is just the book you want in your beach bag."
—Susan Wiggs, *New York Times* bestselling author of *Between You and Me*

"Sexy and emotional."
—Carly Phillips, *New York Times* bestselling author of *Dream*, on *Letters to a Secret Lover*

"The pages are practically drenched in the scent of lilacs and fresh paint in this delightful new series debut from Blake... Readers looking for a gentle summer romance with a dose of family secrets will wish they could stay on Summer Island."
—*Library Journal* on *The One Who Stays*

"Toni Blake tells the perfect story for a summer afternoon in *The One Who Stays*."
—*BookPage*

"*Whisper Falls* is the enemy of productivity. You start this novel, and nothing will stop you until you finish."
—*USA TODAY*

## Also by Toni Blake

### Summer Island

*The One Who Stays*
*The Giving Heart*
*A Summer to Remember* (ebook novella)

### The Destiny Series

*One Reckless Summer*
*Sugar Creek*
*Whisper Falls*
*Holly Lane*
*Willow Springs*
*Half Moon Hill*
*Christmas in Destiny*

### Coral Cove

*All I Want Is You*
*Love Me If You Dare*
*Take Me All the Way*

### The Rose Brothers

*Brushstrokes*
*Mistletoe*
*Heartstrings*

*Swept Away*
*Tempt Me Tonight*
*Letters to a Secret Lover*
*The Red Diary*
*Wildest Dreams*

For a complete list of books by Toni Blake,
please visit www.toniblake.com.

# TONI BLAKE

## *the* love we keep

HQN

HQN

Recycling programs
for this product may
not exist in your area.

ISBN-13: 978-1-335-00881-7

The Love We Keep

Copyright © 2020 by Toni Herzog

This edition published by arrangement with Harlequin Books S.A.

For questions and comments about the quality of this book,
please contact us at CustomerService@Harlequin.com.

HQN
22 Adelaide St. West, 40th Floor
Toronto, Ontario M5H 4E3, Canada
www.Harlequin.com

Printed in U.S.A.

To my mother, who passed away during the writing of this book, for a love that will never be equaled and that I'll carry with me always

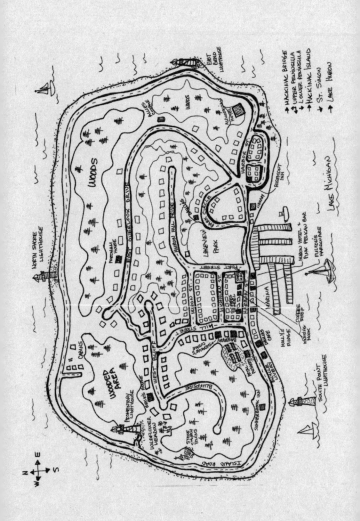

# Part 1

Excerpt from a letter to Suzanne:

*They say adversity builds character. But I believe it builds your very soul. Now, I know what you're thinking—your soul has already put up with its fair share of construction. And you're afraid if it has to endure much more, it might just collapse like a house of cards under the weight.*

*But your soul is stronger than you think. So please don't close it up. Throw open the doors and the windows. Let in the sun and the rain and the snow and the wind. Otherwise you might just miss the rainbows. And I promise you, there will be rainbows. Beautiful, glorious rainbows.*

## CHAPTER ONE

THE DAYS GREW SHORT, but the winter loomed long as Suzanne Quinlan hung a new calendar on the wall, the top part blooming with flowers, the bottom reminding her it was only January. Perhaps clichéd that a florist would select a calendar laden with flowers, but December had been unusually snowy and cold, even by Great Lakes standards, and she longed for color, sun—things that could blossom and grow.

Sometimes she wondered if she'd made a mistake in coming here. A place called Summer Island—it fairly beckoned you, drawing you in with its summertime beauty, the whole place bursting to life with lilacs and trillium and periwinkle, all against a backdrop of lush green trees blanketing the hillsides and shores. Bicycles, rolling past shops and cottages painted in pastels, were the main form of transportation in a place connected to the mainland only by passenger ferry, and life here just felt simpler, easier.

Until winter, that is.

In fairness, *simpler* still held in winter, but *easier* fled the island with the last autumn leaf that blew away before the lake effect snow began. And this wasn't her first winter on the tiny island near the Straits of Mackinac, where Lakes Michigan and Huron connected between Michigan's upper and lower peninsulas. Yet already it felt colder and longer to her than last year's. For December had held romantic heartbreak.

Thank God for her dear friends, Meg and Dahlia—bright spots even in winter. She'd found herself hibernating since Christmas, but Dahlia had declared by text message yesterday that a lunch was in order to start off the new year. If anything would get her through to spring, it would be her friends.

Thus she put on her snow boots and the black calf-length parka hanging on a pegboard by the front door. Adding a scarf and mittens, she headed out into the snow, grateful for some sun and blue peeking through a layer of flat, white clouds. Reminders that winter didn't last forever.

The whole island shut down this time of year—and if you were one of the hardy year-rounders, you relied on Koester's Market and only a handful of other businesses to sustain your needs. One such place was the Skipper's Wheel, the solitary restaurant that kept regular hours all year, weather permitting. The diner-style eatery served all-day breakfast and sported a fisherman's theme of boat wheels, fishing net, and old-time pictures of sailors strewn on the walls as haphazardly as if someone had just thrown them up to see where they'd stick. It boasted the narrowest storefront on Harbor Street but was deep enough to hold a long Formica counter with vinyl-covered stools and more tables than you'd think could fit.

She found Meg and Dahlia at a table in the back, and their smiles warmed her as she shed her coat and traded greetings.

A waitress named Jolene approached to say, "Know what you want?"

The locals usually did. "Blueberry waffles and coffee," she answered, suspecting her friends had already ordered.

"Feels like it's been forever," Meg said, standing to greet her. "Your hair even seems longer." She finished on a soft laugh, reaching to twirl a finger through a lock of Suzanne's dark, naturally curly hair.

"I've missed you so much," Suzanne said in reply. At thirty-nine, Meg was only a year older than her and the two had instantly clicked upon meeting, becoming close friends. But Meg and her live-in boyfriend, Seth, had been away visiting family before Christmas, and since then…well, heartbreak and hibernation.

"Why didn't you come for New Year's Eve?" Meg asked, chestnut hair falling loose and wavy around her shoulders. She was perhaps the most sensible, even-keeled friend Suzanne had ever possessed.

Suzanne pursed her lips, scrunched her nose. "I was in a funk." She'd hated not responding to Meg's invitation to her Victorian home-turned-inn, but…heartbreak. It could really drive a girl to lethargy and ice cream.

"And just how is that funk going?" Dahlia asked. Their older friend sported silver hair and a hippie style, today expressed by a brightly hued sweater and tiny, purple-lensed spectacles.

"Still funky as ever," Suzanne confessed dryly.

"Sounds like we're in need of a serious catch-up," Meg said, reaching across the table to squeeze her hand. Funny how much one small touch could do, especially when there had—lately—been so few.

Suzanne nodded. "I have a lot to tell you." She blew out a heavy breath and tried to smile—tried to *be* a friend even as she *needed* a friend. "And I want to hear all about your holidays and everything I've missed."

At this, Meg smiled widely. "I do have some big news.

Unless—have you heard? But probably not, or you'd have called me for the details." Her smile faded into a scrunched nose. "Or is it insensitive to shove happy news down your throat when you're sad about something?"

That was Meg—always concerned for other people, always seeking a middle ground even if it came at her expense. But Suzanne was glad *someone* had something to be happy about. "No, I'd *love* to hear your news. Maybe it will distract me from my own garbage. Let 'er rip."

"Okay, here goes," Meg said. "Lila and Beck got engaged!"

Suzanne's heart dropped like a stone and she could barely breathe. She tried to hide her reaction, but from Meg's expression, knew it was written all over her face.

"What's wrong?" Meg asked.

Suzanne switched her glance from Meg to Dahlia and back again. Dahlia knew full well what was wrong—she'd been in on every heart-wrenching bit of it while Meg was away. And Dahlia surely already knew Meg's news and just hadn't had the heart to break it to Suzanne. Nor to break it to Meg why her younger sister's engagement wasn't good news for *everyone*.

"A funny thing happened while you were in Pennsylvania," Suzanne said to Meg now. She'd been planning to tell her anyway, of course—just under slightly less embarrassing, painful circumstances.

"What?" Meg asked, her voice barely a whisper beneath glaring overhead lights.

Suzanne swallowed around the lump in her throat. Last summer, when Beck Grainger had been pursuing *her*, she couldn't have dreamed it would turn out like *this*. "I...decided I liked him." The words came out more softly than intended, but she barreled onward. "More than liked him. I decided I was completely and totally smitten. And that I should make a play for him. And when that didn't work, rather than take the hint, I somehow convinced myself I should throw myself at him. Because suddenly he was the one—the one guy I wanted, the one who could help me move past Cal, the one I was sure still had a thing for me, too." Stopping, she pressed her lips flat together and pushed out a tired sigh through her nose—at the memory of her late husband, and the next part of the story. "Only by then, Lila was already here housesitting for you, and Beck had a thing for *her*."

"Oh God." Meg's face went ashen. Suzanne *really* should have told her all this before now—but she just plain hadn't wanted to.

"Though… I didn't know it was this serious," she informed Meg. "Like *engagement* serious." Feeling a little weak, she picked up one of three glasses of water and took a big drink. "But it's great. I'm happy for them. It's wonderful when two people find happiness together."

"You don't have to say that," Dahlia told her.

"You really don't," Meg agreed. "I mean—I had no idea. If I had, I wouldn't have blurted it out all bubbly and overjoyed. Because I'm really happy for my sister—but now I'm also really sad for my best friend."

Overall, Suzanne felt like a heel. "Do I know how to bring down a party or what?"

"It's okay," Meg told her softly, again touching her hand.

But Suzanne suddenly found it hard to look at Meg—who was clearly taken aback, suddenly shoved into an invisible tug-of-war between her sister and her bestie. And having lost the tug, the whole thing left Suzanne feeling a little pathetic.

"And now I suspect *I'm* going to bring the party down even further," Dahlia announced.

Both women flicked their gazes to her, and Suzanne feared she knew what was coming.

"I'm taking a trip," Dahlia announced, a thin smile unfurling on her face. "Heading south for the winter— like the rest of the sane world."

Meg's brows shot up, but Suzanne only sighed. Dahlia had warned Suzanne she might leave the island until spring—but since she was still here, Suzanne had assumed she'd changed her mind. It shouldn't matter so much—and yet it made her feel like a sixth grader finding out her BFF is going away to summer camp while she's stuck at home.

"Why don't you look happy about it?" Meg asked Dahlia.

Dahlia shifted a wisdom-filled gaze back and forth between them. "Because I know you both like having me around, perhaps most of all in winter. And I'm going to miss you."

"Then why exactly is it that you're leaving?" Suzanne inquired.

Dahlia shrugged. "Just a thirst for some sun and sand. I used to see the world, you know." Actually, Suzanne *didn't* know. Dahlia was the sort of woman you instinctively sensed had lived an adventurous life, but she seldom felt the need to talk about it. "I became the stay-at-home type after coming to Summer Island, and I'm ready for a getaway."

"Where specifically are you going?" Meg asked.

For a woman in her sixties, Dahlia just then managed to look downright mischievous. "To be determined as I go. But sandy beaches and an ocean view are definitely on the menu."

This time it was Meg who sighed, rather dreamily. "Sounds lovely." Meg seldom traveled, either, and the trip to see Seth's grandpa last month was the first time she'd left the inn for more than a few days since acquiring it upon her grandmother's death over fifteen years ago.

And a crazy, whimsical idea hit Suzanne. *We should all go!* The ultimate girls trip—Summer Island chicks in paradise. Only she knew Meg wouldn't leave the inn again so soon, and she probably wouldn't leave Seth—their romance was still in the honeymoon phase. And besides, flitting from beach to beach all winter would be expensive, making her wonder if Dahlia harbored secret riches. And… "Are you traveling with Mr. Desjardins, by chance?" Suzanne had been sad to see Dahlia's preholiday tryst, a charming older Frenchman, leave the island. A yes would make her feel at least a *little* better about Dahlia's departure.

"Oh—no," Dahlia said quickly, as if the very suggestion were absurd.

"I really need to get the full scoop on Mr. Desjardins," Meg remarked. She had missed the whole affair, after all.

"There's little to say," Dahlia threw out with a wave of her hand.

"There's a lot to say," Suzanne countered.

Dahlia switched her glance back and forth between them, looking surprisingly impish. "Then you can fill Meg in when I'm gone. But the man is entirely off my mind, I assure you."

Suzanne bit her lip. "Then who are you traveling with?"

"A friend," Dahlia said airily. And when Meg and Suzanne both looked perplexed, she added with a laugh, "You two aren't my only friends in the world, you know."

"Well, who *is* this friend?" Meg asked.

"Her name is Giselle."

Dahlia's shortness left Suzanne itching to ask more, but she feared she came off as nosy when she pried into Dahlia's life. For someone they knew well in ways, she kept a lot to herself. Only when Mr. Desjardins entered the picture had Suzanne started seeing Dahlia through a new lens. She was more than just the wise woman they all turned to for advice—she had an entire past they knew little about.

"When you get back," Suzanne said, "I want you to tell us stories. About your life."

At this, their older friend laughed. "I do have some good ones."

"So it's a deal? We'll gather at the inn or on the deck of the café." Dahlia's Café sat directly across Harbor Street from Suzanne's flower shop, Petal Pushers, and overlooked the water. "We'll drink wine and you'll tell us all the wonderful stories you never have."

Dahlia gave a succinct nod. "It's a deal."

"How's Zack?" Meg asked then. Zack Sheppard was Dahlia's nephew and Meg's ex-love, who'd driven her straight into Seth's arms with his commitment phobia. Meg was well shed of him as far as Suzanne was concerned, but he'd devolved into a dejected lump of surliness since the breakup.

Dahlia gave one of her classic, airy shrugs—even if tempered with a sadness that crinkled the corners of her eyes. "He's still not himself."

"You know we wouldn't have lasted forever," Meg said. "You know he's never going to change." Dahlia had lobbied hard for the relationship. She saw virtues in Zack no one else did—she was his only family, making her devotion something maternal and perhaps also noble, even if Suzanne didn't quite understand it herself.

Dahlia neither agreed nor disagreed with Meg, only

pursed her lips to suggest, "Perhaps he'll rebound come spring." Even if she looked doubtful as she said it. Zack was a Great Lakes fisherman, taking to the water from April 'til November—a major source of contention in his relationship with Meg. The upshot was that he for some reason loved a solitary existence on a little fishing trawler more than he'd loved Meg.

"I do hope so," Meg said solemnly, wistfully. "I want him to be happy."

"I don't believe he really knows *how* to be happy," Suzanne chimed in.

Both women looked at her.

"There, I said it." It was an obvious truth about the man no one ever quite spoke out loud, and she was feeling honest and not overly sympathetic at the moment. She looked to Dahlia. "And it's not your job to fix him, because he can't be fixed." Then to Meg. "And it's not your job to keep worrying about him—you resigned from that position." In her opinion, Zack Sheppard was a lost cause. And she felt fairly qualified to recognize a lost cause because she was starting to think maybe she was one, too.

They all glanced up, their mood cheering when Jolene delivered plates of yummy-smelling breakfast foods, and topics turned lighter. "Time to take down the Christmas tree." "Thank God for a break in the snow." "Who's read any good books I can take to the beach?"

All the while, though, Suzanne sank a little deeper into the malaise she'd hoped this lunch would cure. Her best friend's sister was engaged to the man she'd fallen for. It would drive a wedge between them—how could it not? And her other best friend was leaving, return date uncertain. The people who she'd thought would sustain her through the winter suddenly felt far away even as she sat around a table with them.

After they'd paid and put on their coats, Dahlia pulled them both into a snug embrace. "I leave in two days," she said. As if it were nothing.

Suzanne gasped. "So soon?"

Dahlia raised silvery brows. "Have to go before the lake freezes and the ferry stops running." Indeed, after that a person was literally stranded on Summer Island until the spring thaw. In parting, she hugged them each again, and even kissed their cheeks. "I love you both and will miss you madly. When you find yourself missing me, just think of spring!"

Suzanne had hoped seeing her friends would lift her spirits. But as she departed, she realized the opposite had happened, making each step through the snow a struggle. Dahlia was leaving, Meg had Seth now, and the man she pined for had asked another woman to marry him.

Collectively, it was enough to make her wonder— once again—if she'd made a mistake coming here, moving her business here. Maybe *she* should be the one getting the hell out of Dodge before that last ferry ran.

## CHAPTER TWO

THE INCESSANT BUZZ of his cell phone jarred Zack Sheppard awake. He didn't want to answer—he wanted to roll over and drift back into peaceful sleep. Winter on this godforsaken island should at least be good for that much, but apparently not. Snaking a hand from beneath the covers, he grabbed the phone up from a bedside table, drew it back into the dark with him. "Yeah?"

"Good morning, nephew!"

Of course it was his aunt. She was the only person who called him in winter, and certainly the only one who'd feel the need to do it this early. "Morning, Dahlia." He knew it came out sounding dry. He also knew that didn't bother her one damn bit. That's how things were between them. Dry. But easy.

"I'm calling to say goodbye," she announced.

Oh. Shit. That was today? "Already? This early?"

"It's almost noon. Not so early, my boy."

There was a wink in her tone, but the main thing he heard was the harsh reality of her departure. If she was disappointed that he hadn't bothered getting up to see her off, he couldn't tell. Maybe *he* was the disappointed one. He probably should have treated this goodbye with a little more reverence. But reverence wasn't his strong suit, especially not lately. Even so, he heard himself ask, "Need me to come get your bags to the ferry?"

She still sounded amused as she informed him, "Already got them there."

It didn't surprise him. She was a capable woman, the type who got out and walked more in a foot of snow than most people did on a summer day—so a few suitcases probably hadn't slowed her down any.

"So you're really going on this trip of yours." This damn mysterious trip. To parts unknown, for who knew how long, with someone he'd never heard her mention in his life.

"Of course. Everyone keeps acting so surprised by it, but I'm allowed to take a trip."

"Who's gonna cook for me while you're gone, woman?" He lived in an apartment above her café, and usually a lot of cooking happened *there*—even in winter when she was closed for the season, for the two of them.

On the other end of the phone, she let out a hearty laugh. "If that's your bellowing way of saying you're going to miss me, I'll miss you, too."

It was *exactly* that. Not much got past Dahlia. But he also seriously wondered what the hell he'd eat in the coming months. He wasn't a cook. And his aunt spoiled him when he was in port—with food, and her company, both of which he valued more than he let on.

"Let me get dressed, then I'll head to the ferry to say bye."

"Too late. I'm already gone."

Zack blew out a sigh. "Why didn't you call me earlier? I would've gotten up." *Should've* gotten up.

Another chuckle from her. "Didn't care to make a big to-do over it, that's all." Then she shifted topics. "Did you go to Koester's and get some groceries like I told you?"

His teeth gritted in frustration as he answered,

"Nope." Didn't have a damn thing in the place to eat, as a matter of fact.

"That's a shame," Dahlia imparted in her light, non-chalant way. "It's snowing like crazy out there. I'm lucky the ferry ran. Best get yourself to the store before they decide to close up. We're about to dock in St. Simon, so I have to go. Goodbye, Zack."

"Bye, Dahlia. Be safe."

Rolling out of bed—damn, it was cold in this drafty old building—he nudged the thermostat up a degree or two as he trundled to the bathroom in a pair of worn flannel pants and a gray T-shirt with tattered edges. He tended to wear things 'til they fell apart and only then replace them.

Splashing water on his face, he glanced in the old-fashioned medicine cabinet mirror above the sink to see a hollow shell of the man he'd been six months ago. Back then, he'd had a good life. Well, as good as a guy with serious trust and commitment issues could have.

But everything had changed when he'd lost Meg. He hadn't realized how much that loss would hurt. And now he was stuck on this tiny, snow-covered rock all winter, knowing she was right up the street with her good-looking handyman-turned-boyfriend. He'd known from the start something was going on there, but she'd denied it. Until it had become clear that she was lying, either to him or to herself—most likely the latter, because Meg wasn't deceptive.

*And even then, she gave you a chance.* To love her. To make promises to her. To be there for her. The first had been easy—the other two deal breakers. And now here he was, months later, still trying to claw his way back to the land of the living. She'd been his foundation, the thing that gave his life balance and support. And he hadn't even known it until it was too late.

He didn't bother showering—just pulled on a faded pair of blue jeans he found on the floor and a half-zip pullover Meg had given him a few Christmases ago. Adding a warm coat and boots, he opened the door to see the air swirling with snow against a wintry white backdrop. Stepping out onto the small landing above the wooden staircase that led down the side of the building, he looked south to see Lake Michigan teeming with chunks of ice but not quite frozen. The ferry probably wouldn't run for more than another day or two before the ice severed the connection to the mainland until likely April.

Patting a pocket to make sure he had his wallet, he started down the stairs—and the world dropped out from under him, his foot *whoosh*ing off the step on unseen ice. He instinctively grabbed for the railings on each side but missed—his ass hit hard against wood, and everything rolled past in a blur as he tumbled all the way to the bottom, landing in a heap in the snow.

*Shit.* His lower back hurt. Neck, too. He was gonna be sore for a while. *Just lie here a few minutes and shake it off. Get your senses back.*

But when the cold began seeping through his clothes, he knew it was time to get up. As a fisherman who'd taken to the water at sixteen, this wasn't the first time he'd slipped and fallen. Though maybe such tumbles were a little harder to rebound from at forty-two. Planting his elbows in the snow, then his hands, he pushed himself into a sitting position.

Despite that his back still hurt like hell, he started to stand. Only it didn't work—his legs weren't quite cooperating, so he plopped back to the snow. His right leg tingled with an irksome pins and needles sensation—must have been lying on it funny since hitting the ground.

His hands were cold—he hadn't worn gloves, damn it, which suddenly seemed stupid. But he hadn't expected to be lying around in the snow, either. When a bitter wind stung his face and his whole body suffered the bone-deep chill of winter, he tried to stand up once more. Only, same as before, he crumpled back to the snow, his right leg unwilling to support his weight.

"Zack."

He looked up. Meg—his Meg—stood over him like a parka-clad angel. Was she a mirage? A sweet oasis in a sea of snow? He'd seen mirages before—on the vast Great Lake waters. But he'd never seen one this pretty. *Which must mean she's real.*

"Are you all right? What happened—did you fall?"

In some ways, she was the last person he wanted to see him like this. But in others, she was the *only* person he wanted here right now—maybe the only person in the world who could truly help him.

*Answer her.* "Yes. To the falling part, not the being all right part." He shook his head, tried to form thoughts. "Can't seem to get up."

"Maybe you broke something. What hurts?"

*Think. Just think.* But things grew more foggy than clear. "My lower back. And my neck. Hit 'em both coming down. Slipped on ice." He wished vaguely that he could exhibit some pride—but was also grateful he didn't have to. This was Meg. "Can you help me get up?"

"If something is broken," she said, "you probably shouldn't. We should call the doctor."

Zack shook his head. "Nothing's broken. I've broken bones before—it's not that kind of pain. My leg is just weak. Can you help me try?" he asked again.

Their eyes met, and he knew his probably revealed more than he wanted—a debilitating vulnerability, inside and out. He'd been broken *inside* for months, but suddenly it showed.

*It's okay, though*—this was Meg. His Meg.

No, wait—not his anymore. She belonged to some other guy now. The thought was like a fist squeezing his heart, so he pushed it away. She *was* his. She *had* been for five years. He needed her right now—just as much as he needed to get to his feet and walk away from her.

"Okay," she agreed softly, then stooped beside him. As she put her arm around his back, his own draping her shoulders, it felt awkward, warm, to suddenly be touching again. Even more awkward because of why. He'd never felt so weak with her.

As she began to lift him, he got his left foot under him, not putting any weight on his right yet. Just that—being up out of the damn snow, feeling the ground beneath his boots—felt shockingly satisfying. "You're doing great," she said quietly, encouragingly.

Cautiously, he rested his weight on both legs—then collapsed back to the ground, pulling her down with him. "Shit," he muttered. His leg felt a little numb.

He lay on his back again, looking up at Meg, who now sat peering intently back at him. He missed that, just that connection of their eyes. Hers were green, like marbles. "Zack, you need more help than I can give you." She pulled out a phone. "I'm calling Dr. Andover."

Hanging up a minute later, she told him, "They're sending the snowmobile and sled." Summer Island was a land of bicycles and horse-drawn carriages, no motorized vehicles gracing its shores—except for the few snowmobiles tucked away for emergencies. He suddenly qualified as an emergency.

As they waited, he heard himself say without planning, "I'm a damn clumsy fool."

"It was ice," she reminded him. "Could have happened to anyone."

"In other ways, too," he said. What was drawing out such humbling honesty? Pain? Embarrassment? Or... he'd avoided seeing her since coming into port in November—and maybe he'd needed to say this for months.

When she didn't reply, he added, "I hope you're happy, Maggie May."

"I am," she was quick to answer. But did he see some glint of old emotion glimmer in her eyes at hearing his nickname for her? Probably just part of the mirage.

When the snowmobile could be heard in the distance—its noise grating in the winter silence—he prayed she would come with him to the doctor's office. A year ago, she would have, no question. She'd loved him then. Did love just...dissolve? Melt like a snowman in spring? Damn—spring. He couldn't wait 'til spring, 'til he could get back on the water and away from all of this—away from Meg, and memories, and feelings.

As a lone headlight cut through the snow swirling across Harbor Street—the snowmobile growing closer, louder—he reached out, grabbed her hand. Even through her mitten, it felt so damn good to touch her. Less awkward than when she'd been trying to help him stand. "Will you go with me?"

Meg's heart beat too hard against her chest as Zack held on to her. She'd never felt this before—Zack needing her. The whole five years he'd been in her life and her bed, he hadn't really. But now, suddenly, his need wrapped around her like a snug embrace.

She squeezed his hand instinctively, and her heart wanted her to go. But she told him, softly, "No." She had a man at home whom she loved. A man who treasured her in a way Zack hadn't until it was too late. And she hated sending him off alone, no one by his side—but she couldn't let herself be that close to him anymore. She couldn't be a part of this.

"I'll call Dahlia, tell her to meet you there," she said as the snowmobile pulled to a stop beside them, the smell of exhaust cloying.

"She's gone," he told her. "Left on the last ferry."

Oh. Oh no. "I'll call her anyway. She'll come back."

Climbing off the snowmobile, the EMT asked Zack a few questions, then said, "Let's get you to the doc so he can take a look."

Rather than watch the awkward maneuvering of Zack's body onto the travois-like sled behind the snowmobile, Meg took a few steps away to make her call, the one small bit of help she could give. Frustrated to reach Dahlia's voice mail, however, she left a message. "Please call me back right away. It's an emergency."

After which she had no choice but to return to where Zack lay, his torso and legs secured to the heavy plastic sled with seat belt–like straps. She peered down at him through the falling snow to say, "Dahlia didn't answer. But I'm sure I'll hear from her any minute."

Their eyes met, same as before. She sensed him trying to appear strong and stalwart now, trying to block out her refusal to go. But it didn't work. She wanted to drop to her knees and give him a hug. Or at least stoop down, take his hand once more. Yet instead she only said, "You'll be all right, Zack."

He just nodded. And when the snowmobile began to move forward, the sled with it, their gazes stayed locked, his eyes lonely and wanting.

As she stood watching the sled get farther away, it

reminded her of every time she'd watched his fishing boat sail toward Lake Huron, getting smaller and smaller until he was gone. But this was different. Everything about this was different, making her heart hurt in a different way. It hurt for him instead of for her.

Only when the snowmobile and sled were completely out of sight did she look back toward the Summerbrook Inn. She made out Seth's shape on the front porch through the snow—he lifted his hand in a wave. Returning it, she hoped he could somehow understand the soft spot still in her heart for the other man. But what a horrible thing to ask of someone. Especially since she didn't even understand it herself.

That was when her phone rang and she rushed to answer. While hating to put a crimp in Dahlia's plans, she spoke directly. "Zack has taken a fall down the steps to his apartment."

"Oh no. He's hurt?"

Meg explained, ending with, "Can you catch the next ferry back?"

"Well, I… No," Dahlia answered quietly.

"What?" It came out as a gasp.

"I'm not sure they'll make any more runs today given the weather, and…I have a plane to catch. I'm sorry, but you'll have to handle this in my stead."

Meg just blinked, her jaw dropping. Was this really Dahlia? Dahlia who loved Zack and was always there for him? "I…I can't do that, Dahlia," she said, keeping her voice down. "I can't go to the doctor with him like I'm still his girlfriend. It wouldn't feel right."

"Then…get Suzanne to go with you."

"What?" Meg said again, just as aghast. "Why on earth would I do that?"

"To make it less awkward. And because someone has to do it since I can't."

*Or won't.* Perhaps the ferry *wouldn't* run again today, but it sounded like Dahlia wouldn't come back even if it did.

As Meg stood, speechless, trying to make sense of all this, Dahlia continued to beseech her. "Please, Meg. Just get Suzanne and go, and call me, the three of you together, after he's seen the doctor." And when she still said nothing in reply, Dahlia added, "Meg, no one wants to be alone at a time like this."

Hanging up, it was impossible to ignore the old feelings fluttering around her like the blowing snowflakes, along with the guilt. Dahlia had *always* made her feel guilty about Zack, about not wanting to put up with his neglect, as if she should have. About breaking up with him, as if he'd ever even made their relationship official. But now *she* felt like the neglectful one—even if that was silly because it wasn't her place to do what had been asked of her.

Maybe she shouldn't have come to his aid in the first place.

When Seth had spotted someone out the window lying in the snow, she'd come to look, and even at a distance, even though he was the last person she'd expect to have an accident, she'd known in a second: "It's Zack."

"Maybe we should call somebody?" Seth had asked. "Or you want me to go see to him?"

Her heart had felt ripped down the center. Because Zack would detest having Seth's help, having Seth see him that way. And probably she *should* have just called someone, but instead she'd said, "I should go." And she'd thrown on her snow boots and parka before Seth could blink—or protest. And maybe that had been wrong of her. She wasn't sure right now. Right and wrong seemed forever shaded with gray when pulled between these two men.

Now she texted Seth that she wouldn't be home just yet, then walked through the snow to Suzanne's cottage around the corner, soon banging on the door. When Suzanne answered, wide-eyed, saying, "Well, this is a nice surprise," Meg stopped her in her merry tracks.

"Don't be too happy to see me until I tell you why I'm here."

# CHAPTER THREE

AFTER A FEW X-RAYS, Dr. Andover had ruled out breaks and fractures, presented a pair of crutches, and had Zack fumbling and stumbling around on them. He trundled out into the waiting area expecting to see Dahlia—only to find Meg and Suzanne sitting there instead.

"What the hell are you two doing here?" He knew he sounded snarly, but didn't care. He had plenty to feel snarly about, and what was with Meg's about-face? "And where's Dahlia?" He sagged on the crutches as he spoke.

Both women looked uncomfortable. *That makes three of us.* "She asked us to meet you and to call her when you came out," Meg said, appearing unable to meet his eyes for some damn reason. Maybe the awkwardness from when he'd fallen. He wished he'd hidden his feelings better.

As he slumped onto a nearby chair, she rushed to dial her phone, putting it on speaker in time for Dahlia to say, "Zack? Are you okay? What did the doctor say?"

"That I'll live," he answered shortly. That got no response, though, so he'd have to go on. "Uh, short version is—the numbness and tingling probably means a nerve injury, but since I have feeling in my leg and can put a little weight on it now, the doc doesn't think it's serious. Kinda wanted me to see a specialist on the mainland for an MRI, but I don't want to get stuck there for the winter, so he didn't push it. Biggest problem is it'll probably be a week or two before I can get around on my own, and the doc said I'll need somebody with me around the clock 'til then, so…you on your way back yet?" The situation sucked, and he didn't like trashing Dahlia's plans—but things could be worse. At least he'd be ready to take to the water again by the time the ice melted.

Dahlia replied, "Well, nephew, that's a big relief. You had me worried."

"Yeah," he said, "guess it seemed worse than it was at first. You on the ferry back?"

When she didn't answer right away, his chest tightened slightly. "About that," she began. "Suzanne, are you there?"

Though the three of them had avoided eye contact so far, now they all exchanged glances. "Yeah," Suzanne said cautiously. "Why?"

"I need your help," Dahlia told her.

Suzanne's eyes went wide. "*My* help? With what?"

Dahlia took another moment answering. "I wish I could be there for Zack right now, but I can't. So I need you to take care of him for me."

Zack just gaped at the phone in Meg's hand. Was Dahlia serious? She was the only person he had to rely on and she was leaving him *now*, like *this*? "You're still going?"

"I'm sorry, Zack. But you'll be fine before you know it, and this trip is important to me."

He wanted to yell at her—but he didn't have the strength. And what it came right down to was: she owed him nothing. Maybe it was crazy to have assumed she'd cancel her trip for this. After all, he'd be back on his feet soon enough.

He hated himself for letting it sting, though. Hated himself for assuming she'd put him first. Just like Meg—

she was one more person he'd taken for granted, one more person who wasn't gonna be there when he needed her. Even if he couldn't quite blame her.

When everyone stayed quiet, she added, "I really just need this time away."

He still said nothing. Even if he wondered what the hell it was she needed time away *from*. She loved this place—summer and winter alike. She *was* this place. She was the reason Summer Island had become his home.

"I would think you, of all people, might be able to understand," she told him calmly. "You need time away each summer. You need as much time away as the weather allows."

That was different and she knew it. She was a people person—he was the opposite. She knew how to be a part of a community; she thrived on that stuff. He never had.

"Even if it doesn't make sense to you," she went on, "it's the only way I can explain."

"I didn't ask you to, woman," he snapped, unplanned.

"But I'll make sure you're taken care of."

*I'm not a goddamn invalid.* That's what he almost said. But then he realized...that's *exactly* what he was.

She went on—now talking about him to Meg and Suzanne as if he wasn't even there. "Obviously he can't stay in his apartment—up a flight of stairs. Suzanne's place makes the most sense."

Zack and Suzanne both objected simultaneously. "*Her* place?" "*My* place?"

Then he glanced at Suzanne to see the look of horror that had reshaped her face. She'd never liked him, and now her crystal blue eyes appeared downright icy.

Dahlia's voice, however, stayed completely undisturbed and pragmatic. "You have a pullout couch and the bathroom's nearby. And your house is near the café, making it easy to get anything he needs from his apartment, now or going forward. And Meg, that's where you come in. I'm asking a lot of Suzanne, so can you help by going to Zack's and packing up some clothes and toiletries while Suzanne gets him situated in her cottage?"

Suzanne stayed quiet, perhaps shell-shocked.

"Listen," he said, "I don't blame you for not wanting to have me dropped on your doorstep. I'm not too crazy about it, either. So don't worry about it—I'll get by on my own."

At this, however, she rolled her eyes and said, "I'd love to see how."

"I'll figure it out," he grumbled. "Just buy me some groceries and I'll drag myself up the stairs on my ass if I have to."

And as the two women across from him exchanged looks, he realized his error—that he could barely get up on crutches at all, so taking care of himself really *would* be impossible. *All* of this was impossible. A goddamn impossible mess.

And then Suzanne dropped her gaze to the floor, her countenance suddenly changing—into something softer if even still stunned, as she quietly said, "It does come down to me, doesn't it." She looked toward the phone. "Dahlia's gone." And then at Meg. "And you're living with Seth." And then to Zack. "And you, apparently, have forged relationships with no other human beings on this planet besides these two. So by virtue of living alone and being Dahlia's friend, it comes down to me." She sounded acceptant—and maybe, at the same time, defeated.

"You're also a nurse," Dahlia reminded her. "An orthopedic nurse, in fact. That's why I'm asking this of you."

Zack sat up a little straighter, surprised. "You're a nurse?"

"I was," Suzanne told him. "In a former life."

Still shocked beyond belief, Suzanne searched her soul. She didn't want this. She didn't want this at all. The only redeeming quality this winter had held for her was the freedom to hibernate for a while. She'd thought it would give her time to just…get over things. Over romantic hopes dashed. Over the fact that Beck Grainger would soon join Meg's family, creating a possible disconnect from her friend when she needed her the most. Over everything that suddenly felt wrong. On her own. In peace.

She looked at Zack. The waves in his brown hair seemed more unkempt than usual, the expression in his gray eyes more belligerent. She'd once almost thought him ruggedly handsome—but the fact that he'd made her best friend unhappy had taken away any sense that he might be even mildly attractive. And since the breakup his general attitude had ensured that.

And yet she was a nurse. Once upon a time she'd taken the Nightingale Pledge. And even if that part of her life felt long in the past, for her, commitments ran deep. She had promised to help others heal, regardless of whether she liked them, whether she thought they were stubborn or stupid or difficult.

Of course, she'd never promised to do it in her own home, twenty-four hours a day. But in this moment of seeing no other choice, she tried to push that aside. And much as she loathed this idea, she also wasn't sure how she'd live with herself if she refused.

"I'm doing this," Suzanne announced, "because I'm a good person, I was and still am a good nurse, and it's the right thing to do. And frankly, I hope some of you will take a lesson from that—about the right thing to do."

Maybe she shouldn't have said that, but she meant it—she thought it was wrong of Dahlia to abandon him, wrong of Zack to have not even considered care on the mainland, and wrong of Meg to...well, maybe Meg wasn't at fault here whatsoever, but Suzanne felt a little mad at her anyway. Just because. *Why did I ever encourage her to break up with him? If she hadn't, this would be* her *problem, and she'd be handling it with complete devotion.*

Suzanne could tell they were all taken aback, but she didn't care. "Don't look at me that way—I have the right to be pissed here. Now, we'll need the snowmobile back to get him moved to my place. Meg, would you go to his apartment as Dahlia asked and gather up some things? And Dahlia...enjoy your trip, I guess."

Dahlia's sigh was audible through the phone. "Please don't be mad, Suzanne. This is just something I have to do for myself."

What was up with her? But it hardly mattered at the moment—all Suzanne could do now was throw herself into problem-solving mode, get this ingrate moved into her usually peaceful cottage, and hope he didn't drive her out of her mind before he could walk again.

MEG SCALED THE stairs carefully, gripping the railing tight in one mitten. Then she let herself into Zack's apartment.

While she'd never spent much time here with him—the inn being roomier and more pleasant—it was still jarring to suddenly be in his personal space. The whole place was messier than she might have expected—reminding her he'd been depressed lately. About her. One more reason that made it strange to be here.

She resisted the urge to pick up after him—that wasn't her job. Her job was to go digging through his private belongings and pack a bag for him to live from for a week or two. She blew out a sigh, the task suddenly looming larger than she'd expected. It had sounded like such a simple assignment. But it wasn't.

Because everywhere she looked, she saw...herself. Her life with him. A framed photo of them together on Dahlia's deck still sat on a bookshelf. Plastic containers in which she'd once given him leftovers appeared to still be in use, sitting dirty in the sink.

On the bedroom floor, she found the duffel bag he took with him on the *Emily Ann*, the fishing boat he'd named after his little sister who'd died young. And as she packed sweatpants and waffle-weave pullovers, she recognized them all, remembered washing them for him at times, snuggling up against them on his body at others. Sweatshirts were the same—familiar items she'd once felt were...almost hers in a way, just by virtue of having been close to him for so long.

She'd avoided looking for underwear, but it had to be done. She grabbed a stack of white boxer briefs from a chest and thrust them into the bag, trying not to feel anything. *They're just pieces of fabric, not memories.* And yet, they *were* memories. Warm memories. Hot memories. But also memories of a longing that went beyond sex, which he'd been unable to fulfill.

Her relationship with Seth didn't change the fact that she and Zack had split only a little over six months ago. And normally, she was busy building a new life with Seth, having fun with Seth, having sex with Seth, cooking and eating and sleeping and everything else—all with Seth. But right now, just like out in the snow this morning, she was forced to…feel things. She glanced at the unmade bed, glad she'd never slept here with him— again, all sleeping and other bed activities had taken place at the inn. And yet she could almost smell him in the sheets, in the room, in this whole place.

*Quit standing here. Finish packing and get back to the life you chose with Seth. This is over. Finished. Yesterday's news.* She was simply surprised it was hitting her so hard, like a punch in the gut.

Socks—she'd forgotten socks. Back to the chest— she located the sock drawer and pulled out several pairs. What was it about a man's socks? Maybe it was silly, but somehow she thought she could feel everything from a guy's masculinity to his vulnerability in a simple pair of cozy winter socks. Maybe it was about warmth and comfort and cuddling.

Her chest tightened. *You cuddle with Seth now. You love Seth.*

In fact, she suffered the intense urge to be home with him right now, telling him everything that was happening, about Dahlia leaving and Suzanne getting stuck caring for Zack, and…well, maybe she wouldn't tell him *everything*. It was normal to have old feelings for someone you used to love.

Or…did love really end just because you walked away and connected with someone new? After all, she hadn't parted with Zack because she didn't love him anymore— they'd parted because *he* didn't love *her* enough. And Seth had. The wisest move would be to just forget about all these old feelings suddenly rearing their ugly heads as quickly as possible.

With a last look at Zack's apartment, she exited back out into the cold, bag in hand, and pulled the door shut tight. It instantly felt like a safer place to be—despite the bitter wind and steps still slick with ice. Flipping the hood up on her parka, she carefully descended onto snowy Harbor Street, then made her way to Suzanne's cottage.

Though she hesitated before ringing the bell. Suzanne was understandably upset. Zack was hurting and frustrated, too. And given that Suzanne hadn't been his biggest fan even on his good days, this seemed, frankly, like a recipe for disaster. But she braced herself and pressed the doorbell with the tip of one mitten.

When Suzanne opened the door, her tension came spilling out. "Hey," she said briskly.

"Hey," Meg returned—then held out the bag. "Clothes and toiletries, as requested."

Suzanne took it, replying sullenly, "Thanks."

Meg couldn't see Zack from the door, but asked softly, "How is he?"

"Grumpy. Unpleasant," she said. Then her blue eyes widened hopefully. "Do you want to come in for a few minutes?"

And Meg saw—felt—it was a cry for help. But she couldn't—she just couldn't. The whole day had made her realize she shouldn't be around Zack. For her own sake. And for his, too. So she pointed in the general direction of the inn. "I…should get back to Seth."

Suzanne's eyes settled back into sullenness. "Okay." Delivered with just the tiniest bite. So what Meg really heard was, *I get it. Run back to your sweet new boyfriend while I'm stranded here with your angry, injured old one.*

"I'm sorry. It's…"

"What?"

*Try to explain. Even if you'd rather not.* "It's more

complicated than I expected," she said, still keeping her voice down. "I hate that you're stuck in this position— but I don't think I should be around him. Because he still has feelings for me. And *I* still..."

Suzanne's eyebrows lifted as Meg trailed off. "Oh, you still...too? I just thought... I mean... Seth."

Meg bit her lip. *Explain better now.* She shook her head. "It's just an old, residual thing, lingering memories. Half the clothes in that bag are things I gave him, you know? It'll fade more with time, but right now...it's still weird." She met Suzanne's gaze more fully. "I'm sorry I can't be more help. It's not fair to you."

"I understand," Suzanne said, this time seeming more herself.

"Call me if I can get anything else, though. Or be of help in any other way."

Suzanne nodded.

And Meg reached out to squeeze her friend's hand, promising, "This will be over soon and life will get back to normal."

# CHAPTER FOUR

"DO YOU NEED HELP?"

"No." More of a grunt than a word.

Suzanne watched as Zack hobbled to her bathroom, remembering that a patient's first time on crutches sometimes looked like a baby deer learning to walk. At one point, he accidentally put his weight down on the injured leg and let out a yowl as it dropped out from under him, but he caught himself. Then he banged one crutch into a door frame. *Oh good, I'll get to do touch-up painting after he's gone. This just keeps getting better and better.*

"Are you sure?" she asked, her voice cautious but laced with a tinge of sarcasm.

"I've got it," he snapped.

*Sure ya do.* "Just…try not to break anything, okay? In my house," she added. In case it sounded like she was concerned for his bones. And maybe she should be—but at the moment, she felt more protective of her cute little cottage. She wanted to *keep* it cute. Even if it no longer felt like the private sanctuary it had been only an hour ago.

"Relax," he grumbled. "I'll fix anything I break."

She found that response less than reassuring. But decided to keep that to herself as she went to stir the chili she'd started in her slow cooker back when this had been just a normal winter day. Better to stir than stand outside the bathroom door listening and waiting like some worrywart mom. The chili smelled good, the perfect balm for a cold, snowy afternoon. Or evening—darkness had fallen a little while ago, coming early this time of year. But the comfort food had sounded more comforting back when she'd been planning to eat alone.

A moment later, the bathroom door burst open and Zack and his crutches came trundling out, still flailing and Bambi-like. If Bambi could be compared to a surly man who hated life right now. Seemed unfair to the cartoon deer.

When one crutch literally got away from him, hitting the floor, he cursed, and Suzanne went to help the big lug, whether either of them liked it or not. Moving instinctively, she slid beneath the shoulder where the crutch had been, anchored her arm around his waist, and hoisted him in the direction of the sofa bed where he'd been resting since his arrival.

"Hand me the damn crutch," he said.

"You're not very good with crutches yet, and I'm sturdier. So I think what you meant to say was 'thank you.'"

His indecipherable grumble made her eyes roll. She'd never stood this close to Zack before and he smelled masculine and musky, his body solid against her side. The simple awareness somehow left her feeling even more awkward, and after plopping him down onto the pullout couch, she was relieved to walk away, picking up the crutch to place it with its mate.

"Tomorrow I'll teach you how to use the crutches better."

"No need—I'll get used to 'em."

Another eye roll. "There *is* a need actually," she insisted, crossing the room toward the wide opening to the kitchen. "My need to not have to carry you to the bathroom for a week."

When he didn't reply, she glanced over to see him glowering back. Their gazes met, but she found it oddly unnerving and looked away.

It struck her that they'd never looked each other in the eye before—she knew him only as Meg's one-time boyfriend, Dahlia's nephew. They'd always been at odds and resentment had hung in the air. And now—this. He was in her home. Dependent on her. And clearly resenting *that*.

"Do you want some chili?" The question seemed the wiser, simpler path than continuing down the resentment road.

Though the offer appeared to throw him slightly—he looked confused, and then said, "Oh, that's what I smell."

"I imagine you're hungry. Want a bowl?"

He looked a little less belligerent as he said, "Yep."

And it was only as she turned back toward the kitchen counter, reaching for bowls in an overhead cabinet, that it dawned on her to ask, "How's your pain?"

He didn't answer right away. But as she swirled a big spoon through the tangy-smelling chili, he admitted, "Pretty bad."

That's when she realized how out of practice she was at nursing. His pain level should have been on her mind, much more than how he smelled. "How bad on a scale of one to ten?"

He let out a sigh, appearing to think it through. "Five."

She suspected it was higher but that he didn't want to seem weak—the problem with asking people to scale their pain was that everyone worked on a different scale. He was suffering both muscular and nerve pain, nerve pain being trickier to deal with. Dr. Andover had suggested anti-inflammatories might ease the nerve issues, and prescribed low-dose Percocet for the other, which the drugstore had opened especially to fill. "You can take some pain meds with dinner," she told Zack now.

"No," he said.

She leaned her head back in frustration, blew out a breath.

"I don't need it. Don't want my brain clouded."

She pinned him in place with a glare. "Look, tough guy, that's admirable and all, but we need to control the pain cycle. The longer pain goes untreated, the worse it gets. Managing the pain promotes healing in numerous ways. So this isn't a request, or an option—it's an order."

He shot her a look through narrowed eyes. "You had to go and be a nurse, didn't you?"

"Yeah, I'm regretting that career choice pretty much right now myself."

"I'm going to kill Dahlia when she gets back."

"Get in line."

With that, she turned back to ladling the thick chili into two bowls. She made Zack a tray, including a can of soda and his medication. Carrying it to where he sat, legs stretched out before him, she lowered it to his lap and said, "Pills first. While I watch."

He cast a skeptical glance upward. "Are you serious?"

"Yes," she said. "As a nurse dispensing an opioid, I need to be sure what you've taken."

"Fine," he bit off. Then popped the top on the can, threw the pills into his mouth, and washed them down. "Happy, nurse?"

"Overjoyed," she said dryly. Then left him to find her remote and turn on the TV, suspecting they'd both welcome a distraction.

From her small dining table, she watched the evening news out of Sault Ste. Marie, currently airing a short feature about Great Lakes fishermen biding their time in winter. "Winter is our summer," said a crusty-looking old fellow. "Sure, I s'pose the time off's nice, but most of us got mouths to feed and are itchin' to get back out there early as we can."

"You can say that again," Zack muttered. "Spring can't come fast enough."

It surprised her only because, no matter how great his affinity for the water, she'd have thought he'd be more wrapped up in the matter at hand right now. "What is it with you and fishing?" she heard herself ask without planning.

Zack's gaze shot defensively to hers. "It's how I make my living."

But she was truly trying to understand. "I just mean… you really seem to love it." She tried to speak without accusation. And the distance and low evening lighting made it a little easier to look at him now. "What do you love about it?"

He shoveled another spoonful of chili into his mouth, taking his time with an answer. Finally he said, "Not the fish so much. Not even the work so much. Just…the quiet of it. The dependability of it. Doesn't hold a lot of surprises. And I like my freedom."

He'd sounded almost forthright until the last part, which reverted to defensiveness. She supposed he'd had to spend a lot of time defending his choices to Meg, and maybe to him Suzanne just seemed like an extension of her. After all, that was all she'd ever been to him… until now.

"Mmm," was all she said. It seemed the safest reply. And she had no desire to over-engage with this man while he was under her roof. She was the caregiver; he was the patient.

It was just past seven when she emerged from the kitchen to see he'd fallen asleep, empty chili bowl balanced on his stomach, fingers still loosely wrapped about the spoon handle. It reminded her that an injury could wipe a person out.

Stepping up beside him, she bent to gingerly lift the bowl. As his fingers fell away and she reached over him to grab the tray, the nearness again created that strange awareness. *You've been away from nursing too long.* Being in someone's space when performing nursing duties had never bothered her before—if it bothered you, you couldn't be an effective nurse.

At least a few days' scruff covered his jaw—showing he wasn't diligent about shaving. Maybe it was a winter thing. Or a depression thing. The edge of his sweatshirt currently revealed his lower stomach and the drawstring of his sweatpants, and she thought about pulling it down but stopped—not wanting to wake him and have him see her tugging on his clothes. Again, simple nursing care shouldn't create such concerns—but she supposed this was less than simple, for all the reasons she'd been mired in the last few hours. A smattering of dark hair lay curled across his lower abdomen, above the drawstring. *Why are you looking at it?*

When her phone trilled a text notification from across the room, she flinched, took a step back—and the spoon rattled in the bowl. As Zack shifted in his slumber, she retreated quickly to the kitchen, feeling almost as if she'd been caught at something. Which was silly, of course.

When she returned to the living room, she gave the sleeping man only a quick glance as she passed, then lowered herself into her favorite easy chair, next to the fireplace, currently alight with warm, cozy flames. After muting the TV, she plucked up her phone to find a text from Dahlia. How's Zack?

Sleeping, Suzanne typed back to her.

Another text arrived a moment later. And how are you? Still mad at me?

Suzanne stared at the phone. She'd spent much of her life being a little too quiet and a little too polite. But Cal's death five years ago had drained some of the polite right out of her. The rawness of losing her husband in the prime of both their lives had made her less guarded, more honest.

Truthfully, I'm confused. Why me? The nurse thing aside, there's an island full of people you've known for twenty years.

Dahlia's reply came quickly. The nurse thing aside, I trust you. I trust your loving spirit.

More frank honesty. I don't feel very loving right now.

But you are, Dahlia replied. Like it or not. I thought through everyone who winters on the island, and you're the one I picked.

It's like winning a backward lottery. Like being a Hunger Games tribute.

She could almost hear Dahlia laughing before she replied, I know he can be unpleasant, but you'll both survive this.

Unless I kill him. Where are you?

Atlanta. Layover, Dahlia answered.

Where are you flying to?

Grand Cayman.

Suzanne sighed, thinking how nice that sounded. Sunny days, warm nights, tan skin. How long will you be there?

Undecided.

And this friend of yours is with you? What was her name again?

Giselle. And yes.

Well, have a nice trip.

Suzanne wondered, after she sent it, if it sounded terse. She hadn't meant it that way, but it still stung that Dahlia had abandoned her beloved nephew and dumped him on Suzanne.

I'll be in touch. And, Suzanne, thank you. I appreciate this more than I can say.

A small lump formed in Suzanne's throat when she least expected it. But she didn't answer. She didn't even know why she felt the lump. So she just turned the phone's screen to black and listened to the crackle of the fire as she peered across the room at the injured man on her sofa. Practically a stranger in some ways. And if not a stranger, more an enemy than a friend. Was that why she felt on the verge of tears? Or was it something more?

Was it still the heartache of Beck Grainger choosing someone else? Was it that being confined with someone you didn't like was almost worse than being lonely? Was it feeling distant from Meg—and now Dahlia, as well? Was it winter and whiteness and cold—the sensation of being trapped in a snow globe? Was it wondering how her life before six years ago—when she was a happy florist deeply in love with her handsome doctor husband—had somehow devolved into this?

Maybe it had just been a long six years.

Somberly, she pushed up from the chair, turned off the TV, stoked the fire. Then she walked back over to the sofa bed and once again peered down. Stomach still showing. Eyes still shut. The nurse in her felt glad he was sleeping peacefully. And it was also the nurse in her who reached for the quilt at the foot of the mattress to lay it gently over him.

Unfortunately, it disturbed his slumber enough that he let out a heavy breath, stirred slightly, and opened his eyes.

"Sorry to wake you," she whispered, then made a show of pulling the quilt up, so he'd understand she wasn't just hovering over him like a crazed stalker.

It surprised her when he said, "S'okay," his voice softer than she'd ever heard it before. Then, "The chili was good."

It drew out an unwitting smile. "I'm glad you liked it. Get some sleep."

He nodded against his pillow, and she watched his gray eyes—green in some lighting perhaps—fall shut again. She studied his eyelashes briefly. She didn't know why.

Or maybe it was about…intimacy. Because in one way he was a stranger, but in another, he definitely wasn't. And she was suddenly watching him sleep, covering him up, and standing close enough to notice the way his lashes lay against his face, and the way life on the water had turned his skin slightly ruddy—but that looking a little weathered made him no less handsome, instead only adding character and maybe a few question marks about his life.

*But again, why are you looking at him?*

She flipped off the dim lamp on an end table. Then turned to walk toward her bedroom.

"Thank you."

Caught off guard, she stopped, glanced back, met his gaze in the firelight. "It's only chili."

"No. I mean, thank you."

That was all, but somehow she heard everything he

wasn't saying. He was grateful for her care. And maybe embarrassed that the one person he'd thought he could depend on had deserted him. And hurt that the other person he used to depend on lived with another man now. She heard it all. And felt more empathy for him than she'd known she could.

Nodding an acknowledgment, she said, "Goodnight, Zack. Everything will look brighter in the morning."

SUN IN ZACK'S eyes made him pull the covers over his head. But…he wasn't in his own bed. Flipping them back down, he eased open tired eyes. Shit. He was at Suzanne's. Suzanne, who could barely tolerate him. And he usually felt the same. Of all the people for Dahlia to leave him with.

But she had been…decent to him last night. More than decent. Even if she didn't like him.

He blew out a breath, disgusted by the whole situation all over again. But hadn't she said things would look brighter today? Maybe she was right. Maybe his leg would feel stronger. And he had no idea when his meds were due, but his only discomfort was a dull ache in his lower back. So maybe they'd done what she said— broken the pain cycle.

The aroma of bacon lifted his spirits a little further. Dahlia made him bacon. Meg used to make him bacon. Maybe this was what people meant by comfort food. Without even weighing it, he called out, "That smells great!"

Suzanne's dark, curly head peeked out from the kitchen. She didn't quite smile—but she didn't look as unhappy as she had for most of last evening. "How do you like your eggs?"

"Over easy. Over hard. Scrambled. Doesn't matter—never met an egg I didn't like."

Now she smiled. Even laughed a little. Possible she'd never heard him be very talkative. And he didn't know why he was being that way now. Maybe it was bacon. Maybe it was hope.

"You want to try coming to the table to eat?" she suggested.

When he glanced at his nemeses, the crutches, leaning near the end table, she must have taken his hesitation as doubt, adding, "If you'd rather stick to the bed for now, it's okay—I'll make you a tray."

But the last thing he wanted was to stick to the bed. He wanted back on his feet as soon as possible. "No, I need to use the bathroom anyway, so if I'm gonna get up, might as well sit at the table."

As she walked toward him, reaching for the crutches, he took in her fleecy pink pajamas with gray cat faces on them. Not what he'd expected from the woman he'd always thought smug and self-righteous. "You don't seem like the cat-pajama type," he informed her.

Passing him the crutches, she said, "Then you misjudged me."

When he tried to take them from her, though, she said, "No, wait," and pulled them back. "You're going to learn to use these the right way today."

"C'mon," he protested. "I'm hungry. And I have to pee. It's too early to concentrate."

"Just put your feet on the floor and let me show you the right way to stand up on them."

"For cryin' out loud, woman," he groused. And he was about to object and complain further—when he realized something wasn't right. He'd tried to swing his legs over the side of the bed, but it wasn't quite happening. Now he looked down to see his left leg lying awkwardly across the right one, when he knew good and well he hadn't crossed it over that way.

"What…are you doing?" Her voice came cautiously—and he knew that even as she'd spoken, she'd realized something was wrong. More wrong than it had been yesterday.

Looking down at his legs, he made another focused effort to swing them over the side of the mattress. As a result, the left one crossed over the right even farther—and the right didn't move at all. He blinked, his chest tightening. He tried to get words out, but they stuck in his throat. Breathing was suddenly hard. "My leg…"

"Can…can you move it?"

He tried again. Nothing happened. He shook his head. Then closed his eyes. Maybe this was just a nightmare.

"Zack, do you feel this?"

"Feel what?"

"Do you feel my hand?"

He opened his eyes to see her squeezing his right calf—but he didn't feel a goddamn thing. He blinked, trying to grasp the situation.

"Do you?" she asked, her voice rising with the same panic now entrenched inside him.

He didn't want to answer, didn't want to make this real.

*"Do you?"*

"No." So light a whisper he'd barely heard it beneath the sound of bacon frying. The scent turned acrid now, no longer sweet and inviting. "It's burning," he murmured.

"Your leg?" He looked up to see wide bluc eyes filled with concern.

"No, the bacon."

Her jaw dropped open; she looked confused. "Oh. God. Who cares?"

"Go get it off the stove," he commanded. "Don't burn the damn house down."

He knew the bacon didn't matter—but it felt important to preserve some sense of normalcy, control, even if it was only breakfast. While she was gone, he looked down, tried again—desperately—to move his leg, to make sense of this. Yesterday it had moved fine.

When she came back, appearing shaky, tense, he said, "What the hell is happening?"

"I'll call Dr. Andover."

Zack raised his gaze to her. "You were this kind of nurse, right? An orthopedic nurse. So you know what's going on here."

She hesitated. "We should really—"

"Just tell me what you think, Suzanne." Because he could see in her eyes that she understood this better than he did. And that she didn't want to tell him because it wasn't good.

"I'm not qualified to give a diagnosis, Zack."

"Just tell me, damn it."

He watched her draw in a deep breath. "Sometimes..." She stopped, blinked, then glanced down, clearly uncomfortable. "Sometimes paralysis doesn't happen right when the initial injury occurs. Sometimes it takes a day or two for the nerves to stop sending signals to the brain." He pictured a complex network of nerve endings working like electrical wires, sputtering and blinking on and off before they died altogether. And she was saying his had done that now—died altogether.

"When it only affects one limb," she went on, "it's called monoplegia. It's more commonly the result of cerebral palsy or a stroke, but can occasionally be caused by nerve damage due to an injury. And with nerve damage every case is different, unique and…" Her voice had begun to quiver. "I'm sorry, Zack, but I'm going to call Dr. Andover. Because things like this are rare, and I'm not educated enough about them to be telling you these things."

Zack said nothing. Because his brain had pretty much ceased functioning, right along with those nerves, somewhere between the words *paralysis* and *monoplegia*. He could hear her voice but no longer take in what she was saying. And then he heard her on the phone to the doctor, and then Dahlia, in the kitchen, from where the scent of burned bacon still wafted.

When she re-entered the room he couldn't quite make himself look up at her. "The doctor's on his way. And I let Dahlia know what's happening. Would you…like me to make more bacon?"

Now he looked up—to see her holding a spatula. And realized she'd been right—the bacon didn't matter. In fact, he wasn't sure he'd ever want to eat again. "No."

She blew out a shaky, audible breath. "Sorry." Then lowered the spatula to the dining room table. After which she announced, "I'm going to get dressed," and disappeared into her bedroom. When she came back out, she looked as if she'd been crying.

Ten minutes later, Dr. Andover arrived. The elderly doctor with the jowls of a basset hound did the can-you-feel-this?-what-about-this? protocol, making it all the more clear to Zack that he could feel his left leg just fine—but that his right might as well be gone for all the good it was doing him. Watching the doctor touch and poke that leg and feeling *nothing* made him want to scream. Soon the doctor was using the same words Suzanne had—*paralysis, monoplegia, rare*. "But there *is* some *good* news here," he added, lifting one finger in the air.

Zack would take any good news he could get. "What is it?"

"This could be a lot worse. At least it's only one limb."

Zack just stared. Was this guy serious? Telling him losing the use of his goddamn leg was no big deal? Rather than bite the old man's head off, though, he said, "Listen, Doc, what's the outlook here? Will I walk again? Can I still work my fishing boat?"

The man's brow knit in a way Zack didn't like, and his stomach went hollow. "Again, monoplegia from this type of injury is rare, so it's hard to know for sure. But, son, you need to brace yourself. Some people can learn to walk again over time with a lot of hard work—for others, it's an impossibility. And at best, it's a process that would likely take years. So I'm sorry to say your fishing career is likely over."

Zack shut his eyes, trying to absorb the weight crushing his chest. The water was his life, the only place he'd ever felt whole, safe, relaxed. Even more than with Meg, which was exactly how he'd lost her. And he couldn't blame her—a woman wanted to be more cherished than a damn fishing trawler.

The doctor kept talking, but like before with Suzanne, Zack could barely hear. "Normally, at this point I'd *insist* on having you moved to the mainland, but the ferry made its final run for the season last night—too much ice now. And I made a call as I walked over here, about an airlift, but the weather's no good for that—the ceiling's too low. So my best advice is to mentally prepare yourself for what might feel like a long winter here until we can get you looked at by the right folks come spring."

Spring. When he'd expected to get back on his boat.

But now, spring meant only…a bunch of tests and hassles just to confirm what he already knew. His right leg was paralyzed.

What the hell would his life *be* now?

Nothing. It would be nothing.

# CHAPTER FIVE

DURING HER TIME as an orthopedic nurse, Suzanne had been steady as a rock. Later, after switching gears to work with the elderly, she'd remained steady on the outside, but gone softer inside, somehow less able to shut out her emotions on the job. Now, when called upon to nurse someone in her personal life, she felt like Play-Doh. Too soft. Too able. Too able to be flattened by one good smash of a fist to a table. And Zack's new diagnosis was that fist.

*Bacon? You offered him bacon?* But he'd seemed so damn concerned about it. And she'd had no idea what to do or say. Now she zoomed aimlessly around the house—scrubbing a skillet, straightening a folded afghan on the back of an easy chair. Not looking at Zack because she…couldn't. It wasn't coldness—it was self-preservation. She had to protect herself from his pain and figure out how to function here. She found herself dumping the plate of partly burned bacon hastily in the garbage—then at the last second grabbing a few strips back. She snuck them into a coat pocket—because she was hungry but wanting to eat seemed selfish right now.

And she was halfway up the street to the Summerbrook Inn before she realized she'd just…left him there. With the profound words, "I'm stepping out for a bit," as if it were a beautiful summer day and not the depths of a snow-covered winter when everything was closed and there was almost literally no place to go.

But it wasn't abandonment so much as feeling as if she couldn't breathe. She'd left because she had to figure out how to breathe. She reached a glove-covered hand into her pocket, pulled out the bacon, ate it as she walked. Like some kind of old-time fur trapper chewing on jerky as he trekked through wintry landscapes.

Stepping up on the porch of the big Victorian home, she bypassed the doorbell to bang directly on the door. This was no time to be polite or subtle.

When Seth opened the door and took one glance at her, his stubbled jaw dropped. "Suzanne, you look fraught."

It was also no time to mince words. "Zack is paralyzed."

Seth's bedroom eyes widened. "What?"

"He's paralyzed," she said. "Paralyzed."

At this, Seth grabbed her by the arm. "Come in." Then he turned and yelled through the house, "Meg! Meg, darlin', come here!"

Suzanne watched her bestie stride down the hall from the kitchen carrying a large mug. In a big, cozy sweater and blue jeans, fuzzy socks on her feet, she looked…like what Suzanne longed to be, to have. This serene, controlled life. She suddenly envisioned an entirely different sort of day—one where she settled down here with Meg and her beau to watch movies or play cards. An easy sort of day. She'd thought the winter might bring that—more inclusion back into Meg's life now that she and Seth were no longer brand new. But now that couldn't happen, because of the big, big problem down the street she didn't know how to handle.

"What's wrong?" Meg asked at the look on her face.

Suzanne almost didn't want to tell her. Somehow Meg's eyes, her whole countenance, could make you believe everything would be okay, that any problem could be solved. Maybe that was why she'd come—just for that feeling Meg could inspire, the calm her very presence infused in a room. But deep down, Suzanne knew that even Meg couldn't make *this* be okay.

So maybe she'd really just come out of desperation. And the gut instinct that Meg should know. "It's Zack," she said, more softly than she had to Seth. Because this would wound Meg. That hadn't occurred to her until just now.

"What about him?"

"He's paralyzed."

Meg's brows knit and her mouth formed a silent O as the mug she held dropped from her hand to crash to the hardwood, a brown splash of tea spattering the floor and wall amid an explosion of ceramic. All three jumped back, and Meg immediately crouched to start collecting the broken pieces—until Seth touched her shoulder to say, "That can wait. I'll clean it up."

Meg hesitated—the innkeeper inside her clearly struggled with leaving a mess, even now—and Suzanne understood the rearrangement of priorities brought on by shock. She had bacon in her pocket, after all, and had left a paralyzed man lying there alone with no indication of when she'd be back.

"Be careful," Seth told Meg as she pushed back to her feet suddenly looking like someone else—a lost, broken child who didn't know which way to go. "Let's step in here." He gently herded both women to the old-fashioned parlor where a fire roared in the hearth, but Suzanne couldn't really feel the warmth—everything inside her had gone cold.

And only as the three of them sat down did Suzanne realize what she'd said and rushed to correct herself. "He's not *completely* paralyzed—it's partial. His right leg." Of course, it was still awful, and she went on to explain about monoplegia, and waiting, and uncertainty. "Dr. Andover just left, and I...I did, too." She shook her head. "I don't know why. I just needed to get out of there. And to tell you. And I'm not sure how to deal with this." She shut her eyes tight, blew out a harsh sigh. "Damn Dahlia for leaving. Damn her."

Meg's hand reached out to cover Suzanne's in her lap. "I know, I know. This shouldn't be your problem."

"It shouldn't be...*anyone's* problem," Suzanne realized out loud. "I mean, God knows it would be better if Dahlia were here, but she wouldn't be able to fix it, either. And fair or not, I'll just have to muddle through until the ice melts and she can get home."

"We'll help any way we can," Meg said.

Suzanne tried to smile, but the gesture hadn't reached her eyes. Because, given Meg's history with Zack, and that Seth had taken his place, how much help could they really be? And still a desperate part of her silently beseeched Meg. *You're the one who should be there. You know him—I don't. You loved him—I don't. You care for him—I...don't.* Oh, she supposed she cared in a certain way. In the way you care for a mean animal who gets caught in a trap and suddenly doesn't seem so mean anymore. In the way you care for any human being in trouble.

But if Meg could read her eyes, she never let it show. And Suzanne realized that Meg might as well be camped out on a tropical island with Dahlia right now—she might be right up the street, but when it came to helping with Zack, she was far, far away.

*This is all on you. Only you. Handle it.*

Maybe it was the memory of Cal's caring nature inspiring her, or maybe it was just that nurse thing kicking in—once a nurse, always a nurse. But somehow a quiet resolve stole over her. Nothing in her life was really how she wanted it to be right now, and this was like the rotten cherry on top of a big pile of crap—but she just had to keep her head down and barrel through it. She had to walk back down the street and face the partially paralyzed ogre on her couch and figure out how to get them both through this godforsaken winter.

A little while later, she quietly re-entered the cottage to find Zack asleep. Anger and pain pills could force a body to rest, and it brought her a small measure of calm to see him looking peaceful.

After hanging up her coat, she made her way to the fireplace to warm her hands, and her eyes rose to the framed picture of Cal on the mantel—a professional headshot from shortly before his death. What a handsome man he'd been, her orthopedic surgeon husband. *If you were still here, could you fix what's wrong with Zack? But...if you were still here,* I *wouldn't be here, on this island. I wouldn't even know Zack Sheppard existed.* Oh, the irony.

Dark hair and olive skin on a man with the very Irish name of Quinlan was another sort of irony—or maybe just a reminder of how very mixed together we are on this planet. He'd been big on that—on us all being in this together, on helping our neighbors, on doing what good you could in the world. He'd taught her a lot about being a good nurse when she'd first come into his employ. And then they'd fallen in love and he'd taught her a lot about being a good person.

*And now I have to be that good person, like it or not.*

She glanced to the sleeping man across the room. *But is it wrong if I hope he doesn't wake up for a while?*

"GLORIOUS, ISN'T IT?" Dahlia asked Giselle, studying the sunset before them. Sunsets were one of the things that made her believe in God. Slashes of neon pink and purple coloring the sky couldn't be random accidents in her book. They were God's artwork. Even if she'd sounded glum in the observation.

Which was surely what prompted Giselle to respond from the Adirondack chair next to hers with, "Another mai tai?" She'd suggested the first after Dahlia had hung up with Suzanne. To take the edge off.

Dahlia nodded. "I feel abominably worse now. About not being there with him."

Giselle, a woman in her forties, looked younger in a simple T-shirt and tennis shoes, sporting a mousy brown ponytail. And she was always quick to try to ease Dahlia's mind. "I know. But you couldn't have realized how bad the situation was yesterday."

Dahlia's sigh held equal parts guilt and self-awareness. "Maybe I should have gone to him the second Meg called me after he fell. But you and I had a plan, and I chose to keep it. I've always been that way—once I decide something, I stick to it. Whether it was leaving home for the first time, or quitting a job, or getting married—or divorced. Or opening the café. Once I'm on a set course, nothing derails me. For better or worse."

Giselle patted her hand, the touch calming. "It's okay to put yourself first sometimes."

She'd done a lot of that in her youth, and now she was entirely uncertain she'd made the right decision yesterday. Too late to change her mind, though. "I just don't like to think of him being…afraid. Not that he'd ever let on—that's not who Zack is—but who wouldn't be frightened in that situation?"

"Don't worry—Suzanne will take care of him."

Dahlia let out a cynical laugh. "Oh, she'll try. But he's a handful, to say the least."

"From what I hear," Giselle said with a grin, "nurses rise to the occasion."

Dahlia smiled softly over at Giselle, so busy trying to make light of the situation for Dahlia's sake, even if perhaps taking it a bit far—it was paralysis, not a stubbed toe. But perhaps the point was letting go of what you couldn't change.

A tall, thin woman, Giselle was quiet and pragmatic. Like Meg in a way. Pretty in her simplicity. *Could be prettier if she tried.* But Dahlia suddenly felt past the point of pushing anyone to be any different than they chose to be.

"Just listen to the waves," Giselle suggested. "Let them relax you."

Good idea. She focused on the rhythm of the surf, let it soothe her soul. And then announced, "I think I shall make a study of sunsets. This one, for instance, has so much more pink than some. I like that. So electric. Vibrant."

She watched, listened, sipped the second mai tai that had just arrived—complete with a little green umbrella—and chatted with her friend of many years. "I've gotten sleepy," she soon announced, feeling the alcohol's effects despite a lovely dinner of lemon tilapia.

"You should lean your head back and take a nap," Giselle encouraged her.

"You won't be lonely?"

Giselle laughed, then motioned around them. "Who could be lonely in paradise?"

"SON OF A BITCH."

Suzanne looked across the room. The monster was awakening. And maybe she shouldn't be thinking of him in such harsh terms, but his opening line backed it up.

"Would you like something to eat?"

"No."

"Grumble, grumble," she murmured under her breath.

"What?" he snapped.

"Nothing. But you have to eat, so I'm going to make you a sandwich. Do you need the bathroom?"

No answer. Because surely he did, but just dreaded dealing with it.

Ready to try her damnedest to do Cal proud, she cut him some slack and simply said, "I think our best bet is the crutches."

"Or you can just bring me something to pee in," he muttered, clearly not proud of the request but making it anyway.

"I don't have any receptacles I'm willing to sacrifice to urine, and you need to learn to use the crutches."

"How the hell do you expect me to do that?" he barked. "My damn leg doesn't move! Or haven't you heard?"

She'd anticipated the barking and didn't let it affect her. "I expect you to use the other limbs that still *do* move." She could ask if the clinic had a wheelchair, but she wanted to make him work—get used to working— to get around.

"I can't," he growled.

She drew in a deep, calming breath. He'd just declared defeat before even trying. But even if that attitude might be fair right now—the news was very fresh—she still refused to stand for it. "Yes, if you don't try you definitely can't. But I don't want pee in my mattress—or anything else unpleasant for that matter—so it's time to put on your big boy pants and give it a shot, tough guy."

Propped up on his elbows now, he glared at her. "Who the hell do you think you are?"

Even without the use of one leg, his harsh tone made her want to recoil. But for Cal, and for Dahlia, and even for the gruff, angry man in the bed whom she'd never liked, she instead forced herself forward—until she practically hovered over him. "I think," she began, "that I'm your only resource right now. So maybe you should think about the fact that I'm trying to help you—and have the brains to try to help *yourself*."

With that, she reached for the crutches leaning against the wall and thrust them at him. "Are you ready to do this?"

She met his dark gaze, glimmering beneath the layer of tension weighing down the room, and saw his temple pulsing. But finally he said, "Yeah, I'm ready."

It was grueling getting him out of bed, yet they eventually did, getting him up on the crutches and working out a system.

"Crutches. Left foot. Crutches. Left foot." She repeated the words, watching his useless right foot drag on the floor behind him as he inched forward. But he was inching forward. She'd placed a supportive arm around his waist on his weak right side for balance, aware of the well-toned muscles in his arms and stomach.

"They'll become even stronger the more you use them," she murmured.

"What will?"

"Your muscles."

He glanced over at her—putting their faces close. "Were we talking about my muscles?" He looked confused.

And she *felt* confused. Since of course they weren't—until she'd accidentally noticed them. "No, but…it's good you have them, for using the crutches." She feared she sounded nervous. *Over the fact that he has muscles? Ridiculous.* It was just weird to get so up close and personal with him.

Once they were in the bathroom she said, "Can you handle the rest on your own?"

He lifted his gaze to her once more. "Are you volunteering to help if I can't?"

Heat filled her cheeks. "I most certainly am not."

"Then you better get out 'cause I gotta go."

Suzanne withdrew uncertainly, thoughts whirling. Was he flirting with her? No, closer to being a smart-ass. And the pain meds might be affecting his behavior. And maybe from a nursing standpoint she *should* have helped him—but the very notion made her face burn even hotter as a vague memory floated through her brain: Meg had once told her, after too many cocktails at the Pink Pelican up the street, that he had a nice butt.

A moment later, from outside the door, she heard him going. How utterly bizarre to be listening to Zack Sheppard pee. *Please let him be able to get his pants back up.* Getting them up would be harder than getting them down. She felt about as mature as a fourteen-year-old girl.

A few minutes later, when all was quiet and too still, she called gently, "Everything okay in there?"

"Nope—can't get my damn pants pulled back up."

Crap. It was almost as if she'd willed it. "Well, keep trying." Yep, very mature.

"Aren't you supposed to be a nurse?"

Of all the times for him to make a sensible point. "Yes, but…"

"For crying out loud," he muttered. "I need some god-damn help in here, woman."

She had no choice. *You're gonna have to go in.* "Can you…face away from the door?" Fourteen going on twelve. But this wasn't just a patient—it was Zack.

"Yeah, sure, whatever—consider me faced away."

Taking a deep breath, Suzanne rushed in, bent down, grabbed the waistband of Zack's sweatpants with both hands, and yanked upward. There was a little hang-up in front that made him flinch and her cringe, but soon she was back outside the bathroom, teeth clenched lightly. Over the hang-up in front. Over having touched his bare thighs, hips. And because Meg had been right about his butt.

ZACK LAY ON his side, his right leg flopping limply in front of the left, broken and useless. Darkness had swallowed the cottage a while ago, but day and night felt irrelevant. Suzanne stayed nervous around him, but he didn't give a damn.

His cell phone buzzed, lighting up on the covers beside him. Dahlia. Again. He didn't answer. Again. Across the room, Suzanne watched something on TV. When she'd asked if it was too loud, he'd grunted a response, not even knowing if he meant yes or no.

Three working limbs. He could still pee. And he could still eat. So yeah, things could be worse. But he just didn't know…who he would be now, what his life would be. He didn't want to be a burden to anybody. And he didn't want to sit rotting on this island until he died.

When the phone notified him that this time Dahlia had left a message, he picked it up to listen. "Zack, please forgive me for not being there. You've taken care of yourself since you were sixteen, and it must be hard to suddenly need help. We have that sort of independence in common, you and I. I want to tell you that it'll all be okay—but I can't do that. What I *can* tell you, though, is that I believe in you. I believe in your toughness. I believe in you to always make your way in the world. You always have. You always will. Be brave, and know that I love you with all my heart and am there with you in spirit."

She'd said all the right things. And all the wrong things.

He didn't want to be brave, didn't want to be tough, didn't want to figure out how to make his way. He'd already done that—he'd already been young and alone and without a friend in the world—and he'd made his way, like she'd said. He'd learned a skill. He'd built a life. Some would call it a meager one, but he'd been satisfied with it. He'd already scaled all those mountains, carved out a living with blood, sweat, and tears.

He didn't want to have to do it all again. He didn't have the strength for it.

# CHAPTER SIX

IN SOME WAYS, the week that followed continued to be torturous and awkward and surreal.

Suzanne continued to help Zack with the crutches. She prepared meals, did dishes, did laundry, and she stepped out of the room when he changed clothes. She thanked her lucky stars that the cottage's last owner had installed a shower enclosure with a bench. She'd hated it when she'd moved in, thinking an old-fashioned claw-foot tub would have suited the space much better—but now that bench and the handheld showerhead was the difference between Zack being able to bathe himself or...not. He stayed angry—quiet and withdrawn at worst, grumbly and combative at best. She'd never dreamed she'd prefer a combative man over a quiet one, but when Zack went silent she could almost feel a certain surrender hanging over him.

And in other ways, those days were much the same as any other winter days. She read. She watched TV and movies. Yes, there was a belligerent man lying across the room who refused to join her in such diversions, but she was learning to look past that. He was becoming part of the scenery, a thing that was just there, like a cat who refused to be petted.

One day she even stole away to Petal Pushers, something she generally did several times a week during winter. Stepping in from a still, cold, snow-covered day, she bumped up the heat from fifty to sixty, then proceeded to sow four flats of petunia seeds. The activity wasn't especially efficient, but she liked sinking her fingers into the cool soil and it would save her a few dollars when spring ordering time came. It was a way to make the winter feel a bit useful and keep her head and heart in the game. Today, though, it was more than those things. Today it was an escape into that soil, into the seeds, into the peaceful joy of bringing something to life.

When she was done, she walked to an old refrigerator left behind by Meg's great-aunt Julia, who'd run the shop until her death from cancer. Meg had cared for Julia during her passing and Zack had been there to help Meg through it. It was the one redeeming thing Suzanne knew about him.

But when her eyes fell on the fridge's contents, her thoughts turned back to giving things life. She'd planted the daffodil and hyacinth bulbs in shallow dishes months ago to force them into blooming in February. It was something she did every year—even long before owning a flower shop and nursery—as a colorful, fragrant reminder that spring was just around the corner. Though she disliked the term *forcing* for the bulbs; it wasn't that harsh of an act. She merely made them think they'd endured a full winter before they actually had.

Carefully carrying the dishes from the fridge to the utility sink, she gave each an ample drink of water to keep the roots moist. And as she placed them back into their cool, dark abode, she said gently, "You guys will get to come out soon," as softly as if cooing to newborn kittens.

Closing the door, her eyes fell on a wall clock that brought her back to reality. She'd been gone longer than intended. She'd sunk into the peaceful act of summon-

ing life. Now she had to go back home to a grumbly
man. Who actually had every reason to be grumbly.
She thought again of Cal. And wanting to do good in
the world. *How can I make this situation with Zack better? How can I do the most good?*

When the answer hit her square in the face, she
couldn't believe it had taken her so long to think of it.
Some old books from her nursing days still on her living room shelves would help, along with the internet.
And old friends—specifically, an old colleague of Cal's
came to mind. Tonight, after she prodded Zack to eat
some of the beef stew simmering in the slow cooker, she
would do some research and make a phone call. And tomorrow she would do for Zack what she was doing for
those bulbs—gently force him to start moving forward,
whether he liked it or not.

"It's time to wake up! Good morning!"

The piercing voice cut through Zack's slumber, reminding him of...everything. Sleep was so damn much
better than being awake right now.

"Wakey, wakey—time to get up!"

A low groan left him. What was with her? Usually she
was at least quieter than this, even when she was being a
pain in his side, trying to act like everything was going
to be hunky-dory if he'd just drag his ass—and useless
leg—around the house on those godforsaken crutches.
So now she was going to be loud on top of that?

Her hand curled over his shoulder. She smelled feminine and...sort of flowery. "Zack, wake up!"

Ugh, the damn cheerfulness of her. "What do you
smell like?" he asked, forcing his eyes open to find her
hovering over him in a cozy-looking blue sweater that
hugged her shape.

"Huh?" she said.

"What do you smell like? You smell like something."

She blinked. "What kind of something?"

He blew out an irritated breath to have to say, "Something nice."

She flinched, clearly surprised. "Oh." Then blinked again. "Um, I use a lavender soap—is that it?"

"Yeah, probably." He'd never been particularly aware he *liked* lavender—a man who spent most of his life on the water didn't pay attention to things like that—but it was pleasant, gentle. And maybe it suited her. When she wasn't roaring good mornings at him anyway. "Why are you waking me so loud?"

"Because I have good news. We're starting something new today."

His eyes had fallen shut again, but now he reopened them. "Uh—like what?"

She smiled brightly, almost making him think she might say something miraculous that would fix everything—only to then announce, "Physical therapy!"

"What?" he asked, bewildered.

Her expression remained just as bright. "Physical therapy. Exercises. For your leg."

"My leg *doesn't work*," he reminded her, the words leaving him in a low growl.

"I know that." She sounded completely undaunted.

"I can't move it," he went on, just as surly.

"I know that, too."

He blew out a breath. This conversation was beginning to seem pointless. "How the hell can I exercise something I can't even move?"

"I move it *for* you," she told him.

He just looked at her. "What the hell good does that do?"

"At the very least, it will help prevent atrophy. In fact, we'll be exercising *all* your limbs for that purpose. And best-case scenario, it's possible the stimulation could start the damaged nerves firing again."

His mind raced, but his thoughts were blurry—from sleep and pain meds. She was saying something so optimistic that it made his heartbeat kick up—but...she wasn't a doctor. A nurse, yeah, but... "Are you only saying that to make me do this?"

She answered him just as pointedly. "Do you think I'd torture us both that way only to pass the time?"

The blur made him be honest in weighing his answer. "I just don't want to think something's gonna happen and then have it not happen."

Still standing over him, she let out a sigh. "Listen, Zack, I have no idea if it's going to make anything happen. But it certainly can't hurt anything. And as Dr. Andover said, nerves are mysterious, but stimulating them *can* help them reconnect. If nothing else, it'll keep your limbs active until you can get more specialized therapy come spring. So you can lie there and wallow in your misery, or you can take a shot at helping yourself. What's it gonna be?"

Zack just looked at her. Part of him did want to lie here and wallow. Part of him wanted to drift in and out of medicated sleep. Being awake hadn't gotten any easier since the moment the doctor had told him he might never walk again.

But Suzanne made this sound like a no-brainer, like any answer but yes would be insane. She couldn't know the despair clawing at him, dragging him down like an anchor, making it seem wiser to just take another pill, roll over, and go back to sleep. Even so, he tried to look into the future, to a time when the snow would melt, Dahlia would be home, and maybe mainland doctors would be able to help him. If he went back to sleep right now, and again tomorrow and the next day, sinking deeper into that darkness, he'd become somebody's problem—for life. Dahlia's probably. And yeah, he was mad at her right now—and mad at the world and God and whoever else there was to be mad at—but he didn't want to be anybody's problem. So he mustered the last ounce of courage from somewhere inside him and said to Suzanne, "Okay."

Her blue eyes opened wider; she looked surprised. "Really?"

It was almost tempting to take it back. But instead he said, "On one condition."

She looked worried. "What?"

"No more pills."

"Huh?"

"No more pain pills. Nothing hurts much anymore and I can't think straight. If I'm gonna do your little exercises, I want a clear head."

She nodded. "If you're not in pain, stopping the meds is definitely a good idea. But the exercises aren't little," she pointed out, holding up one finger. "And I think we should get started right now."

At this, however, he shook his head. "No."

"No?"

"Like I said, I want a clear head. Those things make me groggy. Maybe I could…sit up awhile first, eat something. Does that work for you, Suzie Q?"

She laughed—a sound he hadn't heard very much of. "You *must* be groggy." Then she arched one eyebrow. "I'll gladly whip up some breakfast—but I've never been a Suzie in my life and I don't intend to start now."

He tilted his head. "Aw, come on. Are you telling me,

in your whole damn life as Suzanne Quinlan, nobody's ever called you Suzie Q?"

Her eyes narrowed. "Not even once. Until now." She made her way to the kitchen, talking over her shoulder. "And I've only been a Quinlan for twelve years—it's my married name."

Zack tried to do math in his head that he didn't really have the numbers for. But seemed like he'd heard Meg and Dahlia say her husband had died two or three years before she'd come to the island. "How, um, many years were you married before...you know, he died?"

Her back was to him now, at the kitchen counter, hiding her expression. "Six."

"Not many." He hadn't meant to say it out loud, but it was too late.

"Not nearly enough," she replied, her voice gone a little more wooden, making him wish he hadn't pried. It was none of his business anyway. And now he didn't know what to say. So he plowed forward with, "Well, I still can't believe nobody's ever called you Suzie Q."

She peeked over her shoulder as she plopped a bit of butter in a skillet on the stove, looking more bewildered than made sense to him. "Why?"

He raised his eyebrows. "Because of the song."

She'd turned her back to him again. "What song?"

"Are you serious? You don't know the song? The *famous, classic* song 'Suzie Q' by Creedence Clearwater Revival?"

She just shrugged. "Maybe. I'm not sure. I didn't live in dinosaur times."

And at this, he threw back his head and laughed. He didn't know if she was for real or just making fun of him for being more of a classic rock guy than most people his age. But regardless, he couldn't remember the last time he'd actually laughed.

Though he also couldn't let this go without arguing. "If you really don't know the song, you should." He snatched up his phone and did a quick search, turned up the volume, and listened as the old sixties' tune filled Suzanne's little cottage.

She said nothing from where she stood in front of the stove, but before long her hips swayed back and forth to the catchy, twangy guitar beat. He watched the way her ass moved in faded blue jeans as she broke eggs into a pan, then laid some sausage links in another, all without missing a beat—literally. Soon she was flipping the eggs with a spatula and dancing her way to an overhead cabinet to pull out plates and glasses.

She had a *nice* ass. He'd never noticed that before. But the blue jeans curved over it in a way he suddenly couldn't *stop* noticing.

And only as the song ended, the music fading into quiet, did it hit him—this was the first time since the accident that he'd thought about anything else, the first time he'd found something that could steal his focus from it. He couldn't have imagined anything having the power to make him forget, even for a second. But somehow, seeing Suzanne dance around her kitchen while she cooked had grabbed his attention, made him laugh, made him feel something again.

"Glad you liked the song," he told her as she carried two plates of food to the table.

The table. Ah. She was pushing him hard already. Acting as if it was normal for him to come to the table to eat when, so far, he'd had every meal in the wallowing comfort of this pullout couch.

"It was all right," she replied with another shrug, returning to the kitchen for glasses of orange juice.

Fine—he'd go along with it. He reached for the crutches, dragged them over, maneuvered his legs to the floor, steadied the good one, tried to ignore the bad.

"It had a catchy beat," she went on, "but it was pretty old-school."

Using the crutches, he pulled himself up onto his left leg, then nearly lost his balance—but caught himself in time. And informed her, "Your hips tell a different story, Suzie Q."

"Quit calling me that," she said, her eyes swinging over to him—but then they changed, the rebuke leaving them entirely as her voice softened. "You stood up by yourself."

"Well, I wouldn't say by myself." He looked down at the two sticks under his arms.

"I would," she told him.

He tried for a small smile, even if standing suddenly reminded him of the challenges he faced, even if the limp leg he dragged along made him feel weak all over again. "All those trips to the bathroom on these things are paying off, I guess."

Being watched made him feel overly scrutinized—usually she stood beside him when he did this—and he wondered how clumsy he looked from her dining table. But she didn't come to help him, and somehow her faith that he could make it on his own was a balm to his bruised ego. She let him take those hard, heavy, unstable steps himself, until finally he landed in a chair and set the crutches aside.

"Looks good," he said, eyes falling to his plate as he reached for a fork and knife. And if he was honest with himself, it felt good, too. To do something as common as sit at a table, on a chair, ready to eat a hot meal.

Suzanne peeked over at the man across from her. And she considered extending the conversation—whether it be about rock music that pre-dated her, or crutches, or eggs—but instead she just let the silence lie comfortably between them. It felt delicate, this mental move forward. If she pushed too hard, she might break it—and she didn't want to risk that.

The oddest part? It was the most pleasant one-on-one exchange she'd ever had with Zack since meeting him three years ago. Others had been forced, with the underlying obligation of being nice for Dahlia's sake or the underlying accusation that he treated Meg like crap. Now that was all gone, because there were bigger fish to fry...or bigger fish to accept not catching because he would never work Lake Huron again.

Only after they'd both finished did she broach a practical matter. "Your medication was due a couple of hours ago. How's your pain?"

"There's a little," he told her. "But I'd rather feel it."

She nodded, understanding. "Are you ready for exercises?"

He looked up from his plate, eyes wary. "Are you gonna torture me, Suzie Q?"

She blew out a perturbed breath. "I might if you don't stop calling me that."

A half grin snuck out of him. "Probably a good thing I'm tough then."

HALF AN HOUR LATER, Zack had reverted to the grouchy, grumbling man she'd come to know. But he was letting her guide his body through the exercises, and grumbling because she was pushing him was a far cry better than grumbling because his leg wouldn't move.

She tried to ignore the intimacy. Since, like helping him to the bathroom, this required touching. *At least you're not pulling his pants up.* She squelched a burst of sensation at the memory. Of the awkwardness. And his butt.

"Ow, damn it," he groused. She sat beside the bed as he lay on his side facing her. She supported his injured leg with one hand on his thigh and the other below his knee, lifting the knee toward his chest.

"Only nine more to go," she told him. "On this side. You can do the other side with less help from me." Then she lifted the knee again.

"Jesus," he muttered.

"For someone who can't feel this leg, this seems to be hurting you a lot," she said pointedly.

"It hurts other places," he snapped. "My back, for one—my ass for another."

She bit her lip, kept her thoughts inside—that such pain might be a positive sign. Of course, it could also mean only that he'd been lying here sedentary too long or had pulled a muscle. So instead she said, "No pain, no gain—don't be a baby." Then lifted the knee again.

This time he stayed quiet, but she could tell the silence took effort.

"That's better, tough guy," she told him. And lifted again. And in his silence...became more aware of his thigh beneath her palm. Like his butt, it was...nice. *Of all the people I never expected to be touching...*

After ten lifts, she instructed him to scoot to the other side of the bed to exercise the other leg, as well. "It's about balance, and keeping the muscles active and strong."

He didn't object, moving himself over—until she placed her hands back on his thigh and calf. "I can do this one on my own, remember?" he said.

"I still need to guide you—to make sure you're doing it right, at the right speed." Her reply was entirely true—the only secret part being that she didn't really mind helping him. His flesh was warm through his soft sweatpants, his muscles sturdy. *This is sad. It's been so long since you've touched a man that you're enjoying giving one physical therapy.*

*But don't beat yourself up. You're doing what's best for him. So if you've become slightly aware that touching him isn't repulsive to you, it's just a normal, human reaction.*

Though maybe life had been easier back when she'd convinced herself she was content without men, or sex. Beck Grainger had reawakened desires in her that had gone dormant after Cal's death—and this was a hell of a way to be reminded she missed a man's touch.

Soon they moved on to other exercises—ankle rotations, which also involved a hand on his thigh, and toe rotations, which kept her down by his feet and felt less intimate, and mostly like a relief but also slightly like a disappointment. Because she was farther away from him and his thighs. *Which is crazy. Snap out of it. Be professional here. And remember that you and Zack don't even like each other. And that you have serious doubts about him as a human being.*

"Please tell me you're done with the torture, Suzie Q," he said afterward.

"Almost," she said, still cringing a little at the name without quite knowing why. He'd always called Meg by a nickname from an old Rod Stewart song—Maggie May. Perhaps this seemed too similar. Maybe it seemed like…flirtation. Like if she'd advanced to earning such a nickname from him, it meant something.

But it didn't. And it *wasn't* flirtation. In fact, at the moment it seemed a whole lot closer to bellyaching. "Almost? There's more?"

Yep, definitely bellyaching. Though maybe the few exercises they'd done seemed like a lot under the circumstances. "These will be easier," she promised. "I just want you to do some curls to keep the muscles in your arms strong."

She reached for free weights she'd dug from a closet yesterday, glad she'd hung on to them. "We'll start with just five pounds," she said, handing them over.

"Suzanne, I could lift five pounds with my little finger. I work on a fishing boat—I have upper body strength." Spoken as if she were a feeble-minded imbecile.

She blew out a calming breath, then forced a smile. "I'm sure you do. But your entire body—including your back, to which your arms are attached—have been through a traumatic experience. And last I heard—from you—your back muscles are still sore. So we're starting with five pounds."

When he opened his mouth to protest, she impulsively reached out an index finger to shush him, pressing it against his lips. And also his chin. And the rough stubble there.

He looked as stunned as she felt. His breath warmed her finger. She drew her hand back and promptly ignored the unexpected flare of sensation between her thighs.

Then she started talking—rambling really—to distract them both from the fact that her finger on his mouth had felt almost as personal as pulling up his pants. "Who's the medical professional here? Me." She pointed at herself. "And who's the unruly, uncooperative patient? You." Another finger point. "Medical professional overrides unruly patient. And besides, if I gave you weights that challenged you, you'd just claim I'm torturing you, so there." She ended on a sharp nod.

Which seemed to quiet him. Or maybe the whole finger-on-mouth incident had shut him up, but at least he was doing what he was told for a change.

When he'd finished the curls, she announced, "That's enough for today." After which her voice went softer— drawn from the tension and awkwardness back to the realization that…Zack was coming back to life a little. And no matter her past opinions of him, and no matter how grumpy he was, she suddenly harbored a bit of hope for his future. "You're doing great, Zack."

And though it wasn't even yet close to noon, she thought maybe they'd both benefit from a break. So she said, "Koester's should be open today since the weather's clear. Think I'll bundle up and make a trip to the market." And as she put on her snow boots, she thought about how on a normal January day, she'd pay a visit to Dahlia, or call and invite Meg down for a cup of hot chocolate later. But nothing was normal this winter. She'd always heard that the only constant in life is change—and she was beginning to learn that all you could do was roll with the punches. So she would go to Koester's, then come home to the monoplegic man she now shared her home with, and figure out where to go from here. And she'd be thankful that today was better than yesterday—for him, and also, by extension, for her.

"Any special requests from the store?" she asked, pulling on her parka.

"Nah," he said.

"All right," she told him. "Be back soon."

She'd just opened the front door, a rush of cold air spilling in, when he said, "Hey, Suzie Q."

She looked over at him, again annoyed by the name. And he said, "Thank you."

Which took all the wind from the sails of her irritation. "For...what?"

"Caring enough to help me."

She pressed her lips tight together, taken aback by the simple gratitude. "You're welcome," she said quickly, then stepped out into the snow, pulling the door shut behind her. Maybe he wasn't such a bad human being, after all.

## CHAPTER SEVEN

WHEN ZACK'S PHONE rang soon after Suzanne left, he knew who it was without looking. And he still didn't want to talk to her. But he couldn't ignore her forever, so he made himself answer. "What's up, Dahlia?" Probably sounded surly, but he didn't care.

Her joy came through loud and clear when she said, "You answered the phone, that's what's up. I'm happy to hear your voice."

His aunt always sounded so energetic—which, just now, made him feel tired. "I guess you're wanting to know how I'm doing."

"I've been texting some with Suzanne, but I'd like your version, yes."

He'd never been a big talker—and this was a hell of a topic. So he tried to keep it short and real. "Shitty, mostly. Seeing as I can't walk and don't know how the hell I'm gonna make a living. And I'm stuck in a house with somebody I barely know because you guilted her into it. But on the upside, I got myself to the kitchen table today, and I did some exercises."

On the other end, Dahlia released a big sigh. "I know it's a lot. And I wish I could be there helping you. But I'm going to focus on the positive. And I'm sure you know, deep down, that the best possible thing you can do for yourself is what you're starting to do—work your way through it. Dreadful as it is. You have to hold your head up and find the best way to move through your circumstances. And it sounds as if you're ready to do that now."

She made it sound like he'd suddenly seen the light and knew how to fix all this. When all he'd done was take ten steps on crutches without someone holding him up. "I don't know if it's as great as all that. Mainly, I'm just tired of sleeping all day."

"You've been sleeping all day?"

"The pain meds knocked me out. But I'm ready to… at least be awake, I guess." The words, leaving him, sounded so small. *My big goal is to be awake?* A good breakfast and a few laughs with Suzanne had lifted his spirits when he'd least expected it, but reality was slapping him in the face again.

"Well," Dahlia said, "perhaps you *needed* to sleep for a while. But it's good you're ready to move forward."

She was always such a cheerleader—but right now, he just needed her to *get it*. So he said exactly what he was thinking. "I have no damn idea how to do that, Dahlia. No idea at all."

"Zack," she said, her tone going softer, "you've always had the power to overcome difficult things."

The simple words held weight, the weight of a shared family, a shared history, things never talked about but always present just the same. And they still weren't talking about those things now—but it felt as if she'd set them all out on an imaginary table between them. And it reminded him that she'd overcome some obstacles, too. "Maybe I learned that from you," he told her. "But some would say I *ran* from difficult things." Meg, if anyone asked her, would claim he was *still* running.

"Then we both ran," Dahlia said in her easy way. He could almost see the shrug of her shoulders from whatever sun-soaked beach she sat on at the moment. "But running…or searching for better—there's a fine line there, Zack. Be easy with yourself right now."

She had a nice way of putting things, his aunt. He seldom told her so, but he valued what she brought to his life. Maybe it took something this bad to make him really see it.

But enough of this deep, serious shit. "Where are you right now? Drinking some fruity, girly drink with your toes in the sand?"

On the other end, she laughed. "It's 11:00 a.m."

"But you know what they say—it's five o'clock somewhere."

Another chuckle from her. "Still too early for me. I don't imbibe before noon."

"What about the sand? Warm on your feet?" He wasn't sure why he cared—maybe he was just trying to escape the northern winter for a moment.

"I'm not on the beach just now. But I *am* looking out over it. I'll text you a photo after we hang up."

"All right." Then… "Hey, Dahlia, remember when I was little? Remember you always had music playing?"

He'd been seven years old before ever meeting her—Dahlia had lived other places and only came home when her mother, Zack's grandma, had died. She'd stayed for weeks in his grandmother's empty home, becoming a bright ray of sunshine in his young but already troubled life. She'd loved music—sixties' and seventies' mostly—and sent it echoing through the house.

He could feel Dahlia's smile in her voice. "Ah, yes—I played all my old albums on Mom's big console stereo. Which I should've kept—it would be so retro chic now. But I was far too transient then to value large possessions."

"Remember you used to dance around? Whatever

you were doing—cooking, cleaning, anything else—
you were dancing."

"You danced, too—with me," she said. "Do you remember that?"

"A little." He hadn't thought about the memory in a
very long time. "Guess I was sort of a dorky kid."

"Nothing dorky about finding joy in the everyday."

Dahlia, he supposed, had always done that. While
he, on the other hand, had never picked up that particular skill.

"What made you think about that?" she asked warmly.

"Nothing really. Just found out Suzanne didn't know
the song 'Suzie Q.'"

"How is that possible?" Shock tinged Dahlia's voice.

"I don't get it, either. But I played it for her. And she
pretended she didn't like it much, but she did." Her hips
had told him she did anyway. He smiled softly at the recollection. All of life should be that easy. Dancing in the
kitchen. Just like Dahlia had way back when.

Now Dahlia laughed lightly. "Is she taking good care
of you, Zack?"

He blew out a sigh. "As good as she can," he confessed. "As good as I let her."

"You've never been a good patient," Dahlia quipped.
She'd seen him through more than one ailment over the
years. "You're not good at…well, being in any situation
that's not what you want it to be."

Zack took that in. She wasn't criticizing—just thinking out loud. *But for a guy who doesn't want to make
my problems everybody else's, do I do that every damn
day of my life anyway?* He knew he'd been a bear to
pretty much everyone since Meg had broken up with
him. "Maybe I should work on that." The murmured
words snuck out unplanned.

"An enlightened thought," Dahlia replied on a light chuckle. "But no one will blame you right now for being a little moody."

*Ah, Dahlia. You always go too easy on me. Always. Because you know where I've been.* And she'd always given him quiet permission to be...moody, surly, distant, whatever he wanted to be. For better or worse.

"Do you forgive me, Zack?"

Damn. *Way to get serious without warning, woman.* But with Dahlia, he didn't have to rush, didn't have to just tell her what she wanted to hear. They could be honest with each other. So he thought it over and said, "I'm working on it. But I might *always* be a little mad at you for not coming back."

That kept her quiet for a moment. "I had no way of knowing," she began softly, "how bad the injury was."

"You knew I couldn't walk and had nobody to help me—at least nobody I was comfortable with. Even with your trip plans, it still threw me when you didn't come back."

"Fair enough," she conceded on a sigh. "I've always tried to be there for you, and this time I just...wasn't. I can only hope that maybe someday you'll understand why I had to get away this winter."

But he already understood. The two of them were cut from the same cloth—they did what they wanted most of the time, even when it was selfish. Challenges early in life had taught them both to look out for number one. Dahlia just hid that particular trait better than he did. And he'd forgive her eventually, he just hadn't yet.

"For now," she went on, "I'll just take solace in the fact that you're speaking to me again. It's been good to talk, Zack."

Much as the surly side of him wanted to *stay* surly,

the part of him that had just traveled unwittingly back to being seven admitted grudgingly, "Yeah."

"Keep up the good work with your exercises. And be nice to Suzanne."

"I'll do what I can," he muttered.

Though as he hung up, he glanced toward the door, vaguely wondering how long his nurse would be gone. Other days when she'd left, he'd barely been aware, floating in and out of sleep—but now, as the grogginess wore off, his thoughts drifted to: *Wonder what she's getting at the store. Hope she's keeping warm enough in the cold. Her eyes are bluer than I ever noticed before.*

WHEN SUZANNE RETURNED from Koester's, Zack was grumbling about nerve pain. She could have suggested he resume the Percocet, but it didn't relieve that. Little did, and anti-inflammatories hadn't helped much. She found a couple of topical treatments in her medicine cabinet that might help, though, so she handed them over, and said, "Rub these on where it hurts"—because she was *not* doing *that*.

In the hours that followed, he continued to behave almost like a normal person. Normal being subjective— Lord, the man could turn into a grouch at the drop of a hat. But she kept reminding herself: *He's partially paralyzed—you'd probably be grouchy, too.*

At certain moments she almost missed the strange, awkward days of him sleeping most of the time. Suddenly he wanted to watch TV, but not what *she* wanted to watch. When she suggested they might spend some quiet time each reading and offered to select a book for him from her shelves or help him download something onto her tablet, he balked. "I'm trying to wake up, not have something put me back to sleep. And this Dr. Phil show seems pretty wild."

Yet again, she was learning to roll with the punches. So while Zack took in the high drama of Dr. Phil—a new discovery for him—she worked in the kitchen, preparing a hearty chicken and noodle dish, and making brownies.

When her phone beeped, she looked down to see a text from Dahlia. I called Zack and he answered! We had a nice talk.

I'm glad for you, Suzanne replied. While she'd been happy to keep Dahlia up-to-date, she remained in Zack's corner when it came to being hurt by Dahlia's departure.

Clearly, Dahlia read the dryness in her words. I know you're still mad at me, too. And I understand. But for the sake of getting Zack through this, I hope you can set that aside until spring.

Frankly, the whole thing still seemed odd—taking off with a friend none of them had ever heard of for parts unknown. And even weirder after Zack's injury. She texted back, keeping it simple. I'm trying, but you've put us both in such a weird position.

Don't think I don't realize that, my dear. Just please know that I love you both beyond measure.

That pierced Suzanne's heart, just a little. Dahlia was still Dahlia, not just the absent mystery person she'd suddenly become. And yet forgiveness didn't happen just because you snapped your fingers. It could take time. Still, she answered, I love you, too.

SUZANNE HAD BEEN certain that helping Zack exercise would be less awkward the second time around. She'd been wrong.

As she held on to his thigh and calf through sweat-pants the following day, she remained hyperaware of touching him. *You're a nurse—this should be nothing to you. Especially given some of the work you've done with the elderly.*

But the elderly were nothing like Zack Sheppard. His muscle mass was notably more…solid. And he smelled better, giving off some sort of musky, masculine scent. The one thing he *did* have in common with the older people she'd worked with? He was happy to complain and said exactly what was on his mind.

"Goddamn it, Suzie Q, you're killing me."

"Stop exaggerating," she replied.

He let out a low sort of yowl as she pressed his knee toward his chest, gentle but firm, a little farther than yesterday. "You're breaking my damn back."

"Don't be a whiner," she said softly. She knew it hurt—in fact, she was glad it hurt. When it came to physical therapy, *no pain, no gain* was often really true, and stimulating muscles that stretched up into his back meant stimulating the nerves, too. Despite not being a physical therapist, her orthopedic background gave her confidence that she was doing the best thing she could for him right now. Even if, at certain moments, she wished she could ask Cal's opinion. *But that's nonsensical—because if Cal were still alive, you wouldn't be here.*

A thought that made her head spin a little as she progressed from hip rotations into ankle rotations. Because… *If I wasn't here, who would be taking care of Zack right now? Well, Dahlia would have had to come back, that's all.* But Dahlia wouldn't know to do PT with him, or have the skill set that made it easier for Suzanne.

*If Dahlia were here with me right now, she'd tell me everything happens for a reason.* But Suzanne didn't want to believe Dahlia was right to have departed, and she still didn't relish feeling like the pawn here—like everyone else's well-being mattered more than hers.

Raised in a house with a gruff dad and four older brothers after her mom died giving birth to her, she'd spent most of her young life being treated like she didn't matter and feeling as if she didn't belong. *One of these things is not like the others, and it's me.* Only Cal had ever made her feel like she really mattered, like she should be put first. And Meg and Dahlia, too, always made her feel like she mattered. Okay, not so much lately. But mostly.

"Do you even know what you're doing, woman?"

She slanted Zack a look. Possible she'd gotten distracted, but no way would she cop to it. "I am an orthopedic nurse," she reminded him proudly. "You are in the best possible hands on this island that you could be." And she meant that literally, as she gently but firmly rolled his ankle in her grip, thinking: *Reconnect, nerves. Reconnect.*

After the toe rotations, he muttered, "Thank God we're finally done."

"Bad news," she told him. "We're adding a new exercise today."

He looked unamused. "Tell me you're kidding."

"I wouldn't kid about physical therapy. And actually, this is *good* news. The more we stimulate your muscles and nerves, the better off you'll be come spring."

At this, he blew out a breath. She could see the argument held water for him, despite being tired and hurting. "Fine," he bit off. "Torture me a little more."

She smiled. "My pleasure."

The new exercise required him to lie on his back while she lifted his leg, placing a hand on the side of his thigh to help him stretch it across his body. It ranked right up there with the hip rotations in feeling personal, making her a little nervous all over again. And it left her aware of the tight bands of muscles in his legs.

Once more she caught the scent of him, even felt his breath on her face. Hovering over him, she peered down into gray-green eyes somehow angry and docile at once. The position he was in maybe, both physically and mentally. They stared at each other; her heart beat faster. *Say something.* "You're doing great," she heard herself tell him, her voice coming out soft. Softer than intended. Her breath felt shallow, her chest—breasts—achy. From being nervous about all this touching.

Which still didn't make much sense to her. Medical professionals were trained to do this, trained to know we were all just people with bodies and there was nothing to be uneasy about.

"Thanks," he murmured, averting his eyes slightly, looking uneasy, too.

"Okay, other side," she said gently when they finished the reps on his paralyzed leg.

On his left leg she repeated the same movements, but it went differently—all the exercises did—because he could feel those. It made his muscles behave differently, and she had to repeatedly remind him to let *her* guide the motions.

And that was when it hit her. *On this side, he feels it, too—my hands on him. My hands on his thigh, knee. My hands pressing into his flesh.* Heat filled her cheeks. *Why does that matter?* He'd felt it yesterday, too, of course. It only mattered because she was thinking about it. And wondering what *exactly* he felt. Did he feel the intimacy? The weird tension?

Now she avoided his eyes at all costs as she stared down at his leg, the sweatpants covering it, trying to think purely clinical thoughts. She bit her lip and focused on each therapeutic movement. Until finally they finished a set and she decided that was definitely enough for today. "Okay," she said, still not meeting his gaze as she rose up off the bed. "Good work, good work."

Then she headed across the room and stoked the fire. Even if she was sweating a little, the fire was a good distraction—a nice, fake reason to put distance between them until she got over this strange reaction.

Placing a new log on the low flame, she stood back up, her eyes finding Cal's on the mantel. She loved that picture of him. Gray suit, red tie. So classic and handsome. She loved it because it was the Dr. Quinlan the rest of the world got to see—but she got the *real* him, and she knew that sparkle in his eye was only for her. Or *had been* only for her. Sometimes her heart still hurt, physically, for just a quick moment, upon remembering he was no longer…anywhere.

"Can I ask you something?"

She flinched, that quickly having almost forgotten Zack was in the room. "Sure. What?"

"What's the deal with your husband?"

# CHAPTER EIGHT

SHE BLINKED, TAKEN ABACK. "The deal?"

Propped up against pillows on the sofa bed, Zack scrunched up his face slightly. "That was the wrong way to ask, wasn't it?"

She tilted her head. "That depends. On what you're asking. I haven't figured it out yet."

He pressed his lips into a thin line, clearly trying to tread more carefully here. "I know he died. But how? I mean, what's the story of you and him?"

Suzanne just stared at him. Such a normal question, really. And yet anyone seldom asked. Maybe she seemed too fragile. Maybe her clear heartache over the matter made it seem off-limits. Meg knew the answers, and Dahlia did, too—but not because they'd asked. She'd volunteered it one night her first summer here over too many drinks at the Pink Pelican. Maybe people sensed she didn't like to talk about it—because generally, she didn't.

And yet this was quite possibly the first interest Zack Sheppard had ever shown in her as a person. And it seemed a reasonable request on his part—after all, Cal was smiling across the room at him 24-7. If he was curious about Cal, she would tell him. She *should* tell him. He'd died over five years ago and it was time she got better at discussing it.

"He was a doctor," she said.

At this, Zack pulled back slightly, clearly surprised. "Really?"

Funny—to her, Cal was *such* a doctor, down to the marrow of his bones, that she forgot people in her life might not necessarily know.

She nodded. "An orthopedic surgeon. Mainly knees and hips."

His gaze narrowed on her curiously. "Is that why you were an orthopedic nurse?"

She shook her head, eased down into her favorite comfy chair—she might *need* her comfy chair for this topic. "No, it's how we met—I worked at his practice. I guess you could say it's right out of a movie or an old Harlequin romance novel, but…real life is more complicated and the upshot is that…" *He saw something in me no one ever had. He made me feel special. He was my knight in shining armor.*

Yet all that truth felt like…too much. She still barely knew the man on her sofa bed, no matter how much she'd been touching his thighs or pulling up his pants lately. So she just shrugged and said, "We fell in love. He was the kind of man I dreamed of finding someday." She stopped then, backtracked. "And I don't mean because he was a doctor and had money. I mean because he was a great person who really cared about helping people, and at the same time he made me feel like a princess."

Word vomit. Stop. Now she sounded like some delicate flower who wanted to be fawned over and catered to. Which wasn't what her relationship with Cal had been about. "What I mean is…" She stopped, shook her head, got honest. "He loved me. That's all. He loved me and made me happy. And he inspired me to be a better person."

"How?" Zack asked. She appreciated that he didn't

linger over her every nervous word—but just moved forward with what he wanted to know.

"He did a lot of volunteer work," she explained. "With impoverished people and senior citizens without many resources. It inspired me to use my nursing skills in a different way for a while, at a facility for the elderly."

Zack's gaze narrowed further. "A nursing home, you're saying?"

She nodded.

At this, his eyes opened a little wider, even if he still looked tired. "That sounds...a lot harder than working with a knee guy."

A soft chuckle escaped her. He didn't know the half of it. "It was...a challenging choice, for sure. I went home each night tired—but feeling like I'd made a difference in someone's life, even if they didn't always know it." At his confused expression, she went on. "There was a lot of dementia. And a lot of people who were just too deep into their own woes to really acknowledge much else. It was hard but satisfying work. Only—I didn't last long at it."

"What do you mean?"

"It was too emotionally draining. People there told me my heart was too soft for it, that I needed to toughen up. Cal said there was nothing wrong with a soft heart, but warned me not to let it break, to know when I'd done all the good I could there and it was time to go in another direction." She bit her lip. "And then he died."

She'd inadvertently dropped a heavy blanket of tension over the room with the dramatic statement—and with the fact that she'd clearly felt emotional, swept back in time. Zack stayed quiet—until asking more softly than before, "You want to tell me how that happened? Or is it none of my business?"

The answer was: both. But she'd already said way more than planned, let her houseguest see more of her than intended, so why not keep going. She tried to think of it as a getting-to-know-you exercise—maybe it would help if they got to know each other beyond their connection with Meg or Dahlia or his injury.

"He was doing a stint in Doctors Without Borders," she told Zack. "His third."

"Wow," Zack said. Then, "Damn."

She supposed the very words *Doctors Without Borders* plus his having died pretty much told the story. So she could probably just shut up now and be done—but she didn't. "He was in northern Syria, where the government seems to make a concerted effort to obliterate doctors or medical knowledge—part of the war on their people, and a hard thing to understand. There was an air strike. He was in the wrong place at the wrong time. And…that was that."

She chose to push down the rest. Like that being in Aleppo when you didn't have to was *always* the wrong place. And that it still tortured her not to know the details, or what his last words were, or if he knew it was coming or felt any fear. That she'd loved him almost more than life itself—which she'd learned was a very dangerous thing to do with another human being.

Silence filled the space between her and Zack. He'd asked, but now clearly didn't know what to say.

So she said something instead. "It's okay." A lie, but what came out. "Time has passed, and he died doing what he valued, helping people. And life eventually goes on."

Carefully, Zack began, "Mind if I ask you one more thing?"

She did, actually. But wanted him to think she was better with this than she was. "Sure."

"How the hell did you end up being a florist after all that?"

Despite herself, she laughed. At last, something she truly didn't mind discussing. "I had just given my notice at the nursing home when Cal died. I'd been trying to figure out what I wanted to do next in nursing—but after that, I decided to try something entirely new.

"I didn't have a mom growing up," she explained, "but I used to plant flowers with my grandma when I was little, and she taught me about flowers and trees. I always had a green thumb, always had a beautiful yard and flower gardens wherever I lived. So I decided to open a flower shop and spend my energy giving things life—rather than focusing on pain and death. I just wanted to bring more beauty into the world. It wasn't the same sort of giving Cal was dedicated to, but... I needed to start nurturing *my* soul instead of everyone else's."

It almost embarrassed her. *I used to really help people—now I sell flowers.* It felt like more than that, of course, when her fingers were in the soil, when a shoot broke through the dirt, when a bloom opened its petals. But in terms of helping humanity, it sounded pretty weak.

"And that's okay, you know," Zack said.

Her chest tightened slightly in surprise. Zack Sheppard, of all people, understood everything she was saying and feeling. Zack Sheppard, of all people, was absolving her. "Thank you."

"How'd you end up here, though?" he asked. "On Summer Island."

She let out a sigh. "Back home in Indy, it all just felt...too close. I heard from Cal's colleagues all the time. They called to check on me, or invite me places, or they came in to buy flowers. Which was wonderful of them—but just a constant reminder that he…wasn't… anymore. I guess I just wanted a new start someplace where people didn't know about my baggage. Maybe I wanted to hibernate."

He offered a sardonic shrug. "If you want to hibernate in winter, you came to the right place."

*Until my best friend's ex moves in with a leg that doesn't work anymore.* She didn't say that, of course. He was being…well, maybe the kindest he'd ever been to her. He'd set a pretty low bar, but still—this situation wasn't his fault. When it had happened, after all, he'd been hibernating, too. Trying to get over Meg.

That was when it hit her—she and Zack actually had something in common. They were both hibernators. She tried to ignore the irony that they were stuck together now, both on forced hiatus from their chosen hibernation.

"How did *you* get to Summer Island?" she asked.

"Dahlia," he answered simply.

"I already know that part." She raised her eyebrows. "I was looking for more than the one-word version."

"There's not one really," he said. "Everybody's gotta be somewhere. Dahlia moved here around the time I started fishing—it's a good enough home base when I'm not on the water."

Then he stiffened, clearly remembering that he wouldn't be on the water anymore, that everything had changed. Her heart broke a little for him all over again—since she'd just realized one more thing they had in common: knowing how it felt when the life you knew suddenly vanished.

But rather than let him worry about an uncertain and

surely challenging future, maybe it would be easier for him to focus on the past. "What about the rest of your family?" she asked.

She knew from Meg that Zack's childhood had been rough, but Meg had never learned more—because Zack wouldn't tell her. She'd gleaned only that he'd named his boat after a little sister who had died. His unwillingness to open up had been another big ingredient in their breakup.

"No other family," he replied—but that quickly she could see it, an invisible little wall he'd tossed up. His face had changed, his countenance gone darker, his expression more blank.

Yet Suzanne wasn't asking him to open up—she was just trying to make conversation, get a few more facts about her patient. "Relax," she said. "I wasn't digging for your deep, dark secrets—I was just curious why Dahlia ended up with your ever-so-pleasant company. But you don't have to tell me anything you don't want to."

"Good, I won't."

"Even if I just spilled my guts to you about my greatest loss and greatest challenges."

He shrugged. "I didn't exactly twist your arm."

"You asked, though. So I answered. I thought we were…becoming friends or something. But maybe I thought too soon," she said, annoyed.

At this, he tilted his head, appeared to be thinking through how to answer. Given that communicating with Zack often felt like a game of chess, she waited to see his next move.

"Let's just say I don't like to talk about myself," he informed her. Not exactly a newsflash.

"But you expect other people to talk about *themselves*."

Another shrug. "Most people *like* to. Most people don't notice if other people don't."

Yes, she'd observed that, too. But explained, "For the record, I *don't* especially like to. Since we're stuck here in close quarters, however, I thought it might be nice if we learned more about each other. And…maybe I thought it was nice that you cared enough to ask."

Another quiet pause from him, clearly plotting that next move. "Well, I guess it's nice that you asked, too—but my life story's not that interesting. Not a lot to say."

She didn't buy that for a second. She knew he'd left home at sixteen and had been on his own ever since. She knew that when he wasn't busy hibernating here in winter, he was, in effect, hibernating on that fishing boat all summer. And he'd had that little sister who died. There were definitely stories there, and not boring ones. "Try me," she said with a soft, daring grin.

In response, the corners of his eyes crinkled and he let out a light laugh. Huh—turned out his eyes sparkled, too, just like Cal's. She'd simply never seen him smile enough to witness it, and for some reason that unexpected sparkle hit her right in the solar plexus.

"Nice try, Suzie Q," he said, "but I'll pass."

She let out a light *hmmf.* "Fine. See if I tell you anything else."

He pressed an over-dramatic hand to his heart, looking almost playful. "I'm shattered. Not sure how I'll go on."

This earned him a sideways glance. "You're a smart-ass, too."

He glanced toward the kitchen. "This smart-ass is wondering what's for lunch."

Ah, the old change-the-subject chess move—she knew it well as she'd used it plenty of times herself.

Airily, she replied, "Gruel. I'd been planning on hot ham and cheese hoagies with some soup, but now I'm thinking you've earned gruel."

Which earned *her* another laugh. "I'm not worried. Know why? You're too dedicated to the nurse gig." Then he narrowed his gaze on her. "When you're not torturing me with your damn exercises, that is."

"Hmm—maybe I should keep adding new exercises until you get better at talking about yourself."

He lowered his chin. "Are you threatening me?"

She pushed up from the chair and walked toward the kitchen, not bothering to look at him as she replied, "Threat, promise—whatev."

"Where are you going?" he asked.

"To make the gruel."

DAHLIA LEANED BACK in her Adirondack chair and took in the splendor of a neon sunset. "So much orange in this one," she observed to Giselle. "I'm not generally a great fan of the color, but in a sunset, it can be so electric. This is why I could never be an atheist."

Giselle drew her focus from the sunset to Dahlia. "Because of orange?"

Dahlia laughed. "No—because the world is too marvelous for it to be an accident. *This single sunset* is too marvelous to be an accident." Only now did she pull her eyes from swaths of orange, gold, and purple to look at her friend. "We've never discussed your belief system—and maybe I shouldn't ask, but…" She held up the drink in her hand, a nearly empty rum runner. "Inhibitions are down, you know."

Giselle released a soft laugh. "I don't mind. And I agree about sunsets and accidents being two very different things. I believe in God. And angels."

"Angels," Dahlia repeated, tilting her head just slightly. "Now there's a thought I like."

Encouraged, Giselle went on. "I believe they're with us all the time."

"Well then," Dahlia said with a sharp, short nod, "I think I shall start keeping an eye out for angels every day." She lifted her drink again. "And if I keep imbibing these delicious cocktails, I might just start seeing some."

Giselle chuckled once more, sipping on her own drink. "What shall we do this evening? Board games?" They'd played a few recently. Dahlia had long meant to start hosting game nights for her friends and not gotten around to it, but had begun the habit with Giselle.

"Perhaps," she replied. "There's some writing I've been wanting to do and I thought I might start tonight—but it can wait until tomorrow. Perhaps my thoughts will be smartly guided when looking out on a clear blue sky, listening to the caws of the seagulls."

"Board games it is then. Do you mind if I shower first and change into pajamas?"

"Not at all. I'll still be here."

"What are you going to write?" Giselle asked absently, pushing to her feet.

"Some letters, sparked by old memories."

"I'll admit I'm curious about your memories, your life before I knew you," Giselle said, ponytail bouncing behind her.

Dahlia let out a sly chuckle. "There *are* some good stories, I confess. Did you know I left home at sixteen? Zack and I have that in common."

She glanced up at her friend again, who'd gone wide-eyed. "I had no idea."

"It was quite different, of course. He ran away and got a job on a fishing boat. I headed west, hitchhiking—

back before that was considered crazy—and ended up in a VW bus with a bunch of other kids."

"Wow. That sounds amazing. And...trippy," Giselle said, appearing amused to find the perfect word for the hippie-dippie visions Dahlia had clearly just put in her head. "Maybe you'll tell me about it as we play games."

"Gladly," Dahlia promised, and as Giselle departed let out a contented sigh. "I'll just soak up my sunset until you get back."

She'd found that with age, memories grew dimmer and less exact. They became, over time, more like images, flashes and blips, particular feelings—but that the words spoken and the details that went with them got lost in the busy synapses of an active brain.

By the same token, however, she had lately discovered that the more she sat quietly, sinking into recollections, the more that came back to her. She'd always thought it seemed silly when a detective on a TV police drama said to someone, "Let us know if you remember anything else." *Because either you remember or you don't.* But memory, it turned out, was a lot more of an elastic thing than she'd understood: stretch it and it grows.

*DAHLIA'S SUITCASE GREW heavier with every step along the pockmarked, sun-beaten road just west of Toledo on a hot July day. At the sound of a vehicle approaching behind her, she hiked her thumb upward but didn't bother to look, assuming it would pass by like the last ten.*

*When a pale green VW van sprinkled with flower decals pulled over in front of her, gravel crunched and her heartbeat quickened. The side door slid open, the lyrics to "Mrs. Robinson" spilling sloppily out, and she realized everyone inside was singing. A boy with dark, curly hair that hung to his shoulders said, "Where ya headed?"*

*Simple question. The sort of question that should have an answer. But for the first time she realized, "I have no idea."*

*The boy laughed. "Well, if you think Montana might be on the way there, climb in."*

*Montana. It sounded a world away from Michigan. Like a romantic place with sweeping vistas and lots of room to...just be. Like a place with no yelling or slapping or locked doors. She answered by tossing her suitcase inside and taking the boy's hand, letting him help her up into the van.*

*"I'm Dobie," he said, then pointed at the driver, a guy in the passenger seat, and two girls in back behind them. "That's Mulligan, Pete, Linda, and Renata."*

*She held up a hand. "I'm Dahlia."*

*"Cool name," Linda said. And Dahlia smiled. Her mother hadn't given her much, but a cool name was at least something.*

*"Mully's aunt owns a horse ranch north of Bozeman," Dobie said. "Her husband died and she needs help running the place. Room, board, and wages for anybody who wants it."*

*Dahlia let her eyes widen. "Oh, so you're all going to work on the ranch?"*

*"I am for sure," the driver, Mulligan, said. He possessed a ruddy complexion and a fuzzy head of reddish-blond hair. "Dobie's just biding his time, seeing which way the wind blows him when we get there. We're from Wilkes-Barre, Pennsylvania."*

*The girl named Renata spoke up then. "I'm heading to Oregon—got a friend there. But I'm not in a hurry—if I find someplace I dig on the way, I might hang loose* awhile. These guys picked me up near Pittsburgh." She had slick black hair, heart-shaped sunglasses, and a cool confidence Dahlia immediately envied.

Then Linda, a girl with long, straight, silky brown locks, chimed in, "I might try the ranch gig." She shrugged, like she was deciding what to have for breakfast—as opposed to planning her immediate future. "Just needed a new scene."

Dahlia thought Pete, the cute guy in the passenger seat, would weigh in, but he stayed quiet, seeming disinterested. And meanwhile, Dahlia tried not to feel overwhelmed. This was only the second ride she'd gotten since leaving home early this morning—the first from a nice girl in her twenties in a purple Firebird just outside Saginaw going to visit her mother in Toledo. She'd seemed worried for Dahlia the whole while. This crowd was more easygoing, somehow making her feel at home and slightly nervous at the same time. They all seemed so...comfortable in their uncertainty. She would have to learn to be the same.

"You seem young," Dobie observed.

She bit her lip—then tossed a wave of long blond hair over her shoulder, trying to mirror the confidence of Renata. "Is my age important?" They all looked a little older than her—eighteen or nineteen maybe.

"Guess not—you seem groovy enough." Then he reached in a cooler and held out a cold bottle of Coca-Cola. "Thirsty?"

"Sure," she said, still working to be hip, confident—but in fact, she'd been almost woozy from the heat by the time the van had stopped.

She quickly learned the van lacked a working radio, hence the singing she'd heard when the door opened. Linda seemed to be the song leader—by virtue, per-

*haps, of being the only one who cared enough to or-
chestrate the music.* "How about 'Sweet Caroline'?"
she suggested as the van headed west toward Indiana.

As time passed, they sang "California Dreamin'",
"Leaving on a Jet Plane," "Good Morning Starshine,"
"Big Yellow Taxi," and "Woodstock"—but the last one
became a laughter-scattered drone of missed notes and
lyrics no one really yet knew.

Her travel companions were all friendly, sharing
food and drinks—and pot. Dahlia had never had any
before, but when Dobie passed her a joint that night as
they crossed northern Indiana, she tried it. Because she
wanted to be one of them. And she was curious. And on
her own now, so she could make whatever decisions
she wanted.

"You don't have to do that," Pete said, turning all
the way around from the front seat. It was the first time
he'd acknowledged her since she'd climbed in the van
hours earlier.

"I know," she said, still trying to be tough, cool. But
then she looked at him. Her first impression had been
right—he was cute. With dreamy blue Robert Redford
eyes and thick, sandy John Denver hair.

That was all it took. A handsome boy who expressed
concern over her well-being when no one else ever really had. She passed the pot on to the next person and
didn't take it the next time it was offered. She had gone
in the flash of an eye from wanting to fit in to wanting
to impress the blue-eyed boy in the front seat by showing him she didn't have to. And turned out that felt better anyway.

Later that night, the van stopped along a desolate Il-
linois side road. Dobie played a guitar—badly—while
the others roasted hot dogs over a small campfire. Pete

told Dahlia he was from Pennsylvania and didn't want to spend the rest of his life in a steel mill alongside his father and brothers. "So I'm setting out, looking to see what else I can find. What's your story, Starshine?" He'd been calling her that ever since they'd sung the song earlier.

"Things are bad at home," she said, keeping it simple. "So I want to see what else is out there for me, too."

"Maybe we'll see together for a while," he said, and as if to seal the deal, he leaned over and pressed a kiss to her lips. Her first kiss. Because she'd led a life of fear up until this moment. Fear of her mother, who slapped her every time she "smarted off." Fear of men, because so many of them had leered at her like she was a woman when she'd only been a little girl. Fear of the world, because the small bits she'd seen hadn't looked too promising so far.

Three months later, she married Pete in the company of new friends, on the Bar J ranch in Montana, with daisies in her hair. She wore a white cotton halter dress, carried wildflowers, and stood barefoot in the grass to connect with Mother Earth as she took her vows. With Pete, life was full of new hopes, new possibilities, new passions. It held so much more than she'd ever imagined back home in a dumpy little house with a violent mother and an angry sister.

Turned out it was too soon, though. She knew it only another few months later, when she found herself beginning to wonder what lay over the next horizon, when she found herself noticing the new ranch hand, when she began to enjoy the company of Hannah Jasper, the lady ranch owner, more than that of her new husband.

"There are moments when I'm afraid I've made a very big mistake," she confided in Hannah one day as they sat upon a split-rail fence, side by side, watching an untamed mustang buck and snort his way around a corral.

"I feared as much," her older, wiser friend said on a sigh. "Some people do well marrying young—I thought maybe you needed that sense of security, the safety of having a partner in life. But others are just like that bronc out there." She pointed to the glossy black horse who clearly felt trapped, frightened. "You have a bigger spirit than you even know, Dahlia. I think you've spent the time since you got here feeling your way through all the new possibilities you've given yourself. I think you have a thirst for adventure. And I think you're gonna want more and more of it."

"Without Pete, you mean?" she asked to clarify.

"You're the one who called it a mistake."

Dahlia nodded. She'd thought she was in love with him—but she'd been in love with...his eyes, and sex, and the ability to make her own decisions. And he was a good man. Not even just a boy anymore—he was becoming a man before her eyes, same as she was becoming a woman, and his only mistake had been devoting himself to a girl who'd acted impetuously at the first taste of freedom she'd ever known. "What should I do?" she asked Hannah.

"The only thing a free spirit can. Follow your heart."

## CHAPTER NINE

AFTER PUSHING AND prodding Zack through more physical therapy, Suzanne doubled the number of reps for all his exercises. He responded pretty much as she expected.

"Are you trying to kill me, woman?"

"No, I'm trying to help you heal," she informed him, pushing his knee to his chest.

"I thought you said you had no idea if this would fix anything," he groused.

"I don't. But if you lie here like a blob, I can *guarantee* nothing will get fixed. That's fine, though," she told him, backing off, releasing his leg. "If you *want* to lie here like a blob, and if you want to ensure that your *whole life* will be about lying here like a blob, you can. I'll just make your meals and be your maid until Dahlia gets back. Is that what you want?"

He blew out a grumpy breath. "Knock it off with your reverse psychology, Suzie Q. You know that's not what I want."

"Then you have to put in the effort," she said, hands on her hips. "That simple."

"Simple to you," he mumbled.

"It's not simple to me at all. I'm the one who has to put up with you." *And the one who has to keep...touching you. And feeling all tingly and nervous every time.* She kept thinking that would fade. So far it hadn't. She only prayed she was doing an adequate job of hiding it.

She didn't even know what it meant. She was a nurse—
this should not affect her. That was what she kept coming back to over and over again. And the last thing she
needed was for Zack Sheppard to think she was…at-
tracted to him. Even if they almost got along now, the
two of them had been at odds so long that it would be
mortifying if he thought…

Oh. Wait. Was she?

Attracted? Like…physically?

To Zack?

With Beck Grainger, it had made sense. He was a
gentleman. Kind. Polite. Helpful. Classically handsome
and then some. With a substantial career and a lovely
home. What red-blooded American woman *wouldn't* be
attracted to Beck Grainger?

But Zack was…surly. Distant. Selfish. And the career he'd cultivated was pretty much in the toilet now.
Because he might never walk again.

So surely…surely…there was some other explanation for the way her heart raced and her chest tightened
when she touched him. Some other explanation for the
skitter of nervousness that zigzagged through her when
she looked directly into his eyes. Some other explanation
for the tingly sensation that rippled through her when
she caught a hint of his masculine scent.

"Okay, I think we're done here," she told him, rising
up off the bed without warning.

"Suzanne—wait, damn it. I'll do the exercises already."

He looked almost alarmed, and at the very least, distressed. Which threw her—because she was just trying to get away right now. Because she was realizing
the unthinkable and needed space. It had nothing to do

with his grumpiness and everything to do with her body, mind, heart.

"No, it's fine," she assured him. "We've done enough for today."

She started to walk away—when he reached out and grabbed her wrist, stopping her. Her heart lurched to her throat and she looked down—at his hand where it held her. His firm grip echoed all the way up her arm and into her breasts.

"I'm sorry," he said. His tone was slightly grudging—like he just didn't know quite how to apologize, but he was trying. "I don't mean to be an ass. I'll do better."

Good Lord. What was happening? Zack Sheppard was being sincere and humble—at the moment when she could least appreciate it, because she needed to escape before she dissolved into a heap of molten shock over what she suddenly knew she felt. "It's okay," she insisted. "It's fine. I know you're working at this. I just... need a minute."

Pulling her arm free, she made a beeline for the bathroom. She shut the door, lowered the lid on the toilet, and sat down, almost sorry she'd escaped because she missed the touch. The revelation hit her like a slap in the face. She just hadn't seen it. Perhaps she'd chosen *not* to see it. But now she felt thickheaded not to have understood. That she *liked* touching him. It made her nervous as hell, but she liked it. And right now it was hard to unravel the whole roiling, messy, confusing knot of nervousness and awkwardness and pleasure and desire, but no matter how she sliced it, there was suddenly no denying it: she was attracted to Zack.

How utterly unnerving. *Then again, being attracted to a man is* always *unnerving for you.* She'd barely been able to look at Beck—before and after she'd recognized her attraction to him. She'd been nervous when she'd first started feeling that way about Cal, too. *You're just a basket case around men, that's all. Think you'd be used to it by now.*

This seemed harder, though, than the other two. Zack was her patient. Zack was her best friend's ex. Zack was, until very recently, practically her sworn enemy. And to top it all off, Zack was emotionally inept. *Not* a gentleman. *Not* polite. Not any of the things she was normally drawn to.

She blew out a breath. *Okay, make a plan.*

*In the short term, you have to go back out there and act normal. Like you are totally* not *attracted to him. For all the reasons it makes no sense to be.*

In the long term…well, it was hard to think long term at the moment. Suddenly the idea of sharing a home with him for the coming months felt even more difficult than it had last week.

*But you need to focus. On just…acting cool. Like nothing has changed.*

Of course, PT was going to be even harder now. *But don't think about that. Just don't…think. About anything.*

She stood up, turned on the faucet, splashed some water on her face. Then looked at herself in the mirror. *You're a nurse, a caregiver, that's all. Just get through this, one day at a time, and before you know it, it'll be over. For now, do your job. Take care of him, help him exercise, be a pleasant companion—and nothing more. Think of him the way you did a few days ago. Even if you were just as drawn to him then and unwilling to admit it to yourself. Think about how you'd feel if that wasn't true. Fake it 'til you make it.*

Yes, that seemed like a good plan. Remembering her

role here was the only way to keep herself from going down a dark road that could only hurt her.

Because for one thing, he was indeed Meg's ex. You didn't mess with your bestie's ex—you just didn't.

And for another—if she ever again let herself care for a man, he would have to be stable, kind, emotionally intact. One emotional basket case in a relationship was ample—she knew herself well enough to realize she needed someone who had their act together, to balance out her own unevenness.

And for a third—Zack was...Zack. He would never be attracted to her. She wasn't his type. His type was traditionally pretty, calm, steady, smooth-as-silk Meg. Probably because he needed a together person to balance out *his* issues, too. But whatever the reason, she was a far cry from Meg. And she'd be mortified if he ever knew how she felt.

Blotting the cool water from her face, she took a deep breath, let it back out, and opened the bathroom door— ready to be her best caregiving, unemotional self.

"Listen, Suzie Q," he started the second she emerged back into the room, "I really do appreciate all you're doing for me. Okay?"

"Okay," she said. Wishing he'd knock off the sudden niceness. Seriously—for all the times for him to go nice, it had to be now? She let out a quiet sigh, knowing that if she were to fool both of them into thinking nothing funny was going on here, she had to follow her instincts. "Are you ready to do the rest of your exercises then?"

"Yes," he said simply.

She walked across the room and picked up the small free weights. "Do your arm curls, adding one rep of ten to each. And then we'll add two sets of ten leg rotations."

His eyebrows lifted, and he looked almost ready to complain.

"We can make it three sets if you want to argue about it."

At this, he stayed quiet, pressing his mouth together in a thin, straight line. Feeling like a drill sergeant, she gave a succinct nod to let him know she meant business, then passed him the weights.

SUZANNE SAT CURLED in her easy chair near the fire, reading a book, or attempting to—the act required tuning out what they now referred to as "Zack's talk shows." That had become a large part of her existence these days: tuning certain things out.

When her phone notified her of a message, Zack's buzzed next to him on the sofa bed, too. A glance down revealed that Dahlia had sent them a group text to ask, How are you two getting along?

Suzanne thought back to the morning's therapy session—she'd hid her attraction, he'd complained. Business as usual. She typed into the phone: He's as difficult a patient as he is a human being.

Another text followed, from Zack. She's a regular Nurse Ratchet.

Suzanne lifted her gaze from the phone screen to the man across the room. "Ratched."

"What?" he asked, appearing confused.

"Ratched," she said. "You mean Nurse Ratched. From *One Flew Over the Cuckoo's Nest.*"

"I mean Nurse Ratchet," he insisted.

She just looked at him. "From…?" she inquired arrogantly.

"I don't know—I just figured she was named after, you know, a ratchet. Which I wouldn't want to be caught in."

Suzanne just shook her head and sighed. "You don't remember Nurse Ratched from the movie?"

"What movie?"

She rolled her eyes. Then enunciated as if he were hard of hearing. *"One Flew Over the Cuckoo's Nest."*

"Never saw it."

She let her eyes open wider. "Seriously?"

"Seriously. What's the big deal? A person can't see every damn movie ever made."

"I'm going to trust that you haven't read the book, either."

He just gave her a look that said, *You know damn well I haven't.*

"You really should see the movie," she insisted.

"Why?"

"Because it's a classic."

"I've lived without classics this long."

"And...actually," she said, thinking out loud, "maybe it would make you feel better about your situation."

He looked unconvinced as he replied, "Well, let me just dash right on down to a non-existent video store and pick it up on my non-working legs."

"Correction. Only one of them isn't working. And I can probably find it streaming somewhere."

"Lucky me."

"I think you'll actually like it. It stars Jack Nicholson when he was young."

That did seem to catch his attention. She'd noticed he seemed stuck in a time warp, drawn to things from before he was even born. "Oh. Well...then maybe."

When the phones beeped and buzzed again at the break in conversation, they both looked down to see a barrage of texts from Dahlia, which they'd apparently talked through without noticing.

Zack, Suzanne is only trying to help you—listen to her and do what she says.

Be nice to one another.

Are either of you there?

Are you killing each other?

Is this thing on? Tap, tap, tap.

Suzanne couldn't help being amused. She typed: He's lying in a puddle of blood at my feet. Then hit Send.

She slyly glanced at Zack from the corner of her eye, saw him smile slightly. Then he sent a text, as well. I just flung my crutches at her from my puddle.

Suzanne chuckled softly.

But Dahlia replied: That's not funny, you two.

Across the room, Zack typed an answer, and a moment later it arrived. I'm making jokes, so it might not be funny exactly, but it's good in a way, right?

Suzanne's heart expanded in her chest. He *was* right. He'd come a long way in a short time, probably longer than she'd given him credit for. She subtly lifted her gaze to study him—and found him staring back.

As usual for her, that was hard—holding a man's gaze, holding *his* gaze. Fortunately, just as she drew her eyes downward, another text arrived from Dahlia. I hadn't thought of it that way, but yes! That's so very good, nephew! I'm proud of you.

More typing from Zack produced another text to both women. That doesn't mean she's not a Nurse Ratchet, though.

You mean Ratched, Dahlia answered.

THAT NIGHT, WHILE Suzanne popped popcorn in the kitchen, Zack maneuvered himself into one of the two easy chairs facing the TV.

"What to drink?" she called.

"Beer?" he suggested.

"With popcorn?" she questioned.

"Yeah." Like that was normal. Maybe for him, it was.

"Well, I don't have any. There's some wine in the fridge, though." She sometimes drank a glass before bed. Or she had back before her houseguest's arrival had thrown her every routine out the window.

"That'll do," he said.

And so with a big bowl of popcorn on an end table between them, and two glasses of Chardonnay, they watched *One Flew Over the Cuckoo's Nest*.

At first, Suzanne had trouble paying attention. Her focus stuck on the middle-school-worthy concern of whether their hands touched when they reached for popcorn at the same time. Each such occurrence sent an unwanted ripple up her arm, down through her body. Pretty soon she just quit eating popcorn—but she did pour them both a second glass of wine, glad she'd brought the freshly uncorked bottle with her, and Zack kept topping them off because, as luck would have it, it was one of those extra big bottles.

Once she forgot about touching and popcorn, though, she got drawn into the movie. And when it ended and Zack stayed quiet, her mind raced. Was the whole vibe too heavy for a man in his situation? It had seemed like a good idea, but maybe not.

"That was dark," he finally said.

"Too dark?" she asked cautiously. "Because maybe I forgot *how* dark it actually was."

A light chuckle left him. "I've been some dark places, Suzie Q, so it takes more than a movie to bother me."

The words left her curious. *What dark places?* Or maybe she didn't want to know, *shouldn't* want to know.

She was his nurse, after all, nothing more. *Keep telling yourself that and it'll become true—it has to.*

"Then...did it make you feel better? I mean, in comparison, about where you are?"

He grinned, and when she dared meet his eyes, she suspected the alcohol had him a little loopy. "Makes me glad you don't have some sort of shock therapy machine to hook me up to."

And an unwitting trill of laughter escaped her. From the wine. And the grin. *Ignore that part.* But the wine made that more difficult.

Zack reached for his crutches and started to pull himself up onto them—but quickly lost his balance and plopped back down onto his chair. He tossed her a sideways glance. "Bad news, Susie Q. Think I'm a little drunk."

"Uh-oh. Drunk and crutches don't go together. Let me help," she said, rising to her feet—albeit not steadily.

"I think you're a little drunk, too," he announced, pointing at her.

She couldn't deny the accusation. She'd felt fine sitting down, but getting up had been a different matter. "Well, two drunk people with a set of crutches is better than one."

Though as the struggle for him to stand commenced, she realized he was going to need more than a steadying hand to get him to the bed, and suggested, "Let's get rid of this one," taking one crutch away, "and I'll be the crutch." Her work in the nursing home had taught her a lot about moving people.

As she got him to his feet, sliding one arm around his waist as he draped his own around her shoulder, she said, "About the movie, I guess my point is—life can be a lot about perspective." *Her* current perspective was that his body was crushed tight against hers and she felt it from head to toe, most notably between her legs. *But ignore, ignore, ignore. Keep talking, like this is totally normal, like he's just an old man in a nursing home.* "And even though your situation sucks, it could be worse."

He met her gaze, appearing pleasantly intoxicated and maybe a little philosophical. "But it could be a hell of a lot better." And he was *so* not an old man in a nursing home. He was a *strong* man, with taut muscles and a broad chest—the messy waves in his hair and thick stubble on his chin making him all the more sexy right now.

*Because you're drunk. And alcohol has a way of turning a person amorous.* Knowing that should make it easier to ignore. But it didn't.

Still, she tried to concentrate on the conversation as they took slow, lumbering steps toward the sofa bed. "You're right," she said. "It probably isn't fair of me to shove that idea down your throat right now. Whatever you're feeling is valid. And you're doing as well as anyone could be expected to. Which I respect, by the way."

He glanced over at her again as they reached the bedside. "Thanks, Miss Q."

And the shortening of the silly nickname might have made her laugh—except that he kept looking at her, looking right into her eyes, their faces so close that her heart beat like a drum.

"And you're right, too," he murmured softly. "It could be worse. I could be alone right now. But I'm not."

Then his eyes fell half-shut and his gaze dropped to her mouth, her every nerve ending crackling with electricity as she realized he was leaning in to kiss her.

## CHAPTER TEN

WORKING ON GUT INSTINCT, Suzanne pushed Zack lightly onto the bed and stepped back. She had no idea where this kissing notion had come from, but it couldn't happen.

She found him wearing an amused expression as he situated himself up against some pillows. "You dropped me, Suzie Q."

"A hazard of drinking with your nurse," she claimed. Though that near kiss had sobered her up—fast.

Her patient peered speculatively up at her. "Wanna have another drink? You could sit and talk to me some more." He patted the bed next to him.

Oh Lord. He was trying to make this happen even now that they weren't pressed up against each other. And likely angling for more than just kissing. She found herself staring at the spot he'd just patted as heat suffused her cheeks.

"We should both turn in. Goodnight, Zack," she said, then rushed to flip off the lights and head to her bedroom.

She'd clean up the empty wineglasses and popcorn bowl tomorrow, when this would be in the past, like a bad dream. He wouldn't remember—surely he wouldn't remember. They'd never even have to acknowledge it. And things could get back to normal around here. Well, whatever normal was. But normal certainly wasn't kissing and inviting her into his bed.

*Of course* I'll *remember it*. And she had a feeling all those tingling spots in her body were going to remember it, too. Was it really like a *bad* dream? After all, was it so awful for a man she suddenly found attractive to want to kiss her?

Well, in this case, yes—it was. Because the man was drunk. And the man was someone it would be crazy to start kissing.

ZACK'S HEAD SPUN, even lying on a pile of pillows. Had he actually just made a pass at Suzanne? Huh. Too much wine, not enough popcorn.

Truth was, he liked her a lot more than he'd thought. Now he understood why Dahlia and Meg were friends with her—she was a good person who was…well, being a lot better to him than Dahlia and Meg were right now. Funny how things worked out sometimes.

Maybe that vision of her ass swaying to the music had stayed with him. And she was prettier than he'd ever realized. And sorta cute when she got nervous. He liked nervous Suzanne better than the self-righteous, judgmental Suzanne she'd always been with him before the last two weeks. And hell…he'd wanted to do a lot more than talk when he'd patted the sheet beside him. He was sorry she'd gone rushing off.

For more reasons than one, actually. She'd dropped him on the damn mattress so fast he hadn't got to go to the bathroom before getting in bed. And no way he could go by himself in his current condition. He considered calling her—but thought better of it. She'd seemed pretty eager to get away from him, after all. Easier to just hold it 'til morning.

Maybe she just wasn't into him that way. Because of his bum leg. Or because she'd thought he'd treated Meg badly. Or...hell, there could be a million reasons, and it didn't really matter. It had just been...an impulse.

And besides...damn, with his leg paralyzed could he even...?

The question dropped onto him like an anchor. Shit, maybe it was best she'd turned him down. Maybe she'd even already thought of that. He couldn't imagine a worse humiliation than both of them being ready to go, and then discovering he couldn't hold up his end of the bargain.

And yet...her ass in those jeans still swayed in his mind. And when she'd been up against him a few minutes ago, her breast had pressed into his side, full and firm and...

*Aw. Oh yeah. Thank you, sweet baby Jesus.*

He had a semi-erection. Best semi-erection of his life. Even if now he had to fall asleep with *that* distraction, too.

*So I can still be with a woman.* Not that he knew what good it would do him, all things considered. How different and strange and awkward would sex be when he couldn't maneuver his body normally? What woman would want to have sex with him like this?

But he wasn't gonna worry about shit like that right now.

He pushed the ugly questions aside, letting himself remember Suzanne dancing around the kitchen. And he drifted into sleep feeling a little more like a man.

IT WAS ALMOST a weird relief when Suzanne woke the next day to hear Zack grumbling and grumpy. "Woman, do you know the last time I went to the bathroom? I've had to go all damn night." Grumpy Zack she was used to. Flirty, sexy Zack was new and intimidating.

So even as he groused, she just smiled, even laughed. "Hold your horses, grumphead. I'm coming."

And now that he was sober, he was able to take *himself* to the bathroom—but she was glad he'd waited until she got up so she could be nearby if he lost his balance.

Once he was behind the closed bathroom door, she called, "You're doing really well on the crutches. Way better than I would have predicted a week ago."

"Think it's the exercises?" he asked through the door.

"I think it's great you have a lot of upper body strength and good we're keeping it that way. And keeping all your muscles toned and active can only help." As the door opened and he came out, she added, "We'll add more crutch work to our routine. The better you can get around, the happier you'll be."

"You got that right," he said, lowering himself into a chair at the dining table.

His aptitude on the crutches truly impressed her, and she was glad to have turned their conversation to something positive. Another positive? He didn't seem to remember the awkwardness between them last night, or if he did, he wasn't letting it show. Which suited her just fine.

As she moved around the kitchen, letting the skillet heat as she gathered eggs and other ingredients for omelets, he asked, "You like the quiet, don't you?"

She looked over at him. "I guess I do, now that you mention it."

"Don't get me wrong," he said. "I like quiet sometimes, too. Out on my fishing boat there's *nothing* but quiet and I don't mind it. But…you care if I play a little music?"

Suzanne didn't particularly enjoy music first thing in the morning, but if it would keep him contented... "Go for it."

She wasn't surprised when, a moment later, his phone played a clever rock song about signs that sounded straight out of the hippie era. But it had a good beat. "Who *is* this?" she asked as she broke an egg into the frying pan.

"A one-hit wonder called Five Man Electrical Band."

"That's a horrible name." She broke another egg.

"Yeah. Great song, though."

"When was it out—1852?"

Despite herself, she liked that it made him laugh before he replied, "More like early seventies."

"Same difference," she quipped, and he chuckled again.

Then said, "You like it, though."

She stopped breaking eggs and just looked over at him. "What makes you say that?"

"You're dancing a little."

Oh. She was. She hadn't realized. "Hmm. Guess I am."

Why did he look so amused by that? She had no idea, and finally just rolled her eyes and got back to making breakfast.

Do you want to come over this afternoon? Sit by the fire and catch up? Drink some hot chocolate?

Suzanne looked at the text on her phone from Meg. She hadn't heard from her BFF in a while. Though she'd barely noticed, too wrapped up in all the goings-on in her cottage. Zack was a full-time job.

Part of her wanted to be a little standoffish—Meg had

promised Dahlia she'd help with Zack, but they hadn't talked since the day he woke up paralyzed. On the other hand, though, Meg was reaching out to her now, and she loved her friend, so she texted back: Yes, yes, and yes! What time?

After lunch and afternoon exercises, she bundled up and headed down Harbor Street toward the Summerbrook Inn. A light snow fell, but the walk reminded her how beautiful Summer Island could be in winter. Even a glance at ice-laden Lake Michigan, the very body of water keeping Dahlia away and Zack from better medical treatment, didn't bring her down. She climbed the front walk to the inn, eager to see her friend.

As soon as Meg opened the door, Suzanne said, "I've missed you."

"I've missed you, too," Meg replied, "and I'm sorry I haven't called." She stopped, bit her lip, looked uncertain. "I just felt...weird about it all."

"It's okay, and it doesn't have to be weird," Suzanne assured her, then gave her a hug.

As she stepped inside, Meg appeared relieved.

And Suzanne was, too—even more now. "Where's Seth?" she asked, hanging her parka in the foyer. Usually Meg's boyfriend greeted Suzanne when she visited, even if just with a hello from another part of the house.

"He's actually snowshoeing around the island to check on Walt Gardner." When Seth had first arrived here, he'd rented a cabin from the old man who lived on the northern shore. "Ever since Lila found Gran's old snowshoes up in the attic, Seth has been making use of them."

At the mention of Lila, Suzanne steeled herself and tried to do the right, polite thing. "How *are* Lila and Beck?"

The reminder that Suzanne had suffered a wild crush on her sister's new fiancé took Meg's smile from natural to forced. "They're fine."

They moved into the parlor, where Meg already had two mugs of hot chocolate waiting on the mantel. "I assume she's…moved in with him," Suzanne said, picking up a mug, letting it warm hands just pulled from mittens.

"Not officially," Meg replied, taking up the other cup. "She still has stuff here. But she mostly stays at his house, yes. It makes sense, given the distance and weather."

Suzanne nodded.

"They walked down and had dinner with us last night, though," Meg went on as they settled on the sofa. "Then we played cards and watched a movie."

"That's great," Suzanne said, suddenly feeling like the odd man out. It was no fun being the cutoff corner of a love triangle, and now she got to envision her best friend and Seth having cozy evenings with the man Suzanne had so wanted to connect with—along with Meg's sister.

*But you like Lila, remember? You have to get past this, move on.* So she made herself add, "I'm really happy for Lila. And Beck. Both of them." *Fake it 'til you make it.* She lived by those words lately.

That was when Meg bit her lip again. "Oh God, I'm being insensitive by going on about them." She shut her eyes. "I feel like I'm doing everything wrong lately. I'm sorry, Suz."

Meg's honesty made her feel bad about the roadblocks life had put between them lately. It was no one's fault—it just was. "It's really okay," Suzanne promised her. "I'm still getting used to the situation—but I need to. It's going to be part of our friendship now."

"Speaking of getting used to situations," Meg proceeded cautiously, "how are things with Zack?"

Suzanne drew in a deep breath. One thing she hadn't thought about before coming here was… *I'm unwittingly attracted to Meg's ex-lover now.* No way she could tell her that. So she'd just have to leave it out of the equation as she formed an answer—more faking it. "We're… getting along better now. He realizes I'm only trying to help him, and that's made things more cordial. Except for when he's biting my head off anyway, that is."

"That's great to hear," Meg replied, then laughed. "Except for the head-biting part. But given the situation, guess that doesn't surprise me." She lowered her voice slightly for the next question, as if almost afraid to ask it. "How's he doing with everything? With maybe never walking again?"

"Also better," Suzanne told her. "We don't talk about the long-term prospects—I just try to keep him hopeful. And we do physical therapy every day, too. It's helping a lot—not only with strength and mobility, but because it provides some positive structure to the long days."

"Wow—I never thought of that. Your nursing skills are really paying off. You're doing more for him than Dahlia, or I, or anyone else really could."

Part of Suzanne still resented that her old profession made her the obvious person to drop Zack on—but Meg's sincerity made it nice to be appreciated.

Then Meg blew out a sigh. "It does my heart good to know he's doing well. I mean, it's not like I suddenly stopped caring about him when Seth and I got together. I've been sick that he's in this position and I can't be there for him."

Suzanne flashed back on the day Zack first came to her house, how desperately she wanted Meg to come in, help them both get acclimated. But instead of dwelling on old hurt, she said the most direct, sensible thing she could think of. "Well, that's why *I'm* there for him. Since you and Dahlia can't be."

Though only after the words left her did she realize she'd spoken them in an almost proprietary way. *He's not yours to take care of anymore. He's mine. For right now. Even if I didn't want him when all this started. Even if you're suddenly having some kind of weird regrets. Even if now I kind of want him but can't have him. Even if he wanted me last night in a totally meaningless way.*

"Well, I'm grateful he's in such good hands."

Okay, good—Meg hadn't heard the possessiveness in her voice. Maybe it hadn't even *been* in her voice—maybe it was only in her heart. But where on earth had it come from?

"Thank you," Meg said then. "For taking care of him for me."

Suzanne looked over her steaming mug, lips pressed tight together. She'd so missed Meg, so wanted everything to be normal with Meg. Yet they were right back in that awkward place they'd last left each other—with Meg hanging on to Zack emotionally in a way Suzanne didn't like.

Even if, at the same time, she understood. Meg had *loved* him. *Of course* she still had feelings for him. Why did it bother Suzanne so much?

*I'm not taking care of him for you. I'm taking care of him because no one else would. I'm taking care of him because he needs me. You're not part of this, Meg.* Thankfully, she kept all that inside. And from somewhere she mustered up a quiet and awkward, "You're welcome."

It got easier when they turned to other subjects.

They'd both heard from Dahlia, and both mostly quit being mad at her, but agreed there was still something about this whole trip they just didn't get. Suzanne found out Seth was setting up a workshop in the toolshed with the help of some space heaters, where he could paint and refinish furniture, and which he might add on to come spring. They were also planning to repaint a couple of guestrooms—keeping the inn up-to-date was a never-ending project.

When Suzanne politely inquired more about Lila's plans for moving to the island permanently, Meg explained that her sister had accepted a managerial position at the Knitting Nook from the owner, Allie Hobbs, whom they were all friendly with, starting in spring. "And maybe by then," Meg said, "some of the trouble with her old boss will have blown over."

"What trouble?" Suzanne asked.

"Oh my," Meg replied. "So much has been going on, I forgot you didn't know. It's actually all over the news in Chicago—and Lila won't mind if I tell you." Meg then explained that her sister had spoken out after her high-powered boss sexually assaulted her, then fired her, and that she was only one in a long line of victims. "Though of course she doesn't like that word for it, and I don't blame her. She's been through a lot, and I'm proud of her for being brave enough to take a stand so this slimeball can't keep hurting women."

The story left Suzanne flabbergasted and served to remind her that everyone had troubles. Lila might have Beck Grainger, but suddenly Suzanne didn't envy her quite as much as she had a few minutes earlier. And she resolved to give Lila a hug the next time she saw her and truly get past the awkwardness between them.

Now if she could only do as much with her best

friend. Since, after all that, Meg came back to talking about Zack, saying again how much it broke her heart that he had to go through this without her.

*You* chose *for him to go through it without you.* But again Suzanne bit her tongue.

"Was I right?" Meg suddenly asked. "To not be involved? You know I worried it would only confuse things—and I don't want that for either of us. But part of me still wonders if I should have…been around more."

"I actually *do* think you were right," Suzanne said. At the time she'd felt so abandoned, like they should take a team approach. But now…well, now that was water under the bridge, and she and Zack had adjusted and didn't particularly *need* any help.

Meg nodded, even if she looked uncertain.

And when Suzanne announced she should probably be getting back to her patient, Meg said, "Wait—I have something for you to take back."

Left alone in the big parlor, Suzanne soaked up the ambiance of the inn and thought about Beck and Lila falling in love here just last month. She could feel it in the rooms, in the wood and the walls and the very air— that love happened here. It had for Seth and Meg, too. And Meg and Zack before that. And much longer ago, she knew Meg's grandma had fallen in love with Meg's grandpa here. It all served to make her feel lonely.

Meg re-entered the room carrying a covered dish.

"What's this?"

"A chicken casserole. Simple, but Zack always loved it. Of course, maybe it was dumb of me—I know you can cook. I just wanted to do something, and I don't know what else to do." She shook her head.

"No, it's nice," Suzanne assured her.

And it was. Because she knew Meg meant well. *But*

*on the other hand, now I get to go home and say, "Hey, your ex-girlfriend made you your favorite casserole. But don't let that re-ignite your feelings for her or anything."*

# CHAPTER ELEVEN

"WHAT'S THAT?" ZACK asked when Suzanne walked in carrying the dish.

"A casserole. From Meg." She didn't look at him as she set it down, then began to take off her coat and snow boots. "She said it was one you used to like."

"Hmm," he said. "Nice, I guess."

"Yeah," she said, secretly pleased that he didn't seem to be making much of the gesture.

"How is she?"

Suzanne's chest tightened slightly. "Seemed fine."

"You two, uh, haven't been in touch much lately. That's not how I remember things being back...before."

*Back when you and she were a couple.* She was surprised he'd noticed, and wasn't sure how to explain. There were so many reasons—each of them awkward. *Her sister is engaged to the guy I was into. Her ex is living with me. She's avoiding you, and that means avoiding me. I'm still a little put out with her over all of it, even the parts that are completely beyond her control.* Finally, she settled on, "It's an unusual winter—Dahlia's gone, you're here..."

"And she has a new boyfriend keeping her busy."

She looked over at him, shrugged. "That, too."

"You like him?" he asked. "For her, I mean."

She thought it over and met his gaze. "Yes, I do. He

seems like a good guy. He's very devoted, and Meg values that."

Across the room, Zack gave a succinct nod, dropped his gaze, and scrunched up his mouth, before finally saying, "I'm glad to hear it. At first I thought he seemed sketchy, and it worried me. I just want her to…be all right."

Meg had thought Zack didn't love her since he wouldn't commit, wouldn't give up spending half the year on the water, wouldn't talk about his childhood. After she'd broken up with him, they'd all seen that he *must* have loved her because he'd taken it so hard. Now Suzanne had the impression maybe he was coming out the other side of heartbreak. Maybe he simply had bigger things to worry about now, but regardless, if he was starting to get over her, good for him.

"I don't think you need to worry," she told him.

MEG LOOKED UP to see Seth step inside, bundled up but covered in a light layer of snow. She went to help him start peeling off layers. "You must be freezing."

"You could say that, darlin'," he replied, but he still managed a grin for her.

She leaned up, delivered a kiss to his cold mouth, then asked, "Is Walt doing okay?"

Seth nodded. "He's a hardy old guy. Lays in enough food before the first snowfall to last him the winter." Then he let out a short laugh. "Not even sure he was happy to see me. I think he likes being up there alone all winter. Not really a people person." He ended on a wink.

And Meg said, "I'm sure he appreciated the visit, whether or not he let it show."

"Speaking of visits, how was yours with Suzanne?"

"Fine," Meg answered as they moved into the parlor. She took a seat on the sofa while Seth warmed his hands by the fire.

He glanced over at her. "Just 'fine'? Didn't go well?"

She shrugged. "It just stayed awkward at times, which I hate. I got the feeling I kept saying the wrong thing. It's just such a strange situation."

Her handsome beau nodded. "Can't argue that."

"Sometimes I wonder if I'm handling it all wrong."

"How else can you handle it?" he asked.

"I could…be more present. Dahlia asked me to help with Zack and I haven't. I just plain haven't. Short of the casserole I sent home with her." She stopped long enough to roll her eyes at the gesture. "And even that somehow seemed wrong. Like it was such a small effort, why bother? I mean… *I'm sorry you're paralyzed, so here's a casserole*?"

Seth winced. "Okay, when you put it that way…" He pulled his gaze from her back to the crackling fire before him. "But I still don't know what you can really do."

The truth was, even Suzanne's update hadn't quenched Meg's worry. The moment she'd refused Zack's request to go to the doctor with him played in her mind. Despite showing up later, at Dahlia's insistence, she hadn't truly been there for him. And ever since, she'd stayed here in her warm, happy inn with her sexy, loving boyfriend, whiling away the winter like nothing was wrong.

"What's happening over there? You look upset."

She met Seth's gaze. "I just feel like I'm letting down people who I care about. And Zack is partially *paralyzed*, Seth. I mean, think about that."

"I *have* thought about it, believe me. I feel for the guy, no matter how much he probably hates me."

"I wish it didn't have to be so uncomfortable between us all," she said.

Seth just shrugged. "It's only natural, darlin'. Your relationship ended."

She nodded, but couldn't help remembering what she'd told Suzanne that first day when she wouldn't go into the cottage. That there were still feelings there. It didn't mean she didn't love Seth—it only meant she possessed a heart that didn't stop caring for someone the second she decided she couldn't see him anymore.

She should be grateful Suzanne no longer wanted her help with Zack. And yet complicated feelings swirled inside her. Something old. Guilt. And something new. The sense of somehow being…left out, unneeded. She'd grown used to Zack needing her in certain ways. And certainly Suzanne had always needed her friendship. Now, suddenly, she wasn't part of their world anymore.

"Seth, would it bother you," she asked, "if I went to see Zack? Only because I fear I've behaved coldly about his injury."

He gave his head a contemplative tilt. "Let's see— you wanna go visit the guy you were with for five years, who can't seem to get over you? Why would that bother me?" He ended on a playful wink.

And she sighed, smiling softly in understanding. "Okay, I see your point."

But he surprised her by adding, "I'm only teasing ya, darlin'. I know where your heart's at. If it'll make you feel better, I don't mind."

"See why I love you?" she said, getting up to walk across the room and slide her arms around his neck. He really *was* amazing. And her heart really *was* with him. Maybe there were still just a few more doors she needed to close with Zack. It felt like the right thing to do, for both of them.

"VERY GOOD," SUZANNE told Zack as he took slow, solid steps on his crutches around the living room. He dragged his right foot, of course, but it was certainly better than having no mobility at all. She'd originally envisioned Zack ending up in a wheelchair, but now she had higher hopes and couldn't help thinking that necessity—his having to push himself to use the crutches those first few days—had led to this much better outcome.

When her phone trilled with a text, she pulled it from her pocket to see a message from Meg.

Can you break away from Zack for lunch? The Skipper's Wheel is open.

It surprised her—she hadn't heard from Meg since her visit a few days ago, and she hadn't reached out, either. Conversely, she and Zack both heard from Dahlia daily now.

Glancing out the window to see bright blue skies, she couldn't deny it might be nice to get out. She only felt sad that Zack didn't have that option.

"Bad news?" Zack asked.

She must be making a face. "No," she told him. "A lunch invitation. From Meg. Skipper's Wheel. Do you mind if I go?"

The corners of his mouth turned up in a half grin. "You don't gotta ask my permission, Suzie Q. But yeah, go. I'm a big boy—I can take care of myself." His wink acknowledged that was only partially true, but she knew he was happy with his progress, as well.

"Okay," she said pleasantly. "I'll bring you something back."

Half an hour later, she was ordering her usual Skipper's Wheel plate of waffles across a small table from Meg. Two other tables were occupied, and a couple of seats taken at the counter—a good crowd for a winter's day.

"So to what do I owe this pleasure?" Suzanne asked after their food had arrived.

"Does there need to be a reason?" Meg replied.

And Suzanne felt stuck. Up until recently, there *never* needed to be a reason. And here Meg was, trying to get back to that, and Suzanne was acting weird. "Of course not," she said. "I'm glad you texted."

Meg smiled, letting it go, and they made small talk, Meg saying that Lila was begging for them both to join her at one of the upcoming knitting bees at the Knitting Nook. Allie held them regularly, even in winter, and Meg and Suzanne occasionally went, mostly for the social aspects.

"That sounds fun," Suzanne said, still wanting to renew her friendship with Lila. Despite being heartbroken when Lila and Beck had gotten together, her preoccupation with caring for a certain monoplegic man was truly helping her move past those emotions. "How's Seth?"

"Good, as always. How's Zack?"

Suzanne nodded, wishing the mere question didn't irritate her. It was normal to ask, would have felt abnormal if she hadn't. So she smiled and said, "Still doing as well as possible."

"That's so great," Meg said—but then gave her head a little shake. "I just keep worrying about him."

Suzanne longed, again, to tell Meg she didn't *need* to worry about Zack, that he was no longer hers to worry over, but she stayed quiet.

And Meg went on. "I think I'm going to pay him a visit."

Whoa. What? And maybe she was making too much out of this—but she heard herself say exactly what she was thinking, without even weighing it. "That's a bad idea, Meg."

"It is? Why?"

"Look," Suzanne told her, "you said you couldn't be involved. So now you're not, and it's really okay. And besides, I can't imagine it would make Seth very happy."

Meg's eyes went wide. "Well, for your information, Seth is fine with it. And maybe I think it's a *good* idea. Why don't you want me to? I thought it would help you."

Suzanne blew out a breath, trying to figure out how to reason with Meg and not make her mad—but at the same time, she was starting not to care very much if she made anyone mad. After all, who was looking out for *her* feelings lately? "Meg, I'm just starting to make some headway with him. And...well, frankly, I just don't need you mucking with his head."

Meg drew back slightly, appearing wounded. "Mucking with his head? You're saying you think I would... what, somehow string him along or give him false hope or something?"

"That's not what I'm saying at all." Or was it? Suzanne wasn't even sure anymore—she only knew she felt strongly about it. "What I'm saying is—"

"It's not like I'm going to walk in announcing I still have old feelings for him. I just want him to know I care."

Suzanne tipped her head forward, feeling slightly combative now. "Isn't it the same thing?"

"No," Meg said.

"Well, regardless, no matter how platonic you try to

make it, I think it might send the message that he still
has a chance with you. Which, all things considered,
seems…cruel. He's spent a long time trying to get over
you."

Meg released a distressed sigh. "I never thought I'd
see the day when you, of all people, would be worried
about protecting Zack."

"Neither did I," Suzanne agreed. "But things have
changed."

She thought that might stop Meg in her tracks, but instead she kept right on going. "Look, I just think knowing I'm concerned might motivate him. Lift his spirits.
That's all."

Suzanne just looked at her, nonplussed. "I'm sorry
to break this to you, Meg, but I think he's finally over
you. And I can't have you doing anything that might
change that."

At this, Meg's jaw dropped. She looked stunned,
embarrassed. "Since when are you such an expert on
Zack?"

"Since I became his nurse," Suzanne said firmly.
"And since we've started making progress. He's *already*
motivated, more every day in fact, even *without* having
you around." She knew she'd probably taken things too
far, but she couldn't go back, so she might as well seal
the deal. "I know you mean well, but it's not what's best
for him. So I have to say no."

She'd never seen Meg appear so astonished. "You're
saying I'm no longer welcome at your house?"

Suzanne's stomach churned and her face went hot.
How had they gotten to this point? Meg was her best
friend, and even though it had been one of those later-in-
life friendships, they'd always clicked on the important
things—and she'd assumed they always would. She'd

never expected Meg's ex to come between them. But then, she'd never expected *any* of the things that had happened in the last few weeks.

"Please don't put it that way, Meg. It's only for right now, until Dahlia gets back. It's a delicate situation and it just makes sense to stick with what's working, and right now things are going well." *Without you.* But she was quick-witted enough to hold that part back this time.

Still, Meg looked hurt. "Is this because I haven't been there for you since Dahlia left? Are you punishing me by shutting me out now? Because you know I feel terrible about that, and I'm just trying to make things right."

"It's not that at all. It's that Zack and I muddled through those first hard days on our own, and we built a rapport, and we have our routines, and he's moving forward. And so it turns out that the way to make things right, at this point, is to just…stay away."

She'd said the words as gently as possible, yet couldn't ignore the resentment on Meg's face.

"Please don't be mad, Meg," she rushed to say. "Please understand the difficult position I'm in. I didn't want any of this—it was foisted on me. But now I have a moral obligation to do what I think is best for Zack." Up to now, Suzanne had been fighting an anger that simmered beneath the surface, because Meg thought she knew best and thought it was okay to just take the reins and do whatever she wanted. But the expression she wore right now tore into Suzanne's heart and simply made her sad—for both of them. "I still miss you. I miss *us*. I miss normalcy. And I hope to God we can get back to that once this horrible winter is over and Dahlia comes home and Zack is no longer my responsibility. I'm sorry if my decisions make you feel left out, or guilty, or anything else. But this isn't about you, I promise. It's about trying to get a man through a very difficult time the best way I can."

Suzanne felt drained. She'd said so much, second-guessing half of it as it left her mouth. Neither she nor Meg were the type to embrace confrontation, and now they sat staring at each other blankly, shell-shocked and not knowing what to do.

"I'm gonna go," Suzanne told her then. Because what she'd hoped might be a healing sort of lunch had turned into just the opposite—the more they tried to fix things, the worse it all got. Sometimes the safest move was to just retreat. So she stood up, grabbed the check in one hand while scooping her coat up from a nearby chair with the other, and made her way briskly to the cash register.

"Everything okay?" asked Jolene as she rang up the order.

"Yes," she lied. "Just in a hurry." *Because Summer Island is such a fast-paced, bustling, busy place this time of year?* No doubt Jolene had witnessed the tension—Suzanne had totally forgotten they were in a public place. Isolation could make one so socially inept.

And as she took her change, she realized she hadn't gotten Zack's to-go order. But she'd have to make him something and hope he wasn't snarly about it. After stuffing the change in her purse, she threw on her parka, shoved her hands into mittens, and pushed out into the cold. She struggled with the zipper as she started through the snow.

She was too shaken to go straight back to the cottage, so she walked in the opposite direction, toward Koester's. Maybe she'd get a brownie mix or a cake mix— Zack would surely enjoy something sweet, and drowning her own sorrows in some chocolate could only help.

Why was Meg so bent on coming to see Zack suddenly? *Should I have let her? Am I off base about this?* And why did Meg get all the boys anyway? And since when was Suzanne jealous of that? When Meg had garnered Zack's and Seth's affections last summer, Suzanne had been very *you go, girl* about it. What had changed? Maybe she just thought Meg's idea seemed more selfish than helpful. And she didn't want it to confuse Zack and stop him from moving on.

Or was she…jealous? She gulped back the avalanche of emotion that spilled forth at the thought. Maybe she was tired of Zack being so enamored of Meg. Maybe she didn't want to share him with Meg. Maybe the drunken pass he'd made at her had stayed on her mind. Even if he'd been tipsy—alcohol often just heightened whatever someone was already feeling. So maybe he…felt something for her. Not just from the wine. Just like she felt something for him.

*But it's just physical, right? What you feel for Zack? It's from letting Beck Grainger reawaken your desire. It's from opening that door that was closed for so long after Cal's death.*

If that's all it was, though, why did her every nerve ending bristle each time Meg expressed an interest in just seeing him? Why did it feel like…encroachment, like those teenage times when you're talking to a boy and everything's going fine until the pretty cheerleader bounces over and interrupts?

Suzanne blew out a cold sigh as she approached Koester's on the sunny winter afternoon. In fairness, Meg wasn't the cheerleader type—it was among things they had innately in common. But Suzanne could no longer deny the suddenly glaring truth—she was jealous. Even if he had only tried to kiss her because he was drunk and was only nice to her because he needed her, he had become…her companion for now. Who she liked touching far too much during their therapy sessions. Who she unwittingly ached to touch even as she pushed through the market's front door.

"Afternoon, Suzanne," said Trent Fordham. Allie Hobbs's fiancé, Trent, operated the bicycle livery in summer and served as the island's resident attorney. Like Suzanne, he was bundled in a winter coat and hat, and he carried two plastic bags of groceries. He grinned. "You looked a little harried. Everything okay?"

She attempted a smile. "Oh, you know how it is—cabin fever can make you a little nuts." She forced a laugh on the end.

Which seemed to convince easygoing Trent. "Don't I know it. Still getting used to that." He was even newer to the island as a year-rounder than she was. Then his smile faded. "Hey, I heard about Zack. Tough situation. How's he doing?"

Suzanne let out a sigh, almost grateful to be brought back to what was really important here—Zack's paralysis. Her and Meg's head games didn't matter much in comparison. "It's rough, but he's getting by. Doing a little better every day."

"Anything Allie and I can do to help, just say the word. I mean that."

She nodded and thanked him sincerely. If anything came up she couldn't handle on her own, maybe it would be nice to have someone else to call besides Meg and Seth.

Though she didn't want to feel cut off from Meg. She truly hoped they could get past this. But as she plucked up a brownie mix *and* a cake mix from Koester's baking aisle, then added ingredients to make chocolate

chunk cookies—because at this point what the hell?—
she couldn't stop revisiting the question in her mind.
Was she turning Meg away for Zack's sake—or for hers?

# Part 2

Excerpt from a letter to Meg:

*Life isn't a fairy tale. It won't be perfect. But then, you already know that. You've suffered too much, lost too much along the way, and it's taken a toll.*

*But neither is it a battleground. Attacking, retreating, defending what's yours, and holding on too tight—it won't work. Holding too tight to anything seldom does.*

*Life is closer, I think, to being a journey—one very long road trip. You'll hit potholes and have the occasional flat tire. But there will be plenty of smooth stretches, and you get to hold the map and decide which way to go. And oh, the views from the scenic overlooks. The trick is to soak up the beauty of every mile you travel—there's something worth seeing in every single one if you pay attention, even when the weather turns bad and visibility grows poor. But the most important part of the journey is who we take it with. The right travel companions are priceless. Don't cut the trip short with the good ones or you'll end up with no one to share the view.*

# CHAPTER TWELVE

MEG SAT IN the tiny pass-through room at the inn her grandma had always called the nook. It was just large enough for a small wall of built-in bookcases and an overstuffed easy chair where she often curled up with an afghan and a book.

Half an hour after returning home from her ill-fated lunch with Suzanne, she had the afghan and book, as well as her calico cat, Miss Kitty, nestled at her side—but she'd read the same paragraph three times before giving up on the mystery novel. Perhaps she had enough questions in her life right now without trying to resolve fictional ones.

A few weeks ago, she'd been happy. She'd had a wonderful new romance with a man she loved, her sister had moved here and they'd become closer than ever before, and she'd looked forward to a quiet, cozy winter catching up with Suzanne and Dahlia after her time away.

Zack had been the last thing on her mind then. He'd been a guy she'd once loved but felt disconnected from, and she'd only hoped he would disconnect and start moving on, too.

Now—somehow—she couldn't stop worrying about him and didn't know why. Among other things she didn't understand: How had she ended up in a big fight with Suzanne? Would Zack ever walk again? Given how few relationships he had, should she be there for him any-

way, no matter what Suzanne thought? And the baf-
fling cherry on top of the question sundae: Why on
earth hadn't Dahlia come back after Zack was injured?

She knew his injury hadn't seemed as life-changing
when Dahlia had left, but she still hadn't gotten past it.
Surely Suzanne struggled with that, too—probably even
more under the circumstances. *Maybe that's why she's
so rigid about all this and I should cut her some slack.*

"I'm trying," she murmured to Miss Kitty, whose
chin she scratched now. "I really am."

She felt as if the whole world was mad at her. Dahlia
had left a distant-sounding voice mail, to which Meg
had replied only with brief texts. Suzanne was obviously
angry with her. And Zack...well, who knew where his
feelings lay since she couldn't see him. She only knew
that even while she'd felt bad refusing to go to the doctor
with him...maybe a part of her had secretly liked knowing he was pining for her. And if he'd stopped now...
well, good for him. But maybe it had been vindicating
to know he'd finally come to appreciate her.

She picked up the phone and called Lila, who answered cheerfully. "Hey, what's up?"

"You're my only friend in the world," Meg said sullenly.

Lila stayed silent, likely stunned. In the history of
their relationship, *she* was usually the dramatic one.
"Want me to bring down a bottle of wine?" she finally
asked.

"I've never been much of a day drinker," Meg replied doubtfully.

"If I'm your only friend in the world, sounds like a
good time to start."

Despite herself, Meg laughed softly. "Good point.

Bring the wine. And I'll bring the whine. Like, whine with an *h*. Get it?"

"At least despair hasn't dimmed your quick wit," Lila said. "I'll bundle up and head in your direction with Koester's finest vintage."

SUZANNE RETURNED TO the cottage, baking supplies in tow, ready for a quiet afternoon in the kitchen. Pushing through the front door, she glanced toward the sofa bed, ready to say hello—only to see it empty, just a pile of tousled sheets.

Was he in the bathroom? She discouraged him from going when she wasn't home. But she'd been gone much longer than planned. Which suddenly seemed horrible.

"Zack?" she called as she circled the bed—and caught sight of his legs and one crutch on the floor, visible through the wide kitchen entryway. "Zack!"

He didn't answer even as she rushed toward him, rounding the corner. He lay half-propped against the lower kitchen cabinets, a look of disgust on his face—one crutch rested right next to him but the other lay farther away, out of reach. The makings of a sandwich scattered the floor—lunch meat, lettuce, bread smeared with mustard—and a can of soda lay on its side on the counter, cola dripping down one of the cabinets to puddle on the floor.

Oh God. She'd been away too long and he'd gotten hungry. "I'm so sorry," she said. "I should have been here. Please forgive me."

"No." The angry, guttural word slammed into her like a punch in the stomach—until he added, "Not you. Dahlia should be here. Dahlia."

Oh. He wasn't blaming her. He was reverting to blaming the person they'd all been holding accountable, even

as they tried to forgive, since the moment she'd left. And
something in his voice dug into Suzanne's chest, turning her a little panicky.

She rushed to get things back to normal—back to
*their* normal, the normal they'd started building together.
"Well, I'm to blame, too—I shouldn't have been away
so long." She shook her head, nervous, repentant. "I
wasn't thinking. But let's get you up. Then I'll remake
that turkey sandwich. I'm sorry, but I didn't get your
to-go order—and it looks like you smartly gave up on
that anyway. I did get some stuff to make brownies,
though, and cookies, and a cake—so I'll whip up something fun this afternoon."

"I don't want anything," he said, his voice so sullen
that it stole her breath.

"What do you mean? I can make something else if a
sandwich doesn't sound good."

He gave his head a morose shake. "I said I don't want
anything."

"But…why not?"

"Because I don't," he snapped—the first time he'd
even approached sounding grumpy. And grumpy suddenly seemed preferable to a Zack so despondent that he
barely formed words. *But he'll break free of it—maybe
snapping at me is a good sign.*

"Let's get you up," she suggested again, a little more
quietly than before.

"Whatever," he said.

Though getting him to his feet became a struggle.
He'd only fallen a few times, and he could typically
pull himself up using nearby furniture. But everything
in the galley kitchen was too high for him to reach from
the floor, and he was too heavy for her to lift, especially
since he wasn't putting much effort into it.

"Try to…here, put your arms around my neck…okay, that's not working, We'll come up with something else," she said. She stepped out into the next room, looked around, and grabbed one of the solid oak chairs from her dining table. She had dipped into problem-solving mode—but her heart pounded in her chest. Something had changed drastically here. Because he'd taken a fall? Because she hadn't been here to help him or feed him? All of that? She wanted to cry into her hands, but she couldn't.

*I should have been here. Or hell, maybe I should have taken Meg's help and considered it a blessing and not a problem. Or I should have called on other friends for backup, whether or not Zack would like it. But I knew he wouldn't. I knew it was hard enough for him feeling helpless just in front of me. And I thought I could handle it. I thought I could do this on my own.*

"Here." She braced the chair against the cabinets next to him. "See if this helps." She situated herself on his opposite side, and together they slowly managed to pull him up, up, up, until he was able to plop himself onto the chair.

The effort left them both panting, and after catching her breath, she picked up his crutches and put them in his hands. Only he just sat there—for so long that it became awkward.

She asked, "Do you want to head to the table, or the bed?"

His eyes were downcast—he stared at the kitchen floor. "I can't."

She drew in a deep, fortifying breath, seeking strength, patience. Everything had been fine this morning and now each fragile gain she'd made seemed…lost.

And had apparently been more fragile than she'd even realized. "What do you mean you can't?" she asked gently.

He raised his gaze only slightly. "I can't do it, Suzanne. I can't get myself around. I can't do this, damn it."

She pushed out another tired sigh, leaned her head
over into one hand, and tried to think how to proceed.
Given that she couldn't carry him herself, all she had at
her disposal was tough love. "You've done it dozens of
times before, so you can do it again."

"What's the point?" he asked her.

Yet one more sigh. All she could do was boil this
down to practicality now and deal with the bigger picture
later. "The point is you can't sit in this chair forever, and
I can't move you. So you're going to have to do it yourself. And the point is also that you've been getting better and better at moving yourself around, so I don't get
it. You fell. You dropped a sandwich and spilled a Coke.
Big whoop. But whether it's now or whether it's whenever you get sleepy or have to pee, you have to move. So
do it whenever you want. Meanwhile, I'm going to clean
up this mess and make you another sandwich. Which
you can eat or not. Then I'm going to make some brownies. Which you can also eat or not. I'm doing everything
I can for you, Zack—you have to do the rest yourself."

He looked at her like she was an uncaring shrew. But
she didn't know what else to do. She simply turned away
and unrolled a bunch of paper towels from the holder
on the counter. She didn't look at him again—just went
about the business of methodically cleaning up the mess,
soon throwing pieces of the sandwich and sopping paper
towel in the trash.

When she heard him stir, planting the crutches on the
floor, using them to pull himself to his feet, she didn't
look then, either. She just let him do his thing while she

did hers. Though she noted he bypassed the table for the bed. A tiny victory followed by a tiny defeat.

Still, she remade his sandwich, put it on a plate with some chips and potato salad, grabbed another can of Coke from the fridge, and carried the late lunch into the living room. Where she found him lying on his side, facing away from her. Rather than leaning the crutches against the wall like usual, he'd left them abandoned on the floor.

"Lunch is served," she said, trying to sound upbeat.

When he didn't respond, she added, "And again, I'm sorry. About being away so long. I know you must be starving."

Still nothing.

"Why don't you sit up and eat. It'll make you feel better. I can turn on the TV—it's almost time for your talk shows. Then I'll make those brownies. How's that sound?"

How that sounded was as if she were trying to cheer up a belligerent child. But maybe we all acted and felt like children under the right—or wrong—circumstances. She knew she certainly reverted to the mindset of a high schooler more often than she liked lately. It was easy to go backward into insecurities when life grew challenging.

When Zack still said nothing and didn't move a muscle, she decided not to beg him. Just like getting back up on the crutches, he'd snap out of this when he was tired of the alternative—in this case, hunger. "Okay— I'll leave the plate here on the end table for whenever you want it."

She then quietly made her way to the other side of the bed, to see if his eyes were open. No—shut. He'd checked out, at least for now. Despite surely being hun-

gry, maybe some rest would do him good. Maybe he'd bounce back after a short nap—or even a short, fake nap.

That was when her eyes fell on his cell phone, atop the covers near where she stood. He'd clearly not taken it with him to the kitchen. The screen lit up just then, drawing her eyes to an app update message—and the unlocked screen beneath it, showing multiple unanswered text messages to Dahlia.

Hey, did you get my calls? Need to talk.

Where are you?

Having too much fun at the beach to give a damn about anything else, I guess.

Suzanne's heart fell. On one hand, it had only been a few hours. But on the other…now that she thought about it, Dahlia had made contact less frequently the last couple of days. And…okay, maybe you can't expect someone to look at their phone constantly when traveling, but her nephew faced some challenges here, so if there was a time Dahlia should be checking her phone, it was now.

"Damn it, Dahlia," she whispered.

ZACK LAY ON his side, staring blankly at the wall across the room. He smelled something from the kitchen— hadn't Suzanne said something about brownies? Yesterday that might have distracted him, at least a little. But today she could be baking shit pies for all he cared.

He didn't want to move. His whole body felt heavy, lethargic, as useless as his bum leg. He'd been trying his damnedest, putting on the brave face, finding other things to focus on, grabbing on to any distraction…but everything had gone to crap after Suzanne had left for lunch. And it had brought home a grim reality.

She wasn't gonna be here taking care of him forever.

So this almost-palatable situation wasn't…real.

What would happen when Suzanne's forced servitude came to an end? Was he gonna spend the rest of his life being a burden to Dahlia? Who wouldn't even answer his damn phone calls? So maybe she'd take over or maybe she wouldn't, but even if she did...what kind of life was that? For either of them? She hadn't signed up for this, and maybe he couldn't blame her if she ran from it.

That was the problem. *No one* had signed up for this. And Dahlia could twist it however she chose, but they both had a history of running away from whatever didn't make them happy. Maybe she would run away from Zack the same way she'd once run from her mother, the same as he'd run away from his.

He didn't mind being alone. He hadn't ended up the solitary fisherman on a small trawler from spring 'til fall by accident. It had always felt easier, safer, than being with anyone who might start to...depend on him. But the kind of loneliness that came without the open water, or even two good legs to stand on...well, he wasn't a man who could cope with being weak and incapable forever.

Suzanne kept saying how much he was progressing, but how much further could it go? Get really skilled on crutches? And sure, some men could make a satisfying life that way. If he was smart enough to be a lawyer, like Trent Fordham, or a doctor who could heal people with what they knew, like Suzanne's husband, maybe then. But he made his living—his life—outside. Using his hands, and his legs.

And somehow, being here with Suzanne had started to seem...easier than he could have dreamed the morning he'd awakened unable to control his right leg. She'd made him believe trying, working, putting in effort, was going to pay off and lead somewhere. But as he'd lain sprawled like an injured animal on the kitchen floor, suddenly unable to even make a damn sandwich, he'd been forced to wonder: Where? Where is it leading that's so much better?

And to remember, again, that staying here with her was temporary, and whatever came next, whether it was with Dahlia, whether it was doctors and nurses on the mainland…it would mean starting all over again. And never really feeling whole or capable again…forever.

"Oh good, you're awake."

Suzanne had entered his field of vision, but he felt too dead inside to even shift his gaze from the wall.

"Want a brownie while they're still warm? I can heat one in the microwave later, but it's never the same as when they're fresh from the oven."

He didn't answer. But she just stood there, waiting, looking as calm and fresh and hopeful as always. It was almost enough to inspire him. It had before. But right now it seemed easier to keep lying here in the dark place that had started swallowing him up this afternoon.

"Okay then," she said, sounding only slightly discouraged. From his peripheral vision he saw her clasp her hands together. "If you don't want a brownie, maybe we should move on to some physical therapy since we missed your afternoon session."

When he again didn't answer, she stepped toward the bed, clearly ready to dive right in on pushing and pulling his legs like he was a rag doll, and it yanked from him a snarling, "No."

"Come on, Zack. You've had a rotten afternoon that feels like a setback—I get it. But you'll feel better if you snap out of it. Eat a brownie. Do your exercises. Keep moving forward. How about we start with some ankle rotations?" With that, she placed her hand on his right foot. Which he could see but not feel. So strange to watch someone touch a part of your body and not register it in your flesh.

"I said no," he growled at her. "What's the point?"

"Well, the point, as I keep telling you, is to strengthen your muscles and allow your nerves to—"

"Stop it," he cut her off. He hadn't been looking for an actual answer and was tired of the one she kept feeding him. "I know what *you* think the point is—but I don't anymore, so just leave me alone."

She simply stood there, finally dropping the false cheer for a look of discouragement. And then he used his sock-covered left foot to lightly push her hand away from his right one.

"Oh," she said, sounding hurt by the gesture. It made his heart contract slightly in his chest, but then it closed up a little tighter—until finally she walked away.

# CHAPTER THIRTEEN

SUZANNE WAS FED UP. Ready to throw in the towel and give up on the Neanderthal on her couch. The only problem with that plan? It didn't get him *off* her couch or out of her cottage, or get her out of the position of caring for him. So giving up was not an option—not because she was determined or noble but simply because she was stuck.

So as the early darkness of winter fell over Summer Island, she did two things.

First, she texted Dahlia, irate. Look, I don't know where you are or why you're not answering Zack, but he's had a major mental setback. I accept that you're not here, physically—but I need you to be present with him, Dahlia. He's officially despondent now, and I'm not sure what to do. Please call him as soon as you see this.

Second, she made a delicious dinner. Remembering that Dahlia had once mentioned Zack loved her meatballs, Suzanne got out the recipe, which Dahlia had given her along with others, and started squishing ground beef into a mixture of bread crumbs, minced onion, Parmesan cheese, an egg, and some spices.

She took her time, since he clearly needed his space. But she also knew that he eventually had to eat. She'd taken away the sandwich plate a little while ago—the bread had hardened, and the meatballs would be a better lure anyway.

While they baked, she cooked the pasta and prepared garlic bread—hoping it wouldn't be a dinner for one. She soon carried two lovely plates of classic spaghetti and meatballs to the table, placed a platter of hot garlic bread in between, and even opened a bottle of wine. Wine had led to trouble last time, but after the day she'd had, she deserved a drink. Or five.

Things had been going so well up until today. For Zack anyway. For her, maybe not so much—being at serious odds with her best friend, fighting an unwanted attraction to her patient. But Zack had done incredibly well, motivating her to just keep pushing forward and making the best of the situations in which she found herself.

As she pulled out her chair and sat down, she called over, "Zack, are you awake?"

No response. No surprise.

"Listen, you haven't eaten since breakfast and it's nearly eight o'clock. You have to be starving."

Just when she assumed he still wasn't going to answer, he let out a low, grudging, "Kinda."

She smiled to herself. Then told him, "I made spaghetti and meatballs. Dinner's on the table."

"Bring me a plate," he demanded in his typical, grumbly way.

"No," she said.

"Why not?" he groused.

"Because I know you can come to the table."

A low groan left him. "I don't feel like it. Why can't you just make me a plate?"

"Because I care about you, and I'm not going to let you just lie there and regress."

"Regress?" he muttered. "What the hell is regress? Can't you just use normal words?"

She smiled again, amused, as she glanced over at his back. "It means to go backward. We've both worked too hard to let that happen. So if you want to eat, come to the table."

When he still didn't move, she said, "Well, *I'm* going to eat—I don't want mine to get cold. You can do what you want, but if you're hungry, you'll have to get up—that's all there is to it. So it's just a matter of whether you want to eat your dinner hot—or cold." And with that, she cut into one of the meatballs lying atop a bed of spaghetti—then took a yummy bite and washed it down with a big sip of wine.

When the body on the fold-out couch stirred and he began to sit up, she kept eating, not even glancing over—yet her heart sparked with joy. Thank God. It didn't mean everything was repaired, but it was a big step in the right direction.

She continued to eat as he struggled to get the crutches up off the floor, banging one into her end table, soon pushing up onto his left foot, using the crutches for balance. He stayed that way for a moment, taking it slow, likely remembering his fall earlier, but then began with the same careful steps he'd been getting better and better at taking.

After maneuvering himself into the chair across from hers, he surveyed the meal before him. She thought he might tell her it looked good, but instead remarked, "Wine?"

"You drove me to drink," she answered matter-of-factly.

He said nothing in reply—just picked up his fork and knife, diving into the pasta like a man who hadn't eaten in a week instead of less than a day. They both stayed quiet, but she remained pleased—he'd come to the table and was eating vigorously. Mission accomplished.

After a few minutes, though, she decided to say what she was thinking. Maybe she shouldn't—maybe it was the wrong move—but possibly the wine was stealing her ability to strategize wisely. "Will you do me just one favor, Zack?"

He hesitated, looking wary as he swallowed a bite, then asked, "What's that?"

"Just…talk to me," she said. "Tell me what's going on. That's the least you can do. I mean, I thought…we'd become friends. Or something like friends anyway." The uncertainty forced her mind back to their near kiss. What if she hadn't pulled away? But thank God she had. *Today has proven he isn't emotionally stable, so you definitely made the right call—especially since you've never been into casual sex. And he lives with you—it's not like you could just do it and walk away regardless. So you made the only reasonable decision. No matter how delicious the temptation had felt for one fleeting moment or how much it's stayed on your mind.*

Just when she thought he wasn't going to answer and that she might have to smash a meatball in his face out of frustration, he lowered his fork long enough to swipe a napkin across his mouth and say, "Guess it just hit me fresh. That I'm probably never gonna walk again."

Oh. He was talking. Opening up to her. Fresh hope bloomed in her heart.

"Sure you are," she argued. "You're walking now. On crutches. And that's amazing given where you started just a couple of weeks ago."

"I mean the normal way," he told her. "And that I'm never gonna be out on my boat fishing again. And that I don't know how the hell I'm gonna make a living. And that I don't even have decent insurance. I've been float-ing along here, letting you take my mind off things with all this exercising, but…shit, Suzanne, I don't know what the hell I'm gonna do."

She took another sip of wine before answering. She wanted to tell him it would all be okay. She wanted to paint pretty pictures about miracles and believing that anything is possible. But it had been a long, rough day, and in her gut, she knew that wasn't what he needed to hear. And she wasn't sure what he did need to hear— but she spoke from the heart. "I understand," she said. "I would be afraid, too."

"I didn't say I was afraid," he protested.

But she ignored that and went on. "I can't pretend to know what it feels like to be you right now. And every-thing you just said—yeah, it's huge, heavy, scary stuff. And you're gonna have days when you want to give up because you feel overwhelmed by it all. But the impor-tant thing is…that you get up again. Like you just did, coming to the table."

"Let's get something straight." He narrowed his gaze on her, one brow pointedly arched. "I came to the damn table because I'm hungry and you wouldn't bring me anything to eat. It wasn't some big, grand, symbolic act—it was that I didn't have any other choice."

"I think you just made my point for mc, Zack," she said quietly.

"Huh?"

"You got up because you didn't have any other choice. And that's how it's going to be every day. You get up because, in the end, it's easier than lying there starv-ing or not being able to go to the bathroom. You get up because you have to. That doesn't mean it's easy, or pleasant, or that you'll be happy about it. But you do it anyway. And the more you do it, the more you'll forget that it took extra effort, the more it'll just become your new normal."

Zack lowered his gaze, refocused on his dinner, and took another bite—but he looked uncomfortable. "This…those—" he pointed to the crutches leaning nearby "—will never feel normal."

She didn't want to argue with him, but… "Other people have gone through what you are and worse, Zack. And even if it's hard to believe, it becomes normal."

"I don't *want it* to feel normal," he snapped. "I want my goddamn leg back."

The statement filled the air between them. So simple. So impossible.

"I want my husband back," she said softly. Then bit her lip, almost regretting the response. "I know it's not the same thing—but I understand that feeling. That feeling of just wanting what you used to have so damn bad and not knowing why God or the universe took it away from you and it seeming like a nightmare you can't wake up from. I thought life would never feel normal without Cal. And I had more than my fair share of days when I didn't get out of bed, when I couldn't see the point, when I couldn't face having a new kind of life.

"And again, I know it's not the same thing. Maybe, to you, right now, having my husband die seems like… nothing, mere child's play on the big scale of life-changing misery and pain, but he was the only thing that had ever really, truly made me happy. I don't like admitting that—but it's true. And I thought we had another forty or fifty years of that to go. When he died, I…" She stopped, shook her head. "I didn't know how to go on. Sometimes I still don't." She blew out a breath.

"But I get up every day. That's the one thing I do—I get up every day, to make sure I can."

She stopped, raised her gaze cautiously to the man across the table. Crap. Where had all that come from? Self-pity had not been on the menu here. But it had come pouring out of her heavy and thick and…embarrassingly honest.

Zack replied softly, "I don't think it's nothing, Suzanne." An almost shocking compassion filled his eyes. "I've never loved anybody that way, and I don't think I know how to, but…there are moments I wish I could."

"Why," she began gently, "do you think you can't?"

He sighed, blinked uncertainly, and pointed vaguely in the direction of the Summerbrook Inn. "Look at how I screwed things up with Meg. She made everything easy, and I made it all hard. I always knew I was better off alone and that pretty much proved it."

For some reason a lump gathered in Suzanne's throat. Maybe from spilling her guts about Cal, or maybe what Zack had just shared made her sad. "Why would you think that? That you're better off alone?"

He shook his head. "It's complicated. But…well, I didn't grow up in one of those nice families where you go shopping for school clothes every fall and get visits from the tooth fairy."

"Neither did I," she informed him.

His face changed. "You didn't?"

She shook her head. "My mother died giving birth to me. I had four older brothers and a father, but…it wasn't like they looked out for their baby sister. I wasn't really one of them—they bossed me around. We lived on a farm in rural Indiana, and I cooked and cleaned and washed the clothes. My dad was…old-school about certain things being women's work. He didn't know how to relate to a daughter, and I think he resented me for taking my mother away. All in all, I felt like an alien in my own home."

"I guess you didn't stick around any longer than you had to?" he asked.

She knew he himself had left home as a teenager, but she didn't know why. She shook her head. "I worked hard enough in school to get a scholarship. I picked nursing because...because..." She hadn't thought about this in so long, and it made her unexpectedly emotional. Damn wine.

"Why?" he asked.

"Because I always wondered what my life would have been like with a mom. And if anything could have been done to save mine. I wanted to be a labor and delivery nurse, thinking I'd save lives and make sure babies had their moms. But..." She stopped, smiled softly. "I got interested in orthopedics and took a different path. Maybe, deep inside, I got afraid. Of being in delivery rooms, and how it would feel if something bad happened. Nurses—they need to be tough. Tougher than me. That's why I didn't last in the field and just wasn't a very good one."

"Don't say that, Suzie Q."

She met his gaze. "Why not?"

"You're a good nurse, trust me. I know from first-hand experience."

She replied dryly, "Yes, I felt very accomplished when my only patient curled up in a non-responsive ball this afternoon. Let me just add that to my résumé." She regretted the words as soon as they left her, though—so she kept talking, to keep him from thinking about his woes. "Nope, I was happier after I gave up nursing. It's a florist's life for me. It sucks when a plant dies, but no one has to mourn it."

"Well," he said, looking almost sheepish, "I still think you're a good nurse."

And for some reason, this time the compliment brought a flash of warmth to her cheeks. She felt almost bashful as she said, "Thank you, Zack." Then took another sip of wine before asking, "Why did *you* leave home?"

He narrowed his gaze and said, "That's top secret information. I could tell you but then I'd have to kill you."

She couldn't help thinking the answers were at the heart of what made Zack Sheppard tick. It would help her care for him better if she understood him more. And beyond that, just like Meg, she simply wanted to know. What she'd said so casually before dinner was true— she cared about him. Despite herself. "Come on," she prodded playfully. "I told you my sad tale—now you have to tell me yours."

"Nah," he said, dropping his gaze to his nearly empty pasta bowl.

She considered it at least a small triumph that he wasn't replying as combatively as the last time she'd asked about his past. Which encouraged her to keep trying. "Why not?"

He smirked pleasantly. "Let's just say it's not fit dinner conversation."

She raised her eyebrows. "Is any of this?"

A small laugh left him.

And she let a wide smile unfurl across her face. "You laughed," she said. "You actually laughed. Proving that life is, in fact, not all doom and gloom after all."

"Damn you, Suzie Q. You did it again."

"Did what?"

"Got my mind off my troubles." Though his expression turned more wooden then. "Even if saying that takes me right back to them."

"Well…just don't go there," she said quickly.

"Can't avoid thinking about the crap forever. That's the problem, Miss Q. At the end of the day, it's always gonna be there."

But at this, she just shrugged. "So is everything else, including reasons to laugh, and Dr. Phil, and meatballs. You just have to focus more on…the meatballs. Were they good?" she inquired with a hopeful smile.

He gave her a small grin. "Yeah, they were. I was just mad and didn't want to say so."

"Good—because we'll have leftovers."

"I'd, uh, take a second helping."

"Will you still have room for brownies?"

"That's a crazy question. I've never turned down a brownie in my life."

"You did earlier."

"I was asleep."

"Liar."

"For a nurse, you're kinda mean," he said, gray eyes pinning her in place, the corners of his mouth curving up in a slight smile.

She had to look away, though she wasn't sure why. She pushed to her feet, reached across the table, and grabbed up his empty plate. "For a patient, you're kind of impossible."

"You're not the first woman who's called me that."

"I don't doubt it."

Talk went on as Zack ate his second plate of spaghetti while Suzanne cleaned up the meal. Good Zack was back. She still couldn't believe she'd *found* a good Zack, but…well, life was about perspective and this was certainly a better Zack than she'd known before recently, even if he still held some deep dark secrets close to his chest.

Despite herself, she continued to have trouble meeting his eyes—they were doing that sparkly thing she'd noticed on other occasions. *Probably just low evening lighting messing with your head. He's probably not flirting—even if it feels that way in certain moments.*

Regardless, she still found it easier to talk to him from the kitchen while she worked. Even if her breasts tingled slightly. Even if the crux of her thighs felt heavy with wanting. From the non-flirting and the not-really-sparkling eyes.

"Hey, nurse," he called playfully, "I'm getting up to go to the bathroom."

She glanced at him through the doorway. Normally she'd shadow his movements, be ready to provide balance if he started to lose it—but she wanted him to get his confidence back. "I'm here if you need me," she said, and continued to bustle around the kitchen.

He said nothing in reply, but just got to his feet and started taking careful steps toward the bathroom.

"Want some brownies when you get back?"

"Yep," he said. "And more wine."

They'd both had a couple of glasses with dinner. But one perk of living on Summer Island was no driving to get home—and in this situation, no one even had to walk.

Though… Zack, crutches, wine. She dropped what she was doing and stepped out of the kitchen—to see him making his way steadily to the bathroom. Okay, apparently the big dinner had kept the wine from going to his head. All the more reason not to balk about either of them drinking a little more, so she opened another bottle.

While he was gone, she grabbed a knife and the pan

of brownies she hadn't gotten around to cutting yet. Then refilled both their glasses and sat down at the table awaiting his return.

But as he came out of the bathroom, he said, "Turns out I'm kinda tired, nurse."

"After all the sleeping you did today? And the physical therapy you skipped?"

"Yep, afraid so. You mind if I eat my brownies over here?" he asked, heading for the sofa bed instead of the table.

If he was tired, better he not push himself and end up falling again—but she felt oddly disappointed. They'd been…having fun. Connecting. She'd thought it would continue—had been ready to suggest they watch a movie or play cards—but it was not to be. Ah, big disappointments, small disappointments—life was full of them. From a dead husband to a tired houseguest. So be it. "No problem," she said, then carried the tray and knife over, lowering it to the mattress before fetching their wineglasses.

He plopped down, leaning his crutches against the wall, his pleasant expression fading when he had to use his hands to lift his right leg onto the bed.

She tried not to let the sight tug at her heart too much. She'd seen him do that plenty of times before, after all, and she'd done it many times herself. Yet something about it left her more emotional than usual. She'd pulled him back from the brink—or he'd pulled himself, depending upon how you looked at it—and they were moving on with dinner and brownies and laughter, but what he'd said was true. In the end, he still had to deal with this.

Then his eyes fell on the brownies, and he let out a small laugh. "The whole tray, huh?"

"I didn't get to cut them yet," she said, glad he'd light-ened the mood that fast.

And as she stood awkwardly nearby, realizing she didn't quite know what to do with herself, he said, "Well, you're gonna have a hard time cutting 'em from over there, and you don't want me to do it—I'll make a mess of it."

Okay, she'd been avoiding the bed, but clearly that was silly. So she took a seat facing him on the mattress like it was the normal thing to do. And really, it was. She sat on the bed for some of their exercises every single day.

She'd grabbed some napkins, too—helpful as they began to indulge in the chocolate deliciousness. "Hope you like them as gooey as I do," she said, reaching for her wine on the end table up by Zack. The move put her breasts at his eye level, and only a few inches away—igniting the usual ripple of awareness—and she drew back as soon as the glass was in her grasp.

"For sure," he said. "Otherwise, it's just chocolate cake."

She smiled. "Finally, something we have in common."

"Aw, now," he said playfully, "seems to me we're finding a few things in common."

She tilted her head thoughtfully. "We're finding things we don't hate about each other," she replied, "which is not the same as having things in common."

He just chuckled, and took another swallow of wine. "Whatever you say, Suzie Q."

They laughed and talked some more. About the deso-lation of winter here and how the whole island shut down after the Harbor Street Christmas Walk. Dahlia had vol-unteered Zack to head up the technical end of the tree-lighting ceremony just last month, so Suzanne asked him how he'd enjoyed doing that. "Organizing twelve thousand lights? It kinda sucked," he said.

From there, discussion somehow led to Trent Fordham's law office above the bicycle livery—and wondering if he'd had even a single client since hanging up the shingle. "All I can say is," Zack remarked, "good thing the guy rents a lot of bikes come summer."

"Meg told me her sister took a management job at the Knitting Nook," Suzanne said, thinking of island hot spots and jobs.

"Heard she got engaged, Meg's sister."

Suzanne nodded. "Yep."

"Heard you had a thing for that guy, too—the one she's marrying."

Swell. "Yep." Heat filled her cheeks, and she took a quick sip of wine to somehow try to hide it. Though she was pretty sure it didn't work.

"You over him?" Zack asked. "Or does it still sting?"

She bit her lip, thought through it. And answered honestly, "Both." Then dared to meet his gray-green gaze. "But mostly the first, I guess. There's been…a lot to take my mind off the situation since the new year."

At this, he laughed and said, "You're welcome."

Even yesterday, Suzanne wouldn't have dared ask him this, but since they were going down that road and the wine and brownies were flowing, she said, "How about you? Are you over Meg?"

His expression darkened slightly, but he appeared to think it over before saying, "Same answer as yours, I guess. A couple of weeks ago, I'd have said no. A couple of weeks ago, having her around—or not—still seemed like the most important thing in the world. But guess the accident has taken my mind off her a lot."

Suzanne lifted her glass and said, "To silver linings."

Zack laughed, perhaps a bit cynically, but agreed, clinking his wineglass against hers. "Silver linings."

Suzanne couldn't have explained how, but from there talk shifted to the weather (it was supposed to snow tomorrow) to Koester's Market (Suzanne filled Zack in on the few people she'd seen there earlier) to Dahlia's fried chicken (Zack claimed it was the best he'd ever eaten.)

"Is that really high praise, though?" Suzanne teased. "You're on a boat half the year, and on this island the other half. How much of the world's chicken have you really sampled?"

He shrugged, conceding, "Fair enough." And just as she worried that her thoughtless reference to his life on a boat might bring him down, his countenance indeed darkened.

Prompting her to ask gently, "What's wrong?"

"Just…Dahlia," he said. "Every time she comes up I get a little mad."

Ah. There was so much to be tiptoed around these days. "I get it," she said. "I keep trying not to be angry with her on your behalf, but…I haven't quite managed it."

He pointed toward the far corner of the bed, where his phone lay facedown. "Can you hand me that?"

Passing her wineglass into his spare hand, she leaned across the bed, which also meant stretching her body across his legs. At which point she succeeded in knocking the phone *off* the bed and onto the floor, which sent her scrambling across the covers like a little kid until she could bend over and scoop it into her hand. Rising back up sent a rush of light-headedness through her, and as she spun to face Zack she said, "Whew, the wine might have me a little tipsy." She shoved the phone at him as she collapsed onto the mattress, her head landing on the pillows beside him.

"Careful there, Miss Q," he said with a light laugh. "If you get too drunk to walk, I can't carry you to bed."

Then he looked at his phone only to mutter, "She never called me back."

"Dahlia?" Suzanne asked.

He nodded.

"I haven't heard from her, either." *Even after I told her you needed her, even after I practically begged her to get in touch.* Something in Suzanne's soul deflated.

Setting his phone and her wineglass on the table, he rested his head into the pillow, then turned on his side toward Suzanne, their faces only a few inches apart. "Truth is, I don't even know what to expect for sure when she comes back."

"Oh, Zack," she rushed to say, "I'm sure she'll be there for you. Whatever's going on with Dahlia right now, it'll pass."

He let out a troubled sigh, his eyes still locked on hers. "Maybe. But maybe not. Because… I thought the one person in this world I could depend on was her. And she didn't come back. I know I could still feel my leg then, but…I still couldn't believe she left me."

In Zack's voice Suzanne heard something she never had before. It was honesty. It was vulnerability. It was fear. This man who made a great show of not needing relationships…needed at least one.

She wanted to keep acting like it was okay, like it didn't mean anything. Truly, she believed Dahlia *would* come back in spring and *would* take over Zack's care. But she wasn't certain. What *was* she certain of? The hurt Zack was finally allowing her to see, *choosing* to let her see. So rather than just keep feeding him assurances born of sheer hope, she instead said, "I couldn't believe it, either. And I know that must hurt, and that it must...must..."

"It scares the shit out of me," he whispered, and their eyes locked and she saw the darkness of being a strong man admitting he wished he had someone like... a mother.

Suzanne didn't know why Zack had left home so young, but she knew he'd never gone back. And so they had another thing in common: neither of them had a mom. And the closest thing Zack *did* have to a mom had abandoned him when he needed her most. Succumbing to the urge to comfort the little boy inside him, Suzanne lifted both her hands to cup Zack's stubbled cheeks and simply murmured, "I know. I know."

But when she connected with his eyes again, that little boy had vanished and all that remained was the virile man—whose mouth opened slightly, whose gaze dropped to her parted lips, who was about to kiss her.

And this time she wasn't going to push him away.

# CHAPTER FOURTEEN

SUZANNE'S WHOLE BODY longed for the kiss when it came, and his mouth pressing down on hers felt sweeter, wilder, than she could have imagined. Why had she pushed him away before? She couldn't remember anymore, but whatever the reason, it had vanished now, too. Nothing mattered but surrendering to a desire that came barreling through her like an avalanche.

Her breasts, the small of her back, the crux of her thighs—every sensitive spot on her body ached with wanting as his hand curved over her hip and the kissing deepened, his tongue pushing into her mouth to meet her own. She gave herself over to it, leaning closer, close enough for her breasts to brush his chest, for her pelvis to align with his.

That, however, sent questions racing through her mind. What if he…couldn't? And yet he was kissing her, and he'd wanted to before, so did that mean…? It was the first time it had crossed her mind to wonder, too involved in her own longing to even think about *his* side of that.

But she got her answer when the hand on her hip pulled her firmly to him—and oh! He could. He definitely could. A gasp of pleasure left her.

And part of her wanted to be…who she'd always been, in bed. She wanted to lie there letting him take the lead, make the moves. Her backward upbringing had led her to believe that at their core men desired a docile woman between the sheets—and that had always fed into who she was sexually. But maybe she'd changed because right now she wanted to do more than just lie there—so she followed the urge.

The urge to loop her leg up over his hip. Though it was his right hip, so did he feel it? She didn't know. The urge to press her hands to his chest and push him onto his back. And the urge to straddle his hips, longing to feel that hardest part of him where she was the softest. The sensation rushed from her center outward, vibrating electricity through every inch of her flesh.

"Sure you want to do this, Suzie Q?"

The question halted her, alarmed her. Her heartbeat pounded in her ears. They were going to talk about this? "Do you?" she asked.

"Hell yeah."

"Okay—me, too," she told him before he could say anything that might make her stop. She hadn't had sex since Cal died. She'd kissed a few guys who'd turned out to be losers. And she'd suffered her big crush on Beck Grainger, a pursuit which had led to no kisses at all. But this was more than kissing and her body craved the connection.

As he pushed up her sweater and she helped him off with his hoodie, she experienced a profound rush of gratitude for what they'd been through together the last few weeks. It was the strange intimacy they'd shared that made it feel safe, right, for him to suddenly see her in her plain pink bra, for him to lift his hands to the sides of her breasts, stroking his thumbs across their peaks. That same intimacy made it okay for her to run her palms over his muscled chest.

At times, brief bursts of shock broke over her: *This is*

*Zack! How can you be touching him this way? How can he be touching you?* But each time, she pushed it aside. *It's because you both want each other.* And oh God, how had she never really seen how hot he was?

Being mildly, pleasantly intoxicated helped. When her bra was gone and she bent toward him, lowering one breast to his waiting mouth, she simply closed her eyes and sank into the sensation washing through her. When together they pulled down her blue jeans and panties, she surely blushed, but again she shoved the timid woman she'd once been into the furthest corner of her mind and let hunger guide her.

"I'll need you to help me," he said, regarding his own pants. Did it embarrass him to ask? She hurried to pull them down, to show him she didn't care about his leg being different and that he was still every bit a man to her.

Of course, that left him naked. That left her eyes flitting downward, left her gasping slightly, left her body longing and aching. She rose to her knees to lower herself onto him.

"Look at me," he murmured.

She did, their gazes locking as their bodies slowly joined. Her every nerve ending sizzled, even as she felt the need to say, "It's been a while. It might be difficult—"

Before she could finish the thought, though, his hands, fingers, were curving past her ass, helping to part her until she sank down and—oh, he was inside her and the sensation stole any other thoughts.

Her body moved on him in tight, rhythmic circles. As he molded her breasts in his hands and they kissed some more, she got lost in it all—until bliss broke over her like a dam bursting, the pleasure nearly crushing her. It shook her to her core, left her collapsing atop him, had her kissing his neck and wanting to somehow just crawl inside him and be a part of him.

She vaguely wondered if maybe they'd change positions now—but just as quickly realized that without the use of his right leg, maybe this was it. And that was okay. To make sure he knew that, she raised upright on him again, gazed down, bit her lower lip. He thrust up into her, making her moan as he drove upward—*deep, deep, deep*—until he was coming inside her, both of them crying out.

Part of Suzanne wanted to crumple over onto him, cuddle with him. She'd just remembered at least one of the reasons this was probably a bad idea—sex, for her, equaled attachment. Sex for *most women* equaled attachment—it was a physiological fact. She already suffered that aching bond; it was in her now and there was no going back.

But she couldn't let *him* see that, couldn't turn into a Stage Five Clinger. Because they'd just had very undefined sex, and the one thing she knew about Zack? He didn't like relationships or, God forbid, commitments. And so despite the innate longing to press her body closer to his, she instead summoned the strength to roll off him, lie beside him.

He looked over at her. "I think you're too drunk to walk to your bedroom, Suzie Q. Better stay here for the night."

She smiled, relieved. Because how strangely awkward would it be to do this and then go sleep in her own bed? "Just so you know, though," she told him, "this didn't happen because I was drunk."

He met her gaze. "Good. Me, either."

ZACK OPENED HIS eyes to the sun, aware he was cold in one way but warm in another. Cold because the fire in the hearth had gone out overnight. Warm because Suzanne was curled into the crux of his arm, her naked body pressed to his.

Damn, he hadn't seen that coming. Sure, he'd wanted it—but he hadn't thought it would really happen. He hadn't thought she would *let* it happen.

And there was no denying it was the best damn thing to happen to him in a very long time—despite having a bum leg. He glanced down at her sleeping form, remembering the moment they'd clicked wineglasses earlier. *Silver linings.*

He'd slept better than he had most nights since the accident, and even if the wine had played a part in that, so had having a warm, sexy woman at his side. But he *was* cold, and he also needed a bathroom trip, bad. "Nurse," he said, "I have to go to the bathroom."

Her eyes fluttered open, allowing him to see the surprise there as she remembered exactly where she was. "Oh. Hi."

He grinned softly. "Hi. And I'm sorry to break this up, but I really gotta go."

She sat up—then hunkered back down under the covers. "It's freezing in here."

"I think the woman who tends the fire hooked up with some hunky guy last night and fell asleep on the job."

A gentle laugh left her. "She should be sternly reprimanded."

"Well, I might let it go if she can warm it up in here."

"Tell you what," she said. "I'll make a mad dash for some cozy clothes in the bedroom, then we'll get you to the bathroom, then I'll work on the fire and some breakfast. Deal?"

"Deal," he said with a short nod. Though he felt the need to add, "Sorry. That you have to do everything."

She only shrugged. "Not like you have a choice."

True, but after last night, well…maybe he just wished he could feel like he used to, like a capable guy who took care of things. He wished that all the time, but right now in particular, it would've been nice to take care of Suzanne a little.

He couldn't deny enjoying the view as she scurried naked across the living room before disappearing into the bedroom. While she was gone, he reached around under the covers and came up with sweatpants, which he managed to get on, and located his hoodie on the floor next to the bed. She soon came back in leggings and a pastel hoodie of her own.

"Think it's gonna be a shower day for me," he told her, "once it warms up in here."

"Sounds like a plan," she said as he maneuvered his legs over the side of the bed and pulled himself up onto his left leg, balancing with the crutches. "And…I need to ask you a question. About last night."

Uh-oh. It had been great, and he wouldn't mind it happening again, and again—but not if she was gonna make a big thing of it. He'd just gotten out of a relationship like that with Meg, and he knew women liked to know where they stood and all that crap, but he'd just hoped this might stay as easy as it had felt last night. "Sounds serious," he said—trying to be light, but also wary.

"It's about…your hip," she said.

His eyes narrowed. He had no idea what she was talking about, but maybe he'd jumped to the wrong conclusion? "Huh?"

"When we were…you know…were you, uh, able to lift your hip?"

"I...guess."

"The reason I'm asking is—it seemed like you were... thrusting."

He arched one eyebrow. "That's usually how it's done."

"But that requires you move your hip. So this means you can use it. It moves. When you want it to."

He blinked. "Oh. I guess *so*," he said, seeing the relevance now.

"Could you before? Like a week or two ago?"

He tried to think. They'd focused so much on his leg, he hadn't thought much about where exactly the feeling started or ended. "Not sure."

She appeared to think it over and said, "Well, either way, it's good." Then she stepped closer and poked his hip with her finger, hard—and a jolt shot through him.

"Ow," he said.

Then their gazes met—and they both smiled. "You can feel that," she said.

"I can feel that," he confirmed. "It tingled, though. And hurt more than you'd think."

"Like nerve pain?"

He nodded. "Yep."

At that, she poked his other hip in the same way. "Did *that* hurt?"

"Nope."

She looked like she wanted to smile again but was holding it in.

"What?" he asked.

"I wonder if our hip rotations are reactivating those nerves," she said. "I mean, maybe they've been like this all along, but...maybe they haven't."

Now Zack was the one holding back a grin, as unsure as she was. He didn't want to get excited over nothing.

That would be too damn easy to do here. So he just replied, "Maybe. And I'm about to explode, so…"

"Be on your way," she said merrily, shooing him.

Of course, the whole time he was in the bathroom, he found himself poking different spots on his hip. Each poke produced different sensations, some more noticeable than others. And even if he didn't want to get caught up in false hope, he came to the table feeling pretty good. Although the unexpected sex wasn't exactly hurting his mood, either.

His seat provided him a view into the kitchen, where Suzanne flipped pancakes on a griddle. "Smells good, Suzie Q," he said—just as his phone rang and he looked down to see his aunt's face on the screen. He glanced to Suzanne before answering. "Dahlia."

"This should be interesting," Suzanne replied.

He swiped to answer. "Hey, Dahlia."

"Zack, my boy, I'm so sorry. I've been ill, completely out of commission. And I'm still not back to full strength, but somewhat better and I'm just now getting your messages."

He instantly believed her because she sounded… weak. "Sick how?"

"We suspect food poisoning."

"Well, I hope you feel better." He meant it. He couldn't remember Dahlia *ever* being sick, so it threw him a little to hear her sounding frail. She stayed as chatty as usual, but he could tell she was tired. He added grudgingly, "And sorry if I got snotty."

She let that go, proceeding to, "Now, how are *you*? Your messages worried me."

He kept it simple. "I'm fine. Better than yesterday."

"Good—I'm relieved to hear that. It's easy to get

down at a time like this—I know. But it's important not to stay there. It's important you pull yourself back up."

"That's what Suzanne said, too."

He could almost feel Dahlia's smile at his giving credit to Suzanne. "I trust that she's taking excellent care of you."

At this, an unplanned jolt of laughter leaked out.

"That's funny?" Dahlia asked.

"No. And she is," he assured her.

"Then what were you laughing about?"

"Nothing," he insisted.

"Something. I didn't just fall off a turnip truck, you know."

He wasn't sure how to respond, felt put on the spot. "We're just…getting along fine," he told her. "Better than I expected. That's all."

"Well, indeed that's a surprise," Dahlia said. "No more Nurse Ratched?"

"No. And that's Ratchet," he teased.

"Ratched, silly," Suzanne said from the kitchen, hearing only part of the conversation. "Ratched, Ratched, Ratched."

"She sounds merry," Dahlia observed.

"I guess," he said.

And a quiet moment later, Dahlia declared, "My stars. I never would have believed it, but there's something going on between the two of you, isn't there?"

Damn perceptive woman. Then again, his own fault for laughing in the first place. "Uh, listen, Dahlia, breakfast is ready, so I gotta go."

"Don't you dare hang up on me, young man. I fully intend to find out exactly—"

"You're breaking up, Dahlia—talk to you later. Bye."

DAHLIA LEANED BACK her head and laughed. What unexpected and glorious news.

"Um, did you just laugh?" Giselle asked.

Dahlia smiled over from her bed. "Indeed I did. Listen to this. There's romance brewing between Zack and Suzanne. Or sex. Or something in between—I'm not sure. I only know that it's exactly what they both need right now, so I'm elated. A good love affair can sweep you off your feet, you know." Then she stopped, frowning at her choice of words. "Well, perhaps I should have said that a different way under the circumstances—but regardless, it can take you away from your troubles."

Dahlia looked back to her phone to send Suzanne a teasing text. I know what's going on between you and Zack. Brava, my dear. Brava. She added a line of smiling emojis.

As she set the phone aside, feeling more joyful than she'd dreamed possible a few hours ago, Giselle asked cautiously, "Do you feel like getting up? Putting your toes in the sand?"

"Not yet, I'm afraid." She pointed to a nearby table. "But pass me that album please." She'd started to show Giselle some old pictures just before taking to her bed.

When Giselle placed the book on her lap, Dahlia ran her palm lovingly across the cover done in seventies psychedelic. "I've never been one to save a great many photos—I'm more of a live-in-the-moment woman—but just now I find myself glad to have these."

She opened the book to the first page, to faded snapshots from her time in Montana. "There's Pete," she said, pointing at her sweet, young ex-husband. "Oh, and that's Mulligan and Dobie on the horses." She laughed, drawn back there again. "Dobie found that big straw hat in the bunkhouse and made it his. He wore it everywhere, even though it was too big on his head."

"What did *you* do on the ranch?" Giselle asked.

"I cooked. That's another thing my mother gave me—she taught me to cook. So—an interesting name and cooking skills—that's two points for her. Needless to say, my love of cooking eventually led to the café."

Having eased down on the bed beside her to see the pictures, Giselle let out a small gasp and pointed at one. "Is that you?"

Dahlia laughed. "Yes, I was once a blonde." The messy golden locks fell loose over her shoulders as she sat next to Pete on the sofa in Hannah's sprawling ranch house.

"I can just barely recognize you," Giselle said. "It's in your eyes. And your smile. The blond lights up your face."

Dahlia studied the old photo. "I suppose it does at that. But for all things there is a season, and when my hair began to fade, I didn't fight it." She'd chosen to embrace her gray—a thought she knew some women found horrifying, others empowering, and still others just simpler. To each her own. For her, it had started out being about the ease—she'd never been one to trifle with inconveniences she could avoid; life was too short. But the transition to what had become a rather lovely shade of silver had, in a quiet way, brought an unanticipated strength.

"As women, we can *become* our hair, let it tell the world who we are, identify with it so deeply. Even when I chose to let go of that symbol of youth, I thought saying goodbye would be harder. But in the end, it was as simple as…letting it happen. And I suddenly felt like…me. Like some under layer of the real me had been revealed.

"And here's a secret. People think you're wiser with gray hair. They can see, I suppose, that this isn't your first trip around the block, or maybe that you simply know who you are by this point. Regardless, they start listening more if you say what you think—as long as you do it with some sense, mind you." She finished with a wink.

And Giselle said, "Or maybe you're just actually wise."

Dahlia laughed. "Yes, or that." Then turned the page.

Her eyes fell on the ranch woman who'd been a blessing in her life, a mentor. "Oh, that's Hannah. Dear Hannah." Without planning, Dahlia found herself reaching down, touching the photo, as if she could touch Hannah's face with her fingertips. "She was the most beautiful woman I've ever known." She thought back. "She was in her fifties. And back then, many women that age resigned themselves to…a societal standard of aging where fashion and style were for the young. By the time they reached their forties or fifties, they had long since started cutting their hair into boring, sensible shapes and putting on frumpy day dresses and polyester pants. But not Hannah. I'll never forget the moment I met her.

"She wore a long, tiered Western skirt with sturdy ranch boots underneath, and her ex-husband's work coat, which was certainly too big on her and yet she sported it with total ease. Her hair was even longer than mine, somewhere between blond and gray, and her face was weathered and wrinkled and…still beautiful. How can I explain that?" she mused aloud. "I'd never before seen a woman with wrinkles who still exuded beauty and light and, oh, such confidence. She was…a woman of her own. And she taught me to be one, too."

Unthinkingly, she touched Hannah's face again,

pulled back in time, feeling almost as if it were yesterday that they'd last talked. "Hannah taught me, among many other lessons, that youth and beauty are two very different things." She looked to Giselle. "Such qualities really are in the eye of the beholder, you know?"

Giselle smiled. "Hannah would be proud of you if she were here. You make me see youth and beauty in different ways than I did before, just so you know."

Dahlia's heart warmed. "That's a supreme compliment, my friend."

She turned the page to find a photo of her and Hannah together. She'd forgotten it existed, but it made her heart dance. Did Hannah have a copy? Did she ever look at it? Did she remember Dahlia as fondly as Dahlia remembered her? But then, no. Probably not. For a rush of reasons that blew through her mind—just as Giselle asked, "Did you keep in touch with her?"

"No," Dahlia answered, swiftly if a little sadly. "Back then, it wasn't as easy. We didn't have cell phones or computers. We had home phones, so the number changed whenever you moved. And we had pen and paper. It took effort. And someone like Hannah—well, much as I loved her, I think she was used to the transience of the people in her life. Ranch workers came and went. She was content, I think, to let go of people. I've largely been the same way myself. It's that live-in-the-moment part of me. Even if, just now, I'm…wondering why. Why I never wrote to her. Why I never went back to visit."

"Have you ever tried to find her online? On social media?"

Dahlia smiled grimly as a sad, strange truth set in. "She was forty years my senior. I'm sixty-five. So… she's likely long since died. And you know, maybe that's one way life is easier when you lose touch with people.

You don't have to know when they pass, you don't have to mourn them. Up until a moment ago, Hannah had always, for me, been alive and vibrant as ever, in my mind, whenever she crossed it." Then she scrunched up her nose and peeked over at Giselle. "Would it be utterly silly of me to keep it that way? In my mind? Let her just be alive and thriving there?"

"I think it's a very nice idea," Giselle said. Then she tilted her head. "What about the others? Pete? Dobie? The girls? Do you know where any of them ended up?"

Dahlia just laughed. "Not a one of them. And no, I don't want to look them up online."

"Because you prefer to live in the moment," Giselle finished for her.

"Correct," Dahlia said. "And besides, I don't want to find out any of them have died, either. That way, they can just keep living on inside me, too."

"You never told me what happened after the ranch. Or how things ended with Pete."

Dahlia thought back, turned another page. She let out a laugh, seeing that the album had just left the ranch years, right along with her thoughts. "Well," she said, "Pete wanted to have a baby. I was only eighteen and did not. And I did a rather dastardly thing, because I wasn't *quite* bold enough to speak my mind yet, because that doesn't happen overnight when you've often been slapped for doing so. The birth control pill had just been legalized, so I went on the pill without telling him. Until I realized how futile that was, and with Hannah's counsel, eventually told him I didn't know if I *ever* wanted children. And though the marriage had been doomed for me from the start, that was finally the end for him. We divorced and he set out for greener pastures—literally. He was hired on at a ranch in Wyoming. Me, I loved Hannah, and cooking in that big ranch kitchen, and I thought I'd be content to stay there forever. But everything changed when Hannah introduced me to a man named Tom Delaney."

"I trust he's the man you're getting married to in these pictures?"

"Yes," Dahlia said, glancing down. Another barefoot wedding, but she looked so much more grown-up. "It was a sunset ceremony on Hapuna Beach on Hawaii's Big Island."

"I didn't see that coming," Giselle said.

"Neither did I," Dahlia confided with another wink. Then she leaned her head back, sighed.

"You look tired," Giselle said.

"Yes. I suppose my euphoria about Zack and Suzanne lifted me up—but now I'm feeling rather blah again. Would you mind if I take a nap?"

"Not at all," Giselle answered, and Dahlia closed her eyes, vaguely aware of the photo album being lifted from her grasp.

DAHLIA LAY NEXT to a pristine swimming pool looking out over the bluest ocean waters she never could have imagined. She glanced over at the man on the lounge chair next to hers, a big hulking rancher who seemed to think she'd hung the moon. He was getting sunburned.

"He's rich," Hannah had whispered just after introducing her to Tom when he'd come from the next ranch over to have dinner at the Bar J one summer night in 1974. Hannah then explained that he'd bought the Circle D Ranch "on a lark," the man had told her, "'cause I like wide-open spaces," and "the D in the brand matched my name." He hailed from a family of Texas cattle barons, *so he already knew a lot about ranching, "but I always liked horses more."*

*"So basically, he's dabbling in horse ranching," Hannah explained. "Which is only a little irksome to me, since he seems like a nice enough fella. And if he runs the place into the ground, maybe it'll ultimately be to my benefit. My impression is that he's wealthy enough that a failed ranch wouldn't be more than a fly in his soup."*

*As far as Dahlia could tell, he'd moved into the ranch's house, expanded it, and hired people to run the place. He liked the view, and he liked to watch the hands wrangle and tame the horses. He rode a large gelding named Midnight, and after he and Dahlia had started dating, he'd given her a pretty beige mare she'd named Sugar. That had been when she'd known he was serious about her. And the fact that she'd accepted the horse told her she was serious about him.*

*Now they lounged on a Hawaiian beach, whiling the days away. Hannah had hired a cook to fill in during the trip, which had alarmed Dahlia slightly. "I'll only be gone two weeks."*

*Hannah had only shrugged. "I'm not sure you'll be back."*

*"Of course I will. He's invited me on a vacation, that's all."*

*"Well, your job is here when you return. But if something were to keep you away, then I'm covered." She'd winked, and Dahlia had felt as if she were missing the joke.*

*Now, with a moment to stop and breathe and think, she understood. Her relationship with Tom had been a whirlwind—he'd been enamored of her the second they met, wooing her with roses and jewelry and fancier din-*

ners than she had the proper clothing for. He'd bought her everything she was wearing on this trip, in fact.

And she was traveling with a man to whom she was not married. "I registered us as Mr. and Mrs. Delaney," he told her after they'd arrived at the resort. Crossing the country in a VW van with other kids her own age was one thing, but a well-to-do man traveling with a woman who wasn't his wife would be considered scandalous.

"Your lava flow, Mrs. Delaney," a waitress said then.

"Thank you," Dahlia answered, accepting the frothy red-and-white drink and wondering how this had happened. How had a girl who'd left home at sixteen with nothing but a beat-up suitcase and a prayer for a better life ended up in the lap of luxury with a man who adored her?

"I like the way that sounds," Tom said with a youthful grin. He was thirty-one, ten years her senior, but he possessed a boyishness that put her at ease despite the differences in their ages and backgrounds. Then he repeated it. "Mrs. Delaney."

She liked it, too. And when he looked at her, her skin sizzled. Of course, Pete had made that happen, as well. But they'd been so young, just kids. And Tom had a way of making her feel more like a woman than a girl, even when he was grinning at her like a sweet little boy.

He tilted his head and asked in his Texas drawl, "You like it here, doll baby?"

Part of her had wanted to be offended by the pet name, but it had grown organically from her name—at first it had been Dahlia baby, then just doll baby. "How could I not? It's amazing." They'd spent the last week soaking up tropical breezes, swimming in a little cove on the resort grounds, and driving around the island to take in spectacular vistas and more waterfalls than she'd known could exist in one place.

"I was thinkin' maybe we'd just stay awhile. The Circle D can get by without me, and I reckon the Bar J can manage without you—but I'll call Hannah if ya want me to."

Dahlia was stunned. "You can just...do that?"

"I'm a fortunate man, Dahlia. Blessed with the means to do as I see fit. And now I'm blessed with a wonderful woman to enjoy it all with. Can't see a reason to rush back and I'd be obliged if ya'd stay here taking in the pleasures of the islands with me."

Though maybe she shouldn't be so stunned—Hannah had predicted it. How had she known? It made Dahlia feel naive. Just when she'd thought she was so mature. "It's not that I wouldn't love to," she said, "but I can't ask Hannah to hold my job indefinitely. And I need it."

"Not if you marry me and become Mrs. Delaney for real," Tom replied.

Like it was nothing.

She, on the other hand, gasped.

And he smiled. "Dahlia, I wish I could get down on one knee right here and ask ya to be my wife in front of every person at this resort. But seein's as they already think we're married, guess I'd have some explaining to do." He winked in that endearing, boyish way of his— then got more serious. "I've been in love with ya since we met and it just gets better every day. Marry me, doll baby, and I'll make you a happy woman. I'll take care of you the way ya deserve. Will you marry me, Dahlia?"

She blew out a breath, taken aback, her heart threatening to beat right through her chest. She thought she loved him, too. He was kind and affectionate and generous. And Hannah thought well of him, which counted *for a lot. The only thing was...* "This might sound crazy, Tom, but what if...what if I don't want to just be a kept woman? What if I want to do things, and go places, and find ways to make some kind of difference in the world?"

He grinned. "I know you're into that women's lib thing and that's okay. I don't want a lady I can walk on and control. Maybe that's what drew me to ya from the start. Well, that and them pretty green eyes." He winked. "I could see from the first that you had...a spirit that's searchin' the world for meaning. And I got no desire to stop ya from lookin' for it. All I ask is you let me come along for the ride, doll baby. We can have a good life together—me and you."

"Okay," Dahlia said. Just like that. *Because every word he'd said had been just right in his Texasy Tom way.*

"Okay?" he asked, clearly trying to contain his joy.

*She smiled, her heart feeling as big as one of the hibiscuses dripping from vines and bushes all over the island.*

"You just made me the happiest fella in the world, doll baby." Peering over the beautiful crescent swath of golden beach in the distance, he pointed. "We'll do it tomorrow night at sunset, right there. We'll be joined together forever."

*Dahlia bit her lip. Forever. Maybe it was a fast decision. But it seemed far wiser than marrying Pete had been. And forever, with Tom and his love and his willingness to give her everything she could want, including a little independence, sounded like an offer it would be crazy to turn down. Forever, here I come.* "I can't wait to be Mrs. Delaney."

## CHAPTER FIFTEEN

"DAMN IT, WOMAN, are you trying to kill me?"

Some things never changed, and Zack's grousing during physical therapy was one of them. But Suzanne had every intention of continuing to push him. She replied in her normal, calm tone—a habit from her nursing days that had come back recently, especially after learning that Zack's bark was worse than his bite. "You know this is for your own good, and I've told you dozens of times—stimulating the muscles can only help."

"If you want to stimulate my muscles, Suzie Q," he said, narrowing his gaze on her, "I can think of ways to do it that are a hell of a lot more fun."

A familiar heat ascended her cheeks, but now she just laughed. She never would have dreamed the key to relaxing the tensions between them would be sex—but unlikely things happened all the time, and the unlikely truth was that since this morning, even when he was grumpy, the fact that they were suddenly into each other had beamed a light into their forced cohabitation.

She hadn't answered Dahlia's text—simply because she had no idea what to say. Zack's joking avoidance on the phone had certainly left no doubt as to what had happened, but she didn't know how to discuss it because she didn't know what it meant. Was it fun and games? Sexual healing? The start of a relationship? She had no idea.

And she'd resolved to just not think about it. Even

if she already knew that, for her, it was more than fun and games. But she'd taken that leap knowingly, albeit without a net.

What she didn't know was where Zack stood. But if she judged from his past with Meg, where he *didn't* stand was in the relationship zone. Which meant it was one of the other two options—both equating to casual and convenient and good for right now. So she'd just have to go with the flow because there was no other reasonable, sensible choice. *If you wanted sensible, maybe you should have thought twice before just...surrendering yourself to him.*

*And stop being ridiculous. It was more than surrender; you climbed on top of the man.*

But...water under the bridge and all that. Now all she could do was move forward—with physical therapy, a grouchy patient, and, apparently, more sex. Which she would not turn down. Because last night had been amazing. And there was that unwitting attachment thing she already suffered from. So, yep, more sex sounded... downright heavenly. Sexual healing could work both ways. And she'd been trying to heal from losing Cal for a very long time.

Completing Zack's ankle rotations with him lying on his back, she said, "Let's do the new one—where we bend our foot inward 'til our big toe touches the bed, then the other way until our little toe touches."

As she bent over, guiding his left, uninjured leg to remind him of the motions, he said, "First of all, all the feet and toes involved here are mine. Second, it's a waste of time to do this one on my good leg. It doesn't work the muscles enough to be worth the effort."

Her pleasant nurse tone slipped just a little as she said, "Has anyone ever told you you're a terrible patient?"

"Only every time I've ever been one."

"Well, I suggest you remember which one of us is the medical professional."

Zack rolled his eyes—partly from annoyance, partly just habit.

Even if he saw his nurse through entirely new eyes than he had yesterday.

Sure, he'd noticed her charms before—but sex with Suzanne had been mind-blowing. Maybe it was just about the timing, showing him life was still worth living, letting him feel like a man again. He might not be able to work a fishing boat, but at least he could still get it up, and find a pretty woman who wanted him to.

"Okay," she said as he completed the tenth rep on his left leg. "Great. Now ten more."

But the truth was, it felt different than if she'd just been some woman in a port town, or a Summer Island tourist here for bicycles, lighthouses, and a one-night stand. Was it her being his caregiver, and that like it or not, that meant something to him? Or was it the sweet, hungry look in her eyes, the fiery need he'd sensed in her body? He knew she missed her husband—but the way she'd given herself to him had left him feeling like she needed to be cared about, loved, maybe even more than she knew.

Of course, he wasn't the guy for that job—and surely she realized that. Surely they were both on the same page here: it was sex—nice sex, good sex, fun sex. And she only had to ask Meg to know he didn't possess the skills for much more. Not that he was a heartless jerk—there were times he'd been there for Meg, like when her great-aunt was dying. He'd been there by choice—taken care of her in a way that he could. But there were other ways he couldn't.

"Very good," Suzanne said, smiling down on him. "Let's go to three reps of ten today."

The suggestion inspired another eye roll. "Sure, yeah—let's make me do more and more of the ones I don't even feel."

He'd never committed to Meg because…a commitment was a promise; it was putting down a stake. He'd been there for her aunt's death because it had been imminent, something that, however difficult, wouldn't last forever. When it came to bigger promises than that, he wasn't sure he could keep them. And he hadn't wanted to let her down.

And he'd refused to give up his solitude on the fishing boat. She'd asked him to cultivate business closer to home, become a day fisherman, one who didn't stay away for weeks and months at a time. But no matter where he was, getting back onto the *Emily Ann* was the thing he looked forward to, the core of his life that everything else revolved around. It hadn't made sense to give up something he loved in order to have something else he loved. So in the end, he'd kept his first love—the water. And lost his second love—Meg.

*And now you've lost the water, too.*

For five pretty nice years with Meg, he'd had his cake and eaten it, too.

Now, no cake. Only exercise.

And Suzanne's brownies, and other good food, and—last night at least—kisses and touches and slick, hot connections. *No cake—but things could be worse. Remember that.*

Just two weeks ago that kind of logic didn't work on him—but things were changing; *he* was changing. Though when he thought of the loss of his work—hell, that still made his existence feel like a bottomless pit he'd never climb out of.

"Good," Suzanne said when he completed the third rep of ten. "Now the right leg."

The one she had to move *for* him. As she placed her hands on his limp right leg, stretched out in front of him, and began to twist it inward, he peered up at her, his pretty Nurse Ratchet, aware that her hoodie hid the sweet curves underneath. Curves he knew the feel of now. He started getting just a little hard remembering how it felt to touch her, to run his palms up her thighs, to—

"Ow, damn it!" he said as a jolt of electric pain shot through him, yanking him from the sweet, hot reverie.

Her gaze darted to his face. "What did you just say?" Why did she look so dramatic?

"I said 'ow.' Then 'damn it,'" he repeated dryly—a residual echo of pain still arcing through his thigh.

She continued to gape at him. "You're saying…you felt what I just did."

He looked down. This was his right leg, not his left. His injured, paralyzed leg. Usually he complained when she twisted his *left* leg every which way. But this…wasn't that. This was…his right leg. His answer came out more hushed than intended. "I did. I felt it."

She pursed her lips. "Where exactly?"

He pointed, drawing an imaginary line up his thigh. "It kind of…shot up. Into my hip."

Above him, she'd grown very calm, like a doctor wearing a poker face. "I want you to close your eyes—because I don't want visual stimulus to confuse you at all."

He had no idea what she even meant by that, but shut his eyes.

"Okay, good," she said softly. "Now…do you feel this?"

And Zack flinched. From the utter shock of it. She'd just poked a finger into a spot high on his right leg. "Yeah." Then he let out a laugh, a demented sort of sound, but he didn't much care. "I mean, it doesn't feel completely normal—but yeah, I felt it."

He could hear her trying to remain stoic while clearly excited underneath. "Okay, that's great. Keep your eyes closed, and tell me if you feel…this."

He scrunched up his face slightly. Because…so many things. It hadn't felt like he expected or hoped. But still it had *felt*. "A little. Not as much."

"That's okay," she assured him. "That's totally okay. How about this?"

Another flinch—his whole body lurching slightly. "Yep!"

At this, a pretty trill of laughter erupted from her, the sound perhaps sweeter for not being able to see her. No visual stimulus. Maybe that made other things clearer, too—like newfound joy.

She continued poking and prodding various points on his right thigh. Not every spot produced feeling, but many did, even if only slight. "Does it hurt?" she asked, when poking a spot where he'd verified sensation.

He hadn't even noticed that aspect of it, too elated by this turn of events, but, "Yeah, actually. Everywhere you touched hurts some. In that weird, electric way."

"Nerve pain is unpleasant," she said as he opened his eyes, "but in your case good. It means you're having some reconnection. And…"

"And what?" He looked up at her, aware they were both trying not to smile.

"And I don't want to get your hopes up, because I truly have no idea what's going to happen here. But…"

"But?" he prodded when she trailed off.

She bit her lip, tilted her head. "But I couldn't have dreamed even yesterday that you'd have feeling back in any part of your leg this soon. And it could stop right here for all we know—as we keep saying, every case of paralysis is unique. But…" Finally, she let her smile unfurl. "This is a very good sign. A very, very good sign. We have every reason to think you'll continue to regain sensation, whether quickly or slowly."

They looked at each other a few seconds more—until Zack let out a *whoop*, and Suzanne followed with a few yipping sounds, twirling in a circle. He pumped his fists into the air as they both laughed, and she bounced herself joyfully onto the foot of the bed on her knees.

"Clearly our exercises are paying off and I'm a miracle worker," she said with a wide smile, teasingly smug.

He grinned at her, ready to tease back. "Exercises, my ass. It was the sex." Though he was half-serious, too.

She leaned her head back and let out another laugh. "Only a man would say that."

"I'm not kidding," he told her. "It *had* to be the sex. I used, um, muscles that I hadn't in a while—more than just the one between my legs." He winked. "And hell, it's good for a guy to, you know, get to use *that* muscle, too."

She responded by simply tilting her head, tossing him another pretty smile, and saying, "Either way, just call me the miracle worker! Step aside, Anne Sullivan!"

He narrowed his gaze. "Anne who?"

Suzanne rolled her eyes. "Are you telling me you haven't seen *The Miracle Worker*?"

"That's a movie, I'm guessing?"

She let out a playful sigh and said, "That'll be your

next classic film." Then her gaze widened. "Want to watch it now?"

"No," he said, still grinning. Women. They could be so funny. "Right now, I wanna do *this*." He grabbed her wrist and pulled her toward him until she fell into his embrace, where he began to kiss her with every ounce of gratitude inside him. Her palm rose to cup his jaw as their tongues mingled—and he followed the urge to slide his hands up under her hoodie, to her bra.

That was when she pulled back from their kisses, putting a slight crimp in his erection. "What's wrong?" he asked.

"Well, it's…right in the middle of the day."

Zack dryly glanced to the right in the quiet, empty living room, and then to the left toward the window, where fresh snow fell outside. "You have somewhere you need to be?"

She blinked, perhaps starting to catch on to his way of thinking. "Well, no."

He grinned. "Then let's do some celebrating, Suzie Q."

By THE NEXT DAY, they'd had sex twice more and six fresh inches of snow had fallen across the island. But the new morning dawned clear and bright, the kind that summoned the island's winter residents out to the market or the Skipper's Wheel, and Suzanne dragged herself from Zack's bed, kissed him goodbye, and promised to be back soon.

Descending Mill Street and turning toward Petal Pushers, she caught sight of Clark Hayes, owner of the Huron House Hotel, and tossed him a wave. In the other direction came town councilman Tom Bixby on a pair of cross-country skis. "Out getting a little exercise, Tom?" she asked with a smile.

"Absolutely—it's a beautiful day, and my wife's been feeding me too well this winter." He patted his belly through his parka.

"Good for you—keep up the good work," she called as she unlocked the flower shop.

The interior, filled with bare tables and shelves, could almost be depressing to someone already surrounded by the barrenness of a northern winter, but coming in made Suzanne happy. Or maybe there was just already a lot to be happy about.

Zack had feeling in his leg!

And then there was the sex. Almost equally as shocking a turn of events, if not more so. For a long time, she'd thought she'd never want anyone but Cal. And now... when she'd least expected it, Zack Sheppard, of all unlikely men, was filling that void for her.

She shook her head as she approached the refrigerator, still trying to wrap her mind around it. But at the same time, not too tight. *Don't get any more attached than you already are. Remember who he is. Just appreciate him for who he is. A man doesn't have to commit his whole life to you to be worth sharing a connection with.* A new idea for her, but she tried to take it to heart. Zack was giving her something she needed—but he wouldn't be around forever. And that was okay. Because it had to be.

Other things to be happy about: a sunny day in winter, and that after weeks of diligent watering, it was time to move her bulbs out into the light. "Hi, guys," she whispered as she opened the produce drawers in the old fridge, looking down on her shallow dishes. "Guess what? It's showtime."

After another watering, she carried the dishes into the

main shop space, setting them in a spot where they'd receive indirect sunlight. Then she bumped the thermostat up to sixty, where it would now stay. The bulbs' refrigeration since autumn gave them the experience of winter—now, bringing them out into the light and warmer temps would trick them into thinking it was spring. She'd have to water more frequently now, but in two to four weeks, depending on how much the sun chose to shine, she'd have bright, cheerful daffodils and hyacinths.

Though, if she was honest with herself, the days already looked brighter. Sex and reconnected nerves in her lover's leg could really lift a girl's spirits.

Standing next to the bulbs, she ran her fingertips gently through the loose, damp soil that covered them, thinking through the many years she'd made spring come early this way. She'd always been so proud to show Cal her spring blooms in February.

Of course, thinking so concretely about her husband made what she'd done with Zack feel a little like…cheating. Which was silly, of course. Cal perhaps wouldn't love her choice of guy—two men could scarcely be more different—but one thing he'd understood was circumstances, so if he was watching from some other dimension, he was surely pleased to see her finding some joy. He might be worried for her heart—but she was going to surprise them both by turning over a new leaf in that arena, or at least giving it her best shot.

"Goodbye, little bulbs," she said as she wiped her fingers on a towel, put on her gloves, and headed toward the door. "Work your magic while I'm gone."

Stepping back out into the cold, she caught sight of the Summerbrook Inn up the street—pristine and idyllic as ever under a blanket of fresh snow—yet the sight sent an invisible arrow piercing her heart. *Oh no—what have I done?*

It had begun to feel like she and Zack were in a vacuum, the only two people in the world. But they weren't. And she'd had sex with her best friend's ex. Four times, no less. And she'd loved it. She'd loved every hungry, intoxicating, heated second of it.

*You're a terrible friend.* And it wasn't so much the initial act that made her a terrible friend—it was a unique situation and she'd succumbed to a moment of passion, as people sometimes did. What made her a truly terrible friend was that she'd done it again, and again—and that she knew, without doubt, that she was going to keep right on doing it.

# CHAPTER SIXTEEN

"So," DAHLIA SAID slyly to Suzanne over the phone, "what's new with you?"

Curled up in her cozy chair, Suzanne smiled. So very much was new. And part of her simply wanted to hold it all close to her heart. But that was just the isolation talking. It made *everything* feel private, made sharing feel almost foreign at times.

And Dahlia's voice brimmed with so much anticipation that it was tempting to tease her. "Well, I took my bulbs out of the fridge at Petal Pushers."

"Yes, yes, what else?" Clearly Dahlia didn't care about bulbs. But then, why would she—who needed spring when in a land of perpetual summer?

"Um, Zack and I watched *The Miracle Worker.* I couldn't believe he'd never seen it."

"Okay—well, what else?"

"I think it made him count his blessings. Not that he'd ever use that exact phrase, but it made him think. I mean, who *doesn't* think after seeing that movie?" The man in question was currently taking a shower, giving Suzanne the freedom to talk as openly as she wished—or not.

"Well, that's lovely, dear," Dahlia said, beginning to sound impatient. "But I think there's something big you're not telling me."

"You're right, there is. And I hope you're sitting down for this."

"I am."

"Drink in hand, toes in sand?"

"The second one. I'm looking out on a beautiful beach, listening to the waves roll in. Now go on."

Suzanne's heart expanded a little, knowing she was about to give Dahlia far better news than she was even expecting. "Zack has some feeling back in his leg."

"What?" Dahlia gasped.

"You heard me right," Suzanne told her joyfully. "It's painful for him when I move the leg now, but it means nerves are reconnecting! So it's amazing news."

On the other end, Dahlia let out a hearty laugh Suzanne had missed. "Oh, my girl—my sweet, sweet girl— what an incredible thing to hear! You just lifted my heart so high it's zooming circles around the sun." Another laugh, and then, "Zack is encouraged, I'm sure."

"Yes. Now all he wants to do is exercise," Suzanne told her on a chuckle. "I've had to explain that we need to just stay the course, not overdo. But needless to say, we're both overjoyed, and just hoping the progress continues."

After more details on the topic, Suzanne asked, "And what's new with you?"

"Not so fast, missy."

"Huh?" Suzanne had hoped the excitement about Zack's leg might sidetrack Dahlia from her detective work, but apparently not.

"We're not done talking about you and Zack yet."

She feigned ignorance anyway. "We're not?"

"You two seem to be getting along awfully well," Dahlia remarked.

"And what a relief that is," Suzanne told her. "A much more pleasant situation."

At this, Dahlia stayed quiet a moment, then finally

said on a sigh, "Oh, Suz—my dear Suz. I don't intend to pry, truly. You don't have to talk to me about this if you don't choose to. I just thought you might want to." Her tone of voice had gone from merry to more heartfelt, reminding Suzanne once more that Dahlia was more than Zack's aunt, and more than someone who'd dashed off on a mysterious trip leaving them angry and hurt. She was also Suzanne's friend. And given how distant Meg felt these days, it was a nice thing to remember.

"Talk…about what?" Suzanne asked—though her voice went softer, too.

"I thought," Dahlia said, "you might want to tell me you and Zack are an item."

The old-fashioned term drew an unexpected chuckle from Suzanne. And then…honesty. "I wouldn't say we're an item. I would say we're sleeping together."

At this, Dahlia released a peal of laughter, obviously delighted to have sussed out the truth. "Close enough, my girl."

"Well, two different things really," Suzanne pointed out.

"You're snowbound in a cottage together for who knows how long. If you're having sex and enjoying each other's company, that makes you an item."

Suzanne sighed. "Tomato, tomahto."

"Regardless, this is good for you. And for him. My heart is making an extra orbit around the sun because of it."

Another soft laugh echoed from Suzanne. "I knew you'd be happy. And I'm sorry I didn't tell you. It's just sort of a weird thing to talk about. Maybe because you're his aunt."

Dahlia let out an easy, laissez-faire sort of sigh. "You can talk to me about anything, Suz—no need to feel weird. I just hope…well, I know it's been quite some time, and that up until Beck you were quite adamant romance was dead for you. So I hope this is making you happy."

"It is," Suzanne confided, feeling more open now. She'd been putting walls up with Dahlia out of anger and confusion. And she was still confused in a way, but perhaps tired of being angry. "Even if it's…undefined, I feel happier inside than I have in a while." She hadn't quite known that before the words left her, but there it was. Zack made her happy. In a way nothing had since Cal.

"All I can say is, keep doing what you're doing—it's working," Dahlia said. "For both of you, I think."

Suzanne blew out a sigh, deciding to confide even more now that they were going down this road. "I'm not sure where it will lead, Dahlia. You know Zack."

"Everything is changing for him right now," Dahlia said airily. "So maybe neither of us knows him at all."

"What do you mean?"

"He can't work on a fishing boat anymore," Dahlia reminded her.

"I know. But what does that have to do with this? Him and me?"

"Only everything, my dear. He'll have to build a new way of life. And he's going to be very appreciative of all you've done for him."

Oh. Well, even so, Suzanne couldn't let herself start buying what Dahlia was selling. It was too dangerous. "Here's the thing," Suzanne said. "There's some deep, dark secret inside that man that makes him a commitment-phobe. And it's not about his work or his leg. It's something that's been brewing since long before either of those, and it's not the kind of thing that just goes away. I might be able to fix his body, but I can't fix what he won't let me near. Meg's been down this road and suffered for it. So maybe I don't *want* to believe he can change."

"Some people do," Dahlia said, hopeful as ever.

"Most people don't," Suzanne countered.

"Speaking of Meg..." Dahlia trailed off, giving Suzanne's stomach time to churn with guilt.

"I know. I'm a horrible friend."

"Eh—these are complicated times. She'll have to understand that." Dahlia was absolving her? "When are you going to tell her?"

"I was thinking...never," Suzanne confessed.

"What do you mean?" No absolution on this part apparently.

"This thing with Zack will inevitably pass," Suzanne explained. "Very possibly by spring. And regardless, everything about this situation will change then—you'll be back, he'll see doctors on the mainland. We just don't know how events will unfold. But I feel confident things between us will fizzle by then. If for no other reason, because I'm another Meg, a woman who'll want more than he'll want to give. So the way I see it, Meg never needs to know."

"You're so sure?" Dahlia asked.

"About the first part or the second?" Suzanne replied.

"Both."

"Yes to the first," she said. "We're in a cocoon right now, he and I. Once the cocoon opens up and the rest of life comes rushing in, he'll pull back."

"That's a grim speculation," Dahlia observed.

"But realistic, I think. I'm only being honest with myself."

"Perhaps you could just...take it day by day, without thinking so far into the future."

"That's what I'm doing, *mostly*," Suzanne said. "I'm just also preparing for the most likely outcome, rather than ending up heartbroken."

"You won't be heartbroken anyway?"

Suzanne blew out a breath. "Yes. But at least it won't come as a blow—I'll be ready."

"Back to the second part of the equation," Dahlia said. "You truly believe Meg doesn't need to know."

"No, I don't truly believe that. But I've got enough on my plate right now without telling her I'm sleeping with her ex. We're kind of mad at each other already, even without adding that into the mix."

"You and Meg—angry at one another?" Clearly, this stunned Dahlia. It still stunned Suzanne a little, too.

"She wanted to come to see Zack," Suzanne explained, "and I said no, that it would mess with his head and give him false hope—about the two of them."

"You wanted to keep him to yourself," Dahlia said without missing a beat.

"Maybe," Suzanne admitted. "But I also really *didn't* want him confused or led on."

"Understandable," Dahlia said. "I don't want him having any setbacks there, either. I confess that's a by-product I didn't consider when I asked her to help while I'm away. Though…maybe it's a worry of the past. Maybe he's moved on from her at last."

Suzanne took that in, but didn't hold on to it. So much uncertainty floated around her—she couldn't add any more. "Too many questions for me to answer, Dahlia," she replied, "and I need to go make dinner."

"All right," Dahlia said. "We'll talk again soon. Aloha, dear."

"Aloha?" Suzanne repeated, getting up to walk toward the kitchen. "You're in Hawaii?"

At this, however, Dahlia laughed. "Only in my mind. Afraid the sand my toes are parked in at the moment is slightly less exotic."

Despite all the things recently going right for Suzanne amid the depths of winter, the warmth of summer remained a lure. "Still sounds nice, though."

"Take care, Suz. And…give Zack a kiss for me." Dahlia hung up laughing.

LIFE HAD BEGUN to take on a sort of routine. A very different one than Suzanne could have imagined a month ago, but as the calendar page turned to February, it seemed almost normal that she was having sex with Zack on a regular basis. Not every night—some nights they only snuggled—but she'd pretty much quit sleeping in her own bed. And the snuggling nights were, in some ways, just as nice as the sex-having nights. Pieces of a whole that added up to feeling…well, almost like they *were* an item. Even if only for now, in their secret, isolated way.

It seemed almost normal that she got up in the morning, and after a hearty breakfast proceeded into Zack's physical therapy session. It seemed almost normal that she often watched Zack's talk shows with him in the afternoon, then helped with his second round of exercises before dinner. It seemed almost normal that each evening they decided together how to spend it: sometimes a board game, sometimes a movie. She liked continuing to find classics he hadn't seen, and in return, he forced her to watch *Weekend at Bernie's* and *Captain Ron*, which she actually enjoyed but refused to admit out of sheer stubbornness.

"I'll be back in an hour," she promised him now, bending over for a kiss goodbye. Ever since the day he'd fallen, she watched her time away closely and remembered to text or call if she ran late. He never thanked her—more acted as if she were being an overprotective mother hen type—but she knew deep down he appreciated the gesture.

First stop, Petal Pushers to water the bulbs. Upon leaving the shop, she spared a glance up the snow-covered street toward the inn. She hadn't talked to Meg in a while and knew she should. If for no other reason, to let her know about the feeling in Zack's leg, which continued to hold steady, though he claimed the sensation was gradually creeping downward. She feared it was wishful thinking, but never said so, supporting any optimistic thought he wanted to indulge in and believing hope—as much as anything else—led to healing.

She thought about walking down to the inn, knocking on the door, telling Meg everything. Just ripping the Band-Aid off the secrets she'd been keeping from her friend.

*But I told Zack I'd be back in an hour. And I need to go to the market.* So today wasn't the right day. *I'll do it soon, promise.* Though she wasn't even sure who she was promising. Meg? Dahlia? God? Herself? Maybe all of the above.

After a couple of days with dreary, overcast skies and on-and-off snow, this was another of those bright, cheerful ones that drew at least a few folks out of their cozy nests and into the sun. She said hello to Bob and Audrey Fisher, who were heading into the Skipper's Wheel for lunch—and randomly wished she could somehow bring Zack out for something as simple as a meal and a little sunshine. But Great Lakes island life in winter truly came with limitations. If they lived on the mainland and got around by car and shoveled their walkways, he could likely be out and about on his crutches. But going out on them here in the deep snow? Unimaginable.

Josh Callen waved to her from the window of the Cozy Coffee and Tea Shop and then opened the door to call, "I heard about Zack. How's he doing?"

She had no idea how many people knew about his injury, but she supposed word was gradually spreading. "He's doing really well," she said from the street with a smile. "Better than expected."

"That's great to hear," Josh said. Younger than both her and Zack, he was a personable guy with a wife and daughter—so personable that now he tilted his head to say, "Just so you know, I think you're a saint. I've worked with Zack—and I, uh, know he can be…"

Yep, Josh had been forced to help Zack with the town Christmas tree lights last month, which couldn't have been pleasant. Now, though, she simply leaned her head back and laughed. "Actually, he's…mellowed. Or something. We're getting along fine."

At this, Josh flinched in surprise. "Wow. You must have the magic touch."

His choice of words froze her in place, her cheeks heating despite the cold February temperatures. She only hoped she hadn't looked too caught-at-something as she pasted back on a smile and said, "I'll tell him you said hello."

The market bustled with upward of ten customers when she walked in—a veritable stampede for this time of year. Waving to Anson Tate, currently at the checkout, she grabbed up a shopping basket and headed to the deli counter for lunch meat and cheese. After picking up some ground beef and a whole chicken to fry, she was on her way to the baking aisle—Zack had requested more brownies—when she turned a corner and ran into Trent and Allie.

After exchanging hellos, Trent asked, "How's Zack doing?" He'd been another of Zack's unwitting victims on the tree-lighting crew.

Just as when Josh inquired, the question made her smile. "Really good, actually. It's still a very challenging situation, but he's showing a lot of improvement—he even has some sensation back in his leg."

Both of their faces brightened at the news. "That's amazing," Allie said.

"It truly is," Suzanne agreed, still smiling. Was she smiling too much, in fact? Did she sound *too* happy about taking care of a guy who'd been viewed as the town grump since splitting with Meg last summer? *But it's natural you'd be happy about his progress. Quit overthinking.*

"We wondered if you guys had considered having him airlifted to the mainland," Allie suggested. Then added cautiously, "But maybe that's not necessary now?"

The snow and clouds that often prevailed here in winter had kept Zack from getting to the mainland after becoming paralyzed, but indeed days had come—like this one—when the skies were clear. Yet Suzanne had never pushed it—partly because of the expense and Zack's lack of insurance, and partly because of his steady progress. "At this point, it probably makes more sense to wait until the ice melts, especially since he's doing better than expected."

"I hope he's not giving you too hard of a time," Trent said with a sympathetic grin.

She shook her head, perhaps too emphatically. And started to say how wonderfully they were getting along, but then bit her tongue. Her new affection for Zack somehow compelled her to defend his honor, but it suddenly seemed safer not to. So she played down her answer. "He's not so bad. We get along…fine." But she was still probably smiling too much.

"That's…good to hear," Trent replied in a way that made her fear she'd tipped her hand. But she was probably imagining that—she wasn't used to keeping secrets.

"Tell Zack we wish him well," Allie said, reaching out to squeeze Suzanne's hand.

"And hey, tell him if there's anything he needs, or even if he just wants to hang out, to give me a call," Trent offered. "And I mean that."

"I'll let him know," Suzanne said. Of course, Zack might think of it as pity, but if Trent was nice enough to make the gesture after having dealt with Zack's worst self over the holidays, she would pass it on. Reminding him he had more than just her and Dahlia to lean on sounded like a good idea.

But not Meg, of course, even though she'd certainly offered to visit, too. Because that was different, even Dahlia had agreed. *You really have to come clean with her, though.* Every new thought of her began to eat Suzanne alive with guilt.

"Hey, will I see you at the knitting bee Thursday night?" Allie asked.

It reminded her of the invitation that had come from Lila through Meg. "I'd love to," she said, "but I don't like leaving Zack alone for that long." She'd hate to come home and find his spirits dashed by another fall.

But Trent shrugged. "Tell him to invite me over for a beer. We can find a basketball game on TV or something."

She had no idea if Zack would be willing to let anyone else see him unable to get around freely, dragging his leg behind the crutches—but she said, "I'll run it by him and we'll see."

After the friendly couple walked away, she turned her attention to the brownie mixes, and as she added one to the basket looped over her arm, she heard a smooth, deep voice say, "Hello, Suzanne."

And she turned to find Beck Grainger, the breathtakingly handsome man who'd recently decimated her heart. All the air drained from her lungs at the mere sight of him.

"I didn't mean to eavesdrop," he said in his deliciously deep voice, "but I overheard you talking, and I just want to say I know you're in a tough position and hope you're doing okay."

Suzanne forced herself to look up at him, and realized…oh. She was. She really was.

Yes, he was still the tallest, hottest, most handsome drink of water she'd ever seen, but…she no longer pined for him. She'd been taken aback by his arrival—but it had been old embarrassment more than anything else. Her heart no longer went pitter-patter when she peered into his eyes. And now she was actually able to do that— peer into his eyes—without feeling overwhelmed, so she did, saying, "I'm doing fine, thanks—truly."

He smiled. A winning smile for sure, but one that no longer made her skin ripple with longing. "I'm glad to hear that."

She said the next right-seeming thing. "Congratulations on your engagement."

She hadn't intended to make him feel sheepish, but suddenly that was how he looked. "Thanks. I, uh, never planned for anything like that to happen so quickly— it just…did."

But she simply smiled, meaning it when she told him,

"I'm truly happy for you and Lila. You make a great couple."

"Thank you, Suzanne," he said, his expression saying he thought she was a class act. Which felt like a nice switch from a couple of months ago when she was pretty sure she'd behaved like a lovesick lunatic.

"Well," she said pleasantly, "I'd better get back to Zack. I promised him brownies and a game of checkers before his afternoon exercises."

At this, Beck tilted his head. "Oh, that's…great. I thought you didn't get along with him." Hmm, she must have shared that at some point, or maybe Meg had mentioned it.

"Well, I didn't," she said. "Before. But now I do. I mean, it's complicated. But we're good, he and I. Very good." She was nodding, repeatedly, and probably talking too fast now.

And so Beck nodded, too. "Well, that's…good news."

"Have a good…February," she said awkwardly, then rushed away, toward the registers.

Okay, she might have marred her "class act" vibe just a bit there. *Have a good February?* Why did she never shut up with him? She'd always had a babbling problem with him, and even now that she'd gotten over him, apparently it still persisted.

Well, at least it had been good to clear the air. And good to find out she was over him, and really fine with his engagement. She didn't give him another thought as she checked out, ready to head back to her patient with plans for baking brownies, battling him to the death at checkers, and later tonight, pushing him back onto that sofa bed and climbing on top of him.

ZACK LAY WITH Suzanne nuzzled against his chest, one arm wrapped around her, his free hand gently caressing her arm where it rested across his stomach. No sound in the room, just the soft ticking of a clock on the mantel that he'd long since gotten used to. He even liked it during those quiet times when he was alone—something about the forward movement of time reminded him he was still alive and things were always changing.

Of course, it wasn't always that easy. Sometimes, when she wasn't around, he got depressed—even now that things looked more positive than he'd expected. Mainly when he thought of the water—the hardworking days of summer, just him and the whitefish of Lake Huron being hauled up in his nets. Because no matter how much better his leg got, that life was gone now. Now, his grand goal was the idea of walking. He didn't even know if that was feasible, but it was what he dared to fall back on when he felt helpless.

He didn't let his mind float down that despairing river often, though. Hell, he didn't have time to—because the woman in his arms right now kept him so damn busy. Whether it was exercising or eating, watching a movie or playing a game, having sex or…this, just lying here soaking each other up without any words.

Meg had always liked to cuddle—Zack not so much. But this felt different. In his head, he joked that it was because Suzanne had a captive audience in him—that he didn't have the freedom to just get up and walk away. But the truth he knew deep inside was…he just liked it.

Maybe because it simply felt so much better than lying there alone, alone in a way no person with two good legs could ever understand. Or maybe timing was everything. He hadn't appreciated Meg as he should have. All she'd ever done was try to love him—and all he'd ever done was keep her at arm's length, put up a wall around himself that she couldn't penetrate. But he appreciated Suzanne. Because now he knew what it was to need someone, to have no choice in it, to just need them.

He had no idea what she felt for him, if she was dipping into that place where Meg had gone—love. But he didn't worry about it, because it just didn't sound as smothering or possessive as it had with Meg. That hadn't been Meg's fault—she'd given him his freedom. But back then, freedom had been something he could never have enough of. He'd chased it, like a boat sailing toward the unreachable horizon. Now freedom seemed like a smaller, more concrete thing. Freedom was being able to go to the bathroom by himself, dress himself. Freedom would be maybe eventually leaving the cottage when the snow melted.

"Did you give any thought to Trent coming over tomorrow night?" Suzanne asked.

He glanced down at her, having thought she was asleep. As for Trent, he'd been trying to dodge the subject, hoping it wouldn't come up again after she'd mentioned it a couple of days ago. "Aw, I don't know, Suzie Q."

"Might be a nice change of pace," she suggested hopefully. Always so hopeful, this one. Which he'd actually come to love about her—except for when it worked against him, like now.

"Look," he said, avoiding eye contact, "You can go to your knitting party without worrying about me—I'll take care of myself and keep my phone handy. But…"

"Listen, I get it," she said softly.

The simple statement drew his eyes unwittingly to hers. Which were rich and blue as a north woods lake, and filled with an understanding that told him: she really did get it. Even without him giving one word of explanation.

"Once upon a time," she said, "you weren't comfortable with *me*, the way things are now." She chose her words carefully when they talked about this, a small kindness that made him value her even more. "But Trent's a good guy, and I think he just wants to get out, spend some time with a buddy."

"I barely know him," Zack said dryly.

Yet she ignored that and went on. "I realize it feels like a big deal to you—but people really *will* understand, and it'll be okay. And, well, when the snow melts and we all start going outside again—"

"I'll probably stay inside anyway," he interrupted her a bit grimly.

But she playfully patted his chest. "No, you won't. You'll go out. Because you'll want to be outside more than you'll want people not to see you. And you'll quit feeling weird about it." Adding a succinct nod, she concluded with confidence, "And having Trent over will be like...training for that. And I'll feel better going if I know you're not here alone and bored."

Another thoughtful choice of words. Since she really meant "not here alone getting yourself into a situation you can't get out of." But she had a way of making all this feel more normal than it was.

And she had him pegged—he didn't really want Trent, the handsome lawyer who had everything going for him, to see him this way. Zack had always found the younger guy a little too accomplished and good-looking for his own good. But he actually liked him, despite having yelled at his ineptness during the Christmas tree lighting. Being inept wasn't a reason not to like someone—Zack found *most* people inept. And everything Suzanne had just said was true—so finally he relented. "Okay, he can come over. On one condition."

"Hooray." She smiled. "What's the condition? Anything you want."

In response, he shifted their bodies until she lay on her back with him angled over her, and he leaned to whisper in her ear, "I want to be on top."

When he pulled back, her look bordered between amused and confused. And maybe a little aroused. "That's fine with me. I just thought…"

"I know what you thought," he told her. "And you were right. But I think maybe now I can…have my way with you." He ended with a playfully lecherous grin.

Which drew from her a cute and sexy smile, followed by, "Do your worst."

"Oh, I plan to," he promised—and even if he wasn't certain he could maneuver himself the way he wanted, he was damn ready and willing to try. Not that he didn't like Suzanne on top of him. But he wanted to give her more than what might be starting to feel like the same old thing. And he wanted some control. And he also wanted to show her body the appreciation it deserved. So he didn't plan to rush this.

Unbuttoning her pajama top, he kissed his way down her luscious breasts, framing them with his hands, suckling the peaks, loving her little gasps and sighs. Gliding his palms down the curve of her waist, he kissed her stomach—not the stomach of a young girl, he realized, but he didn't *want* the stomach of a young girl. Suzanne was real, solid, with some meat on her bones that was far nicer to squeeze and hold on to than if she'd been skinny. His mouth passed over two tiny scars he'd learned were from gallbladder removal, and a host of freckles and "age spots," she'd once called them. He didn't like the name—he thought *experience spots* might be better. He wouldn't have changed a thing.

Together they removed her pajama bottoms and undies, him all the while dropping kisses across the contours of her hips and the rise of her pelvis—until he parted her legs, licking and kissing until she toppled into a bliss that felt thick and replete as it spilled over him. Or maybe he was the one who felt replete in having delivered it.

Mostly he favored the left side of his body as he moved and shifted, letting his left leg do the work of both. He used it to position himself back up over her, liking when her hands closed over his ass to help drag him upward—without saying a word about why. She made it so simple.

"You have a nice butt," she whispered.

He gave her a grin. She wasn't one to engage in sexy talk, so much so that this struck him as bold. "So do you," he told her. "Especially when you're dancing."

She laughed, confused. "What?"

"That's when I first…you know…started getting attracted to you. Watching your ass sway to 'Suzie Q.'"

And as Zack's erection pressed rigidly against the juncture of her thighs, he knew the moment of truth had come. She couldn't help him do *this*. He prayed his body could muster whatever it would take to let him drive into her the way he ached to.

Gazing into welcoming crystalline eyes, he focused on the wanting. The way he wanted to pleasure her, the way he wanted to pleasure himself, the way he wanted to be the man he *used* to be—strong, sturdy, capable. Gripping her hips, he thrust, felt the tight entry, heard her soft cry of pleasure. And then he gave himself over to it without thought, plunging into her, over and over, being that man for her, the man he wanted to be. He lost himself in every slick stroke into her warmth—and it wasn't long before bliss stole him away, too.

He collapsed gently atop her soft body, burying his face in the curve of her neck, drinking in her feminine scent, and feeling…happy. He'd possessed more control than he'd believed possible.

A thought compelled him to roll off her sooner than he wanted to—but he needed to look at something, look at his leg. Lying next to her in the low light of her living room, he peered down the length of his naked body and tried to move his right leg.

"Suzanne, am I imagining it, or…"

"You're moving your knee," she said quietly.

Just a little, and it took way more effort than the result looked like it should, but…

"You're moving your knee, Zack. You're moving your knee!"

## CHAPTER SEVENTEEN

ZACK'S LATEST MILESTONE had been celebrated with much yipping and howling with joy, and also with brownies, which had been deemed the next best thing behind sex. "Because, sorry, Suzie Q, but it's too soon for me to do it again that fast."

"Don't worry," she'd told him on a laugh, "it's too soon for me, too. I'll go get the brownies and wine." The two most wonderfully mismatched things she could think of for two wonderfully mismatched people to celebrate with.

Now morning had come and they'd started a new day with breakfast and PT, during which he'd continued to succeed in moving his right leg. It clearly took tremendous effort, but Suzanne remained thrilled and amazed. As they sat down in the living room, Zack turned on the TV and Suzanne said, "I'm going to text Dahlia about your knee."

"Sounds good," he replied. Most mornings Dahlia called, but not always and she hadn't today. Suzanne supposed she and Zack had both started taking it in stride, considering Dahlia's recent unpredictability a by-product of her travels.

And Suzanne was also going to tell Meg. Because she should have before now. Despite the current complications in their friendship, Meg deserved to know he was making strides—and perhaps it would provide reassurance that Zack didn't need her, thereby putting all that tension to rest. It would still leave the *other* big tension—the tension Meg didn't even know about yet—but Suzanne would address that soon.

She texted Dahlia: I have amazing news! Zack moved his knee a little last night!

Then she texted Meg: Hey, ready for some great news? Zack has some feeling back in his leg, and he can even move his knee a little! He's been making great progress.

Dahlia texted back right away. Oh my, my, my! Best news I could possibly receive. He's ecstatic, I'm sure.

And before Suzanne could answer Dahlia, Meg replied, too. Really? That's so great! I'm so happy for him! Do you think it will lead to a full recovery?

To Dahlia, she said: Of course. We're both thrilled. He moved it some during morning PT, too!

And to Meg: Only time will tell. But I'll be glad when he can get a real prognosis come spring.

Even if, in a way, she was beginning to *dread* the coming of spring. She'd never dreamed such a feeling was possible. It was…attachment. And loving things just the way they were. Well, except for Zack's injury, of course. And that was why, even while she dreaded spring, she also knew it brought with it hope, and answers.

Dahlia texted again to say, That's so wonderful! Give the boy a big kiss from his loving auntie. Which made Suzanne laugh a little, because she was pretty sure Dahlia knew any kiss from Suzanne wouldn't be aunt-like.

And Meg answered with, Please tell him I'm very happy for him. And thank you for letting me know, Suz. I miss you.

Suzanne took all of that in. Meg still pushing for Zack

to know she cared. But the fact that Meg still missed her tugged at her heart.

She answered Dahlia first—it was so much easier, and she could be more honest. I will. And you'll be happy to know we're still getting along VERY well. She ended with a winking emoji.

Only—crap—she hadn't sent it to Dahlia; she'd sent it to Meg.

She looked at her screen. How damning was it? Not… completely damning. But…well, at least the *I will* part made sense anyway.

Her heart pounded as she stared at the phone, waiting for a reply. It took longer than the others. *God, does she know? Did that one line completely spill the beans?* Then a reply from Meg arrived. I'm glad to hear that. I'm sure it makes the situation easier.

Suzanne read it a couple of times, trying to analyze it, feeling—as usual—all the maturity of a high schooler. Then she looked to Zack. "I'm going into my bedroom to call Dahlia."

He glanced absently from the TV to her. "Why do you have to go in the bedroom?"

"Girl talk," she said.

This time he didn't bother moving his eyes from the screen as he said, "I already know you told her we're doing it if that's your girl talk."

"Oh." She blinked. "How?"

"She quit asking me. She wouldn't have quit asking me if she didn't already know. And actually—" now he shifted his eyes to her "—I guess you did me a favor since it saves me from having to deal with it."

She gave a nod. But then stood up. "I'm still going to the bedroom. Different girl talk."

He arched one brow, appearing amused. "You're not

having sex with anybody else, right? All these errands you go on. Hooking up with the butcher at Koester's? One of the cooks at the Skipper's Wheel?"

But, amused or not, it sounded almost as if he actually considered them…well, an item. "No, it's entirely different girl talk altogether. About other girls, actually. And I wouldn't have the time or the energy to sleep with anyone else—you, Zack Sheppard, are a full-time job." With that, she headed to the bedroom, closed the door, and called Dahlia.

Her older friend didn't bother with a hello, instead answering with, "If you're calling to give me all the naughty details, I'm in."

"I'm not," Suzanne firmly informed her. Instead, she explained what had just happened with Meg. "I'm worried I tipped her off."

She probably should have expected Dahlia's airy response. "Does it matter? She'll find out sooner or later."

Dahlia always handled everything with such a carefree attitude—which was probably something Suzanne should aspire to. As soon as she dealt with this sleeping-with-Meg's-ex situation, which felt pretty dramatic to her even if it didn't to Dahlia. Maybe *nothing* felt dramatic when you were a thousand miles away sipping rum runners in the sun. Maybe that explained Dahlia's mysterious behavior altogether—perhaps she was so far away that everything happening here seemed like a fairy tale or, more accurately, a soap opera.

"Guess I was hoping for later," Suzanne said. "And definitely not over text. I want to be able to explain, make her understand."

"Don't fret," Dahlia replied. "You'll find the right time to tell her, on your own terms."

MEG AND LILA walked up Harbor Street, dusk leaving the snow almost tinted with gray. Both carried baskets of yarn and related tools.

"I'm so excited about this it's ridiculous," Lila said, smiling. Indeed, her giddiness outshone the occasion— but it was her first winter here, and even in the glow of new love, February on Summer Island could begin to wear on a person.

"It's nice to get out," Meg said in a more measured way—even as the lights of the Knitting Nook up the street beckoned warmly. She'd never knitted, but she crocheted a bit, and she'd started a multi-colored scarf at the last bee.

"Then why do you seem so glum about it?" Lila asked.

It irritated Meg that her mood showed—but she and Lila had grown closer lately, so despite that they didn't always approach the world the same way, she decided to confide in her. "There's something on my mind," she said. "Do you think it's possible…anything could be going on between Suzanne and Zack?"

"Why?" Lila asked. Instead of just saying no. Hmm.

Meg explained the weird text she'd gotten from Suzanne yesterday, ending with, "Don't get me wrong— I'm thrilled about his progress. But the other part stuck in my head, about them getting along so well. And the wink. What did the wink mean? It just seemed like maybe…"

"But if that's what she meant, why would she be talking to you about it in a cryptic way, and like it was nothing?"

Oh. Emotion had kept Meg from seeing that very sensible angle.

"On the other hand," Lila began, but then trailed off, peering back ahead.

"On the other hand what?"

"Well, Beck ran into Suzanne at the market one day and got a similar idea. He said she kept smiling as she talked about him. I thought he was jumping to silly conclusions. And maybe he was. Maybe you are, too. Because I'm sure she wouldn't…you know, do that."

Meg tried to weigh it all. Beck's observation gave her pause. But Lila was right. "I'm sure she wouldn't, either. She could barely even tolerate Zack until recently. And even if he and I are history, friends just don't get involved with each other's exes."

"So then maybe the point of her text was—hey, I don't hate him anymore," Lila suggested.

"Yeah, maybe so," Meg said as they stepped up onto the low porch that lined the Knitting Nook and connected coffee shop, also open for the occasion.

Allie opened the front door to greet them. "Come in, come in," she said with a smile. "So good to see my new manager and her lovely sister."

As Meg and Lila followed the usual protocol of shedding their snow boots on a big mat by the door, Meg recognized Suzanne's boots already there. Her stomach churned—despite the earlier invitation, she hadn't expected Suzanne to come, and now she only prayed they could put the awkwardness behind them. And, of course, that both she and Beck had jumped to crazy conclusions and that Lila—not always seen as the levelheaded one—was correct on this particular subject.

Audrey Fisher and the elderly Mrs. Bixby sat in easy chairs in one corner, knitting and chatting, coffee cups nearby. Another group that included Allie's mother congregated in a different corner, and still a few more attendees perused the shelves that lined the walls, filled with every color of yarn. By herself in a small grouping of chairs near the back sat Suzanne.

Suzanne didn't knit, either, despite Lila having tried to teach her on a loom a couple of months ago, so she sat cupping a mug of cocoa in her hands and looking a little lonely. Lila asked quietly, "Do you want to sit with Suzanne?"

"Yes," Meg said without hesitation.

Suzanne looked up as they approached. "It's so good to see you both."

"I'm glad you're here," Meg told her.

"Up to now," she said, "it's been hard to leave Zack. He fell once when I was away, and it became…an issue. But Trent came over tonight with some beer and stuff to make nachos, so I'm happy for a girls' night out."

When Lila let out a laugh at what constituted a girls' night on Summer Island in winter, Meg just smiled and said, "Get used to it."

As they settled in, starting on their projects, Lila again tried to interest Suzanne in working with looms, and Meg focused on her scarf, and things actually felt… normal. Normal when they discussed the weather. Normal when they shared who they'd seen where—a little island gossip was everything by the time February came. And normal even when they talked about Zack's injury and progress in more detail. Meg didn't think Suzanne seemed too smiley at all—she simply seemed pleased in the way any caregiver would. *So I worried for nothing.*

The conversation spread across the room—Mrs. Bixby asked about Zack, and Suzanne replied with a more generic but upbeat progress report.

"Trent was glad Zack wanted him to come over tonight," Allie said. "He's still getting used to our winters."

"Him and me both," Lila announced. "Thank God for knitting bees."

"How is Dahlia's vacation going?" Audrey Fisher asked.

And Suzanne answered, "Fine. She seems to be enjoying the beach."

"She's lucky you agreed to look after Zack," Mrs. Bixby said.

"Well…it's convenient that I have a background in nursing."

"I heard that from Allie," Mrs. Hobbs said. "I hadn't realized you were a nurse."

"Don't let it get around," Suzanne said on a laugh. "It's good for emergencies like this, but I wouldn't feel comfortable going around unofficially treating every person on the island."

When the bigger conversation faded and people turned back to their smaller circles, relief washed over Suzanne. Every question had felt like a potential minefield to tiptoe through. And being face-to-face with Meg while a huge secret stood between them had her feeling guilty and on edge. So she resolved to tell Meg tonight. Later, when the crowd thinned. She'd find the right moment, pull her aside, or maybe even into the coffee shop. Regardless of where, though, she *had* to tell Meg before the evening ended.

"Have you talked to Dahlia much?" Meg asked her now.

Suzanne nodded. "Fairly often. Keeping her updated on Zack."

Meg sighed. "She's called me a few times. But for some reason, I haven't felt as comfortable calling *her*. I guess her leaving just still feels…off to me."

"I've mostly moved past it," Suzanne said. "Even if I'll never quite understand it."

"Where is she exactly?" Lila asked.

Suzanne said, "I'm not sure, to tell you the truth. She hasn't said much about it. Or…maybe I haven't really asked, first because I was mad and then later just busy with Zack. But somewhere on the Gulf Coast of Florida, I think. Originally they flew to Grand Cayman, but she recently told me Fort Myers when I asked."

Across a small table where their mugs all rested, Meg tilted her head and said, "She told me the Florida Keys, just last week. Islamorada to be exact."

The three of them exchanged looks, and Meg smirked lightly as Suzanne rolled her eyes. "That's Dahlia for you. Lately anyway."

"Maybe they're moving around a lot, not staying in one place," Lila suggested.

"And speaking of they," Meg said, "did you ever find out any more about this Giselle person?"

Suzanne shook her head. "I know she makes a mean mai tai, but that's about it." Then she let out a sigh, remembering a conversation from the last time she'd been here with Dahlia, in December. "I guess Dahlia won't finish her blanket this winter after all."

"Oh, that's right," Lila said. "She declared she was going to. Well, maybe next winter."

"Maybe," Suzanne said. "Or not." For some reason, she just didn't feel as if Dahlia's heart was in the same place as it had been before the holidays.

"Could this all be about Mr. Desjardins?" Lila asked.

And Suzanne sat up a little straighter. She'd been in the debonair gentleman's corner the whole time he'd been smitten with Dahlia last fall.

"You don't think she's really with Mr. Desjardins?" Meg asked. "That there is no Giselle?"

Lila shook her head. "No, just that...well, maybe she regretted her decision. Maybe it put her in a funk."

Suzanne shrugged. "There was a time when I thought she'd really begun to care for him—right before she sent him packing and wouldn't talk to me about it. So... maybe."

That was when Allie walked up with a smile and said, "I'm so glad you felt comfortable leaving Zack to come out tonight, Suzanne."

She nodded. "Me, too." And left it at that. It had been nice to leave the minefield behind for safer ground and she didn't particularly want to return.

"When Trent and I saw you in the market, it just made our day to hear how well he's doing. And it was clear to see how happy it makes *you*, too."

*Okay, the minefield is getting more dangerous.* She barely knew where to step. "Yeah, I never expected him to progress so much before spring."

"Well, it was obvious how much you care about him. You couldn't stop smiling when you talked about him. We both think you're exactly what Zack needs right now."

*Kaboom.*

At some point, Suzanne's eyes had glazed over—she kept looking at Allie but couldn't see her anymore. She could only feel...horror. Allie clearly didn't understand what she was saying. Did she not know how much Meg used to love Zack? Did she not know about the tragic breakup just last summer? Maybe she *didn't*—she was younger than them, only a casual friend despite being a lifelong islander. She obviously meant no malice, her tone pleasant and kind.

When no one said another single word, however, Allie finally caught on. Way too late. "Oh—I hope I'm not speaking out of turn. Forget I said anything." It came out playfully, though—like she'd just spilled the beans on a sweet secret that Meg and Lila would now gush over and congratulate Suzanne on.

And as Allie flitted away, Suzanne couldn't look at either Sloan sister. Now would be a good time to have some knitting to focus on. As it was, she stared into an empty hot chocolate mug at the little brown dregs in the bottom. And that was what she felt like. A dreg.

When Meg's voice came, it was low, strained, disbelieving. "You and Zack?"

Suzanne began to sweat, her body heating up from the inside out, her face feeling as if it might melt right off. She tried to raise her gaze to Meg's, but she didn't make it, couldn't force it, and stopped at the half-knitted scarf currently abandoned in her best friend's lap. When she summoned the will to speak, it came out sounding mouse-like. "Kind of."

"Kind of?" Meg repeated accusingly.

The two little words sucked all the air out of the space between them. Or at least Suzanne, for one, struggled to breathe. She kept trying to look at Meg, but still couldn't—unable to face the hurt and betrayal glimmering in Meg's eyes.

"How could you?" Meg asked, her voice quiet but venomous. "How could you do that to me?"

As if the act was a direct stab at her. As if it had anything to do with her at all. And even though Suzanne had completely expected this reaction, the words somehow offended her. "Well, it's not like I waltzed up to him at a singles bar and asked what his sign is. I didn't put the moves on him or anything. I didn't even want him in my house. It just…happened."

One daring glimpse of Meg's eyes revealed that she remained livid. "That's what everyone says who's been with someone they shouldn't have. How long? When did it start?"

Suzanne shook her head, trying to think. Days ran together in winter here, even now with all the unlikely events happening in her cottage. "A couple of weeks?"

Meg's jaw dropped and she appeared even more aghast, if that was possible. "Oh my God—and you kept it from me? For that long?"

Suzanne had lived a relatively careful, crime-free life, and she'd never felt so put on the spot. "I didn't know how to tell you. I was worried how you'd react, and I was right."

"Well, can you blame me?"

*No, of course not. I'm a miserable excuse for a friend. You have every reason to be angry.* All along, those were the things Suzanne had expected herself to say at this moment. She'd intended to fall on her sword, admit her transgression, and beg Meg's forgiveness. But now that it was really happening, she no longer felt that way. Perhaps, deep down, some hidden, hopeful part of her had believed Meg would forgive, say it was okay. Up until lately, Meg had always been even-keeled and understanding, sometimes even when she had every right not to be. Maybe she'd been praying that part of Meg would return.

And Suzanne had always wanted Meg to stand up for herself, not let Zack or anyone else push her around. But *she* didn't want to be pushed around, either. And it was a big ask, a *huge* ask, but she wanted—so, so badly—for Meg to just understand. "Well, maybe you could just…

try to be happy for me. Maybe you could remember that my husband died years ago and I've been so afraid— afraid of sex, afraid of romance, afraid of feelings. And I've been...alone. Not just without Cal. But without you, Meg. I'm so glad you found Seth—you deserve that kind of happiness—but it hasn't been the same between us since he came along. We've never said so, either of us, but surely you know that. And it's okay. I understand. But I've missed you. And when you left in December, that was the worst. I had only Dahlia to turn to—and now she's done *her* disappearing act, too, and...who did that leave me, Meg? Who did it leave me?" She shook her head helplessly. "It left me the paralyzed man on my couch, who needed my help. So I'm sorry if somewhere along the way during the weeks we've spent isolated to- gether, he and I built a connection. I'm sorry if I started caring about him. I'm sorry if I fell in love with him."

Across from her, Meg blinked. "You love him?"

It was as big a shock to Suzanne as to Meg. Her heart threatened to beat right through her chest. "I guess I do," she said softly. "But don't worry. I know who he is. I know he won't be around forever. Even without the use of one leg, I know he'll leave. And I'll be alone again. But for right now, maybe it's just nice to think someone gives a damn about me."

Meg appeared too stunned to speak, and next to her Lila sat still as a stone. In fact, the entire yarn shop had gone silent—and Suzanne realized everyone stared in their direction. This was a nightmare—one she didn't know how to get out of. She was mortified in front of every woman on the island, brokenhearted over what was surely the final straw in this friendship, and shell- shocked to have admitted—not only to everyone else but also to herself—that she'd fallen in love with the last man she could have imagined. Her chest hurt and her stomach ached as she set down her mug, stood up, and said, "I'm sorry if you hate me," as she started for the door.

Except—crap. She had to put on her boots before she could leave. Great, just great. She fumbled with them, hands trembling, as the room remained quiet enough to hear a knitting needle drop. She kept her eyes on her boots, on her hands. Then reached shakily up to a coat tree, snatching off her long parka and tossing it around her shoulders, thrusting her arms in the sleeves. *Grab your scarf, your hat, your gloves. Deal with the rest once you're out the door.*

This wasn't the first long, awkward exit she'd made on this island—in fact, it was beginning to feel like a hideous sort of pattern, one she desperately hoped to break. For now, she just needed to get the hell out of here, with or without her dignity. Though she was pretty sure it was the latter.

## CHAPTER EIGHTEEN

EVEN AFTER THE Knitting Nook door slammed, the tension remained. It was Allie who finally spoke. "Should... someone go after her? Make sure she's okay?"

Meg didn't know the right answer. To anything, it seemed. Yet Allie was looking at her as if she were in charge. She gave her head a lost, helpless shake—and Lila responded for her. "I...think she'd rather be alone."

Allie nodded. "I'll text Trent in a bit—to be sure she got home all right."

Meg only realized that she was staring at her hands, fisted on top of her unfinished scarf, when Lila reached over to touch one of them. "Maybe we should call it a night, too."

She felt frozen in place, still trying to process what had just happened. Suzanne was sleeping with Zack. Suzanne loved Zack. And everyone on the island knew Meg was upset about it. Talk about dirty laundry. "Yes," she said quietly.

And as they stuffed their yarn in their totes, Allie crossed the room to ask Mrs. Bixby, "Is this sweater for your granddaughter?" and people began chatting again, about surface topics like knitting and recipes, all clearly thankful to do so. Meg was grateful, too, as it allowed her and Lila to exit a little less dramatically than Suzanne.

Though as they hit the porch, Allie called behind her, "Meg?"

They looked back to see Allie standing in the doorway. "I'm so sorry if I assumed things I shouldn't have." She gave her head a short shake. "I thought you were…" Another headshake. "I'm so sorry."

"It's okay," Meg said. "You didn't know." *That I didn't know my best friend was sleeping with my ex. And that I would be devastated to find out.*

"Take care," Allie told them, still looking fraught. "Be safe walking home."

"Goodnight," Lila said. And as they stepped down off the porch into the snowy street, she looked back to Meg. "I guess Allie thought you'd be okay with it. She was raised here—maybe having such a small dating pool gives people a different perspective."

Meg was still trying to catch her breath over the whole thing. But the part that weighed on her the most was… "Why *do* I care so much? Don't I want them both to be happy? And if that happens to be with each other, why does that matter to me?"

Lila let her off the hook. "You had very strong feelings for him. And now she has what you once wanted. It's natural." But it stung that Suzanne couldn't see it that way. Despite the pardon, Meg still felt selfish. And, at the same time, wounded.

"*Maybe* she has what I wanted—or maybe he'll ultimately not want anything real with her, either," Meg reasoned. "But even if that's the case, I'm still just as hurt."

"Because she broke the girlfriend code," Lila said as they trudged through the dark, snow-covered night up the silent street. "She put bros before hos."

Meg just looked at her. "Did you really just say that?"

Lila shook her head. "Sorry—I'm on edge right now.

I'm trying to be comforting, I really am. It's just hard because…she broke the code, for sure, and yet…"

Meg blinked. "Yet what?"

"Yet…this is such an extreme situation. He's partially paralyzed. And they've been forced into this really strange, really intimate position. And…maybe I feel bad for her because she cared for Beck and he ended up with me. And it's not like you're alone—you have Seth, hottest guy west of the Mississippi. And…and…if they were celebrities, people would start calling them Su-Zack, which is kind of cute, and please don't hate me for saying that, too."

Oh God—it *was* kind of cute. Meg's heart plummeted further. "So you think it's okay, her being with him."

"I don't know *what* I think," Lila admitted with a brisk shake of her head. "I'm not sure there's a right or wrong here, Meg. But I know it hurts you, and I get why. And I'm sorry."

Meg reached out her free hand, looping it around Lila's elbow. Even through thick coats, it made her feel a little less alone right now. "And you know what sucks on top of it all? Now I have to go into the house I share with a man I love and try to hide that I'm upset. Because if he knew why I was upset, he wouldn't understand, either. But hiding it from him is like lying to him. So I'm damned if I do and I'm damned if I don't. Everything is just a mess."

Lila stayed silent for a long moment. Then finally said, "Want my advice?"

A few months ago, Meg would have answered with a hard no. But her little sister had grown up a lot lately, and tonight in particular it felt as if they'd changed places completely, as if Lila was the mature, steady one and

Meg the helpless, emotional one. Well, if she didn't count the bros and hos comment anyway. So she said, "Sure."

"If I were you right now," Lila said, "I'd go look deep into Seth's eyes and remember what made you choose him over Zack. I'd put everything else out of my mind and just soak that up. And maybe also have some rockin' hot sex while you're at it as, you know, kind of a cherry on top of an appreciation sundae."

Meg looked over at her. "When did you get so wise?"

"I think I'm just…rising to the occasion or something. Someone has to steer this ship and if you can't do it, I'm forced to take over."

"I want to take the wheel again, believe me," Meg said. "I'm just not sure how I'm ever going to get over this. I never imagined things could turn out this way."

SUZANNE WALKED IN the door ready to force a smile, hopeful that low nighttime lighting might hide her expression.

"You're back sooner than I expected," Zack said from where he and Trent sat watching basketball.

How to answer. Especially knowing that Allie would surely tell Trent everything. But for now, she'd keep it simple. "Things started breaking up early." Not even a lie. Since the scene she'd made surely had all the knitters scattering for home by now.

"Have fun?" Zack asked.

Talk about a loaded question. She turned her back to unzip her coat, hang it up. "It was nice to get out." Also not a lie—it *had* been nice, until all hell broke loose. "Did you guys have fun?" She still didn't look over at them, taking off her snow boots.

"Yep," Trent said. "Zack here is way better company when there aren't Christmas lights involved."

She laughed in spite of herself, glad things had gone well.

Zack shored that up by saying, "This guy makes some mean nachos, Suzie Q. Almost makes up for how bad he tangles up light cords."

Once free of her boots, there was nothing to do but walk over to the sitting area and try to keep acting normal. Though she was grateful when Trent took her return as his cue to leave. "Guess I'd better pack up my nacho tray and head home," he said with a grin.

"Don't feel like you have to rush off on my account," she said anyway, to be polite. Like she normally was. When she wasn't freaking out in the middle of yarn shops.

But Trent said, "Eh, game's a blowout anyway." He stood up, giving Zack a hearty handshake in parting. "Was good to hang out, buddy."

"Yeah, thanks for coming," Zack said. "You and your nachos are welcome anytime."

After Suzanne shut the door behind their guest a moment later, she said, "So, great nachos, huh?"

Zack picked up the remote and muted the TV. "What's wrong, Suzie Q?"

She turned to face him, taken aback. "Nothing."

"Something."

She pursed her lips, walked over, and sat down in the chair Trent had just vacated. "How can you tell? I thought I was hiding it so well."

He shrugged. "Guess I've gotten to know you. Your face was a little pinched up."

She blew out a long sigh. "I had a confrontation with Meg."

His brow furrowed. "What about?"

"You," she said simply.

He balked. "What about me?"

Men. They could be so thick at times. "Because we're sleeping together."

His eyes narrowed in deeper confusion. "So?"

She gave another tired sigh. "So she's your ex."

"Yeah," he said. "But…she's the one who ended things." He tilted his head slightly. "Am I the only one who remembers that part?"

"It doesn't matter," Suzanne explained. "She once cared about you and that makes you off-limits."

He drew back a bit. "Huh. For how long?"

Suzanne scrunched up her mouth, first this way and then that. "Pretty much forever."

At this, he raised his eyebrows and said, "That's not really gonna work, now is it?"

"No, it would seem not," she said quietly. "But I still feel awful."

He shook his head. "Not sure I get it."

She tried to concoct a way to make him understand. "Okay, think of the first girl you ever fell completely in love with. And then think about, after you broke up, how you would have felt if your best friend was with her. Does that help?"

"Nope." He shook his head.

"Why not?"

"Never really had a girl like that. Or a friend like that."

Oh. Wow. No wonder he couldn't grasp it. It merely reminded Suzanne once more how closed off he was to relationships. *What you and he share—that feels like a relationship. But when it comes right down to it, Zack doesn't know* how *to love someone.* And she still had no idea why—she only knew it made it that much worse that *she* loved *him.*

"So Meg is really mad at you over this?" he asked, still appearing utterly perplexed.

"Yes," she said. "And just so you know, we made a scene. At the Knitting Nook. And by 'we,' I mean mostly me. I ranted and raved, and if the party broke up early it's because I did the breaking. Which I mention because...well, first, I'm mortified. And second, after tonight pretty much the whole island will know we're sleeping together. So...sorry."

He shrugged. "Doesn't bother *me*. I got bigger things on my plate than island gossip."

It reminded her to ask, "Did everything go okay while I was gone?"

He gave a relaxed nod. In fact, everything *about* him seemed more relaxed than she'd expected after having a visitor. "Once he realized I could get myself around okay he quit hovering, and after that I pretty much planted my ass in this chair all night so neither one of us would have to worry about it."

It made her happy, calmer, to know he'd had a good night, perhaps found a real friend. "Maybe he'll come back again to watch another ball game or something." Then she made a face. "If Allie isn't afraid of me now."

Zack gave her a look that reached down into her soul. "Listen, Suzie Q, whatever happened tonight, people on this island know you and love you. It'll be all right."

"Thank you," she said softly. She'd needed that simple reminder. "I handled things badly, though. Instead of apologizing, I got defensive."

"Regardless, I'm sorry to cause a fight between you. I know you and Meg are close."

"Used to be," she said glumly. "Things have changed lately. Not just because of this—even before. I just kept trying to ignore it. Now I can't anymore."

"WHAT HAS YOU SMILING?" Giselle asked.

Dahlia peeked up at her. "Look at that sunset. Would it be totally clichéd to call it God's handiwork?"

Giselle shook her head. "Not at all."

"Still, I like to think of myself as being more original. People see me as having flair, not falling back on clichés."

Giselle just shrugged. "Clichés are only clichés because they're true, and I'm not sure flair and clichés are always that far apart."

Dahlia refocused on the sunset. So orange it was nearly scarlet—a slash of color that felt full of power, not serene at all. "Perhaps it's God saying, 'Look at me! Here I am! You people say you can't see me, but I'm right here, a swoosh of neon before your eyes.'"

Giselle smiled. "Now that was flair. Thought-provoking flair."

And Dahlia smiled as well, if a bit smugly. "Good to know I've still got it."

"Working on your letters?"

Dahlia looked down at the stationery and pen she'd forgotten in her lap when the sunset grabbed her attention. "Yes—I started them while you were napping."

"When I was young, I had a pen pal. From England," Giselle said, giving her head a thoughtful tilt. "I can't tell you the last time someone wrote me a letter."

"A forgotten art," Dahlia replied.

Giselle pointed into Dahlia's lap. "You're using a purple pen."

She held it up between them. "Flair."

"I promise you, Dahlia, that no one would ever accuse you of not having flair. More of it in your little finger than most of us have in our whole bodies." Giselle took a seat in the Adirondack chair next to hers, then glanced to a book on a nearby table. "If you want to get back to your letters, I can read."

Dahlia set the stationery and pen aside, saying, "Finishing the last one can wait—I don't want to squander this sunset. I'm very eager to see how it evolves, how exactly it fades into night." She pointed toward the horizon and said, "Such a sunset reminds me of Hawaii. I don't know if they're truly more vibrant there—or if that's just in my head."

Giselle slanted her a look. "Speaking of Hawaii, you never did tell me about your second husband."

Dahlia smiled wistfully, thinking back on that big, loving hunk of a man. "Never the most handsome," she said to Giselle, holding up one finger, "but the most guileless and the most giving of perhaps the purest love I've received. He asked little and rewarded me with much. He was the kind of rich that poor girls like me could only dream of. And for entirely different reasons, my favorite of my three husbands—which is why I went back to using his name later, long after he was gone from my life."

"What happened? What's the story of you and Tom Delaney?"

Dahlia sighed, remembering the whirlwind of it all in just a few seconds. She'd never understood how someone's entire life could flash before them when they faced death, but maybe it was something like the way her entire marriage to Tom flashed in her mind as she began describing it to Giselle.

"He gave me the world. Literally. Spain, Belgium, Italy, the Maldives. We spent the first three months of our marriage in Hawaii—I learned to hula dance and he *tried* to surf, but was, sadly, too big and tall a man. I admired his spirit for attempting it, though. Later, we spent a month in Alaska, but it was too dark for me—we went on a lark, during the wrong time of year.

"We stayed in London for a period. And Tuscany—ah, Tuscany. The hill towns captured my heart and whisked me back in time. He was a great fan of Paris—I suppose most people are—but I never felt as embraced there as I did most places we ventured. And it rained for a great deal of our stay, which just puts a damper on anything if you're not a fan of it.

"We came back to his ranch in Montana, but I was quickly bit with wanderlust again, and we spent a winter in Puerto Vallarta sipping tequila and soaking up the sun. The following summer we rented a cabin in the Canadian Rockies—and oh, the lakes in that region, Giselle. Have you ever been?"

Giselle shook her head. "No."

"Put it on your bucket list. You've never seen water so vibrantly blue. It's the minerals in the lakes that make them that way. Feels like canoeing across heaven. And then..."

"Then?" Giselle prodded.

"Then he began to get tired. He was older than me. Not old, mind you, but in my opinion people got older faster back then—they considered themselves over the hill far too young. He wanted to stop traveling, become more involved in running the ranch.

"I thought I would be happy enough, but I wasn't. He knew it even before I did. And as I said, he gave me the world—but when the world ran out, there didn't seem to be any particular glue that held us together. Perhaps I should have been more patient. I'd been more patient with Pete. But then, that patience had, ultimately, felt like wasted time. And I didn't want to waste Tom's time any more than my own. I wanted him to find the kind of woman who could be content on a big ranch in the middle of nowhere for the rest of her days so he wouldn't end up alone. And I wanted…whatever I suddenly wasn't finding with him.

"Soon came more adventures, another man, and then a year later, my mother died around that time. And I went home for the first time since leaving. In one sense, I was a very different person at thirty than I'd been at sixteen. In so many ways I just had my shit together. I knew how to function in the world. I'd become confident, capable. And yet, I wasn't quite…whole. I was still running, still running away from home even all those years later. I realized that when the travel stopped—that I was still trying to get away from something, afraid to stay in one place too long."

"Wait—back up. I have to ask you a question," Giselle interrupted, eyebrows slyly raising. "What about the money? You said he was rich. Or was there a pre-nup?"

Dahlia shook her head. "No pre-nup. I could have taken half, but I'm not that greedy. I took less than he wanted to give me, bless his heart, but more than I could have conceived of ever having before I met him. It was…a nest egg. It went into the bank. At times he even added to it without telling me. I used some of it when I needed it, but mostly, I just saved it. Part of my new life was…living normally, not like a rich divorcée. In fact, my third husband never even knew about that money."

Giselle blinked her surprise at the statement. "And how did you meet *him*?"

"I moved to New Mexico. And I became a waitress."

Giselle just shook her head, smiling. "All that money, and you waited tables?"

Dahlia shrugged. "It was never about money and things for me—it was about adventure and the journey.

I thought it would be a good way to meet people. Turned out I was right. I hadn't been on the job two weeks when a man named Blake Browning walked into the restaurant where I worked and swept me right off my feet."

*"WELCOME TO BIG PORTER'S STEAKHOUSE, home of the best porterhouse this side of the Pecos," Dahlia said. Her uniform included blue jeans, a red-and-white checked shirt topped with a brown suede vest, and a red neckerchief.*

*"I love your hair."*

*Dahlia looked down at the customer. This wasn't the usual response to the spiel she was required to give at Big P's. And her hair wasn't much different than many women's. Current 1983 styles called for it being flipped back on the sides, a line of bangs curled under across her forehead, and her blond locks now hung only to her shoulders. But the cow-eyed party of one in a rumpled business suit gazed up at her like she was Rapunzel.*

*"Thank you," she said with a dry, obligatory smile. "What can I get you to drink while you look at the menu?"*

*"I'm stumped on that, see," he said. "Thing is, I've had too much to drink already."*

*That explained a lot.*

*"I'm in town for a convention, the kind where the alcohol flows, and I'm afraid it's got the best of me. And so here I am suddenly faced with the most beautiful cowgirl in the world, and I want to make a good impression on her, so I figure I better sober up fast. I'm not much of a drinker," he continued, "so I've never had to sober up fast. What do you suggest?"*

*Oh, so many things. A taxi back to your hotel room and a good night's sleep. A gallon of water. A better* pickup line. *She settled on, "I'll bring you a big cup of coffee and a glass of water." Then turned to go before he could reply.*

*"Oh my God, what a cutie," said a waitress named Lorena as Dahlia reached the drink station.*

*"Where?" Dahlia asked absently. Many of her new friends at Big P's were girls on the hunt for love. Dahlia wasn't sure what she was hunting for, but she didn't mind playing along.*

*Lorena giggled beneath the bi-level haircut that made her look like a punk rocker. "Your customer, silly. The one you were just talking to."*

*Dahlia flicked her gaze from the coffee cup she'd just picked up back to Mr. Cow-Eyes across the room. And...oh. He actually was. With dark brown hair and a classic chiseled jaw, once you got past those mooning eyes and the slightly skewed tie, he was quite handsome. "I hadn't noticed."*

*Lorena laughed as if Dahlia were kidding. But it had been a long night in too-tight cowboy boots on swollen feet. Thirty more minutes and she'd be in the car, heading home to her apartment. She could afford better with the money from her divorce, but she was saving that for a rainy day. Or...maybe she didn't think she deserved better. Having left a good man who loved her. Having taken less than he wanted but still more than felt fair.*

*Lowering the drinks to Mr. Cow-Eyes's table—hopefully her last of the evening—she pulled out her order pad, smiled pleasantly, and said, "What sounds good?"*

*He peered up at her in the same adoring way—only this time, something in his gaze appealed more. And normally when a man stared at her so openly it made her feel ogled, and a little creeped out. But his gaze held*

*admiration tempered with...dare she think respect? Or
was she tired and just being wooed by a pretty face?*

"That's a dangerous question to ask a man not in
full control of his faculties," Mr. Cow-Eyes said with a
surprisingly endearing grin.

"I'm sure you won't make me regret it," she offered
optimistically.

"I may be intoxicated, Miss Beautiful Cowgirl," he
said, "but I'm still a gentleman." Then he tipped an
imaginary hat, making her laugh when she least expected it. "I'll have the twenty-ounce rib eye, medium,
with mashed potatoes and green beans. See if it won't
soak up some of the liquor."

*She wrote it down and said,* "That sounds like a
good idea." *Then, against her better judgment, asked,*
"What's the convention for? What do you do?"

"I'm an accountant for Goldwater's in Phoenix. It's
an accounting convention."

*Different answer than she'd expected, and she let out
a laugh.* "The accountants party hardy, huh?"

*He shrugged, grinned.* "Our big chance to cut loose.
And have a killer hangover."

*She pointed to the water glass.* "Drink as much of
that as possible. It'll help."

"Hope so. I have a couple more sessions tomorrow—
then heading back home."

"I'm sure your wife and kids will be glad to see you."

*He shook his head.* "Oh, no wife and kids for me.
Not yet anyway."

*He wasn't wearing a wedding ring, but he looked
older than her, mid-thirties at least, and by that age most
men had a family—especially the handsome ones with
the steady jobs. And intoxication and flailing attempts*

*at flirtation aside, this guy was suddenly striking her as, indeed, the steady type.*

*"Why not?" she asked, head tilted.*

*He looked up at her, a little less cow-eyed, a little more somber. "Haven't found the right girl. I've tried," he announced, holding up one finger. "But I haven't found her. Truth is, Miss Beautiful Cowgirl, I'd love nothing more than to settle down with my soul mate and raise a family. It's how I always saw things going, you know?"*

*Yes, she knew. The American dream—nice home, nice car, married with kids, a nine-to-five job with a pension, and time to grill out in the backyard on the weekend. It had never been her dream exactly—but she saw the appeal. And his disappointment made her sad.*

*Until, that is, he smiled flirtatiously up at her and said, "You applying for the job?"*

*From most men, that would have hit the creep button, but she'd actually started liking him more and more. Typically, drunk men were obnoxious—but this one was just...genuine. The alcohol had knocked down any walls inside him, had him being honest and forthcoming with a woman he'd only known for three minutes.*

*"Afraid not," she answered on a light laugh.*

*He was quick to smile his endearing smile and say, "I'm striking out already? You should give me a chance now, not count me out so fast. I'm not usually drunk and forward. If you met me in real life, you might just like me."*

*His honesty drew the same from her. "I think I might—but I just got divorced. I'm in no hurry to get married again, if ever. In fact, I've already screwed it up twice."*

He cast a puzzled look. "That's impossible. You're too young to be divorced twice."

"I just turned twenty-nine, and I agree—two failed marriages before the age of thirty is a pretty bad track record."

He still eyed her curiously, and she could tell that rather than turn him off, this new information had intrigued him, made her more of a mystery he wanted to solve. "What two imbeciles could have been stupid enough to divorce Miss Beautiful Cowgirl?"

She gave him a sweet smile, truly finding it hard not to like him. "As it happens, the decision was mine, both times."

He tipped his head back. "Ah, now that I believe. You leave a trail of broken hearts behind you."

"I wouldn't go that far," she said. Though she knew she had broken the hearts of both her husbands, she didn't like thinking about that.

"Let me buy you dinner," Mr. Cow-Eyes said.

"What? No. I mean, I'm working."

"When do you get off?"

"Soon, but..." She looked around the restaurant. "I can't just sit down and have dinner with a customer."

"All right," he said, nodding. "Then cancel my order."

"What?" She blinked.

"Let's go somewhere else," he suggested eagerly.

"Oh-h-ho no," she quickly replied. "Sorry, but you're going to be sleeping alone tonight, mister. Or at least not with me."

At this, he shook his head. "You got me all wrong, Miss Beautiful Cowgirl. I just meant let's go somewhere else to eat."

"Oh." She'd jumped to conclusions—a mere two weeks of smarmy men devouring steaks had jaded her.

He pointed out the window, across the street, where the golden arches of a McDonald's lit the night in a strip of neon retail. "Meet me after you get off. Big Macs are on me."

She simply stood there shaking her head, trying to figure him out. "You'd rather eat fast food than steak?"

"Correction," he said. "I'd rather eat fast food with you than steak alone."

Good answer. And almost tempting. But she still asked, "Why?"

"You've got mystery in your eyes. I want to play detective."

Oh, that was good, too. He was hitting his stride. Still, she said, "I don't know. I'm tired, my feet are killing me, and there's a bubble bath calling my name."

He just peered up at her and said, "See, there are so many things I could say to that—about giving you foot rubs or sharing baths, but all I want to do is eat a hamburger with you, Miss Beautiful Cowgirl. That's all I'm asking." With that, he got to his feet, pulled out a wallet, and slapped a five-dollar bill on the table. "For the coffee and conversation. I'm gonna go across the street now, and I hope I'll see you there soon." Then he took her hand, raised it to his mouth, and delivered a kiss— that echoed all the way to her sore toes. And only as he walked away did he look back to say, "My name is Blake, by the way. Blake Browning."

# CHAPTER NINETEEN

"AND SO I WENT," Dahlia said, having given Giselle a shorter version. She'd never been one to give everything away—she believed a wise woman had some secrets and was more interested in others than in herself. And she hadn't given everything away to her suitor that night at McDonald's, either. But she'd given him some—some about running away from home thirteen years earlier, some about her heavenly hippie life with Pete, some about world travels with Tom. "And I told him I was a bad bet. Laughingly, mind you, but that's what I told him.

"He said he was coming back the next weekend to take me on a proper date. It was a seven-hour drive, which I pointed out. He said he'd stay the night at a motel. And that's what he did. After that first weekend, I let him stay with me—but there was no hanky-panky, my dear Giselle," she said, lifting one finger in the air. "No, ma'am. I was determined to go slow. After all, I hadn't started over with an eye toward romance—I'd wanted to finally see what life was like on my own. But then along came this wonderful guy, wooing me."

She thought back to her little apartment near Old Town, just a few rooms but each brimming with authentic Southwestern flair. "I liked Albuquerque and wish I'd gotten to stay longer," she told Giselle. "If I could rewrite the story of my life, I would have made

Blake show up a year or two later. But who can say how that might have changed things, and I'm a believer that things unfold however they're supposed to—even now I believe that—and soon it just made sense to pack my bags and move to Phoenix."

"So you still didn't get to live on your own," Giselle said, sounding disappointed for her.

But Dahlia shrugged. "Yes and no. I insisted on getting my own place and continuing not to rush. And bless my sweet Blake's heart, he didn't push me too hard. Though he wanted to marry me. He made that clear from the start. And I held out, committed to being sure this time. I got a catering job, going back to what I was good at—cooking. Only now it was for masses of people. But I was good at that, too, turned out, and I made a decent living.

"The whole time, though, Blake was the man in my life. I met his parents, his siblings, their families. I went to work functions with him. And it began to be…comfortable. But I still kept insisting I wasn't ready to tie the knot. Not yet. Until…I was."

"What changed?" Giselle asked. "What finally made you say yes?"

"Well, that's a rather long story."

Giselle looked around them. "We have nothing but time, Dahlia," she said pleasantly. "Unless you're tired of talking about your life. You've shared a lot with me lately."

Dahlia tilted her head, thinking it through. "Actually, it's…helped me sort some things out. So I'll gladly finish the story—soon. But right now, it's past our dinnertime."

"Ow!"

"Sorry," Suzanne said.

"This sounded a lot more fun than it is."

Zack lay on his stomach and she massaged his butt. Mainly the right side—stimulating tightened muscles in an attempt to relax the nerve pain down his right side. They were managing it with topical treatments—but she wanted to make it better.

"I know," she told him. "But this is going to benefit you in the long run."

He let out a groan. "Damn, Suzie Q—lucky I trust you."

"Lucky I *like* you," she told him, "enough to put up with your continuous complaints."

"Come on, now," he said, "if I didn't complain, you wouldn't recognize me."

"That's true," she said on a light laugh, then scooted back from him on the sofa bed. "Okay, done. Turn over and show me what you can do with that leg today."

Propping himself on his elbow, he took a deep breath as they both focused on his right leg. And he moved it a little. A little more than yesterday, when he'd moved it a little more than the day before that.

"Great," she said encouragingly. "You're doing great."

At this, he reached out, squeezed her hand. Even with progress, she knew it remained hard. And some days she chose to talk with him about that, keep him uplifted. But sometimes a person just had to feel what they felt—so now, instead, she changed the subject as he began his hip rotations. "I tried to call Meg this morning. To apologize."

"And?"

"No answer. So I left a heartfelt voice mail. Saying I was sorry I didn't tell her sooner, sorry for how it came out, sorry for everything I did wrong." She blew out a sigh. It had felt draining to have to be the bad guy. She didn't *feel* like a bad guy—she felt like a person just trying to navigate the twists and turns of life. But she truly regretted the scene at the Knitting Nook, and she was sorry her connection with Zack hurt Meg. Thinking about it bummed her out, though, so she changed the topic once more. "Talk to Dahlia today?"

He shook his head. "Not yesterday, either. She texted me this morning, though. Sent me a picture of another sunset."

Suzanne nodded and said, "She seems quieter lately. Or maybe just busier. And I guess I've forgiven her for leaving, but I miss hearing from her more." She suspected Zack might feel the same way.

"Yeah," he said. Left it at that.

"So who *is* this Giselle person? Do you know?" The question continued to linger.

"Nope," Zack answered as he continued his reps. "No idea."

It ate at Suzanne. "Meg said she'd never heard Dahlia mention her, and neither have I. Where on earth did she even come from?"

Zack stopped exercising to glance up at her. "You don't think she's…Dahlia's lover?"

Suzanne tilted her head, a little caught off guard. "You think?"

He just shrugged. "Dahlia keeps a lot to herself. And she never seemed to find a man who made her happy, so…"

She saw his point. "Fair enough. Who knows?"

"Or maybe I'm barking up the wrong tree," he said. "Just weird how this woman popped up out of nowhere."

"Agreed. I mean, if she wanted a winter vacation, why didn't she invite you? Or me?"

He narrowed his gaze on her. "That's actually a damn good point."

"You were even depressed," Suzanne pointed out. "Seems like suggesting a getaway to *you* would have made perfect sense."

"You're right." But then he shook his head and sighed. "She used to be restless when I was a kid. Maybe she's gotten restless again."

WINTER LOOMED LONGER than usual for Meg. No Dahlia, no Suzanne—at least not in a good way. Before, there had been Zack—and now there was Seth, but he spent a lot more time outside in winter than Zack had. And there was Lila—and that helped—but her sister was busy building a relationship with Beck, at his house, which would be a much closer walk in summer than it was right now with the island buried under a thick layer of snow.

It was too early for spring cleaning or prepping the inn for summer guests. She had a beef stew simmering, but time on her hands while it cooked. And so she sat trying to read, cat curled at her side, but unable to concentrate and instead staring at the icy crystalline designs on the windowpane beside her.

A glance at the built-in bookcases in the nook drew her gaze to her grandmother's treasured diary, and next to it a Bible that made her feel connected to Gran even all these years after her passing. "Oh, Gran," she whispered, "how do I get past this?"

Her grandma had endured the grand drama of a love triangle in this house as a girl—and then she'd picked the right guy and the drama had ended. Meg had thought her own drama would end, too, when she committed to Seth.

But now she realized life was more complicated than that. She'd never known the events that had happened in her grandma's teenage years until Seth had unearthed the diary last summer. Until then, she'd assumed her grandparents had enjoyed a simple, easy courtship—and if the diary hadn't surfaced, she'd assume it still. And probably Gran's drama hadn't ended even then. Only the diary had ended. Only the love triangle had ended. There were countless stories Meg would never know. Surely *everyone* had stories, stories upon stories, that just faded away, lost to time. Life was likely *never* as simple as she'd envisioned her grandma's being—and it made her feel naive to have lived for forty years before figuring that out. Life just kept going, and things kept happening, and you kept dealing with it, making choices, choosing paths.

When her text notification sounded, she hesitated to reach for her phone. Suzanne had left a message for her this morning and she hoped this wouldn't be her again. Nope—it was Dahlia. A little birdie told me you're upset with Suzanne.

Not mincing words today, her dear friend. So she wouldn't, either. Anyone would be. Friends don't hook up with friends' exes.

I would hesitate to call it hooking up. They're in a difficult and unique situation, Dahlia replied.

Meg answered: So then, you think this is a good thing, them together.

I think they're both in need of companionship. It surprised me, admittedly, but it actually makes perfect sense.

Meg let out a little *hmmf*, even with only Miss Kitty there to hear it. Once upon a time, Dahlia wanted *her* with Zack and had gotten miffed when she met Seth. Dahlia was always Zack's champion and defender, and everyone else came in second place. And yes, she was his only family, and everyone deserved at least one person who loved them unconditionally. But Meg couldn't help feeling that Dahlia's absolute support of Zack often came at her expense.

When she didn't answer right away, Dahlia texted again: I know it hurts. But you and Suz love each other. Whatever does or doesn't happen here, don't let it ruin your friendship. You needed her for a very long time before she came. I saw that, felt that.

Meg drew in her breath, bit her lip. Dahlia had never made that observation before, yet it was true. Isolated on the island, Meg had hungered for a friend who looked at the world through a similar lens, someone to lean on and count on and laugh with and cry with. Dahlia had been Meg's friend since her arrival here over fifteen years ago—but only when Suzanne arrived did Meg finally have that soul mate type of BFF she'd always wanted.

Meg typed a reply. That's why I'm so sad. I don't know how I can ever feel the same about her again.

IT WAS A blessedly bright and sunny day when Suzanne bundled up, headed to Petal Pushers, and draped a plastic bag over her now-sprouted and budding bulbs to protect them from the cold as she carried them ceremoniously home. It was the last step—placing them in full light and warmth—and within the next week or so, beautifully blooming daffodils and hyacinths would brighten the cottage, reminding her spring was right around the corner.

Of course, spring held mystery this year, and questions that could only be answered with time. But it did march on, with or without anyone's permission, so her gardener's heart would welcome it same as every year.

She spared a glance toward the inn upon leaving, her

heart still hurting over Meg. Part of her wondered if she should try again. But no. She'd apologized. Meg would either accept that...or not.

She'd just turned the corner onto Mill Street when her phone trilled in her pocket, but with her hands full, she couldn't look at it until she got home. Once the bulbs were inside, on the table, she found a text from Meg. *Getting past this is going to take some time.*

Part of her wanted to crumble—because she just wanted everything to be okay, *now*. She wanted forgiveness. She ached for Meg's blessing. But this was...at least a long-term maybe. So she showed Zack and tried to make the best of it, tried to move on.

"Those are them, huh?" he asked as she unbagged the bulbs, their green shoots pointing cheerfully skyward.

"Yep," she said. "Soon we'll have flowers."

"And soon we'll have lunch, too—right?" he asked with a grin.

It was past their usual lunchtime—she'd lingered at the shop, forgetting it affected someone else now. Forgetting, for just a few minutes, how much he depended on her. It was easy to forget because he'd become so capable, and he was still so much...himself: Zack Sheppard, ruggedly handsome, masculine to a fault. And unable to use his right leg.

"What's your pleasure? Cold sandwiches? Soup and grilled cheese?"

"Soup and grilled cheese sound good," he said, then glanced toward the window. "Is it warming up any out there?"

She walked to the hearth to place a log atop low-burning flames. "No—the sun helps, but it's still cold."

"No snow melting yet then?"

She shook her head. No snow melting. Or ice, either, if that's really what he was wondering. And surely he knew better. The straits rarely cleared before April. Maybe he was longing for a real prognosis. Or just eager for Dahlia's return. She couldn't blame him for either and tried to let go of any emotions the question triggered. She'd fallen in love with him, but that wasn't his fault—or his problem. Whenever this wonderful thing between them ended, she'd cope. Somehow. "Grilled cheese and chicken noodle soup, coming right up."

"While you're working on that," he said, "I'll make a bathroom run." It was still a feat, no matter how good he'd gotten with crutches—because of dragging his foot behind him. It seemed akin to hauling around a useless anchor.

"Okay," she called, entering the kitchen. After fetching what she needed from the fridge, she turned a burner on low and began to heat her griddle over another. She'd just opened the butter when Zack said quietly from the next room, "Hey, Suzanne—can you, um, come here?"

He sounded calm yet uncertain, the latter filling her with concern. She laid down her knife and walked to the living room, where he stood before her on his crutches. "What's up?"

"Watch," he said. And with his weight on his good leg, he moved his crutches forward—and then, with effort, pulled his injured leg up under him, foot almost flat on the floor.

It left her speechless for a moment. He hadn't been able to do this yesterday. Even this morning, for that matter. But like him, she found herself staying very calm, trying to evaluate what she saw. "Are you putting weight on it?"

"A little. Off and on. Hurts when I do. But at least I'm, you know, moving it."

"Yes," she said, beginning to nod. "Yes—you're moving it." She raised her gaze from his feet to his face, smiling. *"You're moving it."*

"Slows me down even more," he said, trailing off.

"But it's worth it," she finished for him.

"Yeah," he said. "It is." Smiling back at her now. Maybe he'd just needed confirmation that he was really doing it, really pulling that right foot forward—another phenomenal advance.

"Take another step," she requested.

He did. And yes, it was a way slower process. But that didn't matter right now. "That's amazing, Zack." She clasped her hands together, trying to contain her joy. "Truly amazing."

When he met her gaze, *his* appeared glassy, emotional. But he covered that up by saying, "One problem, Suzie Q."

"What's that?" she asked, still smiling warmly.

"I really need to pee and the bathroom's seeming pretty damn far away right about now."

She just laughed. "You don't have to use your right leg for every step when you need to get somewhere fast. But we'll add this to our regimen going forward."

"As soon as we finish lunch," he said. "I want to work on it as soon as we finish lunch."

"Sounds like a plan," she told him, then reached out to touch his arm. "I know you have to go to the bathroom, but one more thing."

He looked up. "What?"

"This," she said, then lifted her hands to his stubbled cheeks and kissed him.

She didn't usually initiate—their passion came when they were in bed at night, or in the morning. And if they kissed in between, it was fast, playful. This, though, came from the heart, and as he returned the kiss, it rushed through her like a match hitting a trail of gasoline.

"Sorry," she said as it ended. "For impeding your progress to the bathroom."

He only laughed, the warmth in his gray eyes filling her up inside as he told her, "Kiss me like that, baby, and you can impede my progress anytime."

SPLASHING WATER ON his face, Zack glanced in the mirror—and realized he was smiling like a damn fool. He stared at himself—the crinkles at the corners of his eyes, a face weathered by life on the water, the thickly stubbled beginnings of a beard he'd been shaving away once in a while. He was getting older. Forty-three now. And he had a bum leg and no way to make a living. Basically the same problems he'd had for weeks—and yet... he was smiling like an idiot.

Even if he never worked a fishing boat again, he was making damn solid progress. And hell, maybe it was vain, but if he could learn to balance his right foot, he wouldn't feel like such a spectacle once he got out and about on his crutches. And spring was coming—those green stems on the dining room table proved it—and it would bring...ways to move forward.

And...damn if Suzanne's kiss hadn't turned him inside out. Part of him didn't want to admit that was part of the big, stupid grin stretched across his face, but it was. And maybe that was okay. Maybe it wasn't something to run from. Always had been in the past—but falling down those stairs had changed *everything*. And if everything was different now...well, maybe the way he looked at women, relationships, wouldn't be the same, either. He felt better than he'd ever expected to again—

and most of it, in one way or another, could be attributed to Suzanne.

"Zack—you okay in there? Lunch is on the table."

"Coming," he called back to her, then opened the door, ready to keep moving forward.

## CHAPTER TWENTY

ON DAHLIA'S THIRTIETH BIRTHDAY, she got a dozen red roses (from Blake), a mini-skirt (from herself—they'd just come back in style after a hiatus through the disco era), and a phone call saying her mother had died.

She considered not going home for the funeral. She'd stayed only loosely in touch with her mother and sister after leaving—and life had been easier without them. Family wasn't always what it should be.

But she'd never met her nephew, Zack, who was seven, and her sister had a new baby, too, named Emily. Both kids by different men, both men long gone—and Dahlia supposed she couldn't pass judgment on relationships that didn't last, but she was pretty sure if she'd had any children that the men in her life wouldn't have abandoned them the way Dottie's partners had. And there would be things to clean up—things in the house, things in her mother's life—which she doubted Dottie could handle.

"It might give you some closure," Blake suggested, handing her a plane ticket to Saginaw. He'd offered to come along, but the independent part of her demanded she go alone.

Now she sat at her mother's kitchen table, thinking through where to begin—should she sort it, leave it all to rot, let Dottie have the house and everything in it? She had no answers—but she had a funeral to plan and two *days to do it. Dottie claimed she couldn't possibly help because the baby was sick, and in fact, she was going to drop Zack off to get him out of her hair.*

"I haven't even met Zack and now you're expecting me to babysit him?"

"It's not my fault you haven't been around, and I need the help."

"Well, I need some peace and quiet to plan this funeral."

"I'll drop him off at noon. Mom probably has some cold cuts in the fridge for lunch."

And so when the back door of the little house opened at twelve on the dot and a wary-looking little boy with curly brown hair walked in, Dahlia—who'd expected to feel irritated and awkward—instantly ached to make him feel loved. "I'm your aunt Dahlia—you must be Zack."

"Yup." He carried a backpack as worn as the knees on his blue jeans.

"I'm sorry we haven't met before," she said with a grin, "but I hope we can get to know each other while I'm here."

"Okay." No smile. But no malice, either. This was a little kid who went along wherever life dragged him. But he lacked joy. She saw that in his face, his eyes.

She made a split-second decision. "Apparently there's lunch meat in the fridge, but...how would you like to go out for lunch? I saw a McDonald's on my way here."

At this, the boy's face brightened. "Can I get a Happy Meal?"

"Absolutely—whatever you want."

And so it was that the two most monumental meetings with men in her life that year took place at McDonald's over French fries and hamburgers.

*Her impression was that Zack hadn't laughed a lot in his young life, and without quite planning it, she made changing that her mission. Wearing French fries like walrus tusks did the trick, as did pretending she'd seen the Hamburglar lurking behind a trash can. Zack didn't buy it—stressful upbringings can inject practicality fast, stealing away whimsy and imagination before their time—but her silliness still put the boy at ease.*

*Though returning to her mother's house—a barren sort of place despite being filled with remnants of their lives—forced Dahlia back to practicality, too. She said to her nephew, "I'm supposed to be writing a eulogy for your grandmother. Do you know what that is?"*

*"No." He shook his head beneath that curly mop of hair.*

*"It's something to be read about her at the funeral, about her life." Problem being, Dahlia didn't have much nice to say about her mother. Other than that she'd been a good cook and had made Dahlia one, too. So she sat back down at the old Formica kitchen table, grabbed a steno pad she'd been using to make notes, and wrote that down.*

*Then she looked back to Zack, who had quietly climbed up onto one of the kitchen chairs covered with shiny red vinyl that used to sparkle but didn't anymore. "Maybe you can help me. What memories do you have about her? What kind of grandma was she?"*

*The little boy thought about it. "She made me pimento cheese sandwiches. And she taught me to tie my shoes."*

*"Okay, that's good. What else?"*

*He thought some more. "She smoked a lot and it made her smell bad."*

*"Yes, that's true," Dahlia said. More people smoked than didn't, but growing up in confined spaces with her*

*chain-smoking mother had kept her from ever being
tempted to try it. As fate had it, her mother had been
diagnosed with advanced lung cancer only a few weeks
before her passing. She'd not called Dahlia. Or told Dottie. Or anyone. Until last week when Hospice moved in.
And even then no one called Dahlia. Dottie's way of getting back at her for not being here, she suspected—trying to make her feel uninformed.*

*But the joke was on Dottie—Dahlia was grateful she
hadn't had to make hard decisions about whether to
come try to help, grateful she didn't have to more closely
examine who her mother was, the good and the bad and
the in-between, as she lay dying. Because most people
were not monsters; even those who hurt us harbored
shades of light and dark. For Dahlia, her mother's darkness had made the unknown more palatable than life
at home. But not knowing her mother was ill had released her from being pulled back into that dark, emotional mire.*

*Her mother hadn't given her much, but that—that
was a profound gift. Albeit probably not the sort of thing
you put in a eulogy. So she asked Zack, "Anything else
you can think of?"*

*He appeared to think some more, then shook his head.*

*"Will you miss her?" Dahlia asked.*

*At this, he stayed quiet, lowered his eyes. Already an
honest enough child not to spew out a lie.*

*"It's okay if you won't. I left because we didn't get
along."* She slapped me every time we argued. She made
me feel worthless. *She left that out, of course. But it reminded her why it still felt raw. She liked to believe her
mother had mellowed with age, that she'd been a better
grandma to Dottie's kids than she'd been a mother to*

*her own. But who could say? Maybe her death had saved Zack from what she and Dottie had endured.*

*So when he still didn't reply, she said, "You know what—this is bullshit."*

*He looked up, perhaps a little frightened. "What is?"*

*"Trying to think of nice things to say about someone who wasn't very nice. I'd rather do something fun— how about you?"*

*His countenance brightened as he gave an enthusiastic nod.*

*But what was fun to do? She looked around the house she'd grown up in—then spotted the old console stereo in the corner of the small living room.*

*Not much of Dahlia remained in the house, but she stood up, told Zack to wait there, and walked to the room she'd once shared with Dottie. Opening the closet door, she peeked up onto a high shelf, and under a pile of her mother's handbags rested a stack of her old record albums.*

*Despite careful maneuvers, several handbags fell on her as she pulled the albums down, but she left them lying and carried the records to the living room, spreading them on the pockmarked coffee table. "Has Grandma ever played any of these for you?" she asked Zack, who sat next to her on the couch, studying them. Simon and Garfunkel, The Mamas and the Papas, Creedence Clearwater Revival, Van Morrison, Jefferson Airplane, The Monkees, and more. Back then, she'd saved up any money she got from babysitting or in birthday cards to buy records—because she could close her eyes and let the music carry her away.*

*Next to her, Zack shook his head.*

*"They were mine when I was a teenager. Want to hear*

some?" she asked, eager to share the one bit of magic that had made her life better here.

Now Zack nodded—a child of few words. But she understood why—the quieter you are, the less trouble finds you.

Trying to think about what might appeal to a kid, she plucked up the Monkees album Headquarters, slid the disc from its sleeve, and placed it on the turntable. From memory, she knew "Randy Scouse Git" was the last track on Side B, so she carefully lowered the needle on the spinning record.

As the song took her back in time, she smiled at Zack and said, "Let's dance."

When he didn't respond, she stood up, grabbed his reluctant little hands, and led him to an open space on the floor to begin twirling around the room with him. Before she knew it, they were both laughing.

She stayed three weeks after the funeral, far longer than planned, so long that she lost her catering job. But spending quality time with a child who clearly needed some of that was worth it, no question. Dottie seemed more than happy to let him stay at the old house with her, making every night a sleepover.

They played games from the same closet as the albums—Trouble, Sorry!, and Mouse Trap. She taught him a song to help him remember all the US presidents in order, assuring him it would dazzle his teachers. "Wash, Ad, Jeff, Mad, Mon, Ad, Jack..." They played more records—she educated him thoroughly on the entire collection during her visit—and watched bad monster movies on a VCR her mother had purchased. She noticed he never wanted to go home.

"What's it like there?" she asked one night while they

*waited for Godzilla—they'd found the original 1954 version at a local video rental—to rewind.*

*"Not fun like with you," he said simply.*

*"Well, it would be hard to compete with the constant fun I provide," she quipped. "But records and movies aside, I...hope it's okay there."*

*"Emily cries a lot and I think Mommy hates her," he said.*

*Dahlia's heart sank. Indeed the baby did seem to cry a lot—and Dottie generally appeared frazzled. "That'll get better over time," Dahlia assured him. Then said the words she'd been dreading but could no longer avoid. "I have to go home soon, Zack."*

*His face fell.*

*"I know," she told him. "I'm sad, too."*

*"You could move here," he said in that hopeful, guileless way of children. Perhaps she'd dissolved a little of that shell of practicality that had hung around him—for better or worse.*

*And for a second, she even considered the invitation. She had no job tying her to any place, after all. And she had the money from Tom if she needed it. But she missed Blake. They talked every night, and the longer she was gone, the more she realized how much she treasured him. "There's a man in Phoenix," she said. "I think I'm going to marry him. And he can't move—his job and family are there."*

*"Oh," the little boy said, appearing crestfallen.*

*"But we'll keep in touch," she assured him.*

*"How?"*

*"The telephone. You can call me whenever you want. And I'll call you, too."*

*And so they did. They kept in touch when his baby sister died in her crib at the age of two, and Dahlia went home for another week. They kept in touch when he grew surly and more distant with adolescence, even if it took extra effort on her part. They kept in touch as he grew into a rebellious teenager, and she wondered if Dottie was abusive but was too afraid to ask.*

I should be there for him. *It niggled in her gut—and yet she couldn't be in two places at once. She'd married Blake soon after that trip home and become an attentive wife, on his arm at more work functions, more family gatherings. She liked being settled. She liked the job she took at a local boutique. She liked the middle-classness of it all.*

*They lived in a pleasant ranch house with a pleasant yard. They threw pleasant cookouts and opened pleasant presents around a pleasant artificial tree every December. It wasn't the aimlessness of her ranch life with Pete; it wasn't the extravagance of her jet-set existence with Tom—it was the middle of the road, and she liked it there. As a child of her era, indeed it turned out that the middle-class American dream seemed like the safest possible place to be.*

*And they were happy—until Blake wanted to have a baby. Well, he'd wanted it all along—but when she turned thirty-five, he pushed the issue. And even having gone through the same conflict with Pete years before, she'd thought she'd eventually want that, too. Only she hadn't.*

*"I'm too selfish," she told him one tearful night in bed. Maybe it was the darkness that gave rise to the stark truth, made her able to finally see it, say it. "Too selfish to put someone first, and that's what you do with a child. I'm so sorry, Blake. I'm just not mommy material."*

*She should have left him. Or he should have left her. Because her refusal drove a wedge between them noth-*

*ing could fix. Oh, Blake tried. There were still work functions and cookouts. Now they just came injected with a degree of loneliness.*

*When Zack was sixteen, he called one day to tell her he'd left home.*

*"You can come out here, stay with us," she said. "Tell me where you are and I'll wire the money for a bus ticket."*

*"Thanks, Dahlia," he said, "but I've got a plan."* He'd grown up somewhere along the way, this troubled nephew of hers. *"I got a job on a fishing trawler out of Saginaw Bay."*

*She remembered youth, and plans. But even so... "I'm worried about you."*

*"You left home at sixteen and got by fine," he re-minded her.*

*"I was lucky."* And not as scarred as you. And maybe I shouldn't have told you how many nice people I met. What if you don't meet nice people, too?

*"I can take care of myself, Dahlia."* So certain. So set on his plan.

*"Please call whenever you can," she told him.*

*She didn't hear from him as often after that and it worried her. But when he did call, he was alive and safe and seemed content enough, even if maybe a little empty inside. She worried about that, too.*

*Because contentment was a funny thing. And her own contentment with the conventional had faded. It wasn't just about babies and wedges in her marriage—Blake had gone on loving her, even under the strain. It was the sense that maybe all those work functions and cookouts added up to...nothing.*

*But if she'd learned anything, it was that, in the end, she was more predictable than she ever could have*

*imagined. Maybe after two divorces, she should have
known that relationships and marriage just weren't her
thing. Hello—goodbye—to number three.*

DAHLIA TOLD GISELLE the short version of those years as
well, as they sat side by side in the sand attempting to
build a castle. She left out the sadder parts, though—
because why spread sadness around?

"I suspect," Giselle said, carving on a turret, "that
the end with Blake draws near?"

"Alas, it does. As time passed, I suggested we travel,
or take up a hobby together, to rekindle the magic. But
he thought I was Peter Pan and just didn't want to grow
up. And thus I decided there was more than one way to
grow up, and I thought about what I really wanted—
which was just a beautiful place to carve out a life by
my own standards. I'd started out that way—but a weak-
ness for romance had repeatedly led me into lives I was
no longer defining. Perhaps Zack's youthful courage reminded me I'd once had plenty of that myself. And so I
parted ways with Blake, sorry to feel I'd robbed him of
something, yet not sorry to leave the drudgery."

"And then?" Giselle stopped carving the sand to ask.

Dahlia smiled, the tiny plastic sand shovel in her hand
going still. "I built the life I lead now. I found Summer Island on an old postcard in some of my mother's
things, and after one short visit knew I was done running. And that it would give Zack a home base, and a
family, small though it is. He needed that. He doesn't
*know* he needed that—he doesn't know he was part of
my decision to come back to Michigan—but he deserved
better than what life had dealt him, and it was a good
move for both of us."

"And the café?" Giselle asked.

"I finally used some of Tom's money—to buy the café and the cottage."

"And you haven't kept in touch with him, either. Or Blake?"

Dahlia shook her head. Then sighed. "Makes it all feel…very long ago, though. I do hope they're happy." As the words left her, she realized she sounded sad. Just a little.

"You're sure you wouldn't want me to try to find any of them?" Giselle asked. "I'm pretty handy with online searches." She smiled hopefully, clearly feeling mysteries afoot.

Dahlia shook her head once more. Though what she didn't tell Giselle was—she suddenly didn't know if her choices held water. She'd just spouted about how she'd stopped running, but…what had she ever been looking for? And had she ever really found it? Or had she simply tired of the search? And why did a certain emptiness linger inside her as she thought back over the men she'd once loved?

ONE PERK OF living on Summer Island for Suzanne had been the lack of Valentine's Day. Oh, it still rolled around on the calendar, but there wasn't much fanfare surrounding it. No stores filled with heart-shaped everything, no restaurants for couples to flock to for a romantic dinner, and no roses for anyone to buy for their significant others.

Of course, back on the mainland, Valentine's Day had been big business for Petal Pushers. But she didn't mind not having the hassle here on the island, and as a woman who'd sworn off romance until recently, it had been pleasant for the day to pass by virtually unnoticed.

So it caught her off guard when on the morning of the

fourteenth, as she lay next to Zack in bed, she received a text from Allie Hobbs inviting her to the Cozy Coffee and Tea Shop *for an afternoon of chocolate and chatting.*

She and Allie had always been friendly, but they'd never socialized outside of a group. And so...maybe this was a group thing? What if Meg was also invited? And why on Valentine's Day? It seemed more like a day for Allie to spend with Trent than with friends.

But on the other hand, maybe it would be nice to get out for a while. Because it *was* Valentine's Day. She recalled from Meg that Zack wasn't much of a Valentine's celebrator anyway—which was possibly forgivable here in winter, yet had still irked her on Meg's behalf. Regardless, though, she now lived with a guy in a wholly undefined relationship, which could make a day that used to just pass by feel awkward. So perhaps this would make it less so.

She replied with: What a nice invitation! Will it be just us or are there others?

Allie answered: Just you and me. I hope that's okay.

And then Suzanne understood. Allie felt bad about the embarrassing incident at the Knitting Nook, which Suzanne was simply depending upon time to make people forget.

Yes, of course, she replied. Then learned through more texting that while the shop was typically open only on knitting bee nights in winter, Josh was coming in to prep for a celebration with his wife and had invited Allie to sample the wares. Trent was busy today, so Allie decided to make it more fun with a friend—Suzanne.

Okay, good enough. Suzanne was in.

Very sweet of you, and I'm happy to come.

"Who ya texting there all fast and furious?" Zack asked, peeking over with a sleepy grin.

She smiled back. "Allie Hobbs. She invited me to get together this afternoon."

"Hmm. Sounds nice, I guess. Let's just be sure we get in both my exercise sessions."

"Absolutely," she said. They'd worked on using his foot with the crutches the last couple of days, and he was beginning to put a little more weight on his leg—with less pain. So no way was she letting up now. "In fact, I'll hop up, make breakfast, and we'll get started."

DAY TURNED TO dusk as Suzanne made the trek home from the coffee shop—and snow began to fall. Through the pleasant afternoon, Suzanne felt she'd perhaps added a real friend to her small group of them, an especially nice thought given that Meg's status felt pretty uncertain.

As she'd suspected, Allie had apologized for accidentally starting the kerfuffle at the Nook, and Suzanne had explained her own remorse, as well. Girl talk followed, Allie confiding that she and Trent were starting to plan their wedding for late summer, and of course wanted Suzanne to provide the flowers. Chocolate had been the theme of the day, Josh serving a variety of chocolate desserts he'd whipped up. *And that's as close to a Valentine's celebration as I'll get—but it's fine. Love isn't about hearts and flowers anyway.*

"Hey, Suzanne."

She looked up to see none other than Trent approaching from the other direction. Allie had never mentioned what he was doing today—but perhaps he'd been at the bike shop or his law office. "Hi," she said with a smile. "I just left your fiancée."

He seemed unsurprised. "Heard you two were getting together. Have a nice evening."

Soon she reached her front door—but drew up short

upon hearing music coming from inside. It wasn't even Zack's usual sixties' and seventies' jams—much softer.

Confused, she opened the door, looked around for Zack, didn't see him in any of the usual spots—and then heard him say from her right, "Hey there, Suzie Q."

He stood with his crutches next to the dining room table—on which rested two plates of something Italian, two glasses of wine, a silk red rose in a vase, and a white teddy bear holding a heart that said Be Mine.

# CHAPTER TWENTY-ONE

SUZANNE BLINKED. TWICE. To make sure she wasn't dreaming.

But no. Zack Sheppard stood before her having somehow created a romantic Valentine's Day dinner. "Happy V Day, Suzie Q."

She raised her gaze from the table to the man, awed. "How on earth did you do this?"

He released his hands from the crutches braced under his arms to wiggle his fingers and say slyly, "Guess I'm magic."

"I'm starting to think you might be."

Then he shrugged. "And I called Trent for help."

She let her eyes go wide. "Which involved Allie luring me out of the house today?"

Another shrug from the rugged man before her. "That part was her idea. She'd been wanting to get together." Then he looked to the table. "Ready to eat before it gets cold?"

"Absolutely," she said. "It looks wonderful."

"Dahlia's lasagna recipe."

It smelled delicious—and left her even more stunned. "I didn't know you cooked."

"Desperate times call for desperate measures," he said, slanting her another playful grin as he set his crutches aside. "Trent cooked the noodles and meat, and I learned to layer a lasagna while Dahlia talked me through it on the phone."

She tilted her head, smiled. "Desperate times?"

He still grinned at her across the table. "Well, not desperate. Just a thing I wanted to do. To let you know I appreciate you. And how much you...mean to me."

Suzanne's jaw went slack. Had he really just said that? Still, she chose her response carefully as the Zack she'd always known would certainly recoil at words of deep affection "You've...come to mean a lot to me, too." She shook her head, still trying to grasp this. "And I'm touched you would do this."

He tossed her a teasingly smug look. "Not bad for a guy you couldn't stand when all this started, huh?"

She threw back her head and laughed. "No, not bad at all. Pretty impressive, in fact."

"Trent had to pick out the bear for me from Koester's, and I realize a stuffed animal and fake flower probably aren't your style, but—"

"I love them," she cut him off. No, they *weren't* her usual style, but she loved them with all her heart.

As they ate, they talked about other things—her time with Allie, that it had challenged him to ask Trent for help but he was glad he had, and that Dahlia had sounded tired on the phone—but the whole time, the effort he'd put into this buoyed Suzanne in unexpected joy.

"You even changed up—or should I say slowed down—your music."

He slanted her a look past the silk rose. "I'm not a total oaf," he said, amusing her with his choice of words. "I know I can't seduce a woman with 'Bad Moon Rising.'"

She tilted her head, cast a flirtatious smile. "Is it possible to seduce someone who's already willing?"

"Are you saying you're ready to ditch the dinner and take me to bed?"

Suzanne thought it over. "My plate's empty."

"Then consider me dessert," he told her.

Her skin fairly sizzled with wanting him, so she didn't hesitate to push to her feet. *But wait. Go slow. Even if you want to run to the bed.* She and Cal used to do that— run through the house to fall into bed together. And she wanted to do that now—run playfully, or maybe take his hand and let him lead her. Only he couldn't. And that was okay. She didn't mind waiting.

Sometimes their sex was playful, full of laughter and fun. Sometimes it was hotter, about passion and hunger and reaching pinnacles she'd almost forgotten existed. When they came together on this night, though, it was slower, deeper, silent other than the heated sighs and moans they drew from one another. When Zack pushed his way inside her, Suzanne found herself wrapping her legs around his hips, circling her arms around his neck, clinging to him in a way she never had before. Because it felt safer now. Safer to feel. Safer to care. Safer not to hide it.

"I love you," she breathed in his ear as he came inside her. That felt safe, too. More than safe—it felt necessary. She needed him to know. That he was loved. By more than just Dahlia. Whether or not he ever gained full control of his body again.

*But what did I just do? I said I love you? First? To a known commitment-phobe? Because he made me dinner?* Still wrapped around him, their bodies still joined, she shut her eyes and let more unmeasured honesty tumble out. "Oh God—I'm sorry. What I wouldn't give to take that back."

He lifted slightly to peer down at her. "Why? I love you, too." Said so easily, like she should have known.

Her heart skipped a beat. "You do?"

"Yeah, Miss Q, I do."

"I didn't see that coming," she confessed.

"That makes two of us." He rolled off her then, until they lay on their sides, facing each other. "Wanna know one thing that makes me love you?" he asked, eyes half-shut.

She nodded.

"You never make me feel weird. About...this." He motioned vaguely toward his right leg. "I mean, I know our sex isn't...the same as it would be if I hadn't fallen."

"If you hadn't fallen," she pointed out, "we wouldn't have any sex at all. So this is much better than that."

He gave her a gentle grin. "See what I mean? You make it okay."

She bit her lip, pressed her palms to his broad chest. "It really is, Zack," she promised. "I mean, sex is more than just...the act. And I feel more connected with you having the use of one leg than I probably would if you had two—because...I know you must really *want* me, and *trust* me. For me, sex is an enormous act of trust—letting someone see your most intimate responses. And I love that you've trusted me with that—especially now."

Oh, so much truth she was putting on the table. And he loved her, too? He really loved her? It was a lot to take—and a lot to give—when she'd expected nothing more than another normal night. The weight of it pressed down on her as she let her gaze drop away from his.

Using one bent finger to lift her chin, he asked, "If you love it so much, what's wrong?"

Sadly, the answer was one she'd known all along. "Loving you is...dangerous."

He didn't pretend not to understand what she meant. "Because of what you know from Meg? That's ancient history, Suzie Q."

Ah, of course he would blow it off with a throwaway line. Perhaps Zack's depth could only extend so far. She didn't fault him for it—she loved him for who he was. He wasn't Cal. He wasn't Beck Grainger. He wasn't her usual type. But if he asked what was on her mind, she would tell him. "It's that…you're not content in one place for long. And I can't handle that. I can't handle loving someone who keeps leaving—not again."

His eyes widened. "Again?"

Crap, what had she just said? Now maybe *she* was the one who didn't want to go so deep. But she'd opened this can of worms, so… "It's just that Cal, you know, did the Doctors Without Borders thing."

"Yeah," he said, clearly not understanding. And how could he? She'd told him very little about it. It wasn't her favorite subject.

"He went three times," she said. "Willingly. And I hated it. I didn't want him to go."

"Oh." Now he was getting it. Cal had died in the noblest of endeavors—it never occurred to anyone that maybe she hadn't *supported* that endeavor. "Did you ask him not to?"

She drew in a deep breath. Talk about hindsight being twenty-twenty. If only she had. And yet… "No—I couldn't. I wanted to, but it seemed so selfish. *Hey, don't go save war-torn people on the other side of the globe because I'll be lonely in our great big house.* So I just told him how much I missed him when he was gone, hoping maybe that would be enough… But he was so driven to help others. It was his way of giving back—to God or fate or whoever gave him such a good life. He wanted to leave the world a better place. And so how could I ask him not to do this thing that fulfilled him?" She shook her head. "Simple—I couldn't. I just kept hoping he'd see how it worried me, see how desperately I didn't want him to go. I think," she went on, eyes narrowed absently on Zack's chest, "maybe it's how I got the way I am now."

"The way you are?"

"I generally say what I mean, let people know what I think—and once I get started on something, I have trouble shutting up. Like now, for instance."

He grinned softly. "It's okay—go on."

She couldn't have stopped if she'd tried. "Back then, I was much more...well behaved. I was a good nurse, and then I was a good doctor's wife. I was...appropriate, the kind of person you could take to a party full of sophisticated people without worrying I'd say the wrong thing. These days I can't even get through an evening at the Knitting Nook without making a scene."

"Well, if it's any consolation, I probably like the you who isn't afraid to make a scene better than the you who wouldn't."

She bit her lip, thought about that. Cal would have loved her anyway, appropriate or not. And Cal would have loved her just as much if she'd asked him not to go to Syria. "I wish now, of course, that I'd spoken up and said what I was thinking. But I also wish..."

"What?" he asked when she didn't finish.

The spot between her eyebrows began to crimp painfully as tears threatened. "I wish he wouldn't have *made* me ask. I wish he'd just looked into my eyes and let that be enough of a reason not to go. If he had, he'd still be alive. And I'm just *so damn mad* at him for leaving."

As she heard her own words, her chest gone tight,

she gasped with horror as tears leaked free. "Oh God—I never realized I was actually *mad* at him," she told Zack. "And what an awful thing to be mad about. And now I feel horrible. Because he's gone, and he loved me."

Zack lifted one hand to her cheek—used the other to gently wipe away her tears. "It's okay, it's okay. I mean, a husband is supposed to put his wife first, right? And I'm no expert on that kind of thing, but…well, I think it's okay if you're upset."

She reached up, curled her hand around his wrist. "But, Zack, he helped people so much! People who really needed it! He operated on people's knees, and hips, and he helped people…" She stopped, gasped. "He helped people walk again." She spoke more quietly to add, "How can I be angry at that?"

But even after this new information, Zack supported her. "I don't think you're mad at him for that," he said. "You're mad at him for putting himself in danger. Without considering what it risked for you, too."

"Oh," she said. Because yes, that was it. Cal hadn't been the only one with something to lose, and she wasn't sure he'd ever acknowledged that with more than a smiling, "Don't worry, honey—I'll be fine."

"Anyway," she said, swallowing past the lump in her throat, "that's why I'm gun-shy, about you…and me. Cal left me alone, even if it was for a good cause. And you left Meg alone for half the year. And now I finally understand why that grated on me so much. The upshot is…you're going to have the same problem with me that you had with Meg. I don't want to love someone who's going to keep leaving me."

Without missing a beat, he said, "You're forgetting one big thing here, Suzie Q. Everything's different than when I was with Meg. Everything." Then he grinned that cute, sexy Zack grin. "I can't even get to the bathroom at top speed, so just where is it you think I'm going? In fact, looks like you might just be stuck with me."

Part of Suzanne filled with cautious hope. And true enough—he could no longer just hop on a boat and sail off into the sunset. And maybe such an intense change of circumstance should be enough to reassure her—and yet... "Zack, why does it take paralysis, literally losing the ability to move, to make you stay in one place?"

Zack looked at the woman next to him who he'd grown so attached to. *Tell her. Just tell her.* He tried to imagine summoning the words, telling her the thing he'd never told another living soul, not even Dahlia. But the very notion made his heart beat faster, his chest ache. There was a reason people didn't go around spilling their ugliest secrets. Finally, he said, "If you knew, you might not want me around."

The last thing he wanted was to drive her away, but what had just snuck out was the truth, the words floating around his tired head. He hadn't liked watching her cry over something that hurt her—and God knew he didn't want to be *another* something that hurt her.

If she could just trust him not to run away from her, and if she could just let all these questions go, he almost thought they'd have a shot at happiness. He had no idea for how long—he'd never been skilled at looking into the future—but what he felt for Suzanne went...well, soul deep. God knew he hadn't been looking for something like that—he hadn't even known he could feel that—but how could he not see everything in her that was lovely and sweet, tough and strong? How could he not love her and want to be with her every day?

Next to him, she propped up on one elbow, the very move punctuated with a determination he'd grown used to in her. Her tears had dried now, her tougher side—the side that said what she meant—returned. "Zack, I'm not asking you for promises or commitments or anything you don't want to give me. What would be the point of asking *anyone* for something they don't want to give? That's not really giving, you know? But I just want to understand you. I want to know you. I'm not going to judge you, I promise. And, well…" She stopped, her countenance softening as she looked over at him. "You just made me lasagna with your bare hands. Something I'm guessing you've never done for another woman, true?"

He couldn't deny that. "True."

She glanced toward the dining room table that still screamed Valentine's Day. "You gave me a teddy bear that says Be Mine. Anybody else got one of those from you?"

He sighed. She had him there, too. "Nope."

"Then I have to conclude that I must be pretty damn special to you. I must be someone you're comfortable with. I must be someone you can open up to and say anything."

He got the point—if he couldn't tell *her*, who could he tell? But that was *his* point, even if just in his own head: *no one* should hear this story, ever. And having a shadowy bad memory lurking in the recesses of your mind was a whole different thing than having to talk about it.

Meg had tried to get him to, but he couldn't. And now Suzanne was making a big freaking deal out of it, too? This was why he and Dahlia had always gotten along. She knew bad things had happened to him as a kid, but she'd never pressed him to talk about it. He knew the same about her but had also never pressed her. They both understood that life was easier without constantly dredging up the bad shit.

"Maybe it feels like I'm keeping something from you—but it's not like that, Suzie Q. It's just… I went through some stuff as a kid that I'd rather not think about, okay?" There, that sounded reasonable—he'd explained it, not just shut her out. Surely she'd understand.

"But…" she began, "if it's the reason you have trouble committing to people, and places, that seems important. And…fair that I know. I mean, if you ever cut and run, I'd like to at least know why."

"Thanks for having faith in me to stick around like I just said I would," he told her dryly.

She shrugged. "Give me a reason to believe."

Women. Why did they have to know every damn thing about a guy? This was starting to remind him a lot of his troubles with Meg, just as Suzanne had said. Up to now, she'd seemed easygoing—but damn, you start throwing the *L* word around and everything gets all serious.

Problem being, though, he did love her. He didn't want to lose the good thing he'd found here with her. It had been…maybe the most unexpected gift of his life. Well, her and Dahlia—Dahlia had come along at a tough time, too, and her presence had been just as powerful.

And so…he would try. Where the hell to begin, though? "You…know I had a little sister, right?"

"Emily Ann," she said.

His stomach contracted just hearing the name out loud. Somehow seeing it painted on the back of his trawler didn't hit him the same way. And when he opened his mouth to talk again, nothing came out. He almost couldn't breathe; his chest had gone tight. An image filled his head. A baby bed Emily had been too big for by then. His mother standing over it. He'd been eight years old.

*Breathe, damn it. Breathe.* He felt a little light-headed, even lying down. And without looking at Suzanne, he said, "I can't. I'm sorry, Suzanne, but I can't."

"Oh," she said from his left. "Okay." The words came out short, soft, and with a chill that swept over him like a cold wind despite the fire blazing in the hearth.

"I'm sorry," he said.

"It's fine."

"It's obviously not."

"It is because it has to be," she said, sitting up in bed, back rigid. "I told you, I don't want anything you don't want to give—so if you don't want to tell me, it's fine."

"Then what's wrong?"

"As I said, it just means there's an important part of you I can't know. And again, that's fine. It's your choice. I get it. I just don't have to feel good about it."

"It's not you, it's me," he said, meaning that with everything in him.

But she simply let out a low, wounded laugh. "I think we've all heard that one before. And it never flies." With that, she got out of bed, grabbing the long sweater she'd been wearing, throwing it on over her head.

"Where are you going?" he asked, sitting up himself.

"To take a shower," she said. "And clean up the dinner mess."

He watched her go, knowing that if he let her walk away, they'd move backward. And he didn't want that. He didn't want that with a fury that burned in his gut. He'd loved Meg more than he'd realized before letting *her* walk away. He couldn't let another woman walk away, even if it was only to the bathroom. It would really be much further. "Suz, wait."

She stopped, looked back, eyes distant, angry. "What?"

"Lie back down with me."

"No."

"Lie down with me," he said again. "I want to tell you. I want to tell you…the worst thing that ever happened to me. And the worst thing I ever did."

# CHAPTER TWENTY-TWO

ZACK WATCHED THE woman he'd fallen in love with pad slowly back across the room toward him. She didn't look happy, though. A lot closer to sad. And as she climbed back onto the fold-out sofa, that big sweater draping around her, she said, "I'm sorry. I know you've got plenty on your plate without me forcing you to re-visit the past." Then she knelt next to him, brow knit-ting. "It's just that…"

He didn't make her go on. Because maybe it was time to finally stop running. From people. From memories. From truth. "I get it, Suz. I do." He sighed. "I mean, kind of, anyway. Because if the situation was reversed, I'd be okay with letting it go—but I'm a guy. And historically speaking, I don't seem to understand women too well once you get past the flirtation and the sex. So if you need to know my deep, dark secrets to be happy, then you need to know them." He ended with a short nod. He wasn't really any more ready to tell her than he'd been two minutes ago, but he had to man up and do this.

She looked almost contrite, and maybe wary, as she whispered, "Thank you." Perhaps suddenly as afraid to hear it as he was to say it.

"At least after this," he told her, "maybe you'll under-stand why I'm…the way I am."

"Surly? Contentious? Hard to get close to?"

When he shot her a look, she cast a teasing smile,

clearly trying to lighten the moment. And he attempted a grin in return, but it was hard to muster right now. "Getting better at the last one, though—right?" he managed. "Being easier to get close to. I'm trying anyway."

"I know," she answered softly.

He took a deep breath, aware that if he had two good legs to walk on, he'd probably get up and leave right now. That's how programmed he was to run away from the bad stuff. But not being able to walk changed more than just your ability to get around. He had to stay here physically—so that meant staying emotionally, too. Like it or not.

"Okay," he said, "here goes." He still had no idea where to begin, but he'd just start spitting it out. *Just get through it, and as long as Suzanne doesn't think you're scum of the earth afterward, maybe you can go back to fun, easy times with her.* "When I was six, my mom had Emily Ann."

"I already have a question," Suzanne said. "What about your dad? I know your mom was Dahlia's sister, but I've never heard anything about your dad."

He nodded. "That's because he wasn't around. My mother got pregnant by a sailor who worked on a freighter stuck wintering in Saginaw Bay. She gave me his last name but he never knew I existed."

Her soft gasp filled the air, and he quieted her before she could start in with questions about that. "And yeah, I'm aware he's probably still out there somewhere, and no, I've never looked for him, and no, I don't plan to. Life led where it led—I have no interest in surprising some old man forty-three years later. It's all water under the bridge."

He could see her wanting to protest badly, so badly that he met her gaze, lifted one shushing finger to her lips, and told her, "That's an argument we can have an-other day, Suzie Q. I can only take so much prying into my life at one time, okay?"

Again, she appeared contrite. "Okay," she said. "I'm sorry—go on."

He blew out a sigh, thinking. Remembering. Feel-ing. Maybe he *should have* let her rant and rave about his mystery dad—an easier subject for him. "Emily's father was a mechanic in Saginaw, who cleared out and moved away when he found out Mom was pregnant. Mom was…" He stopped, shook his head. "She wasn't a good mother, didn't know how to be. Some women get pregnant accidentally and rise to the occasion—and some don't. Mostly her kids were burdens to her." He didn't look at Suzanne as he spoke—his eyes fell ab-sently on his feet.

"My grandmother—her mom, Dahlia's mom—was the same way. There just wasn't much love to go around. I think there was mostly…disappointment, lives that had turned out drab and gray." He raised his eyes to Suzanne then, with a revelation. "That's how I remem-ber my whole childhood, drab and gray. I know the sun had to shine there sometimes—I just don't remember it. I remember overcast skies and trees with bare winter limbs and houses with peeling paint and muddy yards. Except—" he raised one finger in the air "—I remem-ber this one day when the skies were blue, bright blue—a day when Dahlia was there and even though it was winter, the sun was out, and she took me to a park and we played hide-and-go-seek." He smiled at the pleasant recollection he'd nearly forgotten.

"That sounds nice," Suzanne said next to him, her voice gentle, kind.

And it reminded him that he'd gotten off topic—and

he had to get back to it if he was ever gonna get through it. "Anyway, Emily cried a lot. Looking back, maybe there was something wrong with her—maybe she should have been taken to the doctor. Or...maybe she just didn't get enough attention, you know? But no matter how you slice it, she cried a lot. And when I think of her, that's mostly what I think about, the sound of her crying." He stopped, heart pounding. "Until she didn't anymore. Until it stopped. I think of that, too."

*Okay, you're in it now. You're there.* And he *was* there, back in that room, that shadowy room where everything changed. *Just tell the damn story. Tell it so you can be done with it, forever.* He tried to swallow back the lump in his throat, focused on the mound his feet made in the covers. And said, "One day when I was eight, I walked in the door after school and heard Emily crying, same as usual, and my mother screaming bloody murder, telling her to shut up." *Will you shut up? Will you just shut up? Just shut up! Shut up! Shut up!*

"She just kept screaming it over and over—flipping out. And I didn't want to cross her path while she was freaking out or else she'd unleash on me, too. So I just stood there, right inside the door, holding my backpack, staying quiet, not knowing what to do.

"And then...Emily finally shut up." The memory stole his breath. *Don't let yourself feel it—just tell her.* "But it was all at once—one minute she's crying and the next she's quiet. And so is Mom. Everything's quiet. Still as a church. And so I tiptoed toward Mom's bedroom— that's where the baby slept in one of those little baby beds, a bassinet? She was too big for it by then, but it's where she slept. And I stopped in the doorway. And I could see Mom bending over her, but I can't see Emily. Instead I see a pillow—a throw pillow from Mom's bed.

And I see Mom pressing it down, holding it down. And she's smothering her."

Tears rolled down his cheeks now, but he ignored them. He knew Suzanne was crying, too—he could hear it: a whimper, ragged breathing—but he ignored that, too, lost now in a long-ago moment that still felt like yesterday. "And I just stood there. I just stood there watching her do it. I didn't move a muscle. And then I hid. I backed away, quiet as I could, and I ran outside. I remember running up and down the streets in our neighborhood, just crying." He stopped, thinking back. "No one ever even stopped me to ask what was wrong. It was cold out—but there were kids coming home from school, people out checking their mail." He gave his head a slight shake. "I guess a crying kid just wasn't a big deal in our neighborhood.

"I don't know how long I stayed gone. Twenty minutes? An hour? I remember wishing I could call my grandma, but she'd died the year before. And Dahlia lived in Phoenix, so it wasn't like she could come running. And it didn't matter anyway. No one could fix it.

"And when I went back, I remember concentrating so hard on acting normal—afraid she'd kill me, too, if she knew I'd seen. But by the time I got there, cops and an ambulance had come. Mom had called them, and I walked in to hear her crying, saying she'd just found the baby not breathing. That simple. Everybody believed it was a natural death.

"And Mom…" He stopped, sighed. "She loved us in her way. So her tears were real enough, you know? She was sorry she'd killed the baby. She just wasn't sorry enough to tell the truth about it." He stopped, chest tight with the barrage of memories. "And so it turned into just one more little tragedy in a poor neighborhood. One more funeral with a tiny casket—that Dahlia paid for because Mom couldn't."

"Did…did you ever tell her you knew?"

For the first time, he allowed his gaze to flit from his feet to Suzanne. She was wiping away tears, her cheeks wet with them.

"When I left. When I was sixteen. I wrote her a note. Didn't even sign it. Just wrote, *I know what you did to Emily.* Figured that said everything. Why I was leaving. Why I couldn't stand to be around her. Why she shouldn't bother trying to find me—not that she would."

"Are you…ever in touch with her now?" Suzanne asked cautiously.

He gave his head a brisk shake. "Hell no. I never spoke to her again. Dahlia lost touch with her, too, after I left home. I don't know if she's dead or alive and I don't care."

He almost couldn't believe he'd gotten it all out. The thing he'd never been able to tell Meg. The big secret of his life that he'd never escaped no matter how long he spent running from it. A fresh wave of shame washed over him. "So now you know," he told Suzanne.

She nodded, her lips pressed tight together, looking tense—as tense as he felt. This was why he didn't like laying his shit on other people. "I'm sorry," she said. "That's…worse than I could have imagined, and I'm sorry you had to live through it and I'm sorry I made you go back there in your head. But I appreciate you trusting me enough to tell me."

He nodded, one ugly question left in his mind. He could only look at her from beneath shaded eyelids to ask, "You ever gonna be able to see me the same way, Suzie Q?"

He sensed the tilt of her pretty head more than saw it. "What do you mean? It wasn't *your* fault."

At this, he raised his gaze to her fully—his surprise overriding the fact that it was hard to face her right now. "Partly it was." The words came out sounding strangled. "I just stood there."

"Oh, Zack," she said, reaching out to take his hand. "Please don't tell me you blame yourself in any way for what happened to your sister. You were a little boy. *A little boy.*"

He just looked at her—and again confessed his ugly truth. "But I knew what she was doing. And I didn't stop her." Shame pressed down on him.

"You were in shock. I'm sure you couldn't even move or speak. Shock can…paralyze you, Zack." The word hung in the air like a strange coincidence and he could see she regretted it. "For lack of a better way of saying it," she went on quietly. "But it can freeze you up inside. Nothing about this is your fault."

Still, Zack gave his head a short shake. It wasn't that easy. "My whole life I've wished I'd just said, 'Stop,' or yanked my mother away. I've wished my sister could have lived."

Now Suzanne's hands cupped his face and she peered intently into his eyes, her voice vehement. "I wish that for you, too—that she'd lived. But it's not your fault she didn't. I promise. You have to let go of thinking that. It wasn't your responsibility—and you never should have seen something so awful. No child should. No *person* should."

He closed his fists around her wrists, pulled her hands down—he didn't deserve to be comforted. And maybe the point wasn't who was right; maybe it was… "Suz, do you get how I am now? Why I'm happier on a boat,

with no people around? Why I couldn't commit to Meg?"
Helping her understand what made him tick had seemed
like the one purpose this might serve.

So it deflated him further to hear her say, "Actually,
no. What does one thing have to do with the other?"

He blew out a tired breath, frustrated that he hadn't
made things clear. "A man is supposed to take care of the
people he loves. And I…" He stopped, shook his head.
"I can't be depended on to do that. I never would have
dreamed I'd let somebody hurt my baby sister right in
front of me. But I didn't stop it. I didn't do a damn thing
but run away. And that's always made me think I'm just
not…" He was so damn spent, and out of words.

"Worthy? Of love?" she asked. That wasn't what he'd
been shooting for, but he couldn't deny it hit home a
little. "You are, Zack. I promise you are. Everyone is."

Everyone? Was his mother worthy of love? He kept
that inside, though. Because he couldn't think straight
anymore. And he wanted to collapse in a heap. He didn't
want to be there any longer—he wanted to be *here*, with
the woman he cared for, the woman who had a knack
for making things better. Okay, she hadn't made *this*
better—no one could—but he wanted to move on with
looking forward, not back. "Can we stop talking about
this, Suzanne?" Their eyes connected, locked. *I kept my
end of the bargain. Now let me off this ride.*

"Okay," she said softly.

"So…you still want me around?" he asked.

"Of course," she said.

And he mustered at least the hint of a grin. "Guess
that's lucky for me. Under the circumstances." He motioned to his bad leg.

She smiled at his joke, then leaned in to kiss him.

It nearly killed him when she pulled back, though, getting up out of bed. "Where ya going, Suzie Q?"

She motioned to the kitchen table. "Still a mess to clean up. You worked too hard on this lasagna to let the leftovers sit out and go to waste."

"Good point," he agreed. He didn't care about the food, but talking about *anything else* made him feel like he could breathe again.

And every other word exchanged before she came back to bed was a lighter one—the buds on the flower stems were growing, big snowstorm predicted for tomorrow, where had the wine cork gone?—and breathing got easier and easier. But he held her very tight as they slept.

OUTSIDE, WIND HOWLED and snow drifted. Inside, Suzanne felt like she'd been hit with a ton of bricks. She went about her business as normal—making breakfast, checking the forecast, discussing the blizzard-like conditions with Zack, and being grateful they had plenty of food in the house. The weather had been relatively calm lately, and it had spoiled her, making her think spring was just around the corner. In reality, it wasn't.

She dialed Dahlia, planning to put her on speaker, but they reached her voice mail instead. "Call us back when you can," Suzanne said into the phone, then glanced at Zack with a sigh. "Clearly romping around the beach today."

He spared another glance toward the window. "Can't blame her. *I'd* like to be romping around the beach today."

"Maybe soon," Suzanne suggested.

He lowered his chin in doubt. "What do you mean?"

"You're doing so well that—who knows—maybe you'll be up and romping before long. Maybe we could take a trip to celebrate." Though she picked her way through the unplanned words delicately, since—no matter what *he'd* said—she didn't feel their relationship could be fully counted on or considered stable.

Because of what he'd told her last night. She simply...hadn't seen it coming. Never mind it being a big enough secret that he'd never told anyone, and that it had clearly pained him deeply to talk about. For Suzanne, it had become simply...a mystery—Zack's secret past. To have him tell her was supposed to feel like a grand victory, a major accomplishment. Somewhere along the way, she'd lost sight of the fact that it was probably something dreadful. Maybe she'd expected it to be something he'd blown out of proportion. But no, the weight of it still hung around them, and she almost wished she didn't know.

Because now a picture lodged itself in her head— Zack as an innocent child, dragged into horror, unloved, and suffering a guilt that wasn't his. And it made her love him more.

And he was suddenly promising he'd stay with her, but now that she'd met his inner demons, she wasn't sure they would ever release him for good.

"Ready for PT," he announced from the sofa bed.

Back to the more optimistic Zack. Good. And the fact that he'd begun bearing weight on his right leg was phenomenal. And surely a much better place for both their heads than where she'd forced him to go last night.

Soon she stood watching him take careful, measured steps on his crutches, putting weight on the right leg. Not *all* his weight, and painful groans he couldn't squelch snuck out with each step—but he kept taking them.

When she'd counted seventeen, he said, "That's it, all I got."

She beamed at him. "You did great. Up five from yesterday."

He looked happily surprised. "Yeah? Damn, I'm good."

She laughed, then told him, "Head back to the bed and we'll start your exercises."

"Can I ask you a question, Suz?" he said a minute later as they began his hip rotations.

"Sure."

"Did you and the doctor ever want babies?"

It caught her off guard. And took her aback. "Yes," she said, suspecting it came out sad.

"Why didn't you have any?"

She glanced down at him. "I couldn't." Left it at that.

"I'm sorry," he said.

But she shrugged. "Water under the bridge. Though…" She sighed. "Sometimes I think about how different my life would be with a child. I'd have done everything differently after Cal died. I wouldn't have moved someplace so isolated. Maybe I even would have headed south instead of north, to be near Cal's parents in Orlando. But…"

"But what?"

She met his gaze again. "Questions like that are pointless—because if you have to ask one, you have to ask others. What if Cal hadn't died? What if I'd accepted the first nursing job I was offered instead of waiting to interview at Cal's practice? What if I'd been raised with a mother, or a more loving family?" She kept her eyes on his, knowing, of course, the big what-ifs of his own life.

But she never expected him to say them out loud. "What if Emily hadn't died? What if I'd gotten home ten minutes earlier? Or later? What if Dahlia hadn't looked out for me? What if my mother had tracked down my dad to tell him she was having his kid?"

"I'm surprised," she said gently, "that you're playing along with me on this."

He released another sigh, confessing, "It's easier than I thought. Maybe it's…a weight off my chest. That I can. That somebody else knows."

That made her smile softly. Another thing she hadn't seen coming. "The problem with those questions is—they don't lead anywhere because there are such an infinite number of them. Trust me—I spent a lot of time after Cal's death wishing I could turn back time and bar the door or tie him to a chair to keep him from taking that trip. But we can't go back. Only forward."

A small smile graced Zack's stubbled face. "I've been thinking a lot along those lines myself lately. I mean, right after I fell I played that game, too—wishing I hadn't headed to the store, wishing I'd seen the ice—but I figured out real fast it was useless. Only *then* I didn't really know how to move forward. Now, with you, I do."

She didn't know if he meant with her help as a nurse or with her hand as a companion—but in that moment it didn't even matter. Either way, it just made her happy inside.

After PT, Suzanne heated up leftover lasagna for lunch, and they turned on Zack's talk shows. She made a shopping list and put chicken breasts and stuffing mix in the Crock-Pot for dinner. And upon realizing Dahlia hadn't called either of them back, she sent a text in their three-way thread. Can you believe Zack made your lasagna for me? Who is this masked man, right? Anyway, it was delicious. You'd be proud.

She saw Zack look at his phone, his expression laced with amusement before refocusing on the TV.

And a moment later, Dahlia replied. That's lovely, dear.

That was it. Nothing more. Suzanne thought one of their phones might ring then, but neither did. The room stayed quiet as she and Zack silently exchanged glances.

She still didn't know what to make of Dahlia's distant behavior. She only knew it kept disappointing her over and over—and it had to be worse for Zack. She tried to make light of it. "Probably just on the go. I'm sure she'll call later."

DAHLIA WAS TIRED and her very bones ached. She didn't want to tell Giselle. She didn't want to think about it herself. She lay in bed, grateful for the lulling caws of seabirds. No matter what, she still had that, the seabirds. And the sunsets.

When her phone buzzed with a text, she reached for it, expecting Suzanne or Zack. She wished she felt like talking. But no—no, it was from Pierre. Pierre Desjardins, the gallant gentleman who'd made her feel so young again this past autumn. She gasped at the very sight of his name, an unexpected rush of adrenaline pumping through her veins. Because it was more than just feeling youthful. More than she'd admitted to anyone—even herself. She'd begun to fall in love with him.

And then she'd asked him to leave.

She opened the message.

Bonjour, my fair flower. Forgive me for saying hello, but I have not been able to stop thinking of you.

Dahlia burst into tears. She'd never been much of a crier, somehow always able to rise above the urge, but now tears flowed down her cheeks, and low sobs shook her body.

"Dahlia, what's wrong?" Through tear-blurred eyes she saw Giselle rushing toward her.

*Nothing.* Normally, that was what she'd say. But the world didn't feel normal right now. So she simply held out the phone, let Giselle read the words, and said through her tears, "Maybe I was wrong. Maybe I should have let him stay. Maybe I...loved him." The confession stopped her—stopped the crying, almost stopped her heart from beating. "But things got so complicated, you know."

"I know," Giselle said, rubbing her arm.

"And I wanted him to have only good memories of me. I didn't want to hurt another man—I've left such a mess of them in my wake."

Giselle's smile was sympathetic. "I suspect none of them harbors any regrets. Sometimes things just don't last forever, that's all."

The words were a balm. "This is why I love you. You get me. And you...absolve me of all of my sins."

"It's no sin to stop loving someone."

"That's just it," Dahlia said. Her mind felt...open, in a brand-new way. Perhaps it came from the medicine she'd been taking the last few days, but it felt like... revelation. "I'm not entirely certain I ever did stop loving them—any of them. Instead, it's more like I just... turned it off, the same as turning off a faucet. I'm not sure I fully appreciated what I had in any of them. Or in Pierre, either."

She looked out on the beach before her. It felt far away now. Other things felt closer. She curled her hands into fists of remorse. "I'm afraid, Giselle. Afraid I've made very big mistakes. Afraid I've done everything wrong. I've pushed so many people away."

"It's not too late," Giselle told her.

"Isn't it?" Dahlia asked, confused by the notion.

"Not for everyone," Giselle said.

Dahlia took that in, sorry she'd wasted so much precious time. Then she picked up the phone abandoned in the bedcovers and used tired fingers to type back to Pierre a simple truth. I miss you, too.

He replied: I would love to see you in the spring, my flower, when the ice thaws.

Something in her heart pinched, and a few more tears fell as she typed back: Yes, yes, that would be lovely. The spring.

# *Part 3*

Excerpt from a letter to Zack:

*We have so much in common, you and I. We carve our path, winding strategically around any bumps in the road, even ones that don't really exist. But don't make the same missteps I did. Don't mistake love for something dangerous to steer past. When love finds you, keep it. Hold on to it. Cherish it. Because I fear in the end we will find that love is all there is, all that counts for anything.*

## CHAPTER TWENTY-THREE

WHEN A FRANTIC knock came on the cottage door as Suzanne and Zack finished dinner, they looked at each other. A blizzard raged outside. Who the hell could it be?

The sound was so shocking as to freeze her in place next to the table, having just picked up her plate before reaching for Zack's. Only when it came again—a booming *thud, thud, thud*—did she set the plate back down and go to the door.

She opened it to find a woman she didn't know, probably in her forties, bundled in a red parka, strands of long brown hair spilling from the front of the hood. Wherever she'd come from, the walk had left her snow-covered, and big flakes blew past her through the open door. Suzanne went back to being frozen—she hadn't known who it would be, but she'd at least expected someone she knew. She said nothing, gaping at the stranger.

"Suzanne," the woman said as if they were acquainted.

Suzanne blinked, flinched. "Yes?"

"I'm Giselle."

"Giselle," Suzanne repeated. Because that made no sense.

"Dahlia's Giselle."

Suzanne shook her head. "That can't be."

"It is," the woman said, "and I need you to let me in. It's urgent."

Suzanne felt herself blinking some more, her chest tightening with confusion—and intrusion. But the woman stepped forward over the threshold, giving her little choice. Across the room, Zack appeared equally stunned.

"Zack," the woman said, her tone again suggesting familiarity, "I'm sorry. I apologize to you both that time is too short for me to say any of this gently. I'm not only Dahlia's friend—I'm her nurse. And she's not at the beach—we've been at her house this whole time."

"Wh-what?" Suzanne asked, leaning forward slightly. "How can that be?"

Giselle went on. "Please brace yourselves. Dahlia was diagnosed with late-stage pancreatic cancer just before Christmas. She asked me to help her die on her own terms, not wanting to burden you. But now she regrets keeping the truth from you both and from Meg, and I've come to take you to her bedside. I called Meg on the way." She shook her head, looking emotional for the first time. "I didn't want to tell her by phone, but I can only do so much in these conditions. I don't know how much time Dahlia has left, so we have to go *now*. I can tell you the rest as we walk."

When they both stayed as still as two pillars of stone, Giselle repeated, "*Now*. We have to go. Put on your boots and coats."

It was Suzanne who finally found her voice. "But Zack…can't…"

"I know," Giselle said. "So you and I will have to help him. We have to get him there."

Suzanne could barely breathe under the shock. Dahlia was *here*? Dahlia was…*dying*? She wanted to collapse into a heap on the floor, but her nurse's training—or some kind of robotic response—kicked in and started her moving. Stooping down, she reached for her snow boots.

"Where are Zack's?" Giselle asked, dripping snow all over the floor.

Suzanne trembled, unable to think. Zack hadn't left the cottage since arriving. She looked around, trying to remember where she'd put such things. "There," she said, pointing to them in a corner.

After which things moved surreal and dream-like, fast and tense and quiet as Giselle helped Zack with his boots and the coat Suzanne handed her as she pulled on her own, zipping and tying and tightening, vaguely aware of Zack pulling a fleece hat onto his head. And then Zack was reaching for his crutches, pulling himself up, but clearly it was awkward in a heavy coat, different than what he'd grown used to. As he moved toward the door, Suzanne caught sight of wetness on his cheeks and reached up to wipe her own with one mittened hand. *How can this be?*

Moving out into the snowstorm felt like stepping into a cold hell. Zack couldn't walk and struggled with his crutches in the deep snow—making progress impossible. And Dahlia was dying. Dying. Even more impossible.

But they had to get there—they had to find a way. So when it became clear that the crutches were useless in an icy storm, Zack flung them down only a few steps beyond the door and the women got on each side to help him. Every step challenged them, but together the three moved forward, fumbling and clumsy. Suzanne supported Zack's weight as bitter wind and blowing snow stung her face. The wintry street, every storefront dark, stretched silent and long before them as she and Giselle focused on keeping Zack upright, but at times they slipped and lost their footing, too. More than once, they *all* fell. But they had to keep going.

When they reached Lakeview Park, it lay like a thick white blanket to their left. On the right, barren docks rimmed the northern end of Lake Michigan. The thick-falling snow blotted out the moon, but the expanses of white on all sides lit their way.

"I know you're both in shock," Giselle said as they walked. "I'm sorry I had to tell you this way. I begged Dahlia to tell you from the start, but she refused to burden you. She thought it would be easier for you to find out afterward."

They trundled forward in more silence, taking that in, until Zack asked, "She didn't even want to try treatment?"

"The survival rate is very low," Giselle said. "And the cancer was quite advanced. I couldn't fault that particular decision."

"But how..." Zack began. "How did it get that bad before she even knew about it?"

Just then, a foot slid out from under him, yet the women caught him. "There were symptoms," Giselle said. "But they came and went, and she didn't think anything was seriously wrong. Stomach pain, fatigue."

"Oh," Suzanne said, struck by revelatory memories. "She complained of being tired around Christmas. I thought she was just...tired, the same way *any* of us get tired." She suddenly felt thick not to have paid more attention.

Giselle went on. "By the time she saw a doctor on the mainland, it was stage four. Late diagnosis is common with pancreatic cancer."

And then Suzanne had another, bigger revelation. She looked over at Giselle, who—nurse, friend, whatever—

she suspected knew a lot about Dahlia. "Is that...why she sent Mr. Desjardins away?"

Indeed, Giselle didn't flinch at the question. "She didn't want to burden him, either."

"Damn her not burdening people," Zack said.

"And so," Suzanne reasoned as they struggled past the park toward Dahlia's street, "this is why she left anyway after Zack's accident. Or pretended to leave." She shook her head within the hood of her parka. "I can't wrap my mind around this."

"She thought it was a gift," Giselle told them. "She's only slowly come to realize she needs you with her now."

As they started up a hilly street toward Dahlia's cottage, Zack asked, "What about the sunsets? And the beaches? She sent us pictures."

"You'll understand when we get there. And prepare yourselves," Giselle said. "She's lost a great deal of weight. She hasn't had much appetite for weeks. Two days ago she quit eating altogether and I had to increase her pain meds." Stark reminders of where they were, that there was no time to adjust to this, no time to ease her toward the end.

"When?" Zack asked, clearly thinking the same thoughts as Suzanne. "How long..."

"No way to know. Could be an hour, could be a day," Giselle said as she slipped on the incline and caught herself—Suzanne supported Zack more as Giselle regained her footing. "But in my professional opinion, she's fading fast. That's why the urgency."

That silenced them. This couldn't be real. But it was.

And this last part of the walk had grown harder, slower. Zack was doing amazingly well—using both his feet—but he slipped or lost his balance frequently, and Suzanne wasn't sure how much longer she could keep holding him up, even with Giselle on the other side. *Just keep going. Take a step. And another. And another.*

"How do you know her?" Zack asked.

"I came to the island a few summers in a row," Giselle said, "and we hit it off and kept in touch. She knew I had hospice care experience, so she asked me to help her through this. Being chosen to assist someone to the end of life is an honor I don't take lightly."

Neither Zack nor Suzanne replied. That big question finally had a simple but devastating answer. Giselle was a nurse helping Dahlia die.

Suzanne wanted to sink to her knees, those last words having stolen any remaining energy. *Keep going. Keep going.* But she struggled to move forward.

When Giselle glanced behind them, Suzanne did, too—to see Meg and Seth approaching at a much brisker pace than their own. They said nothing—what was there to say?—only turned back around and tried to push on. A moment later, though, Seth stepped up beside Suzanne, touched her shoulder, and said, "Let me help."

She didn't hesitate. It was rescue. An answer to an unspoken prayer. She eased out from under Zack's arm and Seth moved smoothly in to take her place. "It's okay, buddy," he said to Zack. "I gotcha."

Suzanne watched from behind as the most unlikely of trios started forward again up the snowy incline. Seth supporting Zack. Zack letting him. The world not ending. Or…was it? Just in a different way. It was the best thing she'd ever seen. For the worst possible reason.

Meg stood beside her, clearly as stunned by the sight, neither of them moving—instead just watching as the other three got farther away, silhouetted by the snow. Suzanne felt frozen in place all over again. Until Meg wordlessly grabbed her coat sleeve and tugged her forward.

ZACK'S BODY FELT NUMB—from cold, shock, exhaustion, emotion—but his brain whirred and his heart ached as the strange group finally entered Dahlia's cottage. No one said a word as they took in what they saw.

Dahlia lay, eyes closed and breathing audibly, in a single bed situated in the living room facing a big screen TV displaying simple video of a beach, the sun dipping toward the water, soft pink clouds turning more electric before their eyes. The surf *shushed* and a passing gull cawed. Pictures had been taken off the walls, replaced by giant posters featuring white sands, seashells, and blue water. Two Adirondack chairs from Dahlia's front yard had been moved inside, their front legs planted in a baby pool filled with sand.

"She really did want to go to the beach," Giselle said. "But she also wanted the comforts of home. So we compromised."

His gaze flitted briefly to Suzanne's in wonder. All those sunset pictures—taken of a TV or a poster. The few shots she'd sent of her or with Giselle had been orchestrated to show a beachy background. Such an elaborate lie. All not to trouble the people who loved her.

Giselle pulled a chair from the kitchen table close to Dahlia's bed. "Here, Zack." He'd been leaning on Seth all this time, soaking in the surreality of the room. So strange to be leaning—physically—on the guy who'd taken Meg from him. Now Seth helped him to the chair.

He peered down at his loving aunt, almost unrecognizably gaunt. And now he knew…everything. Why she hadn't sent any new pictures of herself lately. Why she hadn't called much the last few days. Why she'd "left" in the first place, despite his injury. He'd been so cold to her; he and Suzanne had both been so angry. Anyone would have been, but he still felt awful for it. And now a dam broke inside him and he couldn't stop the tears from spilling out—they drenched his cheeks, and he bent his face into his hands.

"Don't cry, my boy. Don't cry."

He lifted his head to find she'd opened her eyes. He could see in them that she wasn't fully the same as she'd been before, but she wasn't gone yet, either—she was straddling existence, holding on but letting go at the same time.

"Dahlia," he said. Just that, her name.

"I'm so happy you're here." She didn't smile, but he believed her anyway.

"Me, too," he told her, but then shook his head as he dried his eyes on his coat sleeve. "I mean, I'm not—because I can't believe this—but I am, because…damn it, woman. I don't want this to be happening." He wiped his nose now, and someone shoved a handful of tissues into his fist.

"Of course not," Dahlia said. "Me neither." Her voice was too quiet, like an echo of itself. "I'm sorry. Sorry I didn't tell you."

Zack didn't know what to say. There were a million things. About loving her and being loved by her and being so angry at her for stealing these last weeks he could have spent with her—except, no, he couldn't have. He'd been paralyzed and neither of them was very portable right now. So *life* had stolen these weeks. Life had stolen a *lot*, from both of them, always it seemed, and he was mad as hell but there wasn't time for that to-night—there just wasn't time. And so he simply looked at her, reached out to take a hand turned frail and bony.

"We're here *now*," Suzanne stepped up to say. "We're here with you, and we love you." She stood across the bed, reaching down, touching Dahlia's arm through fleecy pajamas laden with pink flamingoes.

Meg approached as well, beside Suzanne. "I'm here, too, Dahlia."

"Sweet sounds, those. Your voices. I love them so," she said. Her eyes flitted to each of them, her head unmoving on the pillow. "You're all quite wet." She let out a small laugh.

And they laughed, too—just because it was such a nice surprise, that little burst of joy. "It's snowing like crazy out there," Suzanne told her.

But Dahlia moved on to the business of dying. "There are letters for each of you. And, Zack, the important papers are in a purple metal box in my office at the café. I think you have keys to everything, but I've given mine to Giselle and marked what they go to."

"I don't care about any of that right now," Zack said.

"It's important, my boy. The things I can pass on are important to me."

"Okay, okay," he said. "Purple metal box in the office. And keys with Giselle."

"Oh, and the blanket. Giselle, can you get the blanket?" As Giselle stepped away, Dahlia went on. "Girls, I finished the blanket this winter, as promised. I worried I wouldn't make it, but I did."

"What blanket?" Zack asked, confused.

"She's been knitting a blanket," Suzanne said, wistfully, "for three years. She vowed to finish it this winter."

Giselle returned from the bedroom carrying a fluffy multi-colored blanket of browns, purples, and greens, which she laid on the foot of the bed.

"Zack, it's for you."

"You really made this?" She was a woman of many

talents, but she'd only seemed to dabble in knitting, so
the pretty blanket truly surprised him.

"Yes—and turned out quite nice, I think."

"I'll love it forever, Dahlia."

"Now I'm very tired—but I have things to say."

Zack's chest tightened at the reminder that this was
suddenly the end. It made no sense.

"Meg, my dear, come close."

At this, Suzanne stepped back, allowing Meg to take
her place.

"First, I know you've seen more than your fair share
of cancer."

Zack tried to swallow past the lump in his throat.
Meg had survived leukemia in her youth—a fact he'd
tried never to think about, but suddenly it seemed more
real, and he knew he shouldn't have run from facing that
part of her life. And of course together they'd nursed her
great-aunt Julia to her death.

"Don't let it haunt you, Meg," Dahlia said. "Life is
too grand for that. Your heart is large, I've loved you
like a daughter, and I believe the life of your dreams
is finally at your fingertips. I know what you're going
through is hard. You have every right to be hurt by Zack
and Suzanne's relationship, and hurt that she didn't tell
you. You're so strong, Meg, that sometimes people forget you can be fragile, too. And I have no idea if these
two have what it takes to make it—but either way, you
have to keep loving Suzanne and move on. You have to
see the bigger picture. For your sake as well as hers."

She stopped, took a deep, labored breath, then looked
to Suzanne. "Now Suz."

Suzanne hurried back closer, and Zack's heart
clinched watching the love in her eyes for Dahlia, and

the pain they were all trying to muddle through right now in order to be there for her.

"Sweet girl, I have adored you since the moment you arrived here on our lovely little rock. I've watched you struggle, I've watched you grow, I've watched you take chances and come out stronger for it even when the result stung. I've also seen you make mistakes that hurt others. It happens to the best of us, trust me. We all want to be loved for who we are, without conditions. And yet we put understandable conditions on the ones we love. It's quite a conundrum at times. The important thing is to keep loving, even through the conflicts.

"I love you for many reasons, but I love you most now for taking care of my nephew when I couldn't. Who knows where miracles come from—but I credit his amazing progress to you, and I leave this world more peacefully believing he'll walk again. Even if on crutches or a walker, he'll have a far better life than I feared six weeks ago. And more than that, you've opened your heart to him. And you've allowed in unexpected joy under extraordinary circumstances. And though I've not gotten to spend time with either of you since this occurred, my heart says there's much joy and companionship there for you both if you allow it.

"Which brings me to you," she said, shifting her focus back to Zack on the other side.

He met her gaze, stroked his thumb over the back of the hand he still held. "My boy, my dear boy. You didn't get the family you deserve. And neither did I. But we found each other, didn't we?"

He nodded. Stroked her hand again. Answered small, because tears threatened. "Yes."

"You've been the light of my life, Zachary Sheppard. You're the child I never had. The flip side is that I've spent most of your life worried for you. Worried for hurts you haven't let go of, wounds that never healed. And I worry, frankly, how you'll get by in a world I'm no longer in. But a funny thing happened on the way to my demise." He flinched at that, but kept holding her hand, muscles tensed, back rigid, as he peered down into her loving eyes. "You hurt yourself so badly I feared no one and nothing could fix it. And then...Suzanne fixed it." She stopped, blinked, sighed, let that sink into him.

"I'm no expert on matters of the heart, matters of romantic love. It's been my downfall in life." As her gaze shifted to each of them, Zack suspected they were all surprised by the words. "I've long talked myself into believing I was just too strong and independent to be with one man forever, and that I left a string of broken hearts behind me. And it's true, I did. Only I've come to have regrets. I've walked away from great loves, and...why? Ah, those conditions we put on each other, I suppose. Even if I just called it a thirst for freedom.

"Love came easy to me—perhaps too easy, and therefore I didn't value it as I should. I had three lovely marriages, and yet I always wanted more. More what? Some perfect, unattainable, unsustainable passion? An existence of wine and roses and perfect compatibility twenty-four hours a day? Only now do I realize that it doesn't exist. And that I didn't appreciate what I had in those men. We all have our path and I carved mine. I can only conclude it was all meant to be—even having to say goodbye to Pierre when I discovered I didn't have much time left. But if I can give you, my dears, any lessons, it's that I don't want you to miss out on what *I* missed out on. Love is rarer than people think. Hold on to it, my dears. Hold on to it. Don't throw love away. Listen to me, all of you. I don't want you to reach the end of your life and look back with misgivings as I am right now. I thought I was strong enough to do this on my own, die on my own. But that's the thing I've learned. In the end, it's the people you love that make life seem…like it mattered."

She stopped then, shut her eyes. Zack's throat threatened to close up with emotion, but he said without forethought, "I love you, Dahlia. I love you." It wasn't his usual way—had he ever even said those words to her before? It suddenly seemed a shameful oversight, but he knew she'd always known, and at least she was hearing them now. "I love you," he said again.

She squeezed his hand. Then whispered, eyes still closed, "Love you, too."

"We all love you," Suzanne said. "So, so much."

"Yes," Meg added. "We love you, Dahlia. We love you."

Dahlia went quiet, the room bathed in only the rhythmic sounds of a rolling, shushing tide on the TV they'd all forgotten about. She had no more energy to focus on her imaginary beach, but Zack hoped maybe the sound brought her some comfort.

Yet then she began to stir, flinch, jerk her hands away from being held.

"Are you in pain?" Giselle asked from where she stood next to Seth.

"Mmm," Dahlia responded, appearing unable to say more.

"I'm increasing her medication," Giselle said. "I don't want her to be in pain." And a moment later she came to the bed holding what looked like an eyedropper.

"What is it?" Meg asked.

"Morphine. We just put it under her tongue." Giselle

leaned down. "Dahlia, open your mouth for me. Can you open your mouth, love?"

Dahlia appeared to struggle with even that, still trembling, convulsing slightly. Zack struggled to hold back tears as Giselle gently maneuvered the little tube into his aunt's mouth. "There we go," she said soothingly, as if to a small child. "There we go. Better soon."

Dahlia had clutched at Giselle's wrist as she gave her the morphine, and appeared distressed as the nurse pulled back. That was when she whispered two words. "Hold me."

And Zack bounded up on his good leg and bent over, taking her frail body into his arms. "I'm here, Dahlia, I'm here." Just like saying I love you, he wasn't sure he'd ever held her, either. "I'm here," he whispered again.

His heart beat too hard as it broke inside him, and it would have been easy to…slip away himself, in a different fashion—to pull back from it all in his head, view it from a distance, like he was watching a movie and not really a part of it. That was what he'd done through most bad things in his life, his natural response to enduring the unendurable.

But he couldn't do that now. Dahlia needed him. He had to be here for her, he had to love her through this until it was over.

Only when her body went limp in his arms and he realized the medicine was taking effect and also taking her in to sleep, did he gently rise up and sit back down, watching her breathe.

"She looks peaceful now," Suzanne said.

With Meg's great-aunt, he'd gone to the next room, left Meg with her aunt and the hospice nurse. He'd told himself it was a private thing, death, that he didn't belong there. He was pretty sure he'd been wrong, though, because if Suzanne were to walk away right now, he'd feel as alone as that little boy who'd watched his mother do the unthinkable.

An hour after they'd arrived, all sitting in chairs around the bed now, Dahlia's breathing began to change, becoming even more audible.

Zack found himself leaning down near her ear, whispering the words in his heart. "I don't want to say goodbye." As if he'd believed such a declaration could change the outcome. But nothing changed. He squeezed her hand, hoping she would squeeze it back—but she didn't. He began to rub her arm ever so gently. Just in case she could feel it, in case it brought comfort.

And indeed, Dahlia seemed to rest easier, relaxing back against the pillow, and Zack watched as a small smile graced her face. She opened her mouth to murmur, "There are angels in the room."

Meg reached for Seth's hand—and Zack would have held Suzanne's, but she was too far away, so they locked eyes and that was enough. After which he found himself glancing around, at the ceiling and into shadowy corners, for the angels. He didn't see any, but wanted to believe they were there.

He was still searching when Suzanne asked, "Is she still breathing?"

He looked down at Dahlia. They all watched, imaginary waves the only sound, as Giselle moved in with a stethoscope, pressing it to her chest. And Zack kept waiting, waiting for his aunt to take another breath, because surely it wasn't quite time for this, surely she would be with them just a little while longer. *Just a few more minutes, Dahlia. Just a few more, and maybe then I'll somehow be ready to say goodbye.*

But then Giselle stood up straight and said, gently, "I'm sorry. She's gone."

# CHAPTER TWENTY-FOUR

SUZANNE WOKE UP to the sun shining in nearby windows. It felt normal at first—she lay next to Zack, it was wintertime, he was rehabbing, they were lovers. But then the sharp blade of memory pierced her heart. Nothing was normal at all. Dahlia had died last night.

At the crushing weight of it, she dissolved into silent tears. Having grown up in a house where the simple act of crying could bring down the wrath of her father in an instant, she had perfected the art of quiet crying, and the old impulse kicked in automatically now—she didn't want to wake Zack and make him cry, too. So she rolled to face away from him and let the tears trickle onto her pillow, reaching for a tissue box on the end table. There'd been no gentle easing into this.

The snow had ended for the strange, sorrowful walk home—and despite the hour and strange circumstances, Giselle hadn't given them a choice, pretty much insisting they go a short while after Dahlia's passing. "It's best," she'd said. As they'd left, Giselle had handed out letters from Dahlia for each of them. No one had read theirs; they'd all taken them home for later.

Suzanne had pondered calling for the same snowmobile that had originally carried Zack to the doctor, but it had felt somehow as if it would add insult to injury. And so despite their utter exhaustion and the difficulty of moving him, the strange party of four had set out in the snow—Seth and Suzanne supporting Zack, and then eventually Seth and Meg when Suzanne could no longer carry his weight.

She'd walked behind them then—Zack flanked by his ex-lover and her new boyfriend—feeling as if she'd stepped into a nonsensical dream. Were they all thinking about regrets, as Dahlia had advised? Or were they just muddling through, trying to get home where they could all collapse and mourn and try to wrap their heads around this? Suzanne attempted the former but only succeeded at the latter.

Every time she thought she'd gotten a grip on her tears, they returned. *Stop it, stop it now. You have to be strong, for Zack.* She turned to watch him sleeping. And thought again about everything Dahlia had said to them. *Are you going to let me love you, Zack? In a forever sort of way?* God knew he'd been through enough lately that maybe he'd really changed, but she wasn't sure how to trust that yet. *Are you going to forgive me, Meg?* She prayed Meg would take Dahlia's advice to heart, but last night they'd been like estranged sisters being cordial only for the greater good of the family. And hearing Dahlia's words had reminded her—Meg had suffered a lot. That could be easy to forget because Meg usually glided through life so smoothly, not letting it show. Maybe she was done living life gracefully, done turning the other cheek. Maybe she was mad as hell and not going to take it anymore.

Inhaling a fortifying breath, Suzanne quietly forced herself up and out of bed. She wasn't sure if Zack would eat, but she intended to make breakfast anyway because it was healthy to stick to routines. Mostly the routine of his exercises—he had to keep doing them, no matter

how devastated he might be—and the routine of breakfast seemed like a good start toward that.

Though she, too, feared how Zack would survive in
a world without Dahlia—the one person who'd given
him unconditional love. Would he be the same man Suzanne had come to know after this? He'd just lost the
very foundation of his life.

It was cold, so she built up the fire, starting with orange embers left from overnight. Padding to the kitchen
in yesterday's socks, she pondered what to cook. Eggs
and bacon? Pancakes? Omelets? What would be the most
restorative? The most comforting?

*What are you thinking? Food can't fix this.*

Then she covered her mouth, stifling a gasp. *Dahlia
is gone. Dahlia is really gone.* As a barrage of new tears
came, she rushed to the bathroom, closing the door behind her. Lowering the toilet lid, she sat down and buried
her face in her hands as sobs overtook her. She couldn't
stop them. She might have been skilled at quiet crying
as a girl, but when Cal died, she hadn't *had* to be quiet,
and for the first time in her life, she'd learned to cry out
loud. And now she couldn't hold back, giving in to the
sorrow until she sank off the seat and onto the floor.
*Dahlia—why? Why did you have to go? I thought you'd
always be here. Why?*

When the bathroom door swung open, she looked up
to see Zack on his crutches, peering down on her. "Why
are you in here?" he asked simply.

She bit her lip, reached to wipe her eyes. "I had to
cry, but I didn't want to upset you."

He gave his head a short, sad shake. "You don't have
to hide from me, Suz. We're in this together."

She blinked, heartened by the sentiment even if she

said, "But it's…worse for you than me. You've loved her a lot longer." *And she's everything you had.*

"Yeah, but…you loved her, too. And it's okay. Okay to cry."

She nodded and, realizing she remained inelegantly sprawled on the floor, started getting to her feet.

"I'd offer to help you, but…" He loosed his hands from the crutches just long enough to point at them.

"Yeah," she said, trying to smile. Then asked, "What sounds good for breakfast?"

He let out a sigh, looked lost. "Nothing," he said with a shrug.

"I get it," she said, "but we should eat. You especially. It's important to keep your strength up and your energy level high."

He raised his eyebrows. "I hope you're not expecting me to exercise today."

She thought it over and replied, "I'll give you a day, but no matter how hard it is, tomorrow we have to get back to it. You've come too far to stop."

Pressing his lips tight together, he let out a sigh and said, "I don't know if I believe in heaven and all that, but I guess if Dahlia is some kind of an angel now, if I drop the ball on this she'll come down here and kick my ass."

Suzanne got closer to a smile this time. "You're right, she will."

That was when he leaned back his head, shut his eyes, and she saw him remembering again everything they'd experienced last night. It came out sounding a little choked when he said, "I'm gonna need you to help me get through this, Suzie Q."

"I'm here," she assured him. "And you're right—we're in this together." She reached a hand up to his stubbled cheek, then rose on her tiptoes to deliver a gentle kiss to his mouth.

And as they emerged from the bathroom, a ray of hope shot through Suzanne's heart. Zack could have easily crumbled over this, but she truly believed he would somehow rise above it and be okay. And he wanted her help with that. In that moment, it began to feel a little safer to love him. He didn't want to be alone in the world—he wanted her by his side.

That was when her nose caught the scent of sweet perfume, drawing her eyes to the dining room table. Where her bulbs had blossomed into bright yellow daffodils and pink hyacinths. "Oh, Zack," she said, "look. Dahlia made my flowers bloom."

THAT FIRST DAY was mostly about mourning, and talking through Dahlia's astounding ruse, and how much they wished she'd let them in, but also how much they knew Dahlia had to do things her own way. They talked about Giselle, who was—of course—so much less mysterious now. They talked about the sadness of Dahlia's regrets.

On the second day, Zack and Suzanne read their letters. They sat across the room from each other, each quietly absorbing what Dahlia had to say. Suzanne's came on pale buttery yellow stationery that, Dahlia wrote:

> …reminded me of the sun and the sun reminds me of you. Perhaps because you give life to things, make things grow. Or maybe it's because I know the winters on the island are still hard for you, that you hunger for the spring.

The letter left Suzanne feeling loved and trying to soak up wisdom. Every message she'd gotten from

Dahlia in the end was about being brave enough to risk loving without fear. Dahlia knew she'd suffered over Cal, and now she clearly hoped Suzanne would find a lasting love with Zack. *I want that, too, Dahlia—and I think it'll happen. I just wish you'd be here to see it.*

When they were both done, Suzanne said, "You know, all this time, I kept thinking if we could just make it to spring that everything would be all right. But I was wrong."

Soon after, though, she pushed Zack to do his therapy. And she noticed the same thing she had on that long, miserable trek to Dahlia's: that he was using his right foot better. "You're putting more weight on it," she pointed out.

He looked down. "Guess I am." Clearly, with everything that had gone on, he hadn't noticed his own progress.

"Does it still hurt when you do?"

He took another step and said, "Not as much."

Despite herself, Suzanne's first real smile in a couple of days snuck out. "This is another huge step forward, Zack—literally." And she couldn't help thinking that maybe, despite their loss, spring would still bring good things.

The third day became about practical matters. Not many people died here in winter—the year-round population was small and most anyone who was sick relocated to the mainland until spring. But they learned Dahlia had already arranged to be airlifted on the first clear day after her death to the mainland, where she would be cremated. And it was indeed the first clear day.

Giselle told them by phone, saying it would be better if they didn't come. When they heard the whir of a helicopter, they opened the front door to watch it touch down in Lakeview Park. An hour later, the whir came again, and they quietly listened to the helicopter fade into the distance. After that, Suzanne bundled up, took Zack's keys, and located Dahlia's purple box at the café, bringing it back to the cottage. As she walked in the door, she heard Zack on speakerphone with Giselle.

"I wanted you to know the airlift went smoothly. And that I stayed behind at her request—to put the cottage back in order. After that I'll move into one of the inns until the ice thaws."

"You don't need to do that," Zack told her. "Unless you prefer it. Stay at the house as long as you want."

"That's kind of you."

A few minutes later, Suzanne and Zack sat down at the kitchen table, the spring flowers between them, and Zack opened the box. In front was an envelope with his name on it, and after so much emotion the last few days, he looked wary—enough that he handed it to Suzanne and said, "You read it."

She braced herself, then broke the seal. Inside, two sheets of old-fashioned stationery with flowered edges. She unfolded them, then announced, "It's a list. Just a list."

Things to do after I'm gone:

Read the will in this box, in which you will find that I bequeath you the cottage and the café. You may sell or keep them.

You will also find statements for two bank accounts, for which you are the beneficiary.

I would like my ashes sprinkled somewhere on or around the island—surprise me!

After they read the list, Suzanne waited for him to start through the rest of the box's contents, but instead he said, "This really tells me everything I need to know right now, don't ya think?"

She agreed, unable to fault his unspoken logic—dealing with details would be easier once the snow and ice had melted, especially if Zack needed to meet with bankers or lawyers. And though she didn't want to pry, she couldn't stop herself from asking, "Do you have any idea what you'll do—with the house and café?"

"Way things look with my leg, I might need the money. Or..." He stopped, sighed. "I kinda hate to sell the café—she built it from nothing and it's an island staple. But what on earth would I do with it?"

Suzanne cautiously suggested, "Run it? In Dahlia's stead? Just not be as hands-on?"

His brow knit. "What do I know about running a restaurant?"

She tilted her head. "Nothing, but...it's something you can do sitting down. Or moving slowly."

His eyes rose from the list to her face. "You think I could? Run the café?"

"I think if you want to try, I'll help. I *do* know something about operating a small business. It's something to think about."

On the fourth day after Dahlia's death, Suzanne went to Koester's for groceries. The sky was blue, the sun shining, and the temperatures above freezing. Dahlia was correct that Suzanne hungered for the sun, and she liked to think Dahlia was making it shine for her right now. Everyone she encountered gave their condolences, reminding her they weren't the only ones who'd lost their dear Dahlia—the entire island had. Dahlia might have ended up with regrets about her romantic life, but there was no denying she'd made a true home here and been part of the fabric of this community.

People said to let them know if there was anything they could do, and to give Zack their love. They also inquired about his health, seeming relieved to hear what positive strides he was making. She promised to pass on their good wishes, and she left the market feeling some of the weight of loss being burned away by the sun.

And she realized...the snow was starting to melt. Icicles dripped from rooftops and gutters, and the trickle of running water could be heard. The snow was deep, of course—and it was only February so it would surely snow more before the spring thaw truly came—but it still assured her winter wouldn't last forever and life would go on. It would be different than before, but it would go on, and summer would eventually come again.

# CHAPTER TWENTY-FIVE

"ARE YOU READY?" Giselle asked Zack, sitting next to him at Suzanne's table. His aunt's nurse had come for a visit, bearing a photo album of Dahlia's.

"Sure," he said. "But I've seen this before."

"Do you know the stories that go with the pictures, though?"

He met her gaze. "I *think* I do. But maybe I don't."

If Giselle had stuff to tell him about Dahlia that he might not know, he was happy to listen. And so over the next hour, he discovered Giselle did have new insights to share that filled in some of the gaps about Dahlia in his mind.

When she finished, he thanked her. And she smiled, adding, "Dahlia opened up to me a lot during our weeks together. She also told me about meeting you—about the two of you dancing in your grandma's living room when you were little, and how much she always worried about you."

Hearing that made Zack glad he'd brought the memory up to Dahlia not long ago. Though he felt bad as he said, "Never wanted her to worry."

"Of course not. But when someone loves you, it's part of the package. She was worried about you now, too—how you would take the loss. But you seem to be…doing better than she thought you would."

That drew a small laugh from him. Dahlia had known

him well. "For her," he tried to explain to Giselle. "I'm trying to be strong because I know she'd want that."

And hell, no wonder Dahlia had been worried. A few months ago she'd been alive and he'd been healthy, and he'd *still* been mired in depression. How was it that he'd lost his only family, his livelihood, and his ability to move freely in the world, but he was somehow more secure and stable than he'd ever been before?

There was only one possible explanation. Suzanne.

He'd loved Meg—but with Suzanne it was different. She had a way of keeping him afloat—even through these darkest of storms. She'd been the tether that had kept him from drifting out to sea. She'd been the light that breaks through clouds after the rain. She'd been compassionate when he'd had nothing to give her in return. She'd given him hope when he'd believed all was lost. And she'd shown him love at the time when he'd felt the least lovable.

Suzanne had ventured out to a knitting bee tonight, though he was pretty sure she hadn't really wanted to socialize and had gone only so he could have time alone with Giselle. That was Suzanne—always doing the right, best thing for others. When he'd been with Meg, and Suzanne hadn't liked him, he hadn't quite understood why—but he supposed she'd been doing the right, best thing for Meg. She loved fiercely, his Suzie Q. He hoped Meg would take Dahlia's words to heart and forgive Suzanne for being with him. Sometimes you couldn't do the right, best thing for everyone all at the same time.

After Giselle left, he was tempted to call Meg, try to talk to her about the situation—but he decided it wasn't the right move. Less than two months ago, he'd still been pining for her. Now he didn't feel that way anymore—and he wouldn't want her to think he did.

Pulling himself up on his crutches, he headed to the kitchen, grabbed a can of soda—and wished he could grab a snack, but he wasn't that skilled yet, so he stuffed the can in the front pocket of his hoodie and returned to the living room. Maybe soon he'd advance to a walker—on which he could attach a sack to tote stuff. It was the little things in life we often took for granted, like the ability to carry something across the room. But he refused to fret. He'd rather be thankful that he was using his right leg better all the time. Thankful to pop open his drink and take a sip staring into a warm, crackling fire. Thankful to reach for his phone and pull up his music app to turn on some early Rod Stewart, then Three Dog Night.

When the door opened and Suzanne stepped in, he asked, "How was knitting?"

She shrugged, unlooping a long, fuzzy scarf from around her neck. "Eh, since I don't knit and everyone wanted to talk about Dahlia—which was sweet, but heavy—all in all, I'm glad to be home."

He gave her a small smile. "You really didn't have to go." He recalled the morning he'd found her crying in the bathroom, trying not to burden him. "We're in this together, remember?"

She nodded pleasantly as she shed her coat. "Guess I'm still getting used to that. How was your evening with Giselle?"

"Good," he said. "I want to tell you all about it. But first, I've been doing some thinking."

She was bent over, unzipping her snow boots, yet now she lifted her gaze. "Oh?" She stepped out of the boots, set them aside, then padded across the room in cozy socks. "Go on."

As she sat down in the chair next to his, he told her,

"Maybe I *won't* sell the café. Maybe I *will* try to keep it going. *Maybe.* Lot of questions still to be answered. I just need to see how some things pan out once the ice melts. But you're right—it's a job I can do without being very mobile. And it would make Dahlia happy."

"That's very true," she responded with a smile.

"Something else I'm thinking about, too," he told her. "You. And me."

"Oh?" she said again—and he could feel her caution. She was still afraid to *really* "be in this together," all the way. And he supposed, given his history, and how alone her own losses had left her, he understood why. But he didn't want it to be that way.

He pressed his lips together, tried to think through the right way to say it. "Thing is—I don't know where I'd be without you, Suzie Q. And I wouldn't want to find out." He paused, took a deep breath. "I've never committed to a woman in my life, Suz—but I love you. And…even with all the stuff we still don't know, the one thing I'm sure of is…you. I want you and me to be…" He stopped again, stuck for words. "Hell, how do you say it when you're a grown-up? I want you to be my girlfriend. I want to go steady," he said on a laugh. "Hell, I'd give you my class ring to wear on a chain around your neck if I had one, but I don't."

Next to him, she cautiously bit her lip and smiled prettily, looking somehow more bashful than he'd ever seen her. "You gave me a bear that says Be Mine." She pointed to the Valentine's Day teddy bear, sitting on a built-in shelf. "That'll work."

"That's it exactly," he said. "I want you to be mine."

IT WAS REAL. Zack loved her. Zack wanted her in a way he'd never wanted another woman. She ached to tell Dahlia. She ached to tell Meg, her best friend. But she couldn't tell either of them. So she held his words close to her heart and occasionally danced around the room a little when he wasn't looking.

She hated that it had taken so much loss and pain to bring them together, but she also knew that sometimes a person had to be stripped bare to rise up and transform into someone new. The Zack Sheppard she'd known six months ago couldn't have made promises. The Zack she'd known six months ago had been an entirely different man.

She, too, was different. Taking care of him had required her to dig deep and shed some protective layers, as well. Finding the part of her that had compelled her to be a nurse had reminded her she was stronger than she knew. And somewhere along the way, she'd let herself learn to feel things again, too. Not just in strong ways, but also in vulnerable ways.

She sat at the dining table, a blank sheet of paper before her, making notes for a memorial service. Dahlia's death had been such a shock, and the conditions here so limiting in terms of funerals, that it had taken them this long to consider such an event, but this morning she'd suggested it, and Zack had agreed. They wouldn't have Dahlia's ashes until spring, but that seemed too long to wait.

Now she gathered the courage to text Meg. A thing that used to be second nature—something she did multiple, easy, mindless times a day. Now it took effort, and precision. We're planning a memorial service for Dahlia. Would you like to be involved?

Meg answered right away. Yes. Thank you for including me. We could have it here, at the inn, if you'd like.

She and Zack had discussed doing it at the café, but the inn might feel more inviting this time of year. That sounds perfect.

And so it was decided that a celebration of Dahlia's life would take place on the first Saturday in March. As word spread across the island, people offered to bring food. Using Dahlia's photo album and pictures collected on all their phones, Suzanne made a slideshow for the TV in Meg's parlor. They took a framed photo from the café of Dahlia holding up the first dollar she earned there, along with a few other framed pictures Giselle located at Dahlia's house, to create a display. Zack insisted on compiling a playlist of some of Dahlia's favorite music, which neither Suzanne nor Meg thought seemed especially reverent, but then he reminded them both, "This is Dahlia, remember? She wouldn't want reverent."

A couple of days before the event, Suzanne took Dahlia's phone, which Giselle had given to Zack, and did what she'd been putting off since the night of Dahlia's death. She simply hadn't had the heart then, and she didn't have it now, either, but it had to be done. As the only one in Dahlia's circle who'd really spent any time with Mr. Desjardins, the task fell to her.

In his contact information she found an email address, which allowed her to say everything she wanted, closing with: I have every reason to believe she had fallen in love with you, and that if her health had not failed her, she would have asked you to stay in her life.

The way Zack had asked Suzanne to stay in his. The way Meg had invited Seth into hers. Of everyone, Suzanne thought that sweet Mr. Desjardins was the one getting the worst of it, because he had no one to soothe him through the loss, no love to hold on to in the end. The very fate Dahlia had warned of.

THE DAY OF Dahlia's memorial service dawned bright and sunny. Snow still covered the ground, but spring was in the air. The sky shone blue, the clouds were fluffy, and Suzanne couldn't help thinking it was the sort of early March day she might normally call Dahlia to suggest lunch.

While she would normally wear black to such an event, she and Meg and Zack had decided to let color rule the day instead—in honor of Dahlia's vibrant spirit and love of bright hues. Guests were invited to wear something colorful that would make Dahlia giddy with approval if she was looking down on them. And so Suzanne chose a hot pink sweater she seldom wore since it felt loud to her—but just right for today.

Zack lacked much in the way of bright clothes— even when she went to his apartment above the café to look. But she returned with a fire-engine red fisherman's sweater, attractive in style, garish in color, that had come as a surprise to her when she unearthed it in the far corner of his closet. "This was all I could find," she'd told him, holding it up upon her return.

He'd sighed, looking wistful. "I hate that thing. Dahlia got it for me to wear at Christmastime, but I never have. It's perfect."

There was no getting around the awkwardness of arriving at the inn. It was awkward getting Zack up the steps, awkward entering her best friend's home but no longer feeling at ease there, awkward because Dahlia was gone. Though Beck and Lila had come early, and there was safety in numbers as they all busied themselves—Meg commandeering the food setup in the kitchen, Suzanne arranging things in the parlor.

Sadness, of more than one kind, crept in on Suzanne as she worked.

*But stop it—Dahlia would hate it if you were maudlin today. She'd want this to be a party.*

And so it was.

Everyone arrived in their bright colors, all with stories and memories of Dahlia, told around the fire.

"If not for Dahlia," Allie shared, "I don't know if Trent and I would be together. I'll always love her for her pushy ways."

"She gave me the courage to ask Michelle out for the first time," Josh Callen said. "Not sure I'd have had the nerve to do it on my own."

"Sometimes," Audrey Fisher said, "when Bob and I would bicker, Dahlia reminded me all the things I love about him. She had a way of making me look past petty nonsense."

Suzanne hadn't planned her words, but when her turn came, she said, "I don't think Dahlia would mind me telling you that on her deathbed, she confided some romantic regrets. But hearing everyone talk here today reminds me that she surely brought more love into the world than she lost along the way. She was my friend, my advisor, my confidante, the person I turned to for wisdom. She saw in me things I couldn't see myself."

Meg's tribute was longer, with a few stories, and the observation that Dahlia always told you what you needed to hear, even when it required harsh honesty or, conversely, a white lie.

When Zack spoke, it was simpler. "She was the best thing in my life, my whole life, since I was a kid. I'm not sure I realized that until just recently. I hope I can be the man she'd want me to be. And I hope I made her life even half as good as she made mine."

There were tears, but then food and music, two of the many things Dahlia loved. And Suzanne felt they'd honored their friend well.

She stood in the foyer eating chocolate cake, chatting with Tom Bixby—when a tap came on her shoulder and she turned to see Meg. "Can I talk with you for a minute?"

"Of course," Suzanne said, then followed Meg to the little round library at one corner of the big Victorian. As blandly cordial as they'd been to each other today, she assumed it was a question concerning the event—but when they were alone and Meg closed the door, she knew this was something else.

At first, her nerves flared, flashing back to the ugly scene at the Knitting Nook—but then Meg removed the cake plate and fork from Suzanne's grasp, set them on a nearby shelf, and took Suzanne's hands in hers. "I've been thinking," Meg began, "about the things Dahlia said."

Suzanne nodded. "I'm sure we all have."

"And she's right. I have to move on and keep loving you."

*"Oh."* Suzanne's gaze widened on her friend.

"Believe it or not, I really *am* happy for you. And for Zack. I really want happiness for you both. And I can suddenly see how well you fit together in ways I just—" Meg stopped, shook her head "—never imagined. Maybe because you hated him," she added teasingly.

"Fair enough," Suzanne conceded.

"And when I really get down to the heart of the matter, what hurt was… I used to be the glue that connected the two of you. And now, suddenly, you're both more connected to each other than you are to me. I felt… brushed aside, forgotten. By both of you."

Suzanne sighed. She'd been so irritated at Meg that she'd never really considered what it felt like from her side. Suddenly *she* felt like the oblivious cheerleader who'd bounded onto the scene. "I'm so sorry, Meg. And you were never forgotten, I promise. I never meant for things to happen this way. And I hate that things are weird between us now. I miss my friend."

Meg's eyes went glassy with emotion. "I know it was just the situation you were put into. And I know it probably seemed like an impossible thing to tell me."

"Exactly. I'm sorry I didn't, though. I should have. I should have found a way. And honestly," she said, "I didn't think it would last, or get serious. Because... Zack."

"So *is it* serious then? Lasting?"

She hoped Meg wanted the real answer. "He's...not the same man he was a few months ago. He's been forced to change, and I think he's lost so much over the last year, you included, that he's realized he doesn't want to lose any more. So...yes."

"You deserve a man who's devoted to you, Suz. And if Zack can really be that man, then I'm happy for you. And...well, I can't guarantee it won't still be a little weird, and I'm not sure we'll be double-dating anytime soon," she said with a soft smile. "But I think I was wallowing in old feelings, and even jealousy. And the moment I realized how little that all mattered was when I saw Seth helping Zack up that hill."

Suzanne nodded. "That *was* a moment."

"Seth didn't hesitate. And it reminded me why I love him, and that I ended up with the right guy. And so what on earth am I jealous about?"

The words heartened Suzanne. Because they made so much sense. "I think we're *both* with the right guy. It's just...a hard transition."

"And maybe it'll go on being hard for a while. But every time it *gets* hard, we need to just step back and remember what matters. I need my best friend back, Suz—for keeps."

They were hugging, teary-eyed, when the library door opened and Seth peeked in. "Uh, sorry to interrupt, but…I didn't want you two to miss what's going on out here."

Still in a loose embrace, Suzanne and Meg exchanged looks. Then they followed Seth back into the parlor—where Dahlia's favorite music still played, and the seating had been pushed up against the walls to create a dance floor, teeming with people in bright clothes.

They both smiled, and Suzanne said, "Dahlia would love this."

"She would," Meg agreed on a nod. Then she took Seth's hand and led him to join in.

Suzanne spotted an unmissable red sweater in a chair near the hearth and walked over. "May I have this dance?" she asked.

He gave his head a questioning tilt. "Never was much of a dancer, Suzie Q, and these things," he said, motioning to his crutches, "make me even worse."

"But it's not impossible," she said cheerfully—just as Wilson Pickett's "Mustang Sally" faded, and "Suzie Q" began. "And they're playing our song."

"Damn it, woman," he muttered, "if this doesn't prove I love you, nothing does." And with that, he got to his feet with the aid of the crutches, Suzanne put her arms around his neck and wiggled her hips, and Zack did his best to dance with her.

# CHAPTER TWENTY-SIX

A MONTH AFTER Dahlia's memorial service, patches of green began peeking through the rapidly melting snow, and enough ice had melted for the ferry from St. Simon to get through.

Life had gone on. Mourning had progressed, Suzanne and Meg's friendship had progressed, and Zack's recovery had progressed. He'd even traded in his crutches for a walker. The more he used his right leg, the stronger it became, and the less pain he experienced.

And damn, it was good to get outside. Good to see the sun. And good to be rid of those damn crutches. They'd saved him in some ways—but the walker made him feel a hell of a lot more independent, especially now that the streets were free of snow and mostly dry.

Despite the ferry restarting runs yesterday, suddenly he wasn't in such a big hurry to reach the mainland. Lots of islanders were—mainland shopping started to seem exotic in winter, and they had friends to see, movie theaters to go to, and haircuts to get.

"You definitely need a haircut, mister," Suzanne pointed out as they walked slowly up Harbor Street.

He just laughed. She was right. "We'll get there soon enough, Suzie Q."

"Happy April, you two!" They both looked up to see Clark Hayes outside the Huron House Hotel, fixing a gutter that had come down under the weight of winter.

"Same to you, Clark," Suzanne called.

Clark smiled—just as Trent sped past on a bicycle, made a U-turn in front of the park, and headed back in their direction, coming to a stop.

"Slow it down," Zack teased him. "There are people with walkers out here."

Trent laughed and said, "Beautiful day for a stroll, huh?"

"Actually," Suzanne answered, "we're headed to see Dr. Andover. He called yesterday, ready to get Zack in with a specialist on the mainland, and when he heard how much progress Zack has made, he wanted to see for himself."

A few minutes later at the clinic, Dr. Andover looked like he'd watched the world's best magic trick as Zack maneuvered across the floor with the walker. "It's miraculous, son. Positively miraculous." He turned to Suzanne to add, "And you, young lady, are to be commended! Whatever you did with him, it worked wonders."

That made Zack laugh, which she ignored as she replied, "Well, he was a surprisingly good patient—very diligent with his exercises."

"I couldn't have imagined you'd regain feeling this quickly," the doctor said. "Let alone be putting weight on this leg or balancing yourself on a walker. It's a head scratcher, for sure." He then plopped down in a chair next to the one Suzanne sat in. "That said, I told you this kind of injury wasn't my specialty, so maybe I overshot, but I didn't want to give you false hope."

Zack saw no reason not to let the old man off the hook. "Maybe it just made me work harder."

"Well, whatever the case," the doctor said with a jowly smile, "I do believe I stand corrected. If you keep this up, you might just end up back on that fishing boat."

At this, Zack's head shot around as he processed the doctor's words.

Though the old man held his hands up in front of him. "Don't know when, mind you. Not gonna happen overnight. But at this rate, you might well have a full recovery."

A full recovery. Maybe it shouldn't have been such a surprise to hear—but it still was. Because he'd been told normal life was a thing of the past for him. And so maybe, no matter how far he'd come, he hadn't been willing to let his mind go there. "Are you serious, Doc? You think I could get back that level of strength? Balance?"

Zack's doubt—and maybe the excitement he wasn't even trying to hide—made the old doctor pull back a little. "Now again, this isn't my area of expertise—maybe you'll reach a threshold. I'm just saying…you've beat the odds on this thing so far."

The very notion left Zack bubbling with unexpected hope. Because even as much as he'd progressed, he was hellaciously far from being able to haul up nets, sort a catch, deliver it to distributors. But hearing the doctor say maybe he could at some point in the future…it was literally having the thing you held dearest taken away and then learning you might get it back.

No. Dahlia was the dearest thing.

And she *wasn't* coming back. That bad dream was one he could never wake up from.

But if there was any way he could really get back out on the water, doing the job that had always given him purpose…well, *that* would be the world's best magic trick.

He beamed at the woman he loved. "Did you hear

that, Suz? Because of you, I might actually be able to fish again one of these days."

Suzanne did her best to smile back. "That would be amazing," she said. Because it would. It truly would. *But what if that happens? What will it mean for me? For us?*

She hadn't thought it possible—even if Zack regained the ability to walk on his own, commercial fishing was hard labor. And maybe the doctor was wrong—but Zack's rate of recovery suddenly made her feel short-sighted about this. If he continued at the same pace, he *would* keep defying the odds. And God knew the man was driven.

Fishing had been an enormous part of Zack's life. She knew how devastated he'd been to think he'd lost it. So why wasn't she happy for him now, as happy as *he* clearly was?

*Because you just got him and you don't want to be without him for months at a time.* Same as Meg. *And you don't want to be afraid he might never come back.* Meg had never feared *that*—for Meg, it had just been loneliness. For Suzanne, it would come with something even worse.

Still, she smiled. *What kind of monster are you if you don't want him to be able to do everything he did before? You have to be happy for him—you have no other choice.*

And so as they left the clinic, walking slowly toward home, she kept smiling. And she reminded herself that whatever happened, it would take time. *Maybe he'll open the café and love running it. Maybe he'll realize working a fishing trawler is a younger, healthier man's game. Maybe he'll realize he just wants to stay with you, that you're enough, and that he doesn't have anything to run from anymore. Please, please, please let it happen that way.*

As they walked up Harbor Street, she wasn't even sure who she was beseeching. God? Dahlia? Whatever angels had been in the room with them that night?

She wanted Zack to be happy. But just like Meg, she didn't want to feel second-best to a fishing boat, or to the inner demons who had always sent him running there. She'd been so sure she'd banished them. But what if she was wrong and they were still inside him, just waiting for a chance to make him start running again?

ZACK STOOD ON a sun-washed dock, watching the ferry carry Giselle away. He'd come to the marina to see her off.

He hadn't really known what to say—she'd been like an angel who'd come floating into their lives, done an important job, and was leaving again. They hadn't gotten to know her, even though she'd been here for six weeks since Dahlia's death. While always pleasant, she hadn't seemed inclined to socialize, even when Suzanne had invited her to dinner. But she'd loved his aunt, and he hoped she knew how much he appreciated all she'd done.

In parting, she'd handed over the keys to the house, and one last letter. "It's to Pierre Desjardins. I found it, unfinished, in a box of stationery. I think she'd want him to have it."

Sorry to know she'd had more to say to the man and hadn't gotten to, he tucked it into a pocket and promised he'd try.

He and Suzanne still hadn't gone to the mainland. He still wasn't in a hurry to get there. Funny, he'd always been itching to get off this island when spring came—but now the mainland felt...foreign. He'd never maneuvered there on a walker. And the mainland held more doctors, which Dr. Andover still wanted him to go see.

But he'd said, "Doc, what can they do to help me get better any faster than I already am?" The way he saw it, it would be opening a can of worms. A bunch of appointments and tests—which would cost a shitload of money—all to tell him what he already knew: he was recovering and he would keep on recovering. Hell, at this point, he'd be almost afraid if some specialist wanted him to try something new. Why mess with success?

So it was settled in his mind. He'd go get a haircut in a day or two, but he'd skip the new doctors and stick with Nurse Suzanne.

Still peering out over the ferry's wake, he caught the sun sparkling on the cold water as the big boat moved past the South Point Lighthouse. The water itself lured him. The Great Lakes had been his home, more than any piece of land, for over twenty-five years. He let out a sigh, still able to see his breath in the cold air and recalling the doctor's prediction the other day.

He hadn't allowed himself to even imagine he'd ever work his boat again. But now he was sinking into the feel of it—the feel of stepping onto the *Emily Ann* and sailing out past the Mackinac Bridge into Lake Huron. Stepping onto that boat was freedom. It had felt exactly the same from the time he was sixteen. As that first trawler had left Saginaw Bay, he'd looked back at the land and known he'd never return, never have to see his mother again, never have to do what anyone told him again. There were no worries, no responsibilities—other than bringing in a catch. It made life so simple.

He could have stood looking out over those waters forever, letting the waves call to him—but using the walker to get around had its limits, made him tired, left his leg achy. As he made his way back toward Suzanne's place, he looked up to see Dahlia's Café, the building seeming to stare back at him, empty and wondering what its fate would be.

Just then, Lou Burgess, the short, stout man who owned the Skipper's Wheel, walked up to ask Zack about his health and how he was doing since losing Dahlia. That was the one thing he hated about being back outside—but he put up with it because people meant well. Once the pleasantries were over, though, Lou reached up a hand to Zack's shoulder. "I'm not a man to beat around the bush, Zack, so I'll keep it plain. I'm wondering what your plans are for the café. And if you'd be interested in selling it."

Zack's jaw dropped. He hadn't seen that coming. He still hadn't gotten around to looking at Dahlia's papers—legal documents sounded like work, like hoops to jump through and stuff to figure out. And there were other reasons he hadn't dug into them, as well. When it came to Dahlia's cottage—well, he liked living with Suzanne. Dahlia's place was a lot farther walk to pretty much *anywhere* for a guy with walking issues, plus Suzanne's was right around the corner from Petal Pushers and the café—so it made sense, even if he decided to hold on to the business. And the restaurant? Dahlia had made it a local favorite, and he hated to think of it becoming something else. And it would make him feel connected to her to keep it going.

But on the other hand—suddenly here was Lou, feeling like an easy answer to a big question that had been hanging in the air for too long. Even so, after a moment, he finally mumbled an awkward, "I don't really know, Lou."

Lou, a decent guy, held up his hands as if backing off and said, "Listen, I don't want to push you to do anything you don't want to. But it's a good fit for me—near the Skipper's Wheel—and I'd give you a fair price for it. I loved Dahlia and loved her place. I'd run it the same, and I'd keep the name, to honor her. She had a good thing going and I'd just be picking up where she left off."

Zack tried to wrap his head around the offer. His mind whirled with the idea of moving forward, of the place being the same without his having to take on the burden, of having a solid nest egg of money to fall back on—something he'd never had before. And damn, if he could fish again…why wouldn't he? It sounded easy— and inviting—in comparison. Who wanted to start over doing something they knew nothing about at his age?

But it was still a lot to take in when he'd least expected it. So even as his heart beat a little faster at the prospect, he finally said, "I'll think about it and get back to you."

ON A DAY too cold for it, Suzanne and Meg sat on the front porch of the Summerbrook Inn, drinking hot tea, refusing to be driven back inside. The South Point Lighthouse glistened in the sun, and diamonds danced on the rippling surface of the water around it.

What remained of the snow lay in clumps and patches that got smaller each day, and even though spring came later this far north than in most of the US, the green stems of daffodils pushed up through the soil, and Meg claimed she'd seen a few wild crocuses blooming near the shoreline. Meg had started her spring-cleaning in preparation for the coming tourist season and Suzanne had been working at Petal Pushers a few hours each day as fresh annuals began arriving from the mainland, along with potted shrubberies and trees. The long winter had truly ended and the island was coming back to life.

"Did you mail the letter to Mr. Desjardins?" Meg asked Suzanne.

She nodded sadly. The debonair man had responded to her email sounding heartbroken, and then she'd had to ask for his address when that letter had surfaced last week.

"Did you read it first?" Meg asked.

This time Suzanne shook her head, admitting, "Part of me wanted to, but it was meant to be private, between Dahlia and him, and I also feared it might make me too sad."

"Good point."

Just then, Allie and Lila went cruising by on pastel-colored bicycles, Lila yelling, "Hi, you two!"

In the opposite direction came a jogger, also waving hello. "Meg! Suzanne!" he called.

"Is that Cooper Cross?" Suzanne asked Meg.

"Oh my gosh, yes. Hi, Cooper! Welcome back!"

Meg had always said that when you first saw Cooper Cross, a seasonal resident, out for his daily run, you knew summer was right around the corner.

"It's nice to be out and about again," Suzanne said, feeling she spoke for all of them.

"Zack's really been getting around on that walker," Meg remarked. "Seth and I can't get over it, especially as grim as things sounded a few months ago."

A fresh sense of joy flowed through Suzanne's heart. Because Meg was normal Meg again—and caring about Zack because he was Suzanne's boyfriend, not because he'd once been hers. She could hear in her voice that things were truly different.

"He continues to amaze me," Suzanne replied, meeting Meg's gaze briefly but then panning out to the water. In case Meg saw more than amazement in her eyes.

Too late. "What's wrong? What don't I know?"

Suzanne bit her lip. Part of her didn't want to tell Meg. It felt like…failure. She'd been so certain that her love had changed Zack, or the winter had, but that regardless of where the credit lay, he'd been transformed. And now she wasn't so sure.

But she was going to tell her anyway. Because she needed her friend's ear, her friend's support. She needed things to be as open between them as they'd been last year at this time. "The doctor told him he might eventually be able to work his boat again."

She didn't have to say more for Meg to get the full impact—her jaw dropped as their gazes met. And she said quietly, "That's incredible and awful at the same time."

Suzanne just nodded.

Uncertainly, Meg added, "What about the café? I thought he was considering keeping it, managing it."

Suzanne sighed. "He was. And maybe he still is." She stopped, shook her head. "I haven't had the heart to ask him lately. Not since the doctor dangled the fishing life in front of him again. Partly because I'm afraid of how he might answer. And partly because…" She looked into Meg's understanding eyes. "It's been such a cold, hard winter. I just want it to be a little easier for a while."

"Of course," Meg said.

So Suzanne went on. "Right now, things are good. He's happy to be back outside, happy to be moving again, and I'm thrilled he can get around. We enjoy each other's company, and even as we're mourning Dahlia, we find things to smile and laugh about. And he's loving. He's sweet and caring and considerate." She hoped she wasn't saying too much—but she wanted to be real with Meg and wanted it to be okay. "And he doesn't say anything about leaving. But he was so happy when the doctor told him he might be able to fish again that I know…if he gets that chance, he will. And there are so many reasons that'll break my heart."

Meg could have said something deflating in the I-told-you-so or he'll-never-change vein. She could have put Suzanne on the spot by asking what she'd do if he left her six months a year—which she'd found untenable when he'd abandoned Meg that way. But in reply, Meg simply reached out between their chairs and took Suzanne's hand in hers. It was exactly what Suzanne needed in that moment—she finally, really had her friend back. And God knew she needed her.

## CHAPTER TWENTY-SEVEN

ZACK SAT ON a bench looking across Harbor Street at the café. Despite not being open for business as it normally would by May, Suzanne knelt in the dirt in blue jeans out front, planting his aunt's trademark dahlias in bright colors.

He wanted to honor Dahlia's memory however he could. And he had ideas he hadn't shared with anyone yet—but that he hoped might take shape soon.

And part of him wanted running this café to be a piece of it—but behind the café lay the water, the water that had given him a life, a living. If he got the chance to return to it, he didn't think he could pass that up. It wasn't that lucrative a career—meager at best. But it was a life he'd always loved. And he doubted he could play master to both and do either well.

He'd been struggling with that, but then along had come Lou Burgess. And the more he thought about Lou's offer, the more it seemed like...guidance.

Suzanne stood up, brushing dirt from her jeans. The sun had been out when she'd started the task, but now clouds rolled in, turning the air colder. Smiling, she called, "All done."

"Looks great," he said.

Rather than pick up her tools and the empty flower flats, she crossed the street and plopped down next to him. "I'm pooped."

"Sorry I can't help with stuff like this. *Yet* anyway. But one day soon, I will."

She tilted her head, giving him a small grin. "I look forward to that. Not so much because I need the help, but because I'll like you being able to give it." Then she peered back across the street at the empty building, painted a powdery blue to which Dahlia had always given the more complicated name of periwinkle. "People keep asking if the café is going to reopen."

He didn't know what Suzanne would think of his decision. He didn't want her to be disappointed in him—but she loved him, so he had to believe she'd want him to follow his heart. "Actually, Lou Burgess approached me about buying it. And I haven't answered him yet, but… it wouldn't make much sense for me to run the café if I'm eventually gonna start fishing again."

Inside, Suzanne bristled. So here it finally came, the talk she'd dreaded. "So you're planning to do that."

"Eventually, yeah. Of course," he said.

Which she knew. So why was she acting like she didn't? It had been inevitable. "I thought you wanted to run the café," she said anyway.

Next to her on the bench under suddenly white, overcast skies, he looked her in the eye. "I don't know if I can, Suz. But I know I can fish—I know how to make a living at that."

"Not a very good one," she said, too snidely. Fishing the Great Lakes these days wasn't making anyone rich—environmental changes had made it a tough way to make a living.

"But I still know how," he pointed out. "And it makes me happy."

Happy. There were so many ways to define that word. Apparently Dahlia had thought it would make her happy to leave all her husbands and in the end she wished she hadn't. Maybe we didn't always *know* what made us happy. And maybe she should come at this from a more constructive angle—but frustration burned in her. Frustration with an old version of Zack she feared still lurked inside him, like an infection that hadn't been completely healed. "Because it's running away from your problems," she stated bluntly. "You told me that."

"Damn it, Suzanne," he said, reacting harshly for the first time. "I thought you of all people would understand. You know what I've been through. You know the life I built for myself on that boat means something to me. I thought you'd be happy for me."

"I *am* happy for you—happy that you're recovering so well. Because I love you and want you to have a full life. But what about *me*, Zack? What about what *I* want?" That had been one of her criticisms of the old Zack— selfishness. He didn't *mean* to hurt or neglect anyone— but he always put himself first.

"I love you, too, Suzanne," he said. "And I'm committed to you. It's not like I'm leaving and never coming back."

Okay, yes, he'd committed—which he'd never done with Meg. Yet, at the moment, his words gouged a deep chasm in her heart. "How do you know?" she snapped.

"What?" He shook his head, clearly confused.

"How do you know you're coming back? Boats sink, storms come—there are no guarantees."

At this, he just cocked his head. "By that logic, there are no guarantees in life anyway. Dahlia showed us *that*. But I promise if I leave, I'll be back. Every time."

"That's what Cal told me, too."

She saw her past register in his eyes. It left him speechless.

But not her. "I've been living for six years with the memory of a man who didn't come home when he was supposed to, who *never* came home. You don't know what it's like to find out someone died, without you, and that you didn't even get to say goodbye." Her eyes ached as tears threatened. "You have no idea how grateful I am that Dahlia changed her mind and called us to her bedside. Because at least we got to say goodbye."

He blew out a shaky breath—then tried to defuse the situation. "Suz, this might not even happen—we don't know. So why are we arguing about it? That's the last thing I wanted."

*Yeah, well, too late, buddy.* "If you think it might not happen, then why are you selling the café?" When that also silenced him, she went on. "I'll tell you why. You're not a guy who wants to just sit around doing nothing. Other than moping over Meg last fall, you stay busy, even when you're in port. You find things to fix or build, for Dahlia or Meg. So if you're selling a business that would keep you busy, it's because you're *counting* on getting back on that boat. And that you're going to do it whether I want you to or not, like I'm not even part of the equation. And, Zack, I'm not sure I can just sit around waiting for that to happen."

She couldn't quite believe her own words, but it was true. She wouldn't be Meg, who'd waited and waited for him to put her first. She wouldn't wait around for him to drown or God knows what else. And she wouldn't bide her time the way she had the last few weeks, hoping it wouldn't happen only to have him announce one day that he was setting off on the *Emily Ann.*

He just gaped at her, clearly as stunned as she was. He narrowed his gaze, looking hurt, defiant, like she was the one causing the problem here. He'd always made it

Meg's problem, too. "So you're going to ignore Dahlia's advice? Throw away love just because it isn't exactly what you want?"

"Maybe *you're* the one throwing it away," she said. "If you can't put love first, is it…really even love at all?"

"Of course it is," he insisted.

"You'll never really stop running, will you?" Maybe it seemed backward or ironic to accuse a man who could barely walk of running, but there it was. "You were happy to stay here with me when you thought you had no other choice, but the second you find out you might be able to leave, you're ready. Running will always be the easier move for you."

She'd said all she had to, her heart was imploding, and she wanted to take their drama off the streets of Summer Island. It was spring, people were out, and she had no idea if anyone had tuned in to their fight, but she was just getting past her mortification over the Knitting Nook incident back in winter and she didn't want to keep looking like the island crazy person who argued in public all the time. So she stood up, crossed the street to gather her things, and marched away, praying she wouldn't run into anyone who wanted to chat or even say hello. So far she wasn't crying and hoped to keep it that way.

As she trudged around Petal Pushers to the back, her anger crumbled into a softer sort of despair. Behind the building, she sank down at a wooden picnic table she and Meg repainted a fun, bright color every spring—currently lavender. Last year Seth had helped, and Beck Grainger had wanted to as well, but she'd pushed him away. Zack Sheppard had been the last man on her mind. Life's unpredictability was one of her least favorite things about it.

And now that she was more sad than mad, she thought

of Zack's past, the reason he ran, the reason he would always run. It was a reason only she knew, a reason he'd trusted only her with. He had no one else in the world now but her. No wonder he'd expected her to understand.

Should she be his new Dahlia, handing out that unconditional love to him? What *was* unconditional love? Did you stick around, continue doling it out even when it hurt? It suddenly seemed a more nebulous thing than she'd realized.

This was the kind of moment when, in a more perfect world, she'd go sit by Dahlia's grave and seek counsel from above. But there was no grave, and they didn't even have her ashes back yet. So she simply looked up at the white sky, wishing she could somehow find Dahlia there looking back—and pretended she did anyway. *What should I do, Dahlia, about that stubborn nephew of yours? I thought he'd really changed, mellowed. But now I think maybe he simply can't, that it's just in his blood to run away from life and love and everything that could possibly make him feel tied down.*

Dahlia didn't answer her. Exactly. Except…words did enter her mind. In Dahlia's voice. *Do what you have to do, my girl. And he'll do what he has to, as well. All any of us can do is what we believe is best for us—the trick is in finding out whether we were right or wrong.*

So maybe that *was* an answer. After all, what was she expecting—a phone call? A video chat from heaven?

She looked around this little corner of Summer Island that she'd made her own. She'd made Petal Pushers, her cottage, this island—her home. And she'd found so much here. Dear, loving friends—though one of them was gone now. And…love. Unexpected love…that was pulling her into a place irresistibly soft and warm and safe—until you were left alone there and trapped in it by yourself.

How much could she lose on Summer Island before it stopped feeling like home?

WHEN ZACK GOT home that night, Suzanne was distant. It pissed him off. He'd done nothing wrong here. Women. In his experience, they just couldn't be happy for long. They created problems out of nothing; they blew things out of proportion.

He'd thought Suzanne was different.

"Want to watch a movie?" he asked after a dinner she'd pretty much tossed on the table like it was garbage.

"No. I'm going to read in the bedroom, then go to sleep."

That was new. It wasn't that they spent every second of every night together—but mostly, they did. Her response begged the question, "Um, should I still come in and sleep *with* you?" Once he'd started using the walker, they'd moved into Suzanne's bedroom and turned her couch back into a couch again.

"Do whatever you want," she said.

Sheesh.

He tried to watch TV, and when he gave up and decided to go to bed, he found her asleep in the dark, and quietly crawled in beside her. He followed the urge to scoot close, wrap his arms around her. And he whispered in her ear, "I love you, Suzie Q."

"I love you, too," she said. Only it came out sounding like something she regretted.

"Don't be mad at me, okay?"

"I'm getting less mad," she said. "And more sad."

"Don't be sad at me, either," he told her teasingly.

She said nothing in reply. And he didn't know what

else to say—he'd never been skilled at this sort of thing. Hell, this was his first committed relationship. Moments like this he remembered why. Moments like this women seemed like mysterious and unpredictable beings. But things would surely look brighter in the morning. So he snuggled against her and fell asleep.

"I MIGHT SELL the cottage and Petal Pushers. And move back to the mainland."

Zack just blinked, then grimaced, sitting in a living room chair after his exercises. The morning had seemed calmer—until this. "What the hell, Suzanne?"

She let out a sigh, appearing as tired as he suddenly felt. "I came here to get away from my problems, my losses, thinking a quiet life on a tiny island would be enough for me. And that I didn't want or need love. But then you came along—and what we've had has been real, and dependable, and consistent. Until now. I didn't ask Cal for what I needed, and it haunts me. So I asked you for what I need—to put me first. And now I know you can't—maybe I always knew. I don't want to settle for that. And I don't want to live a life of worry. I don't want to always be waiting and wondering where you are, when you'll be back, *if* you'll make it back. I don't want to be Dahlia—on my deathbed wishing I'd done things differently."

Zack took all that in. It stung to hear, and he didn't *want* her to suffer. But until yesterday it had never occurred to him she wouldn't support him getting back to what he loved. He'd thought the promise, his commitment to her, was the thing that counted.

"You might end up *exactly* like that if you go, Suz," he told her. "I don't want to live my life alone anymore, and I know you don't, either. Why can't we be together in spite of me getting back to the job I've always done?" Damn sensible question if you asked him.

But she was having none of it. "Because it's not just a job, Zack. It's…escape. And if you want to escape, I can't stop you. But it means we want two different kinds of life."

Zack sat there, dumbfounded. How had this happened? How had it all gone to shit so damn fast? Just yesterday they'd been fine.

Suzanne walked to the shelf that held the teddy bear he'd given her on Valentine's Day, picked it up, and sighed. Crossing the room once more, she shoved the bear holding the Be Mine heart into his hands.

The very act wounded him more than he could even understand. "What's this for?"

"I can't be yours anymore," she said. "Not like this."

# CHAPTER TWENTY-EIGHT

It was only a toy bear, but it felt like she'd given him back an engagement ring.

His heart turned cold in his chest as he flung the stupid toy to the floor, pushed his way to the door on the walker, and left. He didn't need this shit. He didn't need someone who wanted to control him and take away his freedom. He was a loner—always would be.

If ever he'd wished he could move faster, it was now. He burned to put distance between him and that cottage. But he went as fast as the walker would take him, and he didn't even think about where he would go—his path led, as always, to the water. The *Emily Ann* had been put back in from storage weeks ago. It was the only place in the world that was truly his, truly safe.

Of course, he was nowhere near able to use the boat for fishing yet, but right now he needed to be on its deck, on the water. Maybe there he could think. Or *not* think. That had always been the freedom it brought. Maybe it *was* escape, but what was so wrong with wanting to be at peace, away from the troubles of the world? Getting out on the lake would be good for his soul, give him the solace it always had, take him away from everything hard.

Once at the marina, he clanked his way along the planked dock until he reached the *Emily Ann*, thinking the act should feel more familiar—but the fact that he couldn't walk freely, couldn't just hop on and easily throw the ropes off, made it different. More difficult than he wanted it to be. Still, he maneuvered his way on, untied the boat from its moorings, and headed out into the straits.

Damn, he hadn't expected to be on the water this way again. Those months of snow and crutches and fear seemed a distant memory now. The waves held him like a cradle as the trawler sailed into open water. He leaned his head back, grateful for the sun on his face, eager for everything else to float away—replacing it all with freedom, peace, and yes, even escape.

But a knot still tightened his stomach.

What the hell? That never happened, ever. Leaving had always, *always* lifted away every ounce of worry, fear, concern—about everything and everybody.

He looked to the shore. The pastel row of buildings stood idyllically below the peaks and gables of houses dotting hills now spring green with trees getting their leaves back, and also pink and white with dogwoods and redbuds just beginning to bloom.

From a distance, Summer Island had always felt like…a place he'd rather not be. Not when he had a choice. Something about land, buildings, people, civilization itself—for him, it had always represented complications, expectations, things he'd just rather not deal with. But damn if the place didn't look different to him now. Damn if the café's back deck didn't look…welcoming. Damn if he couldn't almost see the misty spirit of Dahlia standing there waving at him. Damn if the Summerbrook Inn didn't appear warm and inviting, not the house he'd once had a love-hate relationship with because of Meg. And damn if…damn if the dark-haired woman walking up the street in a long, flowy skirt didn't

look like…home to him. Suzanne. Suzanne was home
to him now.

Shit. Who'd have thunk it?

Dahlia, that's who.

He knew in that moment he couldn't let Suzanne
leave. He couldn't let her run to…to the nothingness
he'd been running to for years. And why the hell was he
on this boat when he could be there, on the island, with
her? Suddenly fishing had lost its charm.

ZACK PUSHED THE walker up Harbor Street toward Suzanne. He could see her in the distance, but walking away from him in the wrong direction. He had no
chance of catching up with her, and he couldn't let her
get away—not now, not ever. "Suzanne!" he called. He
didn't care how much unwanted attention it got him; he
didn't care about anything but making things right with
her before it was too late. He only prayed it wasn't already. "Suzanne!"

The streets seemed busier than even just yesterday.
Tourists hadn't started arriving yet, but shopkeepers
were open for business, and out washing windows or
planting flowers. Harbor Street bustled with bicycles
and pedestrians alike. "Suzanne, wait!" he yelled again.

*Please wait for me. Don't be the one who runs away
this time. Give me another chance.*

Finally she stopped, looked back. Nearly the length of
a football field lay between them—and he kept moving
toward where she stood appearing almost wary. But he
couldn't let her keep looking that way. He needed to be
the man she wanted him to be, the man she could depend
upon. And so, much as he'd rather keep their business
private, he threw that concern out the window, calling,
"Damn it, Suzie Q, I love you."

Growing closer—he never stopped moving, running toward her now, even if he couldn't exactly run—he saw the astonishment on her face. And he sensed people on the street stopping, watching, but he couldn't worry about that—the only thing important right now was Suzanne. And so he went on, letting his heart spill out of him in a way he never had.

"I love you forever and always. I love you more than the water, more than that boat." His hopes lifted when she began to walk toward him, too. "I want a life here with you. All the time—spring, summer, fall, and winter. I want everything with you. I promise." She walked faster now, tears rolling down her cheeks, and he kept taking steps toward her, as well. "I'm not running anymore, Suzanne. I don't want to throw away our love. I want to keep it. Like Dahlia said. I want to keep it."

And that was when he realized he was crying, too. In front of the whole damn town. He caught sight of Meg and Seth, paused on bicycles, and Allie and Josh on the porch of the knitting shop. And he didn't even give a damn if only Suzanne would just believe in him, in *them*.

When his sweet Suzie Q came to a stop right in front of him in the middle of Harbor Street, her eyes brimmed with emotion. She said, "Are you sure? Sure you can keep that promise, Zack Sheppard? Because it's a big one."

He couldn't blame her for asking, for wanting him to prove they weren't just empty words. He had to make her know this was real. "I was out there just now—on my boat," he told her. "I thought it was where I wanted to be. But then I looked back and I spotted you, walking up the street, and I knew I was in the wrong place. It was—" he shook his head "—a habit, a reflex, where I've always thought I belonged, so I assumed it would still be that way. But it wasn't, Suz. I belong here now. With you."

Even if in his peripheral vision he became aware of Lila Sloan and Beck Grainger holding hands nearby, Trent toting a gallon of paint from the hardware store, and Jolene sticking her head out the Skipper's Wheel door to watch the unfolding drama, he kept his eyes planted firmly on the woman he loved. She covered his hands where they curved around the walker and said to him softly, "Do you know what this means?"

"What?" he asked, hoping, praying.

"Everyone we know is out on this street right now," she told him, "and I'm going to officially cement my title as Island Crazy Person with No Sense of Decorum, because I'm about to kiss you like there's no tomorrow right in front of them all."

And so she did.

## *EPILOGUE*

ON A SUNNY June day, Zack and Suzanne sat on a park bench situated beneath billowing trees rippling with a warm breeze and lilac bushes just starting to bloom. Harbor Street crawled with tourists—bicycles wove between pedestrians, the clop of hooves signaled the island's horse-drawn carriage rolling leisurely past, and the toot of a horn meant the ferry was pulling out for St. Simon. More colorful bicycles leaned against lampposts hung with baskets of flowers, their blossoms spilling over the sides, and sun gleamed off the round roof of the South Point Lighthouse beyond a row of pastel storefronts.

"Hard to believe how much everything has changed in just a year," Suzanne said, looking out over the idyllic summer scene.

Zack nodded, adding, "In some ways, a lot has changed in just the last month."

She couldn't deny it. The moment she'd seen Zack declaring his love for her in front of everyone they knew, she'd understood that things were truly different, that he'd somehow let go of his past and could see a new, better future. "You saw the light," she teased him.

"I saw *you,* Suzie Q." He squeezed her hand in his.

"And then we finally found out about Dahlia's other secret," she said.

Zack blew out a breath. "Still trying to wrap my head around that part, Suz."

Upon finally digging into Dahlia's papers, they'd found more than just a will and property deeds. Suzanne would never forget the moment Zack said to her, "Am I seeing this right?" as he held out a bank statement that showed a far larger balance than they could have dreamed. Later, they'd found out Dahlia's second husband had left her well off. Turned out she was full of surprises, even from the great beyond.

"And you're a businessman now," Suzanne said to Zack.

He'd opened the café last week, grateful for people's patience as he found his footing as proprietor, also grateful for employees that got over it when he groused and grumbled at them. He was a new man in many ways, but Suzanne was pretty sure he'd always wear his grumpy moments on his sleeve. At the same time, he'd sold his beloved *Emily Ann* like it was nothing, to a larger family outfit, seeming glad the trawler would be put to good use.

"I have a feeling," he said to her, "that learning to walk again is gonna seem easier to me than learning to run a restaurant." He tapped the cane at his side.

That was another new thing—a few days ago he'd traded in his walker for a cane. Suzanne had feared he was rushing the transition—but as with every phase of his miraculous recovery, he was acing this one, too, and she could see how happy the new freedom made him.

And if all that wasn't enough, Zack had blown her away by standing up before the Summer Island town council and proposing Lakeview Park be renamed Delaney Park, in honor of Dahlia. The motion passed unanimously on the spot, and the new sign had been erected just last week at a rededication ceremony that Suzanne was certain had Dahlia laughing joyfully from beneath a slightly tilted halo. Zack had insisted the sign be done in a very tasteful purple.

An additional part of Zack's proposal was to convert one corner of the park into a flower garden, with white benches, a fountain, and a commemorative plaque that christened it Dahlia's Garden. It was a work in progress—Suzanne and her newly formed Summer Island Garden Club would plant bulbs in the fall for next spring, and just yesterday they'd put in annuals and some perennials that would last the summer. Suzanne had used a variety of summer flowers, but had of course included plenty of vibrant dahlias.

"There's Meg," she said now, pointing.

Zack looked up as Meg approached on a winding path that led from the street. It was nice to see her—and even nicer to know he felt nothing but friendship and an appreciation for old memories with her now. She'd been good to him—better than he deserved—and he was sorry he hadn't been the man she'd needed him to be, but he was coming to understand that for everything there was a season.

"Ready?" she said to them with a smile.

While the rededication ceremony might have seemed a more obvious time, they'd decided to make this activity private, between just the three of them. As Zack pushed to his feet, he looked over at Suzanne, who held the little wooden box Dahlia's ashes had come in.

And then, unnoticed by anyone else enjoying the sunny Summer Island day, they walked into Dahlia's Garden and took turns sprinkling her ashes there to be part of the place forever. After which they walked down to the Pink Pelican, Dahlia's favorite watering hole, and lifted a glass in her honor.

After the toast, Zack instinctively leaned over and gave his Suzie Q a kiss—then wondered if it was awkward for Meg. But a glance in her direction revealed her waving to Seth, who had just walked in and was coming to join them. And that everything was okay. Everything was…shockingly, almost impossibly okay. They all had someone to love, the right one to love.

He squeezed Suzanne's hand under the table, then looked over at her. She didn't notice, didn't look back—she was saying hello to Seth, flagging down the waitress so he could order a drink. But he just kept looking at her. *I'm going to marry this woman one day. She doesn't know it yet, but when I can walk again, really walk again—no cane, just my two feet—I'm going to marry her in Dahlia's Garden and make her mine forever.*

It had literally taken losing the ability to walk to make Zack stop running. But once he'd slowed down, he'd realized it was okay to quit, to just be, that there was really nothing to run from anymore and no better place to try to get to. Summer Island and Suzanne were his safe place now. Early in life he'd not found many things or places that seemed worth clinging to, but he'd come to understand that Dahlia was right—in the end, what mattered was the love, and the people you shared it with.

\* \* \* \* \*

## ACKNOWLEDGMENTS

WRITING THESE BOOKS has been a true journey for me in many ways. And as we seldom complete long journeys in life without the support of others, I want to thank those who took the time to help me make these books richer.

Thank you to Lindsey Faber and Renee Norris for early feedback on parts and pieces of the manuscripts. Your responses and input, as always, were invaluable to my process.

Thanks to the Mackinac Island Tourism Bureau and the Mackinaw City Chamber of Commerce for answering various questions about wintertime on a Great Lakes island.

Much gratitude to Dr. Yasmeen Daher and Dr. Syed K. Mehdi for suggestions and help on some injury-related issues in the final book. My apologies for any missteps in the writing, with hopes that I represented the variables and possibilities in a true and realistic manner.

It would be impossible for me to acknowledge every website or article I drew some small bit of insight from along the way, but among noteworthy online sources are: Main Line Gardening, Diane Vautier and Care24.

Thanks to Lisa Koester for taking my messy map of Summer Island and turning it into an adorable work of art.

Sincere appreciation to my longtime agent, Christina Hogrebe, for championing the first book, and for supportively and patiently sticking by me through a long illness that sidelined me for a while during the writing of it. And to everyone at the Jane Rotrosen Agency for many years of wonderful representation.

And finally, thank you to my incredible editor, Brittany Lavery, for such an uplifting publishing experience: for insightful and detailed editorial input and for helping me make these books the best they can be. And to the whole team at HQN Books for giving Summer Island an amazing home.